MW00572639

THE
DARKENING
DRAGONS

SARAH EVEREST

The Darkening Dragons
First Edition

Copyright © 2017 by Sarah Everest.

Published by Happy Lil Book Nook Publishing
www.happylilbooknook.com

This is a work of fiction. Names, places, characters, and incidents are either the product of the author's imagination, or, if real, used fictitiously.

Book & Cover design by Happy Lil Book Nook Publishing
www.happylilbooknook.com

Printed in the United States of America

ISBN 978-0692869444

the Peaks of Aristane

Yaveen's Keep

Arshota River

the Bay of Meristane

Aristania

Chapter 1

The one thing Tucker never wanted to be when he grew up was a trucker. Sure, like most little boys, he had been fascinated by the big rigs that blasted past his home on the winding country road. He had enjoyed pumping his arm up and down in an attempt to hear the resounding bellow of the classic semi horn. However, from the first time Tommy called him "Tucker the Trucker" in first grade, the idea of falling into that stereotype had appalled him. As much as he hated to admit it, he once hit a smaller classmate in the back of the head with a binder when he heard the dreaded nickname being muttered.

He had nothing against truck drivers as a group of individuals. After all, his father was a trucker for a logging company, and once brought Tucker out to the woods on a run. He was ten at the time and had spoken to his classmates of nothing else for several days in advance. They left home in the wee hours of the morning, bags packed with sandwiches and thermoses full of coffee for father and hot cocoa for son. Tucker had received the royal treatment by the entire crew. They showed him the inner workings of the process from start to finish, letting him sit up in the cab of the truck as the logs were being loaded.

The drivers were friendly, good old boy types. To them, the title "Tucker the Trucker" was more a privilege than a curse. With a name like Tucker Kenworthy, it fit. Tucker loved his father, and wanted the outing to be a success, but as the dreaded nickname was bandied about he longed for the day to end.

No doubt, Frank Kenworthy had dreams of passing along the family business when he was too old to handle driving the beast on his own. He said nothing on the delivery run, but waited for their drive home to ask Tucker what he thought about the day. Despite his desire to make his father proud, he gave only cursory answers. It was obvious that something had spoiled the outing, but being a man of few words, Frank was unable to discern what the issue was. The next time he invited Tucker to come along, the request was politely refused with no clear reason given. Rather than linking Tucker's discomfort to what he considered good natured teasing, Frank merely accepted that he had failed his son.

There were a limited number of choices for kids growing up in the mountainous region of Northern California. Contrary to the popular belief that the state was jam packed with people in booming metropolitan areas, the vast majority of land was far from urban sprawl. When Tucker looked around at local career options he came up with an uncomfortably short list. He could work in the woods or on a road crew, but both of those jobs involved the dreaded trucks. He could have a little farm in the valley, or teach at the local school, but neither of those ideas appealed to him either. The only solution, besides moving to the trailer park and applying for welfare checks, was to find a way out.

Even before he entered high school he was planning how he would work hard in school, excel in sports, and earn enough scholarships to help him move on in life. He could see that his father was hurt by his attitude, but found it impossible to explain anything to Frank.

The Kenworthy family had been in the logging industry for generations. Frank had managed to save enough to buy his own truck, and made decent money for himself. He wanted the best life for his family, and believed that he was succeeding. To him, Tucker's determination to move on in the world looked like disdain for everything he had worked for his entire life. If he had taken the time to talk to his son, he might have found the root of the trouble and patched up their relationship. Instead, he stepped back and let Tucker be.

Despite all the work Tucker did to distance himself from anything even remotely concerning trucks, the nickname followed him. He had a solid build, even as a young child, and grew more compact with age. He was never overweight, but muscles stacked up, giving him a thick, powerful appearance. In short, he looked like a trucker. On the football field he was nearly unstoppable. It was impossible to escape the shouts of, "Keep on truckin'," that followed him down the field. The wildly cheering fans were oblivious to the way their words propelled him to work harder to escape.

By the time he was a Junior in high school, he was the captain of the football team. It was a small school, but he did everything he could to excel. Those who knew him best could tell he was going places. He had a handsome, outdoorsy look, and an old school charm that increased his popularity with students and staff alike. But no matter what he did to distinguish himself, no matter how many activities he took on, the nickname refused to disappear.

Sometimes he wondered why his mother had chosen the name Tucker. There were thousands, maybe even millions of names out there to choose from. She could have called him something basic like Daniel, something old school like Milton, or something snobbish like Harold. He would have accepted a name connected to some other profession like "Hunter" or "Walker" or some inanimate object like "River" or "Sky." Frank Jr. even sounded decent. But being Tucker the Trucker seemed the worst fate. It was a name that shouted to him that he was ordinary, through and through. It was like a stamp on his forehead stating his destiny.

At the end of football season, Tucker was busy sending applications to schools around the country. He looked at programs in physics and mechanical engineering. He sought out information about philosophy and art programs. He applied anywhere that had a quality football program that could potentially sponsor his fees and allow him to explore whatever dream came into his head. There were so many options once he got out into the world. Endless opportunities swarmed in his head. He would go somewhere far away. He would introduce himself as Tuck, or use his middle name, Wyndham, which was his mother's maiden name. No one would have the chance to conjure up the old curse. It would be a fresh start.

Then, on a Tuesday afternoon in the middle of a history exam, his teacher put his hand on Tucker's arm and told him he was to go to the principal's office immediately. When he saw his mother standing there, her face white, her hands clenched, he knew the unthinkable had happened. He had never figured out how to tell his father that he loved and respected him. Now he was gone, and there would be no chance. They all knew the risks involved in the timber industry, but when it came down to it, the shock was more than Tucker had ever imagined possible.

The rest of the school year went by in a haze. He still worked hard in his classes, still filled out his university and scholarship applications, but there were days when he found himself staring blankly out the window for hours on end, unconscious of the passing time.

It was his mother who got him out of his funk. She needed him to step up and be the man now that his father was gone. There was no life insurance, and the social security payments were scarcely any help. There were house payments to make, and feeding a kid the size of Tucker was far from cheap. He was forced to get a job on a summer construction crew. Thankfully the pay was good, and the men were friendly. Living in a small community had benefits. Frank Kenworthy had been a well respected man. Everyone wanted to help out his son in this hard time.

Even as Tucker worked on the crew he realized that he was going to have to fight even harder to pay for school. A full ride scholarship was the only possibility he had of getting out of the hole he found himself in now. He wondered what his mother would do without him, or if she would be willing to leave the home she had always known and move to the city.

Two weeks before the start of summer everything changed. Tucker was helping to prune some trees from around power lines when a branch swung the wrong direction and sent him falling twenty feet to the ground. The injury was not life threatening, but it was the end of his football career. He would be unfit to play his senior year, and there would be no opportunity for major scholarships.

Chapter 2

As he convalesced, his mother tried to convince him that his dreams were still possible. He had excellent grades. He could get scholarships and grants and they could take out loans for the rest. Tucker, however, was certain that his fate was sealed. He refused to go into debt. He would, instead, do what he had been destined to do since being christened with the name of Tucker. He would finish high school and then he would get his license to drive truck.

The sky was darkening, bringing with it a cloudiness to her mind. She had long since lost track of how many days she had been walking, how many people she had either dodged completely, or observed cautiously from a distance. It would be easier if she had anything conclusive to follow.

A bird warbled in the trees, calling in a complex array of dialects. She tilted her head heavenward, searching for a sign in the jumbled jargon of its song, but it only worsened the aching in her head, which, in turn, revived the rumbling in her belly.

Determined to make further progress before the light failed, she resumed her focus on the way ahead. Her quest had brought her in a wide circle, and as her faith wavered, she contemplated what would happen if she were to give up the search and return on her own to set things right.

Night thickened as she made her way through the tangled undergrowth on the steep hillside. There was a stretch of flat ground, a road of sorts, ahead of her. As she reached the plateau she was struck by a wave of dizziness. Her food rations had run out more than a week ago, but she had continued to push herself, fearing that stopping would spell doom. Even as her legs buckled beneath her, one last vision of hope flashed across her blurry eyes. In that moment she knew that if he was out there, he would find her, otherwise, this was the end.

Chapter 3

Tucker could tell it was going to be a long day. After ten years of driving truck, he could always tell. There was a pain in his lower back that craved attention. The thought of calling in and going to massage therapy crossed his mind. The entire speech presented itself to him. "Sorry Tom. Just don't think I'm gonna be able to make the drive today. Old sports injury's actin' up again."

Tom would snort, mutter some nasty comment under his breath, and warn Tucker within an inch of his life that if he wanted to make it in this business he better stop acting like some cry baby sports hero. Then he would grudgingly agree that there was nothing like a pain in the back to ruin everything. After all, Tom liked to bring up the shrapnel in his back from "the Gulf." He wore the pain in his back like a badge of courage. But the truth was, he knew the agony back pain could cause, and he wanted his drivers to be alert. Allowing one day off was easier than dealing with an accident due to distracted driving.

The phone was in his hand, ready to dial. Then it rang. A picture of his mother standing in the forest behind the house he grew up in smiled up at him. He knew she would be complaining about something. That was why he had carefully chosen a picture that brought back warm memories. After his father passed nothing went right for Nance Kenworthy.

"Hi, Mom," Tucker fought his dread with forced cheerfulness. "What can I do for you today?"

"I think the hot water heater is off," her voice was thin and scratchy like she'd spent the whole night coughing. "You haven't left yet, have you? You can come back and fix it, right?"

"I've gotta get on the road, Ma," there was no turning back. "You know how Tom gets when I'm the least bit behind schedule. Did you try flipping the switch in the breaker box?"

He could hear the phone being jostled around. Tucker sighed. "Mom?"

"I'm sorry, Dear. I know you're busy, but how can I go to the store today if I can't take a shower? It'll never do. People talk," she added.

"You can always call Karla, Mom. She'll be happy to help you out."

"Speaking of Karla," she switched to a conspiratorial tone. "We need to do some talking about that girl. I'm not sure she can be trusted..."

"Mom, you've got to get over this. Karla is only trying to help us out. I've asked her to come by once a week and straighten things up, and she's available to bring you meals every day. It's her job."

He could sense his mother fighting for a response. When Frank was alive Nance was a house making star. She would get out of bed and make him breakfast at whatever awful hour he had to leave the house. There would be a fresh snack packed, and when he arrived home, a steaming plate of something hearty. Dinner was always served promptly at 6 and the house was immaculate despite the dirt that seemed to follow Tucker wherever he went. She made their clothes herself, and was involved in every community project imaginable. Perhaps there had been some weakness in the woman, but Tucker had never been able to spot one. At least not until she was left a widow.

Something broke in her with the loss of her husband. She had stayed strong at first, but after Tucker's accident, everything fell apart. She knew there was nothing she could do to help her only child achieve the dreams he had worked toward for so long. She became suspicious of everyone, and stopped her community involvement. When Tucker had helped her move with him to a small apartment in town she had followed him silently, not even bothering to help with the packing. Having Karla come in to take care of things had been a Godsend to Tucker, but Nance resented having the help.

"If you want, I'll be the one to call her," Tucker offered. "You won't even have to tell her the trouble."

There was a long sigh on the other end of the line. "I guess I can call her. You drive safe now, you hear?"

"I always do, Mom," he said. "Now try to have a good day, and please be nice to Karla. She really is a very kind woman."

He was greeted with silence. "I love you, Mom."

There was another pause. "I love you too, Tucker."

He hung up before she could take a breath and start on something else. He worried about her when he was away, but giving in to all her whims never helped. Besides, it was already 6:30 and if he missed his call in time with Tom he might as well start looking for a new route.

Despite the aversion Tucker had always had to his childhood nickname, the sight of his truck filled him with pride. He never let himself think that the money he had invested in the shiny green Kenworth tractor could have gone toward a year or two at most universities. He knew his mother felt like he had settled, but when the engine roared to life, and he felt the power rumbling through his body he knew this career had been inevitable.

"This is Tucker the Trucker signing in," he reported for duty.

"Mornin' Tucker," Tom was quick to reply. "Glad to hear yer up and runnin.' I was startin' to think you wasn't gonna show."

"Tom, it's 6:32," Tucker rolled his eyes. "I'm not exactly late yet."

"I'm just sayin' is all," Tom snorted. He was a man of few words, like Frank had been. For him to be saying anything meant he was already irritated.

"There anything special I should know about?" Tucker asked.

"You just keep on gettin' on with your business and things are gonna be fine."

Tucker could scarcely contain his curiosity. He seldom knew Tom to string together a sentence longer than five words. He was sure something had the man riled up, but the book was apparently closed.

"I'm on top of it Tom. I'll let you know when I pass the weigh station." There was no response, but that was normal. Tucker had been running the route for three years. Once he was able to purchase his own tractor he had more options about the runs he made. There were times when things were tight and Tom would ask him to do some serious long hauls, but for the most part he was happy with his regular circuit. He had to be at the loading dock by 7 AM, and would complete the route and be home again by 9 PM. It allowed him to keep an eye on his mother, and maintain a regular schedule.

Driving the same road almost every day for several years could very well become monotonous. When Tucker had considered getting into the family trade, this was what he had expected. Much to his surprise, however, he discovered something different. The more he followed the same route, the more he learned about the places he passed. What had once seemed featureless countryside became a detailed backdrop for his days.

His first stop was always the city. He would hook his truck up to the trailer, then back up to the bay doors to get his load. The size varied, but there was something fulfilling about piling boxes into the empty truck, working them into a balanced formation that would remain steady on the drive ahead.

There were days when he missed football. It was the combination of hard physical work, as well as being part of a team that had inspired him. Long days on the road were lonely, but the morning loading time filled him with that sense of teamwork that he missed in other aspects of life.

"Tucker! Always good to see you," Zack Bertram welcomed him into the warehouse. "We've got a big load for you today, hope you had a good breakfast."

"I'm good to go, Zack. Let's get moving."

It was like a dance the way the crew manipulated the freight and moved it into the echoey trailer. They threw boxes onto rolling platforms and formed a brigade to stack and balance them in puzzle-like piles. The men bantered back and forth as they kept time with the fall and subsequent rise of box piles. The process took under an hour and the truck was sufficiently full for the haul.

"Happy driving," Zack pounded Tucker on the back. "See you tomorrow?"

"Of course," said Tucker, turning to the truck and climbing in.

Then he was off, heading onto the next phase of the drive. The city had its share of intrigue; there were people to watch, and architecture to study. However, the heavy flow of traffic required too much attention for him to take in the finer details. The real curiosities began when he moved into the countryside.

When he was a child, long drives were tedious. Living out in the country, every trip to town was exhausting. He would watch the trees for a while, or try to spot animals along the river, but eventually his eyelids would droop and he ended up with drool running down one side of his face by the time they arrived at their destination. In true childlike fashion, the process of getting from one place to another was simply boring; there was no action, no thrill. It only added to his certainty that being a trucker would be nothing but day after day of monotony.

His first few months on the road he concentrated on the technical aspects of keeping the truck in order. He had imagined it would only be a bit bulkier than driving a pick-up truck. He quickly learned that this was far from the case. There were intricacies he could not have conceived before feeling the wheel in his hands and the surging power that rushed through his body when the key turned in the ignition. He had to keep his concentration solely on the task of driving and not running anyone off the road.

By the time he had settled on the route he most enjoyed and secured his contracts, the drive had become routine. He knew every twist and turn in the road, every sound his truck made as it maneuvered around curves and lumbered up hills. It was only then that he began to really pay attention to where he was going.

At first, he noticed obvious things. Rolling fields undulated in the breeze. Heavily wooded forests curved, creating a living tunnel for him to pass through. Scattered dwellings, tucked away here and there amongst the trees, grew closer together into village like communities. His childhood memories of big rigs driving by and blowing their horns in greeting, inspired him to honk at the fist pumping children waiting at bus stops or passing by in cars. Some became regulars during the school year and he invented the stories of their little lives.

Life on the road also gave him a chance to be introspective. There were times when his mind wandered to what could have been if he had been able to escape the title he seemed to have been born to bear. Other times he pondered where the road of life was taking him. It was on those days that he looked closer at the landscape. Slowly, almost imperceptibly, he became attuned to every aspect of the world he drove through. He could sense the changing of the seasons in the flight of the birds and the stages of the crops or the colors of the leaves. He discovered shady dirt roads, and mysteriously winding trails that led into the forests. Rocky outcroppings revealed what might be caves or other hiding places just out of clear sight and completely invisible from a smaller vehicle's perspective. He knew where to expect deer to cross, and how to identify the animals that he saw skittering across the road even from a great distance. The road was a fascinating world of discovery. Every day brought new aspects to light.

On this day, however, he felt strangely low. It was partly due to the conversation with his mother. Things were growing difficult with her, and he worried that he might have to find more help to keep her happy. He wished she would accept Karla, but it was growing less likely that she would. He was also thinking of how many boxes were along on this haul, and feeling the dull ache rising in his back. Despite months of physical therapy, he could never completely escape the damage done in his fall.

Tucker's eyes scanned the countryside as the sun rose higher in the sky. The grain on the hills glowed in the soft light that filtered through fluffy white clouds. By all accounts, it looked like it would be a lovely day. He tried to shake off the feeling of foreboding that had been growing all morning. There was no reason to think the day would be any less ordinary than it appeared.

"Tucker? Tucker? You there?" Flint's voice over the CB broke into his scattered thoughts.

"Tucker the Trucker at your service, Flint," he said, trying to sound upbeat. "What can I help you with today?"

"Aw, nothing in particular Tuck. You know, I just like to check in every now and then, see how life's treating you and all. Thought we might be able to hook up for lunch at Dora's?" He ended with a hopeful question, making it obvious to Tucker that there was more on his mind than he was letting on.

"I think that oughtta work Flint. Got a big load today, but if you can hold out for your break until 1:30 I should be able to get there on time."

"Will do," Flint sounded relieved. "1:30 at Dora's then?"

"1:30 it is," Tucker agreed. "Drive safely."

Flint gave a friendly chuckle as if to remind Tucker that during his twenty plus years of trucking he had logged on fewer than five violations. He was a veritable example of truck driving perfection. The conversation was over, but something about it added to Tucker's uneasy feeling. He closed his eyes briefly, envisioning his bed at home and how welcome a day off would have been.

One of his eighteen wheels hit a pothole that jarred his eyes open in a flash. Day dreams were for break time, not work hours. He was all focus again, looking ahead to the next corner where he would pass a small isolated bus stop. It never failed to amaze him how children seemed to sprout from the ground out here. He had grown up in a small town himself, but after a few years of city living he wondered how these families survived. He might not have had an active social life, but he knew where to meet people when he needed to get away from home. Out here, there was nothing for miles around. It was beautiful country to look at, roaring by behind the wheel of a truck, but not ideal for day to day life.

He noted that the wind was shifting, indicating a chance that the cotton candy clouds above might be joined by something darker and more sinister. He gently rounded the bend and saw the wooden shelter of the bus stop, the boards splintering around the bottom and the shingles looking less than one hundred percent waterproof. The kids were huddled inside, five of them coming from at least three different families. Around the time he started paying closer attention to the things around him, the oldest pair began their school career. He could still recall them standing there on the first day with their mothers: a dark haired solemn boy he referred to as Bill, cringed behind his mother's skirt, while the girl he called Jill sparkled with excitement at the prospect of the future. He knew the elementary school for these outsiders was in a small community another twenty miles away. Even having to travel that distance, the school was a small one. Based on his observations there could be no more than fifty or sixty students between kindergarten and eighth grade that attended the bright yellow school. He had often wondered if there was a disparity of attitudes among the pupils in regards to those who lived close to the school, and these that lived on the outskirts.

Today it was the youngest of the five, a tiny wisp of a girl with long brown braids on either side of her face, who had the privilege of giving him the signal. As always, he gave the horn two long pulls and added a smile and a wave. The children's delight was evident. It was the same every day.

He was still thinking about them ten minutes later when he reached the treacherous corner that began the winding ascent to the next village town. Normally he would check the big lightning blasted tree on the left for any sign of animal life. The hollowed out tree made a great nesting place for various woodland creatures and they brought joy to his day as he geared down for the steep and slow climb ahead of him. Today, however, as he came around the curve he spotted something that brought his foot down on the break. The tires squealed in protest and he could sense the trailer bouncing nervously behind him, but he would not let these concerns prevent him from stopping the truck.

As soon as he came to a complete stop and was able to throw on his warning lights and the emergency break, he jumped out of the truck and hurried to the lump in the middle of the road. At first glance, he had assumed someone had hit a deer, but the instant his eyes came into focus he was certain the shape on the road was not animal, but human. He slowed his step as he got closer, not wanting to cause any unnecessary shock. The body was situated across the white line at the edge of the road and was covered in a coarse, earthy looking blanket or shroud.

"Hello?" he spoke tentatively, crouching down to get a better look. "Hello? Can you hear me?"

The body shifted and he heard a groan. The sound of the truck's mighty engine was clamoring for attention a short distance away, so he had difficulty recognizing if the person was trying to speak or not.

"I'm going to move this blanket to see if you're alright," he said the words loud and clear. "I won't hurt you, I just need to check if there are any injuries." He saw no signs of blood which was a relief. There was no appearance of a hit and run but he was having trouble figuring out why anyone would chose this particular place to curl up and take a nap.

He noticed, with some irritation, that his hands were shaking. He muttered something under his breath about getting ahold of himself, then took a corner of the blanket in his hand and lifted it to reveal the figure underneath. His first and most immediate observation was that there were no obvious injuries, but it was evident that something was wrong with the frail girl curled up before him. Tucker noted that her feet were bare and thickly calloused, her limbs thin, almost to the point of emaciation, and her long brown hair was knotted in heavy dreadlocks.

"I'm going to touch you now, just to make sure nothing is broken," he said, still feeling that something terrible must have happened for her to end up in this situation. She flinched when his rough hands checked the bones in her legs and arms, but her eyes remained tightly closed. She made no sound.

Tucker stood up and took a step back. He needed to think. There was no way he could leave her there, but he had no idea what to do with her either. He could find no evidence of any injury, but felt certain she had been hurt or abused in some manner. He had seen signs for a volunteer fire department in the town he was about to enter, but worried that whoever had abandoned

21

or lost this girl might be nearby with the intent to do more serious harm.

He rubbed both hands across his forehead. It was a nervous action, but also an attempt to clear his mind. "Okay," he spoke aloud. "I'll bring her along in the truck for now, and when I meet up with Flint we can feed her lunch and see if we can talk to her or something."

He stepped closer to the girl and bent down near her face. "I'm going to pick you up now and take you to my truck, okay? I promise nothing's gonna happen to you. We'll figure out what's going on and get you some place safe, okay?"

There was still no response. Tucker waited a moment longer then pulled the blanket over the girl and picked her up gently. He was surprised by how comfortably she settled into his arms. She remained limp, but her head rested lightly on his chest and a protective feeling welled up inside him.

He climbed carefully up on the passenger's side and eased her onto the seat. Her head lolled to one side, but as far as he could tell, she was merely sleeping from exhaustion, not in a coma. The thought that it might be drug induced flitted through his mind, but he pushed it aside. There was an innocence about her delicate features that made it impossible to think ill of her. He strapped her in with the seat belt, then closed the door and hurried to the other side. Before starting the engine he rolled up an extra shirt he had lying around and maneuvered her so that she was resting against the shirt and the door.

Parked immediately around the corner the way he was, he wanted to start moving again before the school bus arrived. The last thing he wanted was to have an accident and increase the risk both to himself as well as the girl, who appeared to be resting peacefully beside him.

Chapter 4

Two hours passed uneventfully. During the first hour, Tucker looked nervously at the girl every minute or so. Just as he had come to know every aspect of the land through endless observation, he absorbed information about her based on his sidelong glances. Two obvious things registered first. She was very thin and had a travel weary look about her.

Tucker had picked up hitch hikers plenty of times in the past. They came in several varieties in his experience. Some were young, out looking for adventure. They wore hardened masks to protect the individuals they dreamed of becoming. Some were societal outsiders. Perhaps they began similar to the youngsters, full of hopes and dreams and ideals, but the pressures of conformity became too much, and they internalized to the point where the general public considered them insane. They were the vagrants, the drifters, the old school hobos that no longer knew how to fit in with social norms, but had plenty of stories to tell. Then, there were the average drunks and drug addicts who ranted and raved and needed to be dropped somewhere to prevent them from doing damage to themselves or others.

Tucker could never put his finger on what drove him to give them a lift. His mother had told him plenty of stories about the risks of picking up hitch hikers, but being on the road with the trucker crowd had taught him a thing or two about how to protect himself and calculate risks. Ultimately, he was intrigued by the wandering souls of the road. Their stories were fascinating, whether real or fictionalized, and their appreciation of the help he provided them with was genuine. They never left his truck without a meal and something warm or cold to drink to sustain them, depending on the weather.

The girl resting beside him had a different look from most. As far as he could tell, it had been a considerable amount of time since her last good meal. During that time, she had no doubt covered a good deal of ground on foot. Her lack of shoes concerned him, as well as the quality of her clothing. The weather was reasonably warm, but the blanket she was huddled in was threadbare in many places and her clothes were equally as worn.

On first glance he thought her to be quite young, perhaps her early teens due in large part to her size. She could not have been more than five feet tall if even that. Her hollow cheeks were smudged with dirt that hid some of her natural beauty. Later, he assessed that she was more likely in her early twenties, making it doubtful that she was a runaway as he had previously surmised. He wondered what could have driven her out on the highways for such a long time, and where she might have come from.

The longer he sat beside her, the more he noticed a distinctive smell. When he had carried her, he had caught a whiff of it coming from her hair. There was an earthy tone to it that was different from anything he had come across before. Unlike the drunks with their sour bitter stink, or the pungent unwashed youths, her scent was shockingly pleasant. Once he was certain that she was sleeping peacefully and in no danger health wise, he allowed himself to breathe in her natural aroma. The more he concentrated on it, the more it deconstructed. There was warmth, like the sun shining on piles of fallen leaves, and a mysteriously floral note, not to mention the rich smell of the earth itself. It brought back memories of times spent wandering in the forests around his home when he was a child, but there were unfamiliar levels to it as well.

After two hours Tucker's mind returned to wandering. He thought about Flint and their upcoming meeting. He enjoyed their get togethers, and wondered what big stories his friend would have today. Then he remembered the feelings of uncertainty he had felt earlier in the day. Looking over at his sleeping companion he wondered if it had been a premonition of someone in trouble. Despite the fact that she did not appear abused, he could tell there was a story to be heard.

Just as he was considering Flint's reaction when he brought this fascinating waif to lunch, he saw her eyes starting to flicker open. He smiled as she shifted on the seat and bleary blue eyes peeked out from under the heavy dark lashes. A split second later and the eyes were no longer heavy with sleep, but wide open and alert to the point of panic.

"Take it easy," Tucker kept his voice low and calm not wanting to startle her.

All the peacefulness that she had exhibited in sleep evaporated. She pulled the blanket tightly around her body and pushed herself as far into the corner as possible. Her breath came out in rapid gasps and her eyes flew wildly around the cab of the truck searching for the best point of exit.

Tucker waited quietly, not wanting to make things worse. Minutes ticked past slowly. He kept his eyes on the road, giving her time to take in her surroundings and to realize that he meant her no harm.

Her breathing regulated and he could sense her tension easing. He wondered if he should try talking again, or wait for her to speak. The last thing he wanted was to have her freak out and hurt herself. He kept both hands firmly on the wheel.

Tucker watched the quiet passing of the trees. He let himself slip into his general observation mode. When she cleared her throat he had become so ensconced in his normal world that it made him jump. He turned slowly, taking in her relaxed posture, but continued to hold his tongue.

She opened her mouth as if to speak, but no sound emerged.

"Forgive me," Tucker's upbringing as a good host came back to him. "You must be thirsty and hungry." He jostled around in a drawer under his seat and pulled out a thermos of hot tea and a mug. "This one's clean," he smiled reassuringly, handing the things to her. She accepted them warily, but once the liquid was in the cup she drank it greedily, filling it twice more and draining the contents.

Without asking, Tucker handed her a granola bar and an apple that he had also retrieved from his snack drawer. She devoured the apple, leaving nothing but the smallest stem and the seeds, however, she looked with confusion at the shiny wrapper on the granola bar. Tucker put his hand out cautiously and waited for her to shyly place the bar in his hand. He tore the wrapper open and handed it back to her. She sniffed the brown oatey mess and tested the metallic wrapper between her fingers, listening intently to the sound it made as she rubbed it back and forth. Tucker was entranced. He had never seen anyone react in such a way. Cautiously, her tongue emerged and she licked the sticky surface. Her eyes rolled in concentration as she processed the sweetness she encountered, and then she sunk her teeth into the bar. By the time she was done, every sugary spot had disappeared from the wrapper. A contented sigh escaped her lips as she settled more comfortably against the seat.

Tucker grinned. Over all, things were going well. He kept quiet leaving her room to speak. The only problem was, she did not speak. She sat quietly, taking in the scenery passing by in a blur outside the windows of the truck. Tucker waited. He was certain she would say something if he gave her enough time. His first break was coming up shortly and he wanted to have at least the beginnings of a conversation with her before he stopped. He needed an idea of how far to take her, and wanted her to feel like she could trust him enough to tell him where that should be. He was more than happy to offer her lunch with himself and Flint, but only if that was in her best interests.

Another half hour passed in silence and Tucker was nervous. The girl seemed peaceful, but he had no way to measure her behavior. All his former riders had been eager to get a word or two in his ear. Even the most sullen ones touted their ideology when given a sympathetic and patient listener. This girl behaved as though he were invisible. Her eyes were alert, scanning the terrain, but had no time to even glance in his direction.

The rest area was rapidly approaching. Tucker cleared his throat. "I'm going to stop up here in a second," he said. "I'd be happy to let you continue on with me, but the choice is up to you, of course."

She looked at him, measuring what his words were worth, but said nothing.

Tucker was nonplussed. He wondered if she was mute, or perhaps, given her somewhat foreign appearance, spoke another language. He pulled off at the exit and brought the truck to a lumbering halt.

When he switched off the engine the silence was almost deafening.

The girl looked around, puzzled, and tried to move but the seat belt restrained her. Panic clouded her features as she began to claw at the belt. Quickly, Tucker sprang into action and pressed the release button, setting her free. The belt whipped back into its place, and she sighed with relief.

"I'm just going to get out and walk around a bit," said Tucker. "If you want to get out too, just pull the handle there." He indicated the metal bar on her door, then demonstrated with his own. She remained silent. Tucker smiled encouragingly, then climbed down and shut the door but left the truck unlocked so she could feel free.

He was gone twenty minutes. He wanted to give her space, and to get fresh air to clear his head. When he got back to the truck he felt prepared for whatever would happen. He would try to speak straight with her, and if she continued not to respond he would take her into town, and drop her off at a rescue mission. If she was in trouble, they would do all they could to help her, and their resources were better than his.

The shiny green door swung open and Tucker was struck by the aroma of his passenger. He hoisted himself inside, eager to see if she would speak, but to his astonishment the cab was empty.

"Hello?" he said, knowing there was no place for her to hide. He hopped back out and walked around the truck. He wished he had a name to call, but he had nothing, and saying "Girl!" seemed inappropriate. She was nowhere to be found, and a battle waged within him. Being a trucker meant sticking to time constraints. He had to be on the move soon in order to make his deliveries, not to mention the meeting he had scheduled with Flint.

There were several cars at the rest area. He looked them over: a family with young children and two dogs, a pair of young men with an overstuffed van on a road trip, two or three people traveling alone. None of them seemed likely candidates for the girl to hitch another ride. He contemplated asking them if they had seen her, but worried there might be repercussions if he did so. The last thing he wanted was to cause more trouble for the girl, or himself for that matter.

He wandered around the rest area grounds twice but saw no sign of his mysterious passenger. 45 minutes had passed since their arrival and he had only moments to spare before he would risk Tom's wrath. Tucker's head hung low as he returned to his truck. He gave one last look around the trailer, then opened the door and swung inside.

He nearly jumped out of his skin when he saw her sitting on the seat beside him. "Wow," he caught his breath. "I looked all over for you. Sure wasn't expecting to find you right where I left you. Is everything okay? Are you ready to go?"

She looked at him quizzically searching his face. Tucker fidgeted with his keys. People seldom paid close attention to him these days. He had stepped away from the lime light after his accident, choosing a solitary life to hide his disgrace. He was about to start babbling again when her look changed to a smile and she nodded.

"All righty then," Tucker beamed. "I'd say that's progress. Maybe you'll even start talking to me next." He could have sworn that she said, "maybe," but the engine roared to life, drowning out all other sounds. The seats vibrated beneath them as he turned the wheel and eased the truck onto the highway.

Unlike his father, Tucker relished a good conversation. He had pulled away from mainstream society, but he sought opportunities for dialogue. He was fascinated by his quiet passenger and could scarcely stand the silence. He resumed his sidelong glances in her direction. She had washed herself up at the rest area. Her hair was a mess, but her face, hands, and feet were cleaner. He imagined the scene she must have caused in the tiny bathroom, and wondered why no one had been saying anything about her when he walked past them.

She was no longer wrapped tightly in the blanket, allowing him a better opportunity to see what she was wearing. Her clothing was unlike anything he had ever seen. It reminded him of medieval attire. Her shirt could be a tunic. It was made of loose fitting fabric and hung down low over the tattered brown trousers. It might have been white once, but it had taken on the color of the road she had traveled and was a dingy gray. She wore a knotted fabric belt around her waist, keeping the shirt from flapping. Despite the grime, she looked put together. Her posture indicated that she was accustomed to high standards in life. He was baffled as to how she had ended up in her current location and longed to engage her in conversation.

The drive was going smoothly. Tucker could almost allow the truck to go on auto pilot, but every now and then he had to focus on taking the right exits. They headed off on a perilous two way road. Many of his colleagues preferred the interstates, but Tucker found ways to beautify his trip that cut down on mileage and never added more than ten minutes to his driving time.

He drove down a winding pass and headed into a ravine. The ground rose steeply on either side of them, some places cutting directly through the rock. Tall trees were rooted into the shallow soil, casting dark shadows over the road. Tucker loved these mysterious forests. He often made up stories about who or what might live in these wild reaches.

They rounded a sharp corner and encountered a breathtaking view of a lake amongst the trees. The mountains opened up to reveal the heart of something truly amazing where little streams converged to fill a crystal clear body of water. There was a pull out beside the road where tourists often stopped to take panoramic photos.

"Stop here."

Tucker clenched the wheel. He felt like one of those people in the Bible who are stopped dead in their tracks by the voice of an angel. As if his body had a will of its own, his foot came down on the brake and he pulled to a halt at the view point.

When the truck came to a standstill he sat staring straight ahead with his hands clasping the steering wheel. He felt frozen, as though time had ceased to exist. It seemed impossible that after so much time had passed she could speak so easily, with such ethereal elegance and purity of sound. Then the idea came to him that perhaps she was an angel. Even as he thought it he knew it was absurd, but everything was so discombobulated inside that he had trouble sorting his thoughts.

An osprey flew across the lake, its wings moving purposefully as it crossed the water. In a flash, it dove and effortlessly lifted out a fish who had launched itself into a magnificent jump after a bug. Tucker was struck by the mixture of cruelty and perfection in the act. Another one of life's endless circles played out before him. Witnessing this natural occurrence shook him from the other worldly experience that had taken place in the cab of his truck. He turned to look anew at the stranger.

"So you can speak," it was almost an accusation and he regretted it, hoping he would not offend her.

She tilted her head and took him in with dazzling blue eyes. They reflected the water and the sky, and flashed with a vitality he had not recognized before.

"Well, what now?" Tucker asked. "We're stopped, is there something else you'd like?"

She turned and first scanned the water, then searched the trees. Her eyes held still and narrowed.

She studied a spot on the hill across the water, then traced a path back to their location.

"Now, we get out." Despite her small stature and evident lack of food in recent days, she spoke with authority. Tucker found his seat belt unfastened and his door halfway open before he questioned the words that hung in the air.

He pulled himself together and faced her. "Now just wait a minute. What exactly do you mean by 'we' get out? Would you mind telling me what's going on here?"

"What's going on," she tested the words as a statement rather than a question. She let out a sigh. "That, I am afraid, is a very long story and we really haven't the time at the moment. You see, I had trouble finding you, and then I was not certain if you were the one I was looking for, but now I am sure and we must continue as quickly as possible."

Tucker shook his head and made his voice as stern as he could. "I have no problem taking you somewhere safe, or even letting you out here if this is where you think you should be, but I'm working right now and I can't just jump out and run around after some crazy girl I picked up from the middle of the road. I mean no offense, but you must see how ridiculous this is."

She took a deep breath, then released it slowly. "I am afraid you do not comprehend the gravity of this situation."

Tucker wondered how someone who seemed unfamiliar with a common granola bar could have such

35

an extensive vocabulary. He had trouble grasping her ability to turn him with every word. There was no possible way he could stop his truck in the middle of his route and go running around creation with some girl, regardless how lovely. He had a full load. People were depending on him. Yet with every word she spoke he felt so compelled to do her bidding that he feared he might succumb.

Her eyes held his and she spoke each word clearly with a slight lilt to indicate that she was not from around Tucker's world. "I promise I will explain everything later, but we have very little time. I have traveled many days in search of you. If you do not come with me now, everything will be lost."

"I'm afraid you're going to have to give me a little bit more than that. I can't say I've lived the most exciting life," he shuddered, "and what you're offering sounds adventurous, but I have responsibilities. If this were the weekend I'd be more than happy to see what I could do, or help you find the person you're after, but I simply don't have time."

"All right," she took another composing breath. "You are correct about a few things. My search was...rather vague. I did not know exactly who I was looking for, or where to find him. That is the reason it has taken me so long to discover you. But after all that searching you appeared. You treated me with deep kindness when I am nothing to but a stranger. Then, to make it more obvious, you brought me directly where we need to be. You must be able to see that this is meant to happen."

Tucker's mind reeled. The more he thought of his daily drudgery, the more he longed to go on this wild goose chase. The fact that the girl had said nothing about her plans, or why he was needed except to prevent "everything" from being lost, he felt compelled to drop everything and follow her. He bit his lower lip in concentration, choosing his words carefully. "You seem like a very nice girl," he sighed. "And I have to admit that just leaving my truck here and hiking off into the sunset with you has a certain appeal, but we must behave like rational adults. I don't even know your name. For that matter, you don't know mine either. How do you know I'm not some crazy psycho truck driver taking you into the back country to make you my slave."

Her laughter shattered the heaviness that had settled into the cab of the truck since the discussion began. It had a tinkling quality that woke him from a deep sleep. "And I suppose next you will say how you have no idea if I have a plethora of knights hiding away behind the trees to capture you and force you into the Gladiator's ring. Right? Well, let me assure you that is not the case. If only we did have more knights these days. Unfortunately, we have become desperate. I am afraid there is danger ahead, but you need have no fear from me. I promise I will tell you everything I can in time, but if we do not hurry we will have trouble reaching the cave before nightfall."

Tucker knew he was staring. He hated himself for it, but with every word that came from her mouth the entire day became more fantastical. "Let's try this again," he attempted to pull things back to earth. "My name is Tucker Kenworthy. I'm a trucker. That's what I do. I drive trucks. I'm pretty much plain and simple and down to earth. Pleased to meet you miss..."

"Ravinna Avilista Meristonia, from the Peaks of Aristone, but you may call me Ravin if that is more palatable. I am the daughter of the hidden Emperor and have many titles that would only bore and confuse at this juncture. At the moment, I am on a quest to find a dragon slayer and that is exactly what I have done."

This was all said in such a matter of fact tone that it left no room for argument. Tucker wanted to disbelieve her. As fascinating as her speech sounded, he would have preferred to put her in a box titled "loony," and taken her where she would not hurt herself or anyone else. However, there was such veracity in her body language, such singularity of purpose in her words, and such beguiling authority in her voice that he found himself believing in the Peaks of Aristone, the hidden Emperor, and an adventure in a cave despite himself.

As he mulled over the possibility that she might be speaking the truth, the words, "dragon slayer" hit him over the head. The idea was inconceivable; completely contrary to the path his life had taken. He fought the urge to laugh. His father had been an avid hunter, when time allowed, but that was another area Tucker had rebelled against. He could appreciate a good steak as much as the next man, but he had done his best not to think too much about the connection between his food and the animals he loved to observe.

"Well, Ravin, this is all fascinating, and I would love to help you, but I just don't think you've found the right guy. If you'd like, I'm meeting up with a friend in a couple hours and maybe he would be more suited to what you need." The idea of "Flint, Dragon Slayer," appealed to him.

Ravinna shook her head and took a breath before continuing. "Tucker," her voice was all seriousness, and the sound of his name on her tongue shook Tucker's resolve. "We could go back and forth on this all day, but it would not change anything. I suppose you have a choice to make. You can continue along in the life you have been living. You can identify yourself with your job, but I see in your eyes that this is not who you are, this is not what makes you happy. Deep inside, you know you were meant for more. So you must choose. Will you trust me, and come, or will you continue on your way and never know the life you were meant to live?"

Her speech conjured up images of his high school commencement ceremony. He remembered sitting there, stone cold inside. There had been so many dreams recently buried, so many emotions threatening to overflow in front of his peers. He had nearly snuck out before being called to the platform. He focused back on the moment and accepted the truth in Ravinna's words. He had been living a life with no meaning, accepting it because it seemed the only option. The woman beside him, completely outside the context of his mundane life, was offering him the opportunity to discover the dreams he thought had expired.

Ravinna had an uncanny way of reading him. Before he could open his mouth to accept her challenge, she was pulling her blanket around her shoulders and preparing to climb out of the truck. He mirrored her movements. Words were not necessary.

They stood side by side, looking out over the sparkling expanse of the lake. "It's time," Ravinna's voice was scarcely above the whispering wind. In a flash, she disappeared over the guard rail. Tucker fidgeted with his keys. He felt uneasy leaving his truck. The repercussions of his actions flew through his mind. He had never let down a client. Even when he was sick, he made sure to have someone else lined up to take his place. Leaving the truck in this precarious location was putting both the vehicle and the cargo at risk. He wanted to radio someone, but had no idea how to explain the situation.

"Tucker," his name was spoken with a mixture of sweetness and authority powerful enough to put him into action. The keys slipped into his pocket and he headed to the guard rail. The ground sloped steeply down before smoothing out into a thick forest. Tucker blanched as he took in the distance between himself and flat ground. Heights had always made him queasy. Ravinna stood at the bottom, smiling at him as though this was the most natural thing in the world. Closing his eyes, Tucker slipped one leg over the railing and then the second, still holding tightly to the sturdy metal. With a deep breath he let go and half ran, half slid to the bottom.

By the time he came to a stop, Ravinna had disappeared into the thick woods. Despite the sunny weather they had been driving through, the trees were so dense that Tucker could scarcely see anything. "This way," the honeyed voice spoke from the darkness. He caught a glimpse of her light colored tunic.

The path they were on was little more than a deer trail. It stayed away from the patches of sunlight that fought bravely to make their way to the forest floor. Tucker's eyes adjusted enough to make out the shapes of the trees which was a blessing for his face, but it was nearly impossible to spot the roots and rocks that sprang up before his feet causing him to stumble frequently. Ravinna, on the other hand, was lithe as a deer. Even in bare feet she hurried nimbly, making him feel oafish.

It was eerily silent in the depths of the woods. Tucker wondered why the birds were so still. He contemplated that they might not settle in such dark regions, preferring the open sunlit meadows where they could enjoy a more beautiful life. It took most of his concentration to remain upright, but whenever the way smoothed out he was overtaken by thoughts and concerns. It was too much to consider where they were going, or what he would be expected to do upon their arrival. Instead, he was muddled with worries about his truck, as well as concerns about the path they were taking. It no longer mattered whether they made it to the cave by nightfall. The forest was as dark as the blackest night.

They had been hiking for a good hour when the path straightened out and entered a thinner patch of trees. The trees were of a leafy variety, allowing more light to filter through to the ground. Tucker gave a sigh of relief, and then remembered he was supposed to be meeting Flint. He had been in such a trance after Ravinna's speech that he had forgotten to cancel lunch with his friend. A fresh list of worries and concerns coursed through his mind.

Ravinna maintained her distance. As far as he could tell, she had forgotten his existence. It was likely that she would arrive at the cave before she realized he was not behind her. If that were the case, she would see that he was not the one destined to save her or kill any mythological dragons. He did an about face, ready to head back, but before he could take two steps in the opposite direction she was beside him.

"Ravin, I'm so sorry. I thought I could do it, but I really don't think I'm the person you want me to be. I have responsibilities. Maybe my life isn't as exciting or interesting, or even as worthwhile as I would like it to be, but I can't just up and leave it without even telling anyone." His head fell and his shoulders slumped.

"Tucker." For the first time she reached out and touched him. The mixture of her voice, her touch, and that otherworldly aroma washed over his senses. He forced himself to meet her gaze.

"Tucker," she said again, "You cannot give up now. I am certain there are people here who love you, who depend on you, and I promise I will not ask you to abandon them forever. I only ask that you come with me now, for this moment, and help my people. In this time the world as you know it, while not a perfect place, is relatively safe. There will be concern about your whereabouts, but in the end things will turn to right when you return. If you do not come with me, however, I fear everything will be lost and the time will soon come when the evil that has settled into my kingdom will spread over to yours as well. Do you want to be the one responsible for letting that happen?"

He thought she might be laying it on rather thick, but each time she spoke there was such gravity in her statements that he feared it would be wrong to doubt her. "Well, when you put it that way..." he gave her a sidelong glance. "But I'm not gonna lie, I'm really not sure about all this. And I have to admit I'm kinda worried about my decision. I've only known you for an hour, and here I am leaving my whole life to follow you into the woods. You have to see how irrational this looks."

Ravinna smiled patiently, then returned to following the trail. They passed through the lighter section, and the trail rose steeply. Tucker struggled to keep up with his wispy guide. She flitted through the trees like a ghost, her tattered blanket flapping behind her. He quickly lost all track of time. Being a truck driver required a certain amount of strength and agility, but this sort of climbing was stretching his muscles in unfamiliar ways. His legs began to burn, and the gain in elevation hit his lungs hard.

"We are nearly there," Ravinna's voice startled him, but the soothing effect it had on him prevented the shock from causing him to fall. The path had become so close to vertical that he felt more like he was scaling a rock wall than climbing a mountain.

Tucker grunted a response and continued to shuffle his way upward. He looked up and caught a glimpse of her disappearing overhead. "Ravin?" he called.

"You are doing perfectly, Tucker," she popped her head over the edge. "You will be here soon."

At this point Tucker realized that he was climbing up a rock face. As long as he believed it to be a trail he was okay, but the reality struck him hard. When he looked up and saw that Ravinna was still twenty feet higher, his heart sank and his fingers gripped the rock tighter.

"Um, Ravin, um, not to be a bother or anything, but I should probably tell you that heights, well, they're not really my thing." Tucker hoped she would miss his tightly sealed eyes.

"Don't be afraid, Tucker. You will be with me in a moment. Just keep climbing."

"I don't think you understand," Tucker was firm. "I know I've gone back and forth on a few things up to now, but this is something different. You never said anything about climbing up an enormous rock. I just can't do this."

"But Tucker," she said patiently, "you already have. Look how far you have come."

"Nope," he knew he sounded about three years old, but he no longer cared.

Everything fell silent. Tucker tried to work out how to get down from his perch. Her words led him to believe that the crazy climbing he had done had put him in the middle of the rock. It had grown darker and a storm was starting. The mixture of darkness, a heavy growth of trees, a large amount of crumbly rock mixed with sand and the choice to blindly follow Ravinna had prevented him from realizing what he was doing. He fought to control the panic that threatened to take over his mind.

There was a scraping sound, and a few small rocks bounced past his head. Since closing his eyes, his other senses grew sharper. "I am coming back down to you," he detected a note of impatience in her voice, but was beyond caring what she thought of him.

"I told you I wasn't going to be any sort of dragon slayer," he muttered. "Just look at me. I can't even climb a rock. How do you think I could kill some crazy flying beast?"

Her laughter took him off guard. His grip on the rock loosened and in a flash he saw his life passing before his eyes. The scene was too short and uninteresting to give him satisfaction. Before he could take everything in, a small hand grasped his with a vise like grip. Everything was a blur in Tucker's mind. One second he was dangling in the air, and the next he found himself on the cold hard floor of a cave.

Ravinna stood over him. Her hair hung down around her face and her dazzling smile seemed to illuminate the small dark space between them. "You really are a wonder Tucker. I might have to keep a better eye on you. If I had not been there you would have destroyed yourself before we made it anywhere."

The air was thick. At least that was Tucker's excuse for not being able to speak. She gave him space and turned her attention to other work. Tucker assessed what had landed him in a little cave in the side of a mountain with an unusually strong and exotically beautiful girl. Nothing added up, and the more he thought the more his brain hurt. In a last valiant effort to make sense of things, he closed his eyes and fell asleep.

Chapter 5

Unlike his pal Tucker, Flint had always wanted to be a trucker. It was in his blood. For as long as there had been big trucks on the road, Flint's family had been behind the wheel: pioneers of the trucking trade. His mother had never been in the picture much. He remembered getting a birthday card from her when he turned six. It had a picture of a little boy sitting atop a horse with the words "Happy birthday" emblazoned in blue on the top. Inside there was something unrecognizable scrawled across the page. He used to believe it said, "Dear Flint, I love you with all my heart and wish I could be there for your special day. You are the best son anyone could ever ask for. Love, Mom." If the scribbling had been his own, that is what he would have written. When he was fifteen he found the card again, tucked away in a book his dad used to read him. On closer perusal he was now certain that there was nothing to be deciphered from the black ink on the page. If anything, he thought he could discern the words "cheese" and "pickles" and perhaps "milk," leading him to believe it was more likely a grocery list.

Instead of spending his formative years under the comforting supervision of a nurturing, loving mother, he spent them in a muddy sweat stained truck. His father even went so far as to install a small steering wheel and side view mirrors on his car seat. Flint had never doubted that trucking was his destiny, never fought to find some other trade.

Flint first met Tucker Kenworthy shortly after rereading the old tattered birthday card. It was the day Tucker joined his father on the truck. Flint considered himself almost a man by that point. He had done his share of time behind the wheel out on the back roads, and could handle a truck better than any of the newer men on the crew.

When the others had donned the kid with the title of Tucker the Trucker, Flint had laughed along with them. There seemed no harm in it to him. Trucking was not only a job worthy of esteem in his eyes, it was the only job worth considering. There was nothing so glorious as listening to the engine of his dad's truck roar to life, feeling it hum beneath his legs, and watching the world pass by through its various seasons. He thought the boy should feel proud to be welcomed into the world of camaraderie, and was surprised when he saw a flash of anger in Tucker's brown eyes as the name was bandied about.

Flint was on the scene the day Frank Kenworthy died. It was a gruesome accident. He was twenty-two at the time, and a full fledged member of the crew with a truck of his own, debt free thanks to years of work for the company. The accident was the type that was safely avoided every day, but that they all realized was a constant risk. They were piling big cedar logs on the back of the truck and a wire snapped. The lift operator did his best to swing the hefty trunks back in the right direction, but one of them refused to behave and went rogue. The massive force of tree hitting metal caused the truck to rock. Frank, fearful that his beloved machine would be lost, rushed out on the scene and leapt for the cab, no doubt hoping he could find some way to bring it back level. Instead, even as he began to open the door a second wire snapped and this time all the logs began to tumble down uncontrollably.

Flint had watched in horror as one of them caught Frank in the chest and carried him heavily to the ground. There was a terrible ruckus as the metal of the truck was twisted and pulverized by falling trees. By the time the dust had settled enough for the men to approach the scene, Frank's life had expired. There were no parting words to be heard, but somehow Flint believed himself charged to look after his colleague's young son.

The funeral itself, was almost as unforgettable as the image of the mutilated body Flint had helped remove from the scene. The casket had been closed, of course, and most of the words the minister spoke were a blur in his ears. What he carried with him was the salty smell of Nance Kenworthy's tears as she hugged him and thanked him for coming, and the steely look of determination in Tucker's brown eyes when they shook hands. He had seldom come into contact with the boy in the years since his visit to the work site, but he had never forgotten the resentment he had seen at the nickname. What he saw at the funeral struck him even more deeply.

Being young and single and living life on the road, Flint had thrown his money about in a number of foolish ways. He was seldom proud of these flings when he was sober. With every hangover he would swear to mend his ways and would leave an unmarked envelope with whatever cash he had left in the Kenworthy mail slot. He followed Tucker's sports victories in the paper, then read with horror about the accident, and increased his giving to the family. All the same, he knew it would not be enough to keep Tucker's dreams alive.

When the time came, and Tucker did, indeed, join their crew, Flint was the first to befriend him. He never once mentioned the money he had given them, or expressed his feelings that he was meant to watch over the younger man. Thanks were not something he needed. Frank had been a good man and Flint wanted to do right by him. He could sense a belligerence in Tucker, but chose to ignore it. Making a big deal out of the issue would be a waste of time. Instead, he welcomed him as a brother, and did everything he could to ease him into his newfound profession.

Flint could never recall when things had changed. He had always enjoyed being reckless. Whenever he got into a mix up his father had bemoaned the fact that the boy had grown up without a mother. This excuse had rescued him from punishment frequently as a child, and when he got older, he used it to win over women. He told them he needed a little motherly loving and was amazed by how well it worked, at least for a short time. On his days off, he could party with the best of them, and had little mothers at stops all along his routes to cheer him on cold nights.

Looking out for Tucker had helped to sober him up for a while. He wanted to be a good example, someone Tucker could look up to and ask for help. They quickly became great friends, but once he could tell Tucker was managing things on his own, Flint slipped back into his wilder ways. He never missed a delivery, but he often had to mask his bloodshot eyes with dark glasses, and had managed to fake more than one urine sample when mandatory drug tests were required.

Flint knew it was just a matter of time before something was going to come undone. He had seen it happen with other men on the crew. Willy Lawson had lost it on some girl he caught cheating on him at a regular truck stop. Never mind the fact that Willy had even more lady friends than Flint. The story went that Lawson was so drunk he forgot to wait until they were out of view of the tavern, and shot the girl and her new boyfriend in plain view of everyone. Flint had a temper, and was well aware that these things sometimes snuck up on a person. The only good thing he knew that came out of Lawson's mishap, was that he picked up a couple better paying jobs for himself and was able to finally

buy the deluxe sleeper cab he had long been dreaming
to own. His new truck had the works, including a
shower, a fridge and a flat screen television. He had
invited Tucker over for a drink to mourn the loss of
Willy and to celebrate the victory of the new truck.

It was around then that Flint became aware that
Tucker helped him more than the other way around.
When he woke up hungover the next morning, Tucker
had already cleaned the place up and made coffee to
help get him ready for his next run. He wished he could
be a better example, but resigned himself to the
hopelessness of that idea, and instead relied more
heavily on the support of his younger friend. Things
were now completely flipped around in their
relationship. Flint was no longer the mentor, instead he
used Tucker as his confidante.

Things had been going pretty well for a while,
and Tucker had helped him out of a little financial
difficulty his proclivity for gambling had gotten him
into, which put him further into his friend's debt. He
still owed a lot of money on his custom truck, and this
fact helped keep him out of some very tempting
trouble. However, the past weekend had been more than
his weakness could take. He had met a pretty little lady
at a stop, and was giving her a tour of his well equipped
lodgings when her husband showed up.

There were two major things Flint had learned
in his years behind the wheel of a truck. The first was
that you never mess with a married woman. This
particular girl had been angry at her man, Flint
suspected she had even been abused by him, and had

been without a ring when he met her. He, therefore, considered himself blameless in this instance. The second thing he knew for a fact was that a trucker should always be armed. He had never been a gun man. He knew quite a few truckers who never drove without a loaded weapon in their glove box. Some did it for a general feeling of protection, and others claimed it was to help the mutilated animals they frequently brought to tragic ends, to leave the world more quickly. He was pretty sure that second line was just an excuse, but he respected their right to having protection. Personally, he was more of a knife man. He had a six inch blade that he always carried on him, and kept sharp enough to slice through just about anything like hot metal through butter.

When the angry husband had pounded on his door, he had tried to reason with him. He pointed out the honesty of his mistake, and was quick to assert that nothing had happened between himself and the little misses. The woman, seeing the fateful error of her ways, had quickly rushed out to plead with her husband not to be angry. When he pulled out a gun and aimed it at her head, Flint felt more than obligated to defend her honor. Come to find out, she was even more of a little minx than he had realized. When her husband fell to the ground clutching what was left of his shooting hand, she shouted at Flint like he was all to blame. Drunk as he was, Flint had started the truck, driven away, and made it thankfully to a rest stop where he had done his best to sleep it off.

He needed help. Things were getting out of control, and he was hoping Tucker would be able to help him sort things through. Flint knew there was more for Tucker than being saddled with the trucker nickname that had become his job title. He saw in the younger man a depth of character and an ability to help people that astounded him. For Flint, life was a plain and simple affair. There was plenty of hard work to be done, but on the other hand there was plenty of fun as well. The only problem was when the fun slipped too far in the wild direction and he found himself in a predicament. That was exactly where he found himself now, and so he pressed on toward his lunch break and the chance to talk it out with Tucker.

Flint arrived at the cafe right on schedule. He was stressed, and his big rig jostled up over the curb and into the parking area reserved for trucks. He saw no sign of Tucker yet, but knowing the roads Tucker liked to drive he figured there had been some sort of delay.

Dora's Cafe had been opening its door to people on the go for more than thirty years. The original Dora still served guests with a smile and a husky laugh that hung around despite the fact that she had quit smoking more than a decade earlier. Her husband, Walt, ran the grill, and their six children had filled in every role possible before moving on to other parts of the world. Every now and then, one of them would come back when life got hard, and they always knew they could put in time at the cafe.

The decor had scarcely changed in all those years. Wide strips of tape held the once cheerful red booth seats together, and the black and white checkerboard floor was so scuffed that it was nearly an even tone of gray. Dora kept the table cloths neat and pressed, so the chipped tables never showed their age to her faithful customers. What the place lacked for in visible appeal, it more than made up for in flavor. No customer ever left hungry or dissatisfied. If there was even the slightest complaint Dora was there to retrieve the unsatisfactory item and replace it with a smile. Her natural generosity of spirit, and her husband's skill in the kitchen, kept the cafe lively, despite its backwater location.

Flint walked in and took a seat at his usual table. Despite his lankiness, the bench seat squeaked beneath his weight and he shifted around until he was comfortable. He idly picked up a menu. There was never any question what he would order, but he liked to look.

"Flint!" Dora had a way of making him feel like his presence was a blessing. "So good to see you again. It's been a while."

"Yes ma'am," he replied with a grin. "But you know every chance I get to come through this way I never pass you by."

Dora's face lit up with a wrinkly smile. "I'll be right over with a fresh coffee in a minute." Then she added in a low conspiratorial tone, "Andrew's back for a while, so we're a bit behind, but it won't take but a minute for me to get things in order again."

Andrew was one of her sons. He had a few bad decisions on his record, and while he did help out around the place, it was hard to tell what he managed to get done.

"Andy, Hun," Dora called. "Andy? Can you go ahead and heat up some fresh coffee?"

A grunt sounded from the back followed by some shuffling about. "Not more than a minute or two," Dora winked at Flint.

"Just so you know, Tucker should be in soon too," Flint said.

"Tucker? Heavens, that boy's always in such a hurry to be on time. I better get his burger on the grill right now. Want me to start your steak?"

Flint laughed. It never ceased to amaze him how Dora could remember so many things about the men who passed in and out of her cafe. He had often enjoyed watching the dance she did with her patrons. They only had to come in once, and they were never forgotten by the remarkable woman. She made them all feel welcome and at ease. When he caught his breath he finally responded, "Go ahead. Tucker said 1:30 so I expect to see him pulling in any moment now."

As he sat there, the clouds lifted from his mind. The coffee was ready promptly, and Andrew managed to be cordial when serving it. There was nothing like a thick juicy steak, cooked to perfection, with a side of steak fries and a slice of Dora's homemade blueberry pie to make Flint feel like he never lost his mother. With Dora's food in his belly and Tucker's listening ear he was sure he would have the whole problem sorted by the time he pulled back onto the road.

A wind rushed past the cafe, sending a chill through Flint's bones. He looked at his watch and noticed that it was already 1:35. He signaled Dora for a second cup of coffee, puzzled that Tucker had not arrived.

"You said 1:30, right?" Dora asked, mirroring his thoughts.

"That's what I thought," Flint scratched his head. "I don't think I've ever known Tucker to be late for an appointment."

Dora poured the coffee and studied the weather out the window at the same time. The day had started out in a blaze of glory, but now dark clouds were blowing in from the west. Something was wrong. "Do you want me to bring out the food?"

"Let's give another five minutes," Flint's stomach growled at the thought. "If he doesn't show by then I might go out and give him a call."

The clouds built up with immense speed. In the five minutes Flint waited, they blanketed the sky. Images of blinding rain storms and sky splitting lightning filled his mind. He wondered what could be keeping his friend. He knew Tucker liked to take the back roads and he reminded himself that it only took one little accident or mudslide to shut things down in those lonely places.

Dora returned as promised, her concern evident. "It's not like that boy to run late," she commented.

Flint nodded. "Let me run out and give him a call to see where he's at. I've got some leniency in my schedule, but he likes to keep things tight. Don't want him to run out of time to eat."

Dime sized drops of rain splattered the ground at intervals as Flint rushed to his truck. He was quick to send out the call. "Tucker? Tucker, you about here? Dora's got your burger up and if they leave my steak on the heat any longer it won't be much good."

Flint paused. The rain thundered down on the hood of his truck. The radio remained silent. "Tucker?" The silence was deafening. Flint tested his equipment but everything was working. He pulled out his cell phone. Something in him generally rebelled against modern technology. When he first started driving truck the CB was the only option. He knew that most of the younger set were tied more to their phones than their radios these days, so he gave Tucker's number a try. It rang for more than a minute, then passed him to voice mail.

"Uh, Tucker," he never knew what to say on such contraptions. "Uh, Tuck, yeah, this is Flint. Just checkin' in. It's about..." he fumbled to look at his watch. "1:42 and I thought you said 1:30...so I'm at Dora's. Gimme a call. Bye." He ended the call with relief which was soon replaced by worry. It was unlike Tucker to go on radio silence on a run. Even on the back roads he always had some form of communication open.

He trudged back through the rain, not noticing how soaked he was getting. Dora held the door open. The look on his face was worrisome enough to alarm his hostess.

"What's happened, Flint? Has there been an accident?" She put a motherly hand on his arm and led him back to his seat.

"I don't rightly know, Dora. I tried to contact him every which way and there was just nothin'. Something's not right. I don't like this at all."

Without thinking, Dora sank down on the seat across from Flint. It was obvious that she was remembering the accident that took Frank's life. She had only known him by reputation, but had followed the story in the papers and said her prayers for the family.

"I'm sure he's all right," Flint took a long drink from his coffee mug. "He's a tough kid. He'll turn up."

"How long we gonna hold this food back here, Ma?" Andrew called from the back. Dora looked at Flint, the question echoed in her worried gray eyes. "Go ahead and bring me that steak," he said finally. "I don't want it like a rock when I eat it. Just keep Tucker's back there so it stays warm. He'll show up. He always does." His voice was void of assurance, but Dora stood and followed his instructions.

The steak arrived, juicy and beautiful as ever, but it went down like cardboard. Flint remembered his secret promise to look out for Tucker and felt like a failure. He had so many regrets, but he knew that if anything had happened to his friend he would never be able to forgive himself. The personal worries of the moment had to be set aside.

The food disappeared and the time moved past two o'clock. Flint knew he would have to hit the road shortly if he was going to make his next stop on time. There was no sign of Tucker at 2:30, and he had to go. He paid for Tucker's meal and tipped Dora generously, then left without another word. The cafe was bustling with lunchtime traffic, but Dora took the time to stand at the door and wave goodbye as Flint headed out.

With his truck in motion, he decided to radio back to Tucker's headquarters and let Tom know something was up.

Tom responded immediately when Flint hailed him over the radio. "What's up, Flint?" he was all business as usual. "Lookin' for a new run?" He never missed an opportunity to get a quality driver on his team.

Flint chuckled despite himself. "Not today, Tom. I was actually checking in to see if you've heard anything from Tucker. He was supposed to meet me at Dora's for lunch but never showed. I tried calling him and got nothing. Just not like him to disappear."

Tom quietly took the information in, mulling over the possibilities. "You're sure you got everything right? The time? The call signal?"

"I even called his cell phone," Flint assured him.

"Thanks for letting me know, Flint. I'll look into it right away." The conversation was over.

Flint drove on through the storm that was growing increasingly more violent by the minute. It was nearly pitch black outside, and the road was slick with fresh rain. Flint focused on driving, knowing that if he let his mind wander toward what had happened with Tucker he would never make his delivery on time. He had done what he could. He knew Tom kept GPS devices on all the trucks driving for him. He would be able to find Tucker and figure out the problem. Worrying would do him no good.

Chapter 6

Tucker stirred in his sleep. A cold wind was blowing in through the mouth of the cave. He shivered and let his eyes slowly flutter open. Night had fallen, and the world outside was black. He could hear rain falling heavily, and the distant booming of thunder. There was a small fire nearby, its flickering flames sending shadow and light dancing off the dark stone walls. Ravinna sat hunched next to the fire to keep warm. She seemed to be studying something in her hands.

Tucker's mind was awash with the realization of what had happened. He was in a cave, in the middle of nowhere, with a girl he barely knew, supposedly on the way to kill a dragon. The absurdity of it all was enough to make him burst out laughing, but he managed to hold it in.

He moved slowly, and was surprised by how much his body was aching. Between the strenuous climb and sleeping on the cold hard floor of the cave, he hurt everywhere.

"You're awake," Ravinna was by his side at once. "Here, drink this. It will help." She reached out and handed him a small wooden cup with a dark and steaming liquid inside.

"What is it?" Tucker asked as the strong smell hit his nose and set his eyes to watering.

"Best not to ask," she smiled and there was a sparkle in her lovely blue eyes. "But it will help to remove the pain from your bones and to give strength for what is coming. The storm has come in, and the mountain is obscured so everything is falling into place."

As if to lend credence to her words, a resounding boom shook the walls of the cave and an even colder wind howled through the opening. Tucker held his breath then tossed the foul smelling liquid straight down his throat. He had never been much of a drinker, but had gone out a few times with Flint just to keep an eye on his friend. He had been obliged to take a shot or two on such occasions but the burning sensation that now filled his entire body from this one swallow was unlike anything he had ever experienced. His eyes flew open and he looked with shock at Ravinna. To his astonishment she was laughing. Between the pain coursing through his veins and the brutal pounding of the storm he could scarcely hear the magical sound of her laughter, but he thought he saw tears streaming down her face as she sought to control herself.

"Is it really that funny?" he gasped, wiping a different kind of tears from his own eyes.

Ravinna nodded as she composed herself. "Come along then," she took him by the hand and pulled him to his feet. "We must be on our way. It appears that animals have gotten into the supplies I left on my first arrival. The only thing they didn't touch was the distilled dragon urine which you have now consumed. I hope it will be enough to sustain you for the next stage of our journey."

Tucker knew it was useless to ask questions. After experiencing the horrifying drink he was beginning to believe it might well have come from a dragon. As he followed her, he could feel the fire subsiding inside and settling into a healing warmth. Exactly as Ravinna had promised, the pain was wiped away leaving him invigorated.

While he slept, Ravinna had made a torch which she lit in the fire. Once it had a good burn going she doused the flames. "We want to leave as little trace as possible," she said. "It is bad enough that animals were able to find the food I stored here, but they are more clever than humans in the art of food discovery." She quickly spread the ashes across the floor, mixing them in with the dirt.

When she was satisfied that they would leave little trace of their presence, she turned toward the back of the cave. The flickering light of the torch made it hard for Tucker to decipher what he was seeing.

When he first surveyed the cave, it appeared to be little more than a walled in curve in the mountain rock. Now, as he continued behind his petite guide, he learned that it continued on into a narrow tunnel. He thought about mentioning their size difference and his uncertainty that his particular bulk was going to fit along the ever shrinking passage way, but he had a feeling that such protests would be fruitless. After moving between some large rocks the space widened, and Tucker was able to breathe a bit easier.

An old memory of visiting a cave in the middle of Montana when he was a kid resurfaced in Tucker's mind. His parents had taken a rare traveling vacation to visit a cousin who lived in the mountains there. Most of the trip was a blur in his mind, but being in the cave brought it all flooding back. The cousin had wanted to give their family a little thrill and took them to the cave during off hours. He had a friend who ran tours there, and was more than willing to have a little sport with a man like Frank Kenworthy who seemed to know no fear. Tucker shuddered as he recalled the moment when the lights went out, leaving them in a darkness so pure that no amount of time was going to reveal even the vaguest of shadows.

Frank had raged against his cousin, insisting that the lights come back on immediately. He had forgotten how, when they were children, he had once locked his cousin in their grandmother's cellar after telling him that it was where she used to torture her children when they were naughty. The family had been helpless for no more than five minutes, but they were the longest minutes of Tucker's young life.

"Tucker," the soothing glow of her voice calmed his nerves and made the cave appear brighter. "Things are going to get tight in the near future. I am sure you will have doubts, but if you trust me, we can make it through."

The reassuring quality of her voice was slightly negated by the meaning of her words. Tucker felt the walls pressing in coldly on his arms. He had nearly tripped over a rock rising from the ground while lost in his reverie, and it was taking all his manly will power to ignore the spiderwebs that clung to his face.

"And it will be a bit darker as well," the bad news flowed peacefully from her lips. "I will have to pass the torch through ahead of us, and I am afraid my body will block most of the light, but it will only be for a short time."

"Um, Ravin," Tucker mumbled, "I'm sure you're a very observant person, and the size of my body in comparison to yours can't have missed your notice. In other words, if you're going to have to squeeze, there's just no way that I'm going to be able to make it through."

She stopped and turned to look at him, the torch flickering warmly in the space between. "I would not have brought you here if you would not be able to follow me," her voice was barely above a whisper. "Do not lose hope now."

Tucker had an undeniable urge to scratch his head, but even as he brought his arm up it scraped against the wall of the cave. The rock was so sharp that it sliced through his skin before he could think to pull his arm back down. A gasp escaped his mouth and he clamped his hand over the scratch. He could feel the warmth of blood on his fingers and felt certain that this incident would be enough to prove his point. He realized it would be difficult to turn back, but the idea of continuing was impossible.

Ravinna passed her hand through the flames to reach his arm. The feel of her small hand on his skin tickled his nerve endings and sent a shiver through him. Confidence circulated through his system. He had trouble remembering why he was so worried. "I promise," Ravinna murmured, as her fingers ran down his arm to his hand, slowly wiping away his concern. The flames flickered around her as she pulled her hand back and turned down the narrowing passage.

Tucker told him himself that the reason he suddenly felt cold was because the torch was no longer warming him. He let his eyes adjust for a minute, trying to catch a glimpse of what lay ahead. The walls of the tunnel continued to constrict to the point that even light was scarcely able to make its way back to him around the slender frame of his guide.

"Put your hand on my shoulder and let me lead you," the mellow voice was barely more than a breath, whispering his worries away. His hand seemed to move of its own accord, balancing gently on the girl's narrow shoulder. A sigh escaped his lips and a tingling sensation ran up through his fingers and down his spine. Despite the heat running through him from the nasty drink, he felt a chill that was far from unpleasant. There was a smile in Ravinna's voice when she spoke again.

"Just don't step on my feet, if you can manage that much."

Tucker laughed at her comment, but a new amazement silenced him. With each step they took, the rocky walls pulled in tighter around Ravinna's body, but when he moved forward behind her they did not touch him. It was unfathomable, just as the idea of there being dragons awaiting him at the end of their journey was unfathomable.

They moved in silence, the walls constricting and stretching invisibly around them as they passed. Tucker lost track of time again. He wondered if he would be able to explain this to anyone. He thought of Flint. He could imagine the worry he must be experiencing at Tucker's sudden disappearance and he hesitated, not allowing himself to consider how his mother would respond.

"What is it?" Ravinna's voice was anxious. "Did you hear something?" He felt her body go rigid under the weight of his hand as she strained her ears for whatever caused Tucker to stop.

"No," Tucker admitted, puzzled by her reaction. "I was just thinking of my friend, Flint. I was supposed to meet him for lunch. I can't imagine what he must be thinking right now. I'm usually the stable dependable one in our relationship. And he sounded really eager to see me, too."

Ravinna relaxed. "I am certain your friend will be fine. I will try to have you back soon. We are getting close, and I should warn you that there are dangers ahead." She lowered her voice further, to the point where he had to hold his breath to hear her.

"When we get to the other side of the cave," she breathed, "we will be in the heart of dragon territory. I should have explained more to you, but I was so desperate for you to come that I did not want to risk your fear."

Tucker wished she would turn around and look him in the eyes when she was speaking. The tension in her voice was infectious, just as her peace could be. Panic built up inside his stomach. "You see, there is not just one dragon...there are many. They are not all to be feared. But the evil has spread through many of them, destroying much of what once was good. This is why it is necessary for you to help us." She paused. "I promise I will tell you everything when we are in a safer place."

Tucker shook his head, trying to take in what she was saying, and felt something fall in his hair. He took his hand off Ravinna's shoulder and reached up to brush whatever it was away, but the rock walls pushed in around him, their sharp edges pricking his skin on all sides. He fought to turn his head but it felt as though he was in a rocky cocoon.

"Ravin," he gasped into the rock filled darkness.

"Try to relax, Tucker," her voice was low, but above the whisper so that the musical quality of it had returned. "Remember, you are supposed to trust me."

He held on to the authority of her words and slowly stretched out his arm toward where she had been standing near him. At first his fingers encountered nothing but rock, and he felt a distinct desire to scream.

69

The image of Flint came to him, and he knew that screaming would be ridiculous. He would never be able to live down a scream. He breathed in musty dirt, mixed with the sweet earthy smell of Ravinna. His hand moved again, and the rocks vanished as he found her steady shoulder.

He chose not to ask more questions, or to speak at all. With a reassuring squeeze to say he was ready, Ravinna understood that it was time to proceed.

After not more than ten steps, the light of the torch flickered brighter around the edges of Ravinna's body. The tunnel opened up into a cave. Tucker let his eyes readjust. On this side of things, the cave sparkled in the torchlight. The rocks were no longer sharp, but smooth and inviting. He kept his hand on her shoulder, but could not resist the urge to turn and see what they had come through.

Again, he came to a standstill. From his perspective it appeared as though they had emerged directly from the wall. There was no hole that he could detect.

"Almost there," Ravinna spoke in response to his hesitance. He wondered if she could read the panic in his posture as he realized there was no turning back.

Tucker did his best to accept that her words were good news, despite her previous warning that they were soon to be entering some insanely dragon infested region. He forced his feet to continue, one in front of the other, keeping time with Ravinna's soft, confident steps.

Light spread around them in a steady flow. Tucker noticed it was no longer the torch lighting the way. In fact, he realized Ravinna was not carrying it anymore. He wondered how he had missed her setting it aside. He kept his eyes open, drinking in each development. Moss grew on the walls of the cave, and their feet splashed in water as they passed through a small stream. A desperate thirst burned his throat, but he was afraid to open his mouth while they were in a dangerous position.

Ravinna stopped and bent down cautiously, as though reading his mind. She tested the water on her fingers, then pulled out the small pouch that had carried the distilled dragon urine. She rinsed it carefully, filled it with water from a small clear pool, then slipped it back into the folds of her tunic. Once it was secure, she wordlessly encouraged Tucker to scoop some of the water into his mouth. She avoided speaking at all costs, so Tucker followed suit and held his tongue.

Tentatively, he reached his hands into the water. It was icy cold, but he paid little attention, greedily bringing the liquid to his lips. He sighed contentedly as it eased down his parched throat and brought sweet relief. Unfortunately, it also caused him to remember how long it had been since he had eaten anything and his stomach growled loudly. Ravinna tensed at the sound and cast her eyes around the cavern, but there was no other sign of life.

With a sigh, she indicated that Tucker should sit. As he settled to the ground, the aches and pains that his earlier drink had burned away, welled up in his body with a vengeance. A wave of exhaustion washed over him and he longed to curl up and sleep, but Ravinna shook her head, seeing where his mind was headed.

She indicated that he take a look around rather than sleeping. After so long in dark tight spaces, he had assumed they had entered an enormous brightly lit cavern, but as he paid more attention, he realized the area they were in was little more than five feet wide and barely any higher than his head. The cave curved ahead, and the light that seemed so bright merely trickled into the area where they sat. Tucker examined the walls. They were smooth and in the areas where the moss did not grow, were covered in strange symbols. His mind flickered back to pre-historic cave drawings he had seen in his school books. These, however, were not the simple stick figures of some mythic cave men, nor were they the stylized hieroglyphics of the Egyptians. What appeared simple at first glance, quickly became intricate works of art that seemed to move as they told their unreadable stories.

He stared in awe, trying to figure out what he was seeing, but before he could take it all in Ravinna was pulling him to his feet, mouthing the word, "later" as she did so.

Reluctantly, he stood and brushed himself off. It was no longer necessary for him to have his hand on her shoulder for guidance, but he wished he could. He held back, not wanting to do anything that she might find inappropriate, but still followed her as closely as possible without actually touching her.

Her body was tense, as they rounded the corner at the end of the cavern. She held Tucker back with her hand, indicating that he should wait. He wanted to see what was around the bend, but her guidance had brought him safely so far and he wanted to keep her happy since she was his only connection to anything resembling reality. She disappeared briefly and in her absence a new smell came to him. As long as Ravinna was nearby her woodsy freshness kept the dank despair of the musty cave from impacting his mood, but now that he was alone he noticed a putrid stench coming from the opening in the cave.

His initial impression of where they were headed had been a place of growing light, something appealing after the pitch black cave. Now, the light took on a sinister design in strange compliance with the stink that was growing exponentially by the moment. There was an eerie shimmer in the air and his imagination ran wild as he worried if Ravinna was some dark angel leading him unwittingly down the pathway to some sulfurous hell in the middle of the earth. He shook to clear it, finding it impossible to connect Ravinna to such a dastardly plan.

Then she was beside him again, a breath of fresh forest air. She took his hand in hers and squeezed it, not daring to speak even in her dulcet whisper tones. With a slight nod and a deep look into his eyes, she beckoned for Tucker to follow her. It was hard for Tucker to grasp how it could be so much easier to breathe when she was around. The reek was in the background, but it became tolerable.

As curious, in a dark sense, as the awful odor had made him, nothing in his mind had prepared Tucker for what he would see upon rounding the bend with Ravinna. As beautiful and peaceful as the cavern where they rested had been, the one they entered next was the polar opposite. It took only a moment for him to locate the source of the malodorous plague on his senses. The origin of the light remained elusive, as they crept into the enormous room that had the appearance of the gaping mouth of Hell. If he had ever tried to picture some ancient village attacked by vicious dragons, the sight that met his eyes would pale in comparison to the blinding horror of reality.

The ground was littered with corpses in various stages of consumption and decay. The dragons pursuit of human destruction was clearly not fueled by a need for food. Tucker blanched and sought wildly for something to look at to distract himself from the horror. He realized that if Ravinna had given him any hint of what they were to encounter he would have passed on her offer. Maybe being a trucker was less than glamorous, but at least it was relatively respectable.

He was so overwhelmed by the cruel vision before him that his eyes were unable to grasp the other fairytale aspect of the scene. As Ravinna tugged on his hand to keep him moving he heard something skidding beneath his feet and realized, with another wave of shock, that the floor was also covered with vast amounts of treasure. Gold coins, sparkling jewels, piles of glittering valuables were scattered everywhere creating mountains of unimaginable wealth. Tucker shuddered, wondering if anything could ever wipe away the sheer terror he felt in that room.

Ravinna squeezed his hand, as tightly as she could, her fingernails digging into his flesh in an attempt to wake him from his stupor. He looked into her eyes and was met by immeasurable sorrow in their shadowed blue depths. As awful as the carnage appeared to him, he realized for her it was dramatically worse. For all he knew, she might be facing the dismembered bodies of people she knew. Even if they were not her intimate friends, they were her people, connected to her in the way the people in his home town were connected to him.

Tucker found himself fully aware of her face for the first time since he had studied her sleeping profile in the cab of his truck. Her eyes, large and luminous had signs of tears welling around the corners. Her full lips were a tight line of determination, and the rest of her features solidified with purpose. He was struck by the thought that this was not her first time passing through this place, and he wished he could be the strong force that would support her in this time, rather than being her bewildered puppy.

He had never thought of himself as a coward, nor had the idea of being a hero crossed his mind. Life had gone differently than he had planned, but that was how life was. In the beautiful tragic face before him, he saw true suffering. He and his mother had mourned the loss of his father. It had altered the course of their lives in many ways, but it was nothing compared with watching an entire world being torn apart.

With a solemn nod, in which he imparted his commitment, his solidarity as it were, Tucker signified that he was ready to proceed and would in no way hinder her, regardless of what was to come. They continued along with as much stealth as possible.
Tucker did his best to avoid the macabre scene surrounding him, and focused on staying upright. It was like hiking over sand dunes as they attempted to pass through the mountainous piles of treasure. The coins shifted and slid beneath their feet making silence impossible no matter how much they willed it.

Tucker figured the cavern must be at least a mile across. He had assumed they were near the opening to the cave, but as they maneuvered their way around he realized that the light source came from the middle of the room. For the most part, the scene was silent, but he heard a bubbling sound coming from the area where the light was strongest. An urge to investigate welled up inside him, but he fought it wisely, putting yet another question into his long list of things to ask Ravinna when they were in the clear.

After what seemed an age, Tucker realized that the environment around them was changing. He blocked out most of the bodies and bones, but noticed when they started diminishing, as did the treasure. It grew darker. The mysterious light was clearly behind them, and they found themselves in a wide tunnel, much roomier than anything they had traveled down previously. Ravinna relaxed slightly, but they were still in a dangerous location.

When the ground was clear of both gold and human remains, she pulled the pouch of water out and sprinkled it over the places their feet had tread. She made Tucker walk in front of her so she could wash away the evidence of their presence in the forbidden dragon lair. The passage opened up on the right and a different light drifted in, but when Tucker headed in that direction he felt a hand pulling him into deeper darkness on the left. He fought the tickling sensation of panic that crept in as he was pushed into another tight dark space. Ravinna doused the opening to their trail before following him.

He could feel her small body pressed close to him as she made her way into the lead. There was no light this time, just the heady aroma of flowers in the sunshine that made her earthy scent so complex. He was drawn after her without a thought in his head.

"Thank you," she breathed into the darkness. Tucker thought he had imagined the words into her soft breathing, but when he nearly stepped on her he realized she had stopped and was facing him. She was surprisingly timid as she reached her hands up to touch his shoulders and pulled him closer to her face so she could let the words waft directly into his ear as she spoke them for a second time.

Then they were moving again, before Tucker could pull his senses together. When the light filtered in this time it was connected to something new, a slight breeze that spoke of life beyond their own. There was a greenish tint to the flickering rays that played before his eyes, and then a sound of water falling.

The sound grew in greater proportions than the light. Tucker imagined that they were going to come out beneath a massive waterfall, and he was not mistaken. When the sound grew to a boom, he was greeted with another unbelievably glorious noise: Ravinna's laughter. She ran ahead of him and he followed her lithe figure through the semi-darkness until they burst through a tangle of dangling green growing things and stood beneath the powerful splash and spray.

Tucker's senses had never been more clear. Each sparkling drop was a precious miracle. Each breath of fresh air was the most amazing gift. Ravinna slipped her hand into his and laughter surged from a place deep inside that Tucker had never experienced before. They laughed together and he experienced the elation that each particle of water felt as it raced to discover all the world had to offer.

"We made it," Ravinna's shout remained little more than a whisper above the clamor of the waterfall.

"Yeah," Tucker shouted jubilantly back. "We sure did." Without thinking he picked her up and swung her in a circle of joy. Ravinna held her reaction in, but when she was firmly on her feet Tucker questioned his sanity. After all, she had straight out told him her father was an emperor.

"One victory down," she said, "but more to come. It will be dark soon. We must push forward if we hope to reach safety before they return."

The light was so brilliant after all the time spent in the cave that Tucker had not realized that what he saw was little more than the day fading into twilight.

He had no concept of how long they had been walking. Ravinna was already moving. He had never experienced such a strong desire to slow time down. There was so much to process, so much to see, but his guide was disappearing through the lacy covering of the waterfall.

Ravinna stopped on a rocky ledge a few steps beyond the edge of the falls, her hair hanging heavy around her shoulders from the spray of the water that was now only hitting her occasionally. Tucker followed her gaze outward and took in the vast landscape before him. His life was filled with contrasts. As much as the massive cavern they had passed through had looked like Hell, the beauty his eyes beheld was more reminiscent of his ideas of Heaven. In a flash, he took in the cliff where they balanced. He traced the water to where it pelted a pool far below. Not wanting to let dizziness get the better of him, he focused his vision past the rolling hills that cycled between forest and farmland to the distant peaks silhouetted against the background of the glorious fire sky that ranged in color from a vibrant gold where the sun was just disappearing, through shades of orange, pink and a dusty purple as it faded into night around the edges.

"Ravin, where are we?" he asked. He turned to her, awe evident in his face.

"This is Aristonia, my home," she sighed, contentment mixed with a slight edge of anxiety. "But we must not linger. Look again," He followed her gaze and made out a dark shape in the sky. It moved with shocking speed, growing frighteningly larger with each

passing moment. Then he realized it was not alone.
"Quickly," Ravinna was a blur of motion.

Tucker refused to let himself think about how precarious their situation was. Between the body crunching fall potential, and the great beasts drifting heavily through the sky, he wondered which death he would prefer when he was not strong enough to keep himself focused on trusting that Ravinna knew what she was doing.

The light was rapidly fading. He was thankful he could no longer see the way the massive dragons would have blotted out the sun if it had been present. "Hurry," Ravinna's voice urged. "Into the trees." As they fell behind the protective trees a strange sound filled him with a dread he had never known. A screeching howl echoed across the valley, reverberating against the rocks. It was greeted by others, each a distinct voice and each equally brutal in its variation. Ravinna grabbed his hands and forced them over his ears, covering her own as soon as she was sure he understood. It was an instant too slow to blot out the undercurrent to the sounds. The screams they overshadowed were all too familiar in their humanity. Visions of the mutilated corpses in the cave surged before Tucker's eyes and he cringed.

Ravinna looked back at him, willing him not to give up but to continue following her. With blind obedience he discovered his body was already in motion. They kept their hands clasped tightly over their ears as they moved deeper into the forest. Darkness was becoming all too familiar. Tucker ignored the scratching of the branches against his face. He no longer wondered when they would arrive or how anything would ever seem right again. His life had lost all sense of reason.

Light flickered in the darkness. Ravinna headed toward it with determination. Tucker responded to the urgency in her movements and picked up his pace. He realized he had been holding her back, and wanted her to feel his commitment to keeping up with whatever pace she chose. They were running then. If he could have moved out of his body and watched their progress they would have appeared as one person, their movements perfectly choreographed, even as they fumbled through the darkness with hands clamped to their ears.

A small structure solidified from out of the darkness. A thrill of joy surged through Tucker as safety reached a hand toward him. A tree root contradicted such thoughts as it hooked itself around his foot and brought him crashing to the forest floor. Ravinna sensed him hit the ground. In a blur of motion, her hands flew to pull him up. He had kept his ears covered, rather than shielding himself from the fall, and he could taste blood mixed with dirt, tree needles, and rocks in his mouth. He tried to process everything happening, but he was yanked from the ground with surprising force. Only when they were safely in the presence of the light, the door slammed shut behind them, did he realize that Ravinna had not acted alone in this rescue mission.

His body sunk with relief to the floor of the small room. There was too much in his head for him to take anything in but the fact that panic was no longer necessary. He was vaguely aware of voices and multiple pairs of hands. A thought crossed his mind that made him want to laugh hysterically. Somehow, he was supposed to be a hero in this story. Ravinna had passed through so much danger and hardship to find him, but all he could do was fade away into oblivion every time things got risky. A chuckle escaped his lips as he berated himself, but there was not enough energy in his body to protest as they settled him into a bed and covered him with something soft and warm. Then he knew nothing.

Chapter 7

Flint would have liked to deny that his hands were shaking when he answered the phone. He had made his delivery in the nick of time, and continued on his way as the day prescribed, but he had been antsy and anxious the whole time. He had the worst feeling about what might have happened to Tucker. In all the years he had known him, Tucker had never been unavailable. Even when the guys were mocking him with the dreaded nickname, Tucker did what he could to keep composed and even laughed along when he could manage.

It was nearly ten PM and he kicked back in his deluxe expanded cab. No expense had been spared when he had upgraded his old truck for this beauty. He had a small apartment where he collected mail, but this truck was his home. He had installed a flat screen television complete with satellite access. There might not be 3,000 square feet to stretch out in, but his bed was big enough and topped with a thick layer of cushy memory foam that felt like his own personal piece of Heaven.

Flint liked to keep up his tough exterior. It was easy to convince people that he was unable to maintain a large closet full of clothes, and he liked the rough way it made him look to wear them until they were threadbare. People might have considered him next door to homeless, but as far as he was concerned, he lived like a king. One of his favorite secrets was his passion for cooking channels. He saved up episodes of his favorite cooking shows and challenges, then watched them on lonely evenings. Being a trucker had been his primary goal in life, but there was a part of him that harbored secret desires to become a chef on the side. He imagined coming into a challenge and knocking the socks off the judges. They would never fathom someone so honestly frightening looking, could make such gloriously divine offerings.

Tonight, however, even his favorite diversions were not enough to keep his mind off his friend. He had resisted the urge to call Tom, and felt downright heartsick when he thought of Nance, Tucker's mom, but he was certain calling anyone would make matters worse. When the phone finally rang, he had to struggle to keep his voice tough, rather than emotionally rough.

"H'lo," he said.

"Flint, it's Tom." He recognized the voice at once, but hearing him identify himself solidified the certainty that bad news was coming. "We, uh, we found the truck..."

By the time Tom pulled himself together enough to continue, Flint had envisioned a thousand scenarios of how it looked. He could picture the ravines it could have tumbled over, or the panic when Tucker must have realized the car hurtling at him was going to run out of time to pull into the right lane, convincing him he would have to swerve and take the fall.

"He wasn't there," Tom muttered, his tone a mixture of sadness and mystification. "Just...gone."

"What do you mean, 'gone'?" Flint asked.

"Exactly that," Tom replied.

"So was the truck burned so badly you couldn't find the remains? Or was he ejected somewhere? We'll have to search. I won't let Nance be left without a body. Not after all she's been through. She needs to be able to say goodbye to her son," Flint could feel the blood pumping through his body. It reminded him of the feeling he got right before a brawl started up.

Tom tried to speak in the midst of the speech, but it was useless. When Flint stopped talking he hesitated a minute before continuing, "You got it all wrong, Flint. I told you we found the truck. Truck's fine. Not a scratch. Load perfectly intact."

"But you said," Flint began to protest.

"I know what I said, Flint," Tom clenched his teeth at the other end of the connection. "We found the truck, but Tucker wasn't there."

Flint had no words. There was silence for a good thirty seconds, long enough to be awkward; long enough to feel a whole lot longer.

When Tom decided he had shut Flint up he continued. "Soon as I got off the call with you this afternoon I looked into it. Checked the GPS. Saw the truck wasn't moving." He took a deep breath. Words were not Tom's strength. Flint held his tongue despite the myriad questions forming in his mind.

"Gotta admit I thought the worse, same as you. Tried to call and got no response. Always knew Tuck liked to take alternate routes, but it'd never been a problem..." his voice broke off. Flint had always imagined that Tom was just about the payload. He wondered if he was worried about Tucker or upset that he was short a good driver.

Tom took a deep breath, composing himself. "Didn't want to scare anyone, so I decided to make the drive myself. Figured if it looked bad when I got there I could call in help. Even on those back roads, people drive by. If the accident was bad someone else was bound to be there." Another intake of breath, this one quick like he had been burned. "The truck was just sitting there," he said, awe in his voice. "Not a scratch. No sign of struggle. Parked at a sort of look out place. Real pretty place actually. All trees and water way down in the mountains. Would've been a bad fall if he'd gone off there. Even looked down just to see, but there was nothing to see. He was just gone."

Flint tried to take in what this could possibly mean. Obviously there had to be something they were missing. "You said no sign of a struggle, so did you look for one?" Flint asked.

"Not just me," Tom's voice was tense and defensive. "Soon as I saw the truck was okay, I called for back up. Brody and Sam were both off today, and Mitch had a run close enough to pass through. You know how the guys are. They couldn't believe it either. Brody even tried to find if there was some sort of trail, like if he went to take a leak and slipped off somewhere. But you know Tucker, Flint. Good guy, but awful scared of heights. Sometimes the guys teased him about how high he was off the ground in his own truck! Just can't see him takin' the risk of running around in that sort of country. Guys get sorta invisible up in the mouths of these beasts, but it's like Tuck just climbed out and disappeared."

Flint's mind was racing. He quickly determined that he would go himself, but it would have to wait until first light. He needed the rest if his mind was going to be clear enough, and he would have to find a replacement driver in a hurry. His own problems had dimmed to insignificance in the face of his friend's peculiar disappearance. "Did you call Nance?" he asked, forcing himself to concentrate on the crucial things.

"Yeah," Tom's voice was low. "Didn't take it too well."

"Can you blame her?" Flint snorted.

"Don't take it so personal," Tom was on the defensive again. "Did all I could to break it gentle. But you know that woman. Few screws left since Frank... Anyhow, she was ready to call in the police, but you know they like to wait a while. Truck abandoned in the middle of nowhere with no sign of a driver ain't quite enough for them to take action. Gotta be 24 hours or some such garbage. I think Nance is calling down to the station now, pestering them within an inch of their lives if I know her."

Flint almost laughed at the thought. He imagined she had done the same to Tom. Nance was no more likely to take this sitting down than he was.
"Thanks for getting back to me," Flint said at last. "You'll let me know if you hear anything more?"

"Course," Tom was relieved.

Flint decided it was best to hang up before things went on any longer. He doubted Tom was responsible for what had happened, but there was something about his reactions that left Flint on edge. It felt like the run was more important than the man. He wondered if Tom had called so many guys just to make sure they had enough hands to move the load off to someone else. He was certain that when he went to investigate on his own the truck would be empty. If the police asked any questions about that whenever they got around to investigating he imagined Tom would defend himself saying that he had a responsibility to his customers, and that there was no missing evidence in the load. Flint sighed, knowing it would probably be the truth, but it made him cringe. It was highly unlikely that he would ever drive a truck for Tom.

He contemplated giving Nance a call. Ideally, he would reassure her, let her know that he was going to do everything in his power to find Tucker. The more he ran the idea around in his head, the more he knew it would play out differently in reality. If Nance was able to hold herself together enough to hear him, she would be such a ball of crazy emotions that everything would get twisted. In the end he might even find himself confessing that he was responsible for Tucker's disappearance.

He rubbed his eyes with his fists trying to hash out a plan. The entire scenario felt wrong. In the background, he heard someone being declared the champion of the show he hadn't watched. They would be taking home ten thousand dollars and making their dreams come true. Flint sighed, knowing how fast ten thousand dollars could be reduced to nothing. He turned off the television and the lights. Sleep was unlikely, but it was necessary if he was going to help his friend.

Chapter 8

Tucker knew he was dreaming. There was no other way to explain anything that was going on around him. His mind was on overdrive, or maybe hyper-speed. He twisted his head tentatively, and opened his eyes a small crack. Everything around him was in technicolor. It was all a touch too vivid, almost glittery.

"Nice," he muttered. The meaning of the word was undecipherable. Thoughts and memories mixed and jumbled. There was a scent in the air that was wrong. "Five more minutes, Mom," he said, plain as day, then flopped his body over and put his arms over his head.

His eyes were wide open then. He was no longer in bed, but was lying on the ground, a dark shadow covering him. Someone nudged him gingerly, with a shoe covered foot rather than a hand.

"Flint?" he squinted because everything was too bright. "What the...?"

Flint pulled him to his feet and Tucker brushed himself off, as though the action would help him clear his head. "A beauty, ain't she," Flint drew Tucker's attention to a shiny black truck parked a short way from where they stood.

Tucker could only stare. The grill of the truck shone in the bright light of the sun; chrome bars that resembled razor sharp teeth. The black paint of the nose rippled back from the front, drawing his eyes up to the darkened windows. They had been tinted so dark that he could distinguish nothing behind them, but the longer he looked the more he sensed a glimmer of something that felt like intelligence behind the closed off eyes.

As he watched, the truck roared to life. The engine growled angrily and smoke billowed from the side stack. Tucker took a step back and Flint let out a wild laugh. There was a grinding of gears, and as Tucker tried to hold his ground, he noticed that the trailer was not at all what he had been expecting. This was no separate entity, but the true body of the beast. As the wheels went into motion the truck spun around revealing a huge scaled body that stretched behind it, eventually dwindling to a spiked tail.

Laboriously, the truck picked up speed and as it did so the wheels unwound from themselves. Tucker's mouth was gaping. The tires uncurled completely and revealed themselves to be powerful legs with sword like talons curving from the feet. The sides of what could scarcely be called a truck undulated, and leathery wings unfurled. With a horrifying screech the truck turned beast lifted itself from the ground, as Tucker fell.

He wanted to scream for Flint to run, but his voice had taken flight with the dragon and he could do nothing but watch as his friend squealed with toddler like delight, clapping his hands and hooting with glee. Frantically, Tucker searched for something, anything, to drive the monster back. It hovered, the grill twisted into a wicked silvery grin.

Flint skipped in circles, tracing the lines of the dragon's shadow. Tucker sensed that they were not alone. A girl stood in the trees. She looked familiar, and he wondered if she had visited his dreams before. The sun glinted off something in her hand, but before he could register what it was she was throwing it directly at him. A spear somersaulted through the air and Tucker prepared himself for the blow that was to come, not noticing that his hand had flown out to catch it midair.

"Isn't it great, Tuck?" Flint called in a singsong voice. "Do you think we can keep it forever and ever?" He giggled and threw a handful of flowers in the air.

Tucker wondered where the flowers had come from, his mind trying to justify what was happening around him with any reality he had ever experienced. The spear vibrated in his hand, drawing him back to what was important. He looked up just in time to see the jaws of the mighty truck beast widen, preparing to clamp down on his unsuspecting friend. Tucker heaved the spear directly into the gaping mouth. Even as he did it, he questioned why he had chosen this particular move. In any book he had ever read involving dragons, there was a soft spot amongst their scales that the hero had to attack. There would be a chink in the armor protecting the area around the heart, or a weakness around the neck that made it possible to decapitate it. He could think of no good reason to throw his weapon into the gaping mouth.

He hit his forehead frustrated by his stupidity. The chrome teeth and vicious jaws would no doubt snap the spear in half. Instead, things slowed down. He looked around and saw everything at once. Flint's arms flopped lazily up and down, the girl in the forest ducked behind the trees for cover, and the windshield eyes of the dragon gaped wider as the spear slipped between its teeth and lodged in the back of its throat. A slow BEEP...BEEP...BEEP and then BOOM, played itself calmly out in Tucker's ears and the truck monster shook violently. The thick black skin became transparent as an orange glow inside exploded, surrounded by billows of smoke.

Tucker oscillated between a desire to cheer or scream. It seemed inevitable that while the beast was defeated, the aftermath was going to destroy everything. He watched as the wall of flames came for him, and was baffled when he felt was a cool hand on his forehead.

There was a soft whisper in his ear, the exhalation of breath tickling him in a pleasant way.

"Tucker," the voice said. "Tucker, you were having a terrible dream, but you are safe now." Instantly, his body relaxed like a deflated balloon. There was authority in the voice.

"Tucker, it is time to wake up." When his mother said those words they always came out as a command. This time it sounded like the most reasonable request ever uttered.

When his eyes came open, he had the feeling that something was still off in the colors, but now they appeared both more subdued and also richer than normal. "Where? Wha?" he mumbled as he tried to sit up. The attempt to speak caused a burning sensation in his face.

Before the world around him became clear, Ravinna's face was next to his, her expression begging him to listen to her explanation. "We were in a hurry last night and you," she hesitated, embarrassed. "You fell. I am sure everything will be fine, but you hit your head, well, your face...very hard."

Tucker wondered how serious the damage to his face must be. Ravinna tried not to grimace when she looked at him. He was sure he must be horribly disfigured. He had never considered himself movie star material, but the girls in high school had liked him well enough when he was a sports star.

"Everything will be fine," she muttered, reassuring herself more than him.

"Maybe I'm not cut out to be your dragon slayer after all," the words hurt him more physically than emotionally. Everything had come back to him. The reality was about as puzzling as his dream, but he was relatively certain he was sane.

"Let me get you something to eat and drink," Ravinna scurried away before he could ask more

94

questions. Her departure from his side gave him space to think. He had trouble making sense of the way her presence befuddled him.

He looked around the room, taking in the meager furnishings. The place he had slept was more of a bench than a bed, shoved up against the wall. He noticed that, while the room was compact, the benches around the walls indicated that as many as eight people could sleep here. The ones sleeping on the door wall and the fireplace would have to be rather short, but the space was clearly intended for housing as many people as possible.

The more he looked, the more he discovered. What appeared to be shelves running higher around the walls were beds as well, and beneath the benches he noticed there were more bedrolls tightly packed in neat lines. He wondered what the purpose of this place could be, but figured there would be time for questions after he had something to eat. In answer to that idea, his stomach growled loudly, drawing a nervous laugh from Ravinna where she was preparing something on the table in the middle of the room.

Tucker ignored his grumbling stomach and continued his perusal of the room. There were pouches for food and water hanging from the higher ring of bed shelves. Everything was carefully organized and prepared for quick access.

A large pot hung over a blazing fire on the side of the room across from him. He imagined witches' brew boiling inside the massive cauldron, but tried to keep at least one foot in reality. The fire provided the only light in the room, casting a cloak of mystery about the place.

The only other furniture was the table. There were several baskets on it, and Ravinna was picking through them for food. A small window in the door revealed that it was still dark outside. Tucker wondered how long he had slept.

The flickering flames tried to lull him back to sleep. He traced the lines of the shadows they cast and noticed something else around the table. There was an animal skin rug there, and beneath it he thought he could detect what might be a trap door. His mind reeled with ideas to explain the purpose of these items.

Ravinna made her way toward the pot over the fire, a bowl in her hands. He avoided looking directly at her, but as she moved into the glare of the flames he realized that she was not the same as before. Not only did her movements appear refreshed, he noted that she had cleaned herself up. Her clothes were no longer the loose fitting rags he had discovered her in, but were figure flattering and elegant. He wondered how the fabric that shimmered around her as she swayed in the firelight might feel.

He realized he was staring when she turned toward him. Their eyes met, and the breath whooshed from his lungs. Indeed, she was nothing like the dirty waif he had lifted from the road and studied in the cab of his truck. Her dark hair was still dreaded, but it was more contained, and her face was so smooth, so perfectly formed, that he wondered how he could ever have thought of her as anything less than a princess. A blush crept across her cheeks and Tucker composed himself. He no longer had any doubt as to why her presence made him feel weak in the knees. Her voice, her smell, everything coalesced with the vision before him.

"The others will be here soon," her words tumbled out as she handed him a wooden platter. The bowl was on one side, filled with a thick dark stew, and there was a large chunk of bread and cheese along with a mug of steaming liquid.

Tucker stammered a quick, "Thank you," as his appetite redirected his focus. The food smelled healthier and more appealing than anything he could remember. It took every bit of his will power to prevent him from gobbling it up like a wild animal. He gripped his spoon tightly, and let the hot liquid flow down his throat. He got a large chunk of hot potato at the same time, but fought the urge to howl with pain and instead puffed his way through it, proceeding with more caution and a large bite of bread. He was thankful Ravinna was not watching him the whole time while he ate, certain he was going to make a fool of himself every second bite or so.

"We need to find you some different clothes," her voice blossomed from across the room. "The others will be here soon, and you will be shocking enough without that."

Tucker wondered what she meant by her comments, but the food was so good that he simply nodded in agreement, certain Ravinna had everyone's best interests in mind. She wandered around the benches until she found what she was looking for. She pulled a leather bag out and began to rifle through its contents.

"You are probably closest in size to Arthyr," she reasoned, pulling things out from the sack. "I have no idea what to do for your shoes, though. Maybe we can wrap something around them to make them less obvious."

Tucker pulled his focus away from the food and looked more closely at what Ravinna was wearing. Her feet were wrapped in green boots that seemed to be more a natural part of her body than clothing. He remembered her filthy bare feet, and wondered if she had chosen to walk that way to blend in better in his world.

"I am just glad Arthyr was the one on guard duty last night. It would have been much more difficult to get you inside otherwise. These will still be a bit...short. We will just have to make do."

She handed Tucker the pile of clothes and he held them up questioningly. If this Arthyr was the closest person around to his own size, there was no doubt in his mind that he would do more than stand out. The shirt looked like it might be about large enough to go around him but the sleeves would not stretch past his elbows, and a wave of doubt washed over him at the idea of exposing his stomach. When he held up the trousers Ravinna laughed.

"Okay," she agreed to his unspoken question. "Perhaps a cape will suffice." She pulled out a long gray cape and handed it to him. "It's quite shapeless, and would trail the ground on any of us, but it might be enough to wrap around you," she offered hopefully.

Tucker swung the cape around his shoulders. It was soft and warm but surprisingly light weight. It did, indeed, wrap easily around him, and nearly came all the way to the ground. Ravinna studied him critically, bringing a blush to his cheeks. She nodded and looked him in the eyes, as if testing his ability to be natural with her this time.

"It will do," she confirmed, and he felt as though he had passed a test. "We don't normally wear these indoors, but they will understand. As it is, the questions are going to be endless."

"And what about my questions?" Tucker ventured. "I do recall you promising to tell me more when we arrived. I'm going to guess we're here, and so far the more time that passes, the more questions I have."

"You are quite right," Ravinna nodded as she hesitantly sat beside him. "Unfortunately your, um, accident, threw off my plans somewhat."

Tucker had forgotten about his face. He reached up gingerly to touch his lips, his nose, his cheeks, trying to assess the damage. The food and Ravinna's appearance had so thoroughly distracted him that the pain had all but been erased.

"I was hoping we would have a few more hours before daylight when the others will arrive, but I know I will only be able to scratch the surface before they come," she pointed toward the window and Tucker noticed that it was not as dark as it had been when he opened his eyes. "We have ten minutes at best, before the first will return."

"Ten minutes is better than nothing," Tucker encouraged.

Ravinna drew in a deep breath then began in a low voice. "Maybe it's best to explain this place first," she absently waved her hand around the room they were in. "If they are calm enough when they return, there are better tellers than I to share the real story at hand. I noticed you observing things and could see the questions on your face. And of course," she laughed lightly, "there is the obvious clothing issue. We are not so very different from you, but I should warn you that I am abnormally tall among my people."

Tucker tried to figure which thought was more absurd, that Ravinna was considered tall, or how the look on her face implied that she felt shame in regards to her outward appearance. The more time he spent with her, the more entranced he became, certain she was the most beautiful creature he had ever laid eyes on. He recalled their time together in the cab of his truck and how he had thought she was merely a child because she was so tiny.

"Beyond the obvious physical differences," she continued without any pause, "we could likely pass ourselves off as average citizens in your world. As the dragon problem increases, that has been suggested by some, but there are those of us who would prefer to maintain our own way of life."

Tucker did his best to focus on the words she was speaking rather than trying to analyze the way her voice warmed him from the inside out. There was a diplomatic quality to her speech, and if he lost control of his thoughts they began to wander to an imaginary scene with her addressing a large and important delegation in some exotic location. A quick swipe of his hand across his face was enough to bring the pain back in a rush, helping him concentrate on the present.

"For many years, we have lived in peace. Sadly, there have been dramatic changes over the past decade that have put our survival into question. Places like this have been set up across the land to provide housing while our warriors seek to deal with the dragon issue. As I am certain you have noticed, this particular stronghold can house up to fifty soldiers when necessary. Currently there are only fifteen in full time residence," she sounded disappointed with the number.

"Besides the faction that would have us leave our homeland, there are also those, like my Uncle Karush, who would have us make unhealthy allegiances. The history of our world is long and complicated, but about a year ago my Uncle managed to use some trickery to remove my father from power and send him into hiding."

Tucker remembered something about a hidden emperor and wished there was time for him to ask questions. "As long as Karush is in power, the outposts are all but abandoned. He has made compromises with the dark dragons," she released a bitter sigh.

Before she could continue, the door burst open and three people entered. It was difficult for Tucker to think of them as men at first. The tallest was scarcely

101

more than four and a half feet tall, but the weapons they held made him take them seriously.

The emotions that crossed their faces at the sight of him ranged from fear to anger to utter incredulity. "Stemoor, stand down," Ravinna's voice carried authority. She stood to her full height to add weight to her words.

"Majesty," he gasped, "What is it?"

"Friend," Tucker watched her word work magic on the warriors. Just as Ravinna's beauty defied reason, these men went against his ideas of their size. He had expected them to look dwarfish like tiny people he had read about in fairy tales. However, their bodies were heavily muscled and perfectly proportioned. The only difference between himself and them was the fact that, at 6' 2," he towered nearly two feet over them.

"Is he...?" the obvious leader of the group seemed unable to put what he was thinking into words.

"Yes," Ravinna clearly needed no further explanation. "That is the plan."

"What happened to his face?" the second voice was higher than the first, and slightly muffled due to the fact that the speaker was hiding behind his leader. A snicker followed the comment as though he figured himself invisible, and therefore safe from the giant's wrath.

"He had an accident when we first arrived," Ravinna admitted, "But Arthyr was here and he patched him up so he should be as good as new in no time."

At the mention of Arthyr, the group visibly relaxed. It appeared that, while they knew they must

obey this voice of power, the one they trusted was
Arthyr. "I sent him to assess our travel options for the
afternoon. He should return shortly."

The mood shifted. "You mean you intend to
travel by day?" Stemoor was shocked.

"Did you hit your head as well, my Lady? It is
not to be thought. As it is, this place is gravely
dangerous in the night, but by day, they no longer have
any respect. You have been gone a long time. Things
have not improved during your absence."

Ravinna's head drooped. "I am aware of the
current situation," her voice was resigned, "but we
cannot wait any longer. I must get Tucker to my father
immediately. He must be trained and ready to kill the
dragon as soon as possible. If not for the fall, we would
have been on our way at first light."

Tucker cringed at the thought that his
clumsiness had caused further problems. He had passed
out in the cave before their journey started, and had
been nothing but trouble since Ravinna drug him
behind her. His embarrassment grew greater when he
heard the men whispering his name, tasting the
strangeness of it on their tongues.

The door opened a second time, and five more
miniature men entered the room, equally well armed,
and instantly bristling with distrust and uncertainty.
Over the next half hour the pattern repeated every five
or ten minutes until everyone had returned and been
informed that the giant in their midst had come to help
in their fight, not tear them limb from limb.

Arthyr was the last to arrive. Whatever rumblings might have been passing between the warriors, they were silenced when their leader entered the room. He was clearly not disturbed by Tucker's presence and even went so far as to offer him a smile. The man was huge in comparison to the others, standing at an impressive 5 foot 3. His arms were bulky with muscle, and his girth was clearly not the result of eating too many sweets. Everything about him exuded confidence and strength, but the sparkle in his eyes spoke of something else as well.

"Greetings Ravinna, Tucker," he said, depositing his weapons in a pile near the door. Tucker made a note of the fact that the other warriors continued to clench their weapons at the ready. Arthyr glanced around the room at the fidgeting men. "What's this?" he asked.

"We have a lady in our home and a brother in arms who has graciously come to our aid in our darkest hour, and you stand here like a bunch of nervous women. Have you even tried the...?" he broke off mid question and turned to face Ravinna, "Have they even tried the stew? And do pardon me for that comment about women, your Highness. What is wrong with you all?" he spun back on the men.

The jaws of several worked furiously in an attempt to defend their actions, but no sound came out.

"I believe I took them by surprise," Tucker's voice surprised even himself, but the impact of his speech on the others was more intense than he had expected. A few of them cowered at the depth of his tone, and those that withstood the booming looked dumbfounded by what he had said.

Ravinna's lovely features twisted into a look of despair and she hid her face in her hands. "Sorry Arthyr, he slept so long I ran out of time to cover everything. Tucker, I am afraid to say that they will not understand a word you say."

There had been plenty of things that baffled Tucker over the course of his time spent with Ravinna, but this took him completely aback. He had taken for granted the fact that this otherworldly girl spoke and understood English perfectly. It had all felt so natural that he never could have imagined the other people in Aristonia would be any different, especially since he could understand them as easily as her.

Arthyr grinned and patted Ravinna familiarly on the shoulder. "Our little Angel," he winked at Tucker. "Sometimes gets ahead of herself without remembering that we aren't all as quick as she. I suppose the first thing out of her mouth when she met you was that she was in need of a dragon slayer, now wasn't it?"

Tucker nodded mutely. His head was spinning the way it did when he found himself balancing precariously from a great height.

"Well, never you mind," Arthyr patted Tucker on the back. Then he turned to his men, "Eat up, boys. We have a real chef in our midst today. You won't believe the magic she's worked on our usual fare." He winked at Ravinna this time, but her face was shrouded by her hair so Tucker wondered if she had even seen the gesture.

"Arthyr, you are too much," Ravinna muttered so low only Tucker could hear. Tucker considered what the relationship between the two might be. Clearly, Arthyr respected her as a natural authority figure, but his familiarity suggested something more. Age was an impossible thing for him to judge, but he estimated that Arthyr was likely in his mid to late thirties, not all together too old for her, and clearly he was a man to be treated with respect. All the same, the thought of them as a couple rankled him, and he found himself hoping it had to do with their military positions rather than anything romantic.

Arthyr rounded the table and picked up a platter like the one Ravinna had given to Tucker. He piled it with bread and cheese, then filled his bowl with stew. His actions broke the spell, and the men set down their weapons and rushed to the table, greedily eyeing the spread with relish.

Their snorts of appreciation reminded Tucker that he had not finished his own meal, nor even tasted the steaming liquid in the cup. He looked into the mug nervously, remembering the last unidentifiable liquid Ravinna had served him, but figured this had to be better. He smelled it, and was relieved by the heady scent. Sipping cautiously he was rewarded with a sweet and fragrant warmth that glided down his throat and left him feeling satisfied and blissfully warm at the same time.

Ravinna took her seat next to him, and watched the men devouring the food she had prepared. Tucker sensed discomfort on her part, but she had nothing to fear. "Is everything all right?" he asked softly, not wanting to stir up any added controversy among the ranks.

"Oh, fine," she sighed. "It's nothing really. Arthyr thinks I am silly for responding this way, but it is so frustrating when they behave in such an unbelieving manner. I have done everything possible to prove to them that I am more than just some useless princess in a tower. I guess I hoped that finding you and bringing you here would make them finally trust me, that's all."

They sat in silence, listening to the sound of jubilant chewing. "Sorry about the language. I didn't exactly forget, but, well, I forgot."

"About that," Tucker shifted uneasily, "What does it mean?"

A smile broke across her face, lighting it up brilliantly. "Before all the madness happened I had such lovely dreams. I have two sisters, you see, and what beauties they are. So lovely and talented and positively sweet that they hold everyone who sees them in the palm of their hands. They are treasures more valuable than dragon's gold, and were even a part of Karush's villainous scheme." Her eyes dimmed and Tucker hoped she would get back to the idea that made her smile so beautifully at the beginning of her story.

"Well," she continued, "I am nothing like them. They are petite delicate creatures with graceful figures and they purely embody sweetness and light. I am the tall gangly awkward one. I think my father was secretly longing for a son when I was in my mother's womb, and when I came out with a mess of dark hair instead of the feathery blond tresses of my sisters, he decided he might as well make the most of me.

"I went through the standard knight training, just to see what it was like, but while I excelled in some areas, I never had the kill instinct. My father praised my ability to track down anything and my endless endurance, but when he watched me compete with the men, even though I was taller than most, he saw that I was not the son he was trying to make me.

"So my training changed. He let my mother have her way, and I went through the ladies side of things as well, but, to put it mildly, it was soon evident that was not my calling either. They were at a loss as to where I should fit in. While my sisters delighted and entertained the kingdom, I went into hiding. I discovered my father's vast library and everything in my world changed. He never told me how he did it, but somehow he had managed to collect books in languages that were not familiar to our little world. Along with my sisters, I had learned the mandatory greetings in the languages of our neighbors to the north and south, but the books I fell in love with were from a greater distance than any of us could even fathom.

"And there, in those ancient volumes, I discovered my gift," her smile radiated joy and warmth, and Tucker wondered how anyone could see an ugly duckling in this exquisite creature. "Although the languages were unfamiliar, I spoke the strange words on the page and discovered that I could understand them. Even more peculiar was when I realized I could speak them and make them understandable to those closest to me, or those with whom I chose to share them.

"It is hard to explain exactly how it works, but I am an interpreter, in an unusual. way. Currently, you are my project. You have a great need to understand what is going on, so I am able to spread my gift on to you. My words sound familiar to your ears, and therefore the words they speak are also within your grasp. However, if I were to leave the room, their voices would be as foreign to you as if they were from a different country in your own world. The problem is that I can only cover one other person at a time. So they must be in the dark in order for you to be enlightened."

The men were sopping up stew from the bottom of their bowls, clearly impressed by her cooking, despite her claims that she was weak in the female arts. As they finished, they piled their platters back on the table then unrolled their bedrolls and were soon snoring blissfully. Within a few short minutes, only Arthyr remained alert amongst them.

When Ravinna was certain the others were completely unaware of their surroundings, she called Arthyr over to them. He finished meditating on the final bite of stew, a contented smile on his heavy lips. He added his things to the pile then joined Tucker and Ravinna.

"They worry about your safety because they value you," he said gently as he sat down on the floor in a pile of furs that he pulled from beneath Tucker's sleeping bench. "They don't want to see you get hurt."

Ravinna snorted. It was a wild sound, and Tucker envisioned her wielding a sword to prove a point. "Perhaps they value my cooking, but that is all."

"Now, now," Arthyr chuckled, "you shouldn't be so hard on them, or so blind to your power in the kitchen."

As Tucker observed the exchange between the two of them, he felt relief. Clearly, this was more of a mentor relationship than anything else. "As long as they never ask me to dance," a sparkle returned to her eyes. Arthyr let out a booming laugh but quickly smothered it with his hands, leaving his shoulders shaking mirthfully.

"You have my word there," he consented when he had managed to pull himself together.

"I might have been able to get a marginal understanding of how to cook soup," Ravinna explained, "but dance lessons were always a point of contention between myself and my mother. I may be graceful with a sword in my hand, but she could never make my body move the way it was supposed to when music was involved.

"All jokes aside," she gave Arthyr a serious look, "we need to catch Tucker up to speed. I want to be on our way by mid afternoon at the latest. We should have a decent amount of cloud cover by then, which will help us reach the Eastern outpost by dawn."

Arthyr nodded grimly, stroking his chin in thought. "You do understand all the risks involved, do you not? They are not foolish in saying you would be wiser to wait for nightfall. You can rest here, and I can send you with a small party to the nearest outpost. Things will not change so much if it takes a week to reach the Emperor, rather than two days."

Ravinna shook her head. "We already discussed this Arthyr. I was gone too long on my search for Tucker. The truth is, if he hadn't almost run me over I might still be out there on the road searching. We have no more time to waste. I have been through the caves." Her eyes were wide and luminous. Tucker could see the flames of the fire reflected in them, but behind that there were the shadows of the horrors they had passed through together. "There are so many, so many. And then there is the wedding to consider..."

With a deep breath that whooshed through his large nose, Arthyr accepted her verdict. "Very well," he agreed. "But you will be no use to anyone if you don't get some sleep yourself. I will speak to Tucker, I will explain what he needs to know."

"But you need me to translate," she protested, even as her eyelids drooped heavily in defiance of her will.

Arthyr kept his laughter low. "I have a few tricks of my own, my Dear. After all, it was I who often helped your father amass his vast collection."

This last comment was enough to perk up her sleepy eyes. "You?" she gasped.

"There will be time for those explanations some other day," he looked at her with fatherly eyes. "Rest Ravinna. The time is short, indeed."

Tucker sensed the internal struggle going on behind the lovely face next to him. She was burning with questions almost as much as he was, but sleep was a strong factor in her decision to let it be for the time being. Even as she assented to his words, her head began to bob and she slipped down onto the bench and curled up in a ball close to Tucker's side. Arthyr pulled a fur from the floor and wrapped it snugly around Ravinna. Her breathing evened, and her features settled into a smooth picture of calm.

"Now," Arthyr sighed, "where to begin with you. Another drink first, I think." He was off the floor in a flash. He fumbled around with a few of the bottles hanging about the room until he found the one he wanted. "Yes," he smacked his lips in appreciation as he took a swig to make sure."This is just the stuff." He poured a healthy dose into his mug and then brought it over and filled Tucker's.

Tucker sniffed the liquid tentatively, remembering the dragon urine again. Arthyr stifled another laugh. "I'm guessing Ravin gave you a dose of something to take the edge off at some point."

Tucker nodded, uncertain if Arthyr would be able to understand his words. He figured he could still understand because of the way Ravinna's hair was brushing against his skin. Arthyr recognized the double meaning to his hesitation. "Never you mind, young friend, I am speaking your own English now. When she sleeps her power travels with her. And have no fears about drinking up either. While this might put a little hair on your chest, it won't make you feel like your insides are going to explode."

Tucker took him at his word and took a sip.
Mead was the word that came to mind when he felt the
warmth on his tongue. He imagined himself in an
ancient castle in a foreign kingdom, so this drink fell
perfectly under the mysterious heading of things he had
read about in the fairy tales of his youth.

"So, Ravinna has told you a little of herself, and
a little of the dragons, but I can see the curiosity
burning in your mind, so I will start at the beginning of
the current conflict. There is not time to explain the
connections between Aristonia and the world you
inhabit, that must wait for another day. For now, you
need to understand the dragons and what I believe to be
your place in our history.

"I am sure much of what you have already
witnessed has come as a shock to you. It has been quite
some time since I ventured into your world, but I can
only imagine how things there have changed. There
was a moment in time when our two worlds were more
alike than not. It was during this stage that I was able to
travel freely between the two. The cave of the dragons
was a welcome place in those days, and passage from
here to there was common."

Tucker stared at him, "but that would make you
like 400 years old or something."

Arthyr laughed heartily, "it's not quite so bad as
all that, but, again, explaining the differences in time
and space is not my place. Let us just say that I am old
enough to know a few things about life, and young
enough to be every day amazed by all there is yet to
learn. You see, time and space do not run in the straight

lines you may believe. This is part of the reason our worlds are now split more fully. There was a love of facts, of progress, of science that served to silence the magic, and we chose to let that other half of life be and to stay in the world where myth and magic and belief could still exist," Arthyr closed his eyes and took a long drink from his wooden cup.

"From your perspective, it may appear we chose a simpler way, something a bit more natural and tied to all that has come and all that is yet to be, rather than what we can create on our own. We did not choose to live in ignorance, but in openness. Though the passage was mostly closed before Ravinna was born, you can see that she does not lack for knowledge."

Tucker struggled to grasp how Ravinna could have been trained in so many things and be so young. Rather than the child he had assumed her to be at first, he realized she might be old enough to be his great great grandmother. Arthyr observed Tucker quietly, aware that there was no way to explain the things of which he spoke. It would be up to Tucker to accept what he could not make clear, and adjust to that which he could not reason his way through. In that moment, he was the very model of science which Arthyr had told him they had sought to stay away from.

"This is only for you to have some concept of what you are dealing with here. You will have to let go of some things your eyes have told you to believe, and go back to stories you thought were fantasy. Do you think you can do that?" Arthyr's voice was low, a mixture of kindness and extreme gravity.

"I, I think so," Tucker spoke directly to the other man for the first time. He felt young, and unprepared for the job at hand. "This wouldn't happen to be Atlantis would it?" he could not resist the question.

There was such joy in Arthyr's laugh that Tucker felt he was laughing with him more than at him. At least, that was what he was hoping for.

"Not exactly," Arthyr grinned. "But at least you get the idea. So now that we have that covered it's time to get on to the crux of the matter: Dragons."

A chill ran down Tucker's spine and caused goosebumps to rise up on the skin of his arms. He felt a mixture of excitement, dread, and fascination. He nodded enthusiastically to cover the twitching of his body, hoping Arthyr would not guess the part about the uneasiness and fear.

"For as long as our history has been recorded, the dragons have been keeping track of things as well," Arthyr turned into a story teller, and Tucker settled back against the wall. "Most of the time, our histories have intertwined peacefully. We worked together to keep Aristonia a beautiful place. There was no animosity between our races.

"They were more than happy to carry us great distances that our legs could not manage easily. We never saw them as pets or servants as the people in your world looked at their beasts of burden. We were on an equal playing field. While their forms of communication, both in speech and in writing down the history of the world, were different than ours, we never doubted that, were things between us to change, they would have the advantage.

"Perhaps it might sound to you that we made this alliance out of fear. That is not the case. The dragons were our friends. Sure, we had a healthy fear of what could happen, but there was no reason to believe it would. The dragons' laws were stricter than our own when it came to the sanctity of all life. There were occasionally those who broke with their ways, but they were quickly removed, and never chose to wreak havoc on us, opting instead for your world I am afraid to say. I am sure even your diluted history has recorded something of their exploits.

"Anyhow, while most of us believed that life would continue to exist as it always had, there were a few who were more cautious. They witnessed what happened when the dragons went askew. They saw the pillaging of villages, the murder of innocents, and they were nervous.

"One man, I believe you would call him a prophet or a seer, had a vision. It was not pleasant. He saw a time coming when something unprecedented would happen. I should have told you that these dragons where herbivores. They lived primarily off wild vegetation, but as part of our partnership we grew crops we knew were to their liking.

"Perhaps this man, Balthazar was his name, had spent too much time documenting the plight of your world. He had witnessed the corruption of men there, as well as the dark side of the dragons. He warned that if we were not careful, those few would turn to many.

When people called him crazy he had the vision. Some believed it was merely a ploy to convince them of his initial dire predictions, but others listened.

"In this vision, he saw a dark force moving amidst the dragons. He was unable to discover how it started, but it soon grew into a beast that drove them into a frenzy. They had always craved treasure, anything that sparkled was an extreme temptation, but they valued life above all else. Balthazar was vague, but he spoke of this beast in frightening terms. It was dark and cold and full of hate. It provoked the others to value only their own lives. It encouraged them to attack animals first, as a show of dominance. Next it focused on humans as the enemy. Ultimately, it turned against any dragons who stood in its way.

"In this final stage of depravity, the dragons lost their sense of balance. Balthazar said there were two things that must happen in order for them to be stopped. He foresaw a great sacrifice on their side, and an outsider with a special spear," here Arthyr winked at Tucker.

"Of course, this prophecy was only a lot of words at the time. Even those who believed that he could see into the future, saw it only as a possible future. After all, the dragons were our friends. Together we celebrated victories as well as defeats. Beyond that, despite many of us having visited your world, the idea of a man with the proportions Balthazar described seemed positively impossible, no offense intended," again he gave Tucker a significant look.

"Sadly, his predictions were more accurate than we could ever have dreamed possible. Unfortunately, it started so unusually that before we were able to make the connection things were well underway. I told you that there were occasionally renegades amongst the dragons, but they were dealt with quickly and efficiently. Their leader, Yaveen, was powerful and honored far and wide. At the first sign of a problem he sought to point the rebel in the right direction. He was just and fair, always giving them a clear choice. His rules were for their good, but if they refused his ways, leaving was the only option.

"Pride is a dragon's greatest weakness. Most of them saw the wisdom of Yaveen's words, and the sorrow in his heart when they were hurting themselves with their willful actions. Those who did not, chose to go to your world. They presented themselves to the people like powerful gods, and demanded praise. They took whatever caught their fancy and plagued the populace until some brave soul stood up to their vanity and vanquished them, or they grew bored and moved to the outskirts.

"Well it came about that, as Yaveen grew older, the leader of his guard became envious. Svyetlo knew that when Yaveen was ready to pass his kingdom on to another, he would not be in the running to receive it, despite all he had done to make their land great. Naturally, Yaveen planned to pass rule over to his son, Adym.

"It is a classic story. Svyetlo was strong and beautiful, a magnificent dragon with scales that

118

sparkled like emeralds. He was loved by everyone and he appeared to be invincible. On the other side, was Adym. He was, perhaps, less brilliant in figure, but in heart, he was golden. Both man and dragon could not help but adore Adym because he was the epitome of all that was wise and good, just like his father.

"It quickly became evident, amongst those of us who remembered the warnings of Balthazar, that a conflict was inevitable. Yaveen, wanting to avoid the worst, sent Adym into your world to discover if there was any way to win back the hearts of those who had turned their backs on their King. He hoped that during this era of separation, Svyetlo's heart would soften, and he would see that it is better to be merciful than cruel. Sadly, without his son by his side, Svyetlo believed Yaveen was weak. He began to speak lies into the minds of the other dragons, convincing them that their King had sent Adym out to the other world as a trick.

"The stories he spread were convoluted. To some, he said that Adym would return with the revolting dragons and strike against the King. To others, he said that a time was coming when the King would no longer lead them with a hand of peace, but would become a tyrant, forcing them to do his will without reason, and using his son as a slave driver with the powerful dark dragons by his side. I heard only bits and pieces of the different plots, but it was enough to assure me that nothing would ever be as it had been. We did not break our allegiances with the dragons at once. We were still certain that Yaveen would do none of these things, and that there might be some way that Svyetlo could be dissuaded from his treacherous course, but it was hard not to think of the prophecies and wonder how we would possibly find anyone who could help us if the hour did turn as dark as we feared it might.

"The dragons began to change. They had always been mysterious to us, but now they became secretive. It is possible that even at the beginning Svyetlo whispered dark words against us as well. He spoke of our friendship as an unhealthy alliance, against the nature of our two species.

"At the same time that he was trying to show them some inability to coexist with us, he also tried to make Yaveen out to be the bad one. He spoke as though he had manipulated them into the position of being nothing more than tame pets, when in truth they were meant to be kings among men, gods even. It broke Yaveen's heart to see the way things were going. He tried to persuade Svyetlo to reason with him, but his former friend would hear nothing of it.

"When Adym returned from his quest, he had changed as well. Despite his sacrifice, despite the love he had extended to the few dragons he had found still living among the men of your world, they would have none of it. They were too much in love with their own mythic power to care about the life they had left behind. So he returned, broken hearted, to his father, unable to offer up any proof that change was possible within the heart intent upon evil.

"His discouragement was nothing compared to the horror he discovered upon his homecoming. Everywhere he looked, he saw dragons on their way to the same fate he had seen those in your world suffering. They were questioning everything. They no longer were satisfied with peace and goodness. Svyetlo had revealed the power of terror to them.

"Just as Balthazar had warned, it started out small. They began by stealing our livestock. Svyetlo used our eating habits against us, claiming that Yaveen had hidden from them the beauty of consuming flesh. We sent delegates to Yaveen with our concerns. He heard us, and agreed, but they no longer listened to him. They believed that Adym's reports were only support of what they had heard from Svyetlo. Clearly, they were each meant to be great, and to serve no king but themselves.

"They were blind to the fact that, as they chose to follow Svyetlo's teaching, even as they spoke against having a king, they merely added to his power. There was no freedom, no individuality in this new life. With each cow, sheep, pig, or horse they stole, the mighty Svyetlo grew in size and darkened in color. The other dragons' once luminescent green scales began to darken, along with his, as they ate the raw meat. I cannot begin to explain the terror in our hearts as we watched this nightmare unfold.

"They struck only at night. They could wipe out a farmers entire herd in a matter of days. Their hunger seemed insatiable. But they soon grew tired of eating simple animals. There was no thrill in the chase. They turned to hunting humans as a sport. Some worked alone, others in teams. Regardless, we are helpless before them.

"In an attempt to protect humanity, Yaveen and Adym sought to protect the passage to your world at the back of the mighty cave where the dragons had always lived. They wanted to contain the violence as much as possible. Yaveen was old, and this action seemed to take the strength he had remaining. If all Ravinna reported is true, you passed by his remains in the cave of treasure. The glowing light in the middle comes from his great heart."

Tucker remembered the light. It had seemed eerie at the time, the undulating green glow that lit the piles of gleaming treasure and the bits and pieces of broken bodies. He shuddered at the thought.

"From what Adym has told us," Arthyr continued, "Yaveen is in a sort of coma. A sleep without dreams. It is Adym's belief, and my hope as well, that if this mess can be resolved the great Yaveen will awaken, and the world will come right again. But it has been hard to keep this dream alive in the face of so much carnage.

"I know this all seems bad, but in the past months things have become even more bleak. Hunting humans for sport, and amassing treasure to pile in their cave has lost much of its thrill. I am afraid I left out the bit about the resistors. Forgive me, I'm getting on in years myself, and sometimes my memory fails in the light of the story. Not all of the dragons were overcome by Svyetlo's treachery. There were a large number who stood behind their King and his son. But as they watched their brothers swell in size, and darken in color, they were afraid. They trusted Yaveen and Adym to do all they could, and in turn, they sought to protect themselves.

"They fled throughout the three kingdoms of men. The warriors among them taught the men how to do battle with the dragons who would hunt them. They knew the best places to attack their brothers, but refused to fight themselves. It was always the greatest crime of all to harm another dragon. Self protection was one thing, but to attack was forbidden. They found their own caves, and created peaceful settlements wherever they could hide. They continued to forage by day and hide at night when they knew the hunters would come out for their vile sport.

"It was during this time when things in our own kingdom began to go downhill. Ravinna's father, the Emperor Karlov, and Yaveen had long been dear friends. They kept one another informed throughout the war that raged against their former alliance. Ravinna was often the messenger between the two of them. She is the only one I know who is skilled in the ways of both humans and dragons. Quite a wonder she is." Arthyr's eyes softened as he spoke of Ravinna, and Tucker had a sudden urge to stroke her hair as she slept beside him, but thought better of it.

"For all the work they did to find a resolution to the situation, Karlov's brother, Karush, saw things differently. He saw the possibility of a darker alliance. In his opinion, the old way was gone, and now was the time for progress. He saw an opportunity for domination not just of the three kingdoms of Aristonia, but of your world as well. He and Svyetlo entered into a crude team. They found ways to overthrow their rightful leaders. Karush did so by convincing the people that Karlov was on his deathbed, and that he had given over his power willingly. He also said that the future belongs to the dragons, and to technology. He developed such an elaborate plot that many of the people accepted him to be an even greater blessing to them than their rightful Emperor had been.

"Once the two of them have all of Aristonia firmly under their control, they intend to reopen the passage between worlds and take everything. They believe that, given the shock value of their coming they would be able to gain absolute power even in the face of your technology," Arthyr cringed at the thought.

Tucker felt certain there was more to the story. He wanted to know where he fit in the plan. "So where does that leave us?" he asked when it appeared that Arthyr was not going to continue.

"Well, at the moment it would seem that leaves us with you and Ravinna. Given her understanding of the dragons, and what might lie on the other side of the cave, she determined to cross over in search of you. Her father warned her against it, but she has a hard head and refused to listen. We had only a few moments to speak when you arrived, so my knowledge of her journey is cloudy at best, but she believes you are the one spoken of in the prophecy. Her goal is to take you to her father in hiding and to make contact with Adym.

"There is actually more to my story, I am afraid. With the aid of Karush, the evil dragons grew stronger. He made dark dealings with men in power throughout the three kingdoms, and he used them to find where the green dragons were hiding. For Svyetlo and his kind, things were about to become even more extreme. The consumption of human flesh had turned their scales into a black so dark it reflected no light. They drifted invisible through the night sky until they found the caves where their former brothers attempted to live in peace. Svyetlo convinced them that in order to become their strongest, the ultimate sustenance was the flesh of their own kind. And so, on a night with no moon, they attacked the dragons and consumed many of them. This greatest of crimes turned their eyes fiery red, a proof of their total depravity.

"Alas, what Svyetlo had told them was true. Eating other dragons did, indeed, make them essentially invincible. The men the green dragons had trained were helpless in the face of their mighty foes. Svyetlo had grown to gargantuan proportions, and what had once been a being of great beauty was transformed into a beast that evoked only horror. They also lost their fear of hunting during daylight hours. I have seen him in the light of day, and it as though a black hole opens up and turns everything that is good and true into a lie. I can think of no better way to describe the experience. They are more than happy to take the daylight as their own, and spoil what little we humans have left."

"So what can I possibly be expected to do?" Tucker lost his resolve of silence. "I can appreciate the fact that there is a prophecy about some dragon slayer, but I'm having a little trouble imagining myself being that guy. My friend Flint, well, he might be able to manage better. He's the rough and tumble sort, if you get my meaning, but me?"

"Do not underestimate the power of what Ravinna has seen," Arthyr said in all seriousness.

"And what, exactly, is that?" Tucker asked.

Arthyr sighed, but even in light of all he had just shared he had a smile on his face. "That is for her to know, and for you to find out."

Tucker let out an exasperated sigh, but could see he was getting nowhere in this argument. The fire was dying down, and the sounds of sleeping men had mellowed to a low purr.

"So the men here?" he asked, "Where does their loyalty lie?"

"I am sure that Ravinna made some comment about her disgust regarding our numbers. When Karlov was in power, he set up outposts to protect the people and serve as a defense against the dark dragons. At that time, they were filled to capacity and worked in double shifts to make sure the villagers were warned in advance of approaching attacks. There were still casualties, but at least we were trying. When Karush took power, he knew the people would revolt if their protection was fully removed, but his alliance with Svyetlo guaranteed that the areas raided would be mutually beneficial, shall we say.

"Those of us he saw to be security risks of one variety or another were sentenced to areas where he continued to condone attacks. And so we are here, in the very shadow of the dragon's lair, a band of men loyal to the true Emperor, but bidden by him to maintain our battle station under Karush."

"So if they're loyal to the Emperor, why don't they like Ravinna very much?"

"It isn't that they do not like her," Arthyr shook his head. "That is a mistake she often makes. It isn't even that they do not respect her. As long as men have been men and women have been women there has been a disparity between the two. An inability on both sides to accept equality if you will. The truth is, one without the other will always be lacking in something. We need balance in life. Male and female is a good example of this balance.

"The problem is when there is any sort of crossover in skills. Ravinna is very much a woman. I have seen the way you respond to her, so I am sure you have no doubt of this. However, her stature and her skills threaten men such as these; men who have been brought up to think that it is their job to protect, and a woman's job to nurture. Her abilities defy their preconceived notions and this threatens them."

Tucker had to agree that most men would feel that way even in his world. Of course, on that side she would be seen as something delicate and rare, rather than a powerful and threatening force. "So will they be willing to do what she says when the situation calls for that?" Tucker asked.

"No doubt about it," Arthyr spoke confidently. "For all that they may protest, when faced with the choice they will support her one hundred percent. After all, she is the daughter of the Emperor, and none of them would dare to refuse her bidding. They might mutter, or make comments about how she would be better off some place safe, but ultimately, they know who she is and what she can do, and would give their lives in her service."

It had been a long day, maybe even two, but something in Arthyr's words struck him afresh. He had seen the bodies in the cave, he had watched the great beasts blotting the light from the sky, and heard their screeching that would have been enough to turn the bravest man to stone, but until that moment the thought of losing his life had never fully actualized in his mind. The talk of fighting dragons was so abstract. The story Arthyr had told was riveting, but fairytale dreamlike.

Arthyr perceived the gravity of it all catching up with the young man before him. "You are right to respect the situation, Tucker," he said. "The prophecy is vague at best. The outcome has never been certain. But I trust Ravinna, just as I trust her father, Yaveen, and Adym."

"Hasn't turned out so well for some of those guys," Tucker pointed out.

"No, not yet," Arthyr agreed, "but the end of the story has yet to be written. And you are here to help us write the next chapter."

Tucker wanted to refute this last statement. He felt an urge to fight all of it. He had been a fool to follow the strangely compelling girl. He had a life. It might not be much, but it was far from over. There was still a chance for him out there. He had a few dreams, even though they had been shoved to the back of his closet. Still, they were there. Even as hairy as driving a truck could be, the chance of him dying on a route was low. Sure, it happened, but this was like jumping in front of the firing squad at a girl's request. Fighting dragons? The idea was suddenly so absurd to him that he wondered how he had ever listened to her. Sure, she was beautiful, he looked down at her face to remind himself just how very lovely, but...but... His mind went blank as her eyes began to flutter open.

"How long have I been sleeping?" asked Ravinna groggily.

"An hour, maybe two," Arthyr answered. "You should both get some more sleep. No worries, I will wake you when the time is right. The daylight hours are intensely dangerous times for travel."

Ravinna yawned and nodded. She shifted to a more comfortable position and fell back to sleep. Tucker doubted he would be able to fall asleep so easily this time, but decided he should try.

"Thanks for telling me everything," he said. "I'm not sure what good it does me, or what good I can possibly do all of you, but I'm here now so I guess the only thing I can do is try."

"That's the spirit," Arthyr patted him on the shoulder and rose to his feet. "When you wake up I'll have everything ready to go."

Tucker thought that might not be the best news, but there was nothing he could do about it. He curled up on the bench, expecting only horrifying images to fill his mind, coupled with endless thoughts of how ridiculous his situation was. Instead, he took a deep breath and was amazed again by just how good Ravinna smelled, and how incredibly soothing her presence was. Sleep took him quickly and fully, his only thought being thankfulness as reality drifted away.

Chapter 9

Flint woke up with a headache. He had experienced more than his fair share of head splitting hangovers, but this was something else all together. He remembered his dad saying his mom had migraines. There was a shadowy picture in his mind of a white skinned woman, pale as a ghost, with dark rings around her eyes, and an ice pack on her head, vomiting in the toilet and then passing out on the couch. He wondered if her icy blue eyes might not be the only thing he inherited. The pain was like nothing he had ever experienced.

He knew there was something pressing he had to do. It was something of utmost importance, but he was having trouble putting his finger on it. The sound of his phone ringing was so excruciating that he saw sparks flying. He contemplated just ignoring it in the way a child considers pretending not to hear the school bell's impatient ringing.

Then, like an ice pick breaking through a thick layer of ice, the block in his brain shattered, and he recognized who the obnoxious ring tone belonged to. It was Nance Kenworthy. The woman might be a bit neurotic, but he had never blamed her for that. When Tucker started driving truck, and Flint had made his role as mentor more official, Nance had taken him under her wing. Since his own mother did his memory no good, he fancied Nance in that role. She often invited him to dinner, and was always more than happy to offer advice about women, or his future plans, or give gentle lectures on the adverse effects of drinking. He took it like a man, and any time Tucker was out of town and she had a problem she knew she could count on Flint to help.

As he fumbled for the phone he regretted not calling her the night before. The truth was, he was surprised she had waited so long to call him. He drew in a steadying breath, then flipped the phone open. "Nance?"

There was a choking sound on the other end of the line. He felt a surge of panic. Maybe they had found Tucker. "Nance?" he repeated, gently, willing her to speak.

"Oh, Flint," she gasped. "Where is he? What is he mixed up in? This just isn't like him, it doesn't make any sense." Her voice crumpled into a choked sob.

Comforting people was not part of Flint's skill set. That was partly why he had left them the anonymous money. It was easier than saying that he had no answers for her sorrow. He had been ready to take action, but trying to console a desperate and broken woman was out of his comfort zone.

He attempted a soothing sound, but felt it came out more like a hiss. Embarrassed, he hoped she had not heard it. When she made no response, he breathed a sigh of relief and waited for her to say something to propel him into action.

"Has he said anything to you that would make you think he was in trouble?" she asked composing herself. "It's taken me forever to get anyone to do anything, and that seems to be the only question the police know how to ask."

"You know Tucker," said Flint in his best encouraging tone. "He's a good guy. I know he wouldn't a been messing around with any of that stuff." He wondered if the embarrassment of his own actions was turning his own cheeks pink. He was glad Nance was on the phone and not in the room.

"So what do we do, Flint?" her voice was serious. "My baby boy is missing. He's all I have left."

The desperation in her voice was like a kick in the head for Flint. He pushed aside the nausea caused by his headache, and gave himself an internal "man-up" speech. "I'll be right over Nance. We'll figure something out."

After hanging up, Flint's stomach sank. What could a grief stricken middle aged mother and a burned out trucker possibly uncover that the police could not. Years and years of self doubt washed over him and the headache demanded pampering. He looked futilely around the cramped room, wishing for answers.

He muttered under his breath and pulled on the jeans he had discarded next to the bed the night before. There was no point in driving the truck. He opted for his motorcycle instead, despite the ceaseless throbbing in his head that he knew would only be made worse by the noisy engine.

Nance had wisely prepared coffee before he arrived. Flint never mentioned the pain in his head, but she sensed it, and moved around him quietly, waiting for him to speak.

The coffee went down, burning yet satisfying. The fog in his brain lifted gradually as he sat on the faded gold and orange flowered seventies sofa in the tiny living room. "Sorry I haven't been over for a while," he said, setting the empty mug on a cluttered side table.

"Think nothing of it," Nance insisted. "You're a busy man, I know how it is. If Tucker didn't sleep here I'd hardly remember he was around." She had meant the words to be off hand, but there was a tremor in her voice at the end, and her hands were shaking around her steamy pink mug.

"So, what do you know?" Flint asked.

"Very little, I'm afraid," Nance sighed. "Tom called me as soon as he and the guys had finished going over the truck. He wanted to finish the route, but I insisted that he leave it there until the police came. There might be evidence. Of course, you know how Tom is. All business. He was kind, but I could tell he was worried about making sure the deliveries were made, and at as little cost to himself as possible. In the end, I think he had one of his guys bring down an empty truck and switch the load over. Even that made me nervous, but I figured that's Tom's jurisdiction, and I'd feel bad to ruin his relationship with Tucker. He's passed him a lot of business, and we need the money."

Nance leaned back in the threadbare blue rocker. She moved as though shifting between two worlds. In one, Tucker was still the baby she sat up with late at night in the very same chair, nursing him back to sleep, and in the other world she was a desperate lonely woman, on the verge of losing everything she held dear.

"The police," her voice shook as she continued. "The police wouldn't do a thing at first. I, I may have hounded them a bit. I realize they're just trying to do their job, and that not every man who pulls off by the side of the road and vanishes into thin air in the middle of a typical work day is a victim of foul play, but they don't know Tucker like I do. He's the most responsible boy, I mean man, that I know. Ever since his father..." she choked back another sob and dabbed her eyes absently with a crumpled and already too wet tissue. "He's always done everything to look out for me. Even when he had his accident and I knew he was hurting, he sucked it up and tried to make me happy."

Flint thought back to those days. He remembered the first few times he and Tucker had really talked. He could tell the kid was in pain. Tucker's priority had always been caring for his mother. He had mentioned wanting to help her meet someone new, someone who could bring joy and purpose back into her life.

"I'm sorry the house is such a mess," something seemed to switch in her brain as she looked with glazed eyes at the dirty dishes on the coffee table that had made it impossible for Flint to put his cup there. "Tucker hired some girl to come in and help out, but...There was just something about her. I sent her home and I was going to get around to clearing all this up, but then Tom called and, and..."

"It's okay, Nance," Flint assured her. "Honestly, I didn't even notice." He almost mentioned the sty his father lived in, but thought better of it, not wanting her to feel like he was making comparisons between her housekeeping skills and those of his father. "So, you said you were finally able to get help from the police?"

"It took most of the night, but, yes. They agreed that if we hadn't heard anything by morning they would go over and take a look. I don't think they run on the early schedule of truckers, though, so I'm afraid they still haven't gotten around to it."

"Do you know where the truck is? Tom made some vague references, but I thought I might go have a look for myself," Flint was getting itchy for action. It was evident that spending much time with Nance was going to settle him into depression rather than making anything better.

She nodded. "Let me see if I can find that paper I wrote it on." She got up and went into the kitchen. He heard her rustling around and took the moment on his own to run his hands through his hair a few times. He was sure he looked like he had been hit by a truck, which was how he felt. "Here it is," she called.

Nance handed Flint the paper with the scrawled out directions. "This is what Tom told me. I was thinking of driving out there myself but, well, it's been a while since I drove."

"You stay here and try to rest. Maybe give that girl a call. I'm sure it would do you good to put your feet up and have someone else take care of you for a change," he stood up, walked over to her, and put his arm around her shoulders.

"Oh, I don't know about that," she looked wary and Flint realized now why Tucker had been so worried about her. The past few years had been harder on her than he had realized.

"Now, Nance, you're not going to be doing Tucker any good if you work yourself into a frenzy and end up sick, are you? Do you have her number? I'd be more than happy to call her myself."

Reluctantly, Nance allowed Flint to usher her into her room and help her into bed. She even begrudgingly gave him Karla's number. He turned the little TV on for her, then went to the other room to make the call.

"Hello?" the voice on the other end of the line was bubbly and infectious. Even in that one word Flint knew he liked her.

"Um, hi," he wished he was able to sound suave rather than like an idiot who had never made a phone call before. "Is this, uh, Karla?"

"Yes it is, and who might you be?" there was no hesitation in her voice, just a natural inflection of cheerfulness.

"Uh, yeah, the name's Flint," he cursed himself internally for being such a bumbling fool. "Yeah, I was, uh, just calling you on behalf of Nance Kenworthy. Do you think you might be able to come over and help her today?"

"Well, of course," she sounded puzzled, "but why didn't Tucker or Nance call? Not to be nosy or anything, I'm just curious."

"Well, see, that's the problem," Flint lowered his voice. "Tucker's gone missing, and Nance is pretty upset..."

"Missing?" Karla was concerned. "Are you sure? I can't believe it."

"Yeah," Flint muttered, "I'm on my way out to check on things, see if I can be any help. He and I were supposed to meet up for lunch yesterday, but when he didn't show I called to check in on him. His boss found his truck parked by the side of the road, but Tucker was nowhere around."

"That's awful. You tell Nance I'll be right over. Is there anything I should bring? I feel so at a loss."

Flint felt at a loss, too. He wondered if it might be best if he stuck around until Karla showed up. He told himself that it was because he wanted to keep Nance company, but there was an itch in him to meet the girl who matched the perky voice.

"I haven't looked around the place much. I know she had coffee. She made me some before I got here, but the place is looking in need of attention, and I'm not sure what she has around here for food." He poked his head into the kitchen as he spoke, then hurriedly walked away. "Yeah, I'd say bringing some lunch would be in order."

"No problem," Karla accepted her mission. "Will you still be there when I come, Mr. Flint? Do you want me to bring you a sandwich as well?"

"Uh," he hesitated. "Well, I was gonna head out, but maybe it would be best if I kept an eye on Nance. I think she was up trying to convince the police to do their jobs all night long, and, uh, yeah. I'll be here."

"Great," the smile was back in her voice. "I'll be there in twenty minutes tops. Tuck's a good guy. If there's anything else you can think of for me to bring, just call me back."

The phone went silent and Flint got to work. One peek in at Nance proved that bed had been just the thing. She was passed out cold, completely oblivious to the witty banter of the morning show hosts on the TV. The head ache had thankfully been banished by adrenaline, and Flint rushed back to the kitchen. The coffee pot was the one thing in the room that looked okay. He decided to brew a second pot, then carried the dirty dishes from the living room into the kitchen to make it easier for Karla.

He was certain that when Tucker was home the house would never look this way, but in the day of his absence Nance had managed to make a mess of things. Again, he was amazed by how much she had lost control.

Once the place was more organized, he hurried to the bathroom to splash water on his face, and reorganized his hair. His face in the mirror was less than satisfying, but the rinse did some good, and he hoped he looked like a man's man, rather than a filthy beast. Most of the ladies he messed around with were the types that hung out in seedy bars and were drunk enough that he looked good, but the voice on the phone made him want to appear normal.

There was a knock at the door then a jingle of keys as Karla let herself in. "Hello?" she called out in the same lilting tone she had used on the phone.

Flint flushed the toilet to cover for his primping, then ran the water to make it sound like he was washing his hands before opening the door. "Karla?" he said hesitantly, emerging into the living room.

"I'm in the kitchen," she called. "Tucker gave me a key so I let myself in."

Flint followed her voice, his pulse beating in his ears faster than normal. He berated himself for being ridiculous. People have long claimed the power of love at first sight, but falling for a voice was silly. He pushed open the door silently, accepting the fact that he might look like a creeper, and watched her work.

It had been no more than three minutes since Karla had entered the apartment, but she had already cleared off the counters and made the kitchen look almost normal. "Looks like Nance was in a cooking mood yesterday," she said without looking up.

Whatever image the voice had conjured up in Flint's head, the reality of Karla was nothing like it.

Perhaps he had pictured a petite blond with pigtails and a voluptuous figure, or a sassy brunette with legs that wouldn't quit. What he saw instead, from behind at least, was a woman with mousy brown hair in a fly away ponytail, of average height and stocky build. Basic. Sturdy. Girl next door in the wall flower sense of the word. The thoughts that filled his head now had him feeling ashamed of the whole gamut of thoughts that came before.

"I brought you a sandwich," she still kept her head down, busy with the task of shining the counters. The voice remained what it had always been, and Flint shook his head to clear the contradictory images in his mind.

"Um, thanks," he remained hesitant in the threshold.

"There," there was a smile in Karla's voice as she surveyed the work she had done. "She forgets that she can't do everything she used to," she explained, finally turning. "She means well, but you saw the results."

For a second time, Flint felt all his impressions being tossed to the wind. Karla was an unlikely candidate for a magazine photo shoot, but her smile lit her face in the most astonishing way, leaving Flint breathless. He was smitten all over again. Her brown eyes, the same color as her hair, sparkled, and the sweetness of her look was conspiratorial. It was as though by offering him a sandwich she had invited him to become a part of her magical world.

"I'm so glad you called me," Flint was overwhelmed by the honesty in her voice. "Tuck and I went to school together, and we ran into each other a couple months back in the grocery store. I moved out here for a job last year, and when it fell through I decided to stick around and see if anything else came up. I don't know why I'm telling you all this," she blushed and the way it colored her cheeks made her all the more alluring to Flint.

"Anyhow," she hurried on, "We got to talking and he told me about his mom. I've been working as a private caregiver for a while now, and I was more than happy to add them to my client list. Tucker's just such a real guy, you know? Like totally earnest and sincere." She sighed, "do you have any idea what might have happened to him, Mr. Flint?"

"Just Flint," he corrected. He was glad she was unconcerned by his appearance, and he was pretty sure she and Tucker really were just old school friends, but he wanted to make certain he came off as friendly and concerned, and not overly anything else. "I really have no idea," he admitted. "I was hoping Nance would know something, or have some ideas, but the most I got from her was the location of the truck. I was going to head down there and have a look, see what I can figure."

"I hope he's okay. I remember when his dad died, and then his accident," her smile faded with the memory. "Like I said, he's a good guy. I wouldn't want anything bad to happen to him. Now, don't you worry at all about Nance. I'll keep a good eye on her, and hopefully you can figure something out to help find Tucker." She was all business again, but with that special sparkle that had inexplicably drawn Flint from the first moment.

"All right," Flint still stood motionless in the door, the slip of paper with the truck's location held tightly in his right hand inside his pocket.

"And don't forget your sandwich," Karla was already returning to work. "My schedule is pretty free this week. Several of my other clients have gone on a group trip, so I can stick around, no problem."

"Thanks for coming, it means a lot. And, thanks for the sandwich," he took a step forward and pulled the sandwich from the bag. "I'll be sure to let you know if I find anything so you can tell Nance. I'll come back to the house as soon as I can. There might not be a good cell connection, but if you need me to bring anything back, well, you have my number now, so don't be afraid to call."

Karla looked over her shoulder and grinned at him in reply. A loud snore emanated from Nance's room, and it propelled Flint to action. He gave Karla a salute and headed out to his bike.

Chapter 10

A small hand gripped Tucker's shoulder and urged him into wakefulness. It seemed that every time he woke up lately it was to a world of uncertainty and questions. He had expected to lie there, contemplating Arthyr's story for several hours. If not that, he had hoped his mind would work things out while he was sleeping. Back when he was focused on education, he had found that if he read over his notes one last time before going to sleep, his mind continued to mull over the information, and in the morning he would have almost perfect recall of even the most baffling concepts.

For some reason, none of these ideas worked this time. He was feeling as clueless when he woke up as he had felt befuddled when he went to sleep. Oddly enough, Ravinna's cool fingers brushing the hair back on his forehead did little to pull it all together, although they did serve to knock his pulse rate up a notch or two.

"I know you are tired," she whispered, "but I am afraid we must be going."

Tucker sat straight up, then cringed as the blood rushed from his brain leaving him momentarily in the dark. "Okay, maybe we don't have to leave that quickly," Ravinna chuckled at his pale cheeks and evident loss of equilibrium. "Arthyr has prepared a meal for us. I will bring some over for you so you don't hurt yourself before we even get started."

If he had been in better control of his thoughts and body, Tucker might have been offended by her teasing, but in the current situation he was so confused by the thought that he had been mistaken for a hero, that he considered it a good idea for Ravinna to see that he was just a normal guy prone to head rushes. As he waited, he tested his face gingerly with his fingertips. It appeared that the swelling had gone down considerably, and the pain was far less intense. Whatever Arthyr had used on his skin was clearly helping.

Ravinna returned a moment later with another tray of hot food and a steaming mug of something that smelled awful. "This isn't...?" he indicated the foul smelling stuff with horror.

Ravinna nodded. "I know it seems odd to you, especially seeing as how many of the dragons are now our enemies, but this is the best thing to drink to give us the strength we need for the next part of our journey. I must be completely honest with you: it will be very dangerous. I know Arthyr told you the dragons have grown bold in their hunting games. Daylight is their favorite hour for sport because they inspire the most fear. Their eyes make them adept at fighting at any time, day or night, with equal ease, but during the day, their victims are totally undone at the sight of them." She shuddered at the thought, and Tucker wondered how many nightmarish images flashed through her mind as she spoke with him.

He decided the best option would be to throw it back in one shot, rather than sipping on the vile drink. Knowing what it was only made it all the more difficult to get it down, but trusting Ravinna in the past had gotten him this far safely. He ignored the fact that trusting her had gotten him into this whole mess in the first place.

The beautiful thing about pain is how quickly it is forgotten. Were this not the case, no one would ever do anything stupid or harmful more than once. While the memory remains all fuzzy in the back of the mind, there is nothing like a vivid repeat to bring it rushing back. All Tucker could think through the intense burning was that the last time there had been less to swallow.

He choked and spluttered and gulped it down while tears streamed down his cheeks. He thought it likely that steam was spouting from his ears like in a cartoon, and he was almost one hundred percent certain that if he let himself belch to relieve the awful pressure, flames would spurt out of his mouth.

"It's like drinking lighter fluid and then chasing it down with a match," he gasped when the cup was empty.

A wicked smile spread across Ravinna's face, and he thought she might start jumping up and down and clapping like a three year old. "You really are brilliant, Tucker," she looked on him with awe. "I have never seen even the strongest men of my acquaintance finish so fast and so well."

"Well, don't get too excited," he warned her. "After hearing all that stuff about prophecies, and the whole mess going on around here, I'm really not certain I'm the guy. I might be on the big side around these parts, but my six pack isn't what it was when I played ball. You know what I'm saying?" Tucker had the horrifying feeling that he might be slurring his words. He had a sudden urge to vomit.

"Quick," Ravinna tried to hide her worried expression. "The eggs. Eat the eggs."

Tucker felt his stomach rebel, but the thought of feeling all that dragon urine coming back up was more than he wanted to imagine. With fortitude he had never imagined himself to possess, he shoveled a heaping forkful of eggs into his mouth. He chewed quickly, not tasting anything, and swallowed them in a huge lump. His first thought was that this was an even bigger mistake than downing the entire drink in one go, but much to his surprise, when the eggs passed down his throat he felt instantly better.

"These aren't magical dragon eggs are they?" he asked nervously.

"Of course not," Ravinna was laughing again. "Our alliances may have changed, but we would never eat the eggs of the dragons. They contain life. These are just from ordinary chickens. No little chicklets inside."

He could tell she was trying to make a joke, and even in his rather distressed mood, he chuckled in an attempt to please her. The eggs tasted delicious once he was no longer considering them making a return appearance in the near future. They counteracted the venomous aspect of the drink without canceling any of its warming and invigorating potency.

He finished off the eggs, with another chunk of the hearty bread and some cheese. Ravinna had a tray of food as well, and they both finished at the same time.

"Where is Arthyr, anyway?" Tucker asked when he was done eating and finally took the time to look around.

"He is worried," Ravinna sighed. "He won't say it, but I know it's true. He trusts me far more than the rest of them, but even he believes I am risking too much by traveling during the day."

"That didn't answer my question," said Tucker, hoping for more information.

"He went to scout around, see where the dragons have headed and what might be the safest route. He should be back any time now. He already packed our bags, so we can leave as soon as he returns."

"Are you sure this is the best idea?" Tucker asked.

For a moment, he thought Ravinna was going to glare at him, but as quickly as the irritated expression began to creep across her face she pushed it aside and attempted to look serene. "Please, Tucker. I know it might look foolish, but we must get to my father. The sooner we can arrive, the better. I know what I am doing."

He decided it was best not to say anything more. He had followed her this far, and he realized then that he might very well follow her to his death. It was a ludicrous thought when he remembered what his life had looked like the day before. He wondered if someone would be able to get a message to his mother if he died in this place. The thought of her sent a sharp pain through his chest and he was glad Ravinna was busy taking care of the dishes. He determined to write her a letter if there was ever the chance. If he failed in this crazy mission, he needed to know he had tried to do the best by everyone. He was sure she was half crazy with worry about his disappearance, and wondered why he had left without contacting anyone.

The door opened and Arthyr entered. His face was grave, but he mustered a smile for Ravinna. "You should leave immediately," he lifted a loaded pack off the ground and handed it Tucker as he spoke. "There are none in sight at the moment. They seem intent on the Southern mountains these days. Karush has taken advantage of the alliance and is vying for his own power play in that direction."

Ravinna's eyes flared at mention of her uncle's name. She moved quickly, tossing a few final things into her pack and throwing it onto her back. "Are you ready?" she asked Tucker.

"Ready as I'm gonna be, I guess," he agreed. The pack on his back was heavy, but it was less awkward than he had expected. He had no idea what a trek through dragon hunting grounds might look like, but he knew being flexible would be useful.

"I know I don't have to tell you to be careful." Arthyr slipped a drinking bottle over her shoulder.

"No," she agreed, "You do not. I do know what I am doing, old friend. In these situations there is always reason to be cautious, but I have come back from more treacherous missions unscathed. I will take no unnecessary risks, especially with Tucker. And you and I both know why time is of the essence."

Tucker took her comment as a sign of his value to the mission, rather than a hint at his lack of skills. He shook Arthyr's hand firmly. "And I'll do my best to stay out of trouble," he added, hoping to come off light hearted and unconcerned.

The twinkle was back in Arthyr's eye. "We're all counting on that, young man," he nodded. "Now be off, and quickly."

Ravinna threw her arms around Arthyr's neck. The embrace was brief, but Tucker found it unsettling. It felt like she was saying more than just, "See you later." Then they were out the door, and Ravinna had eyes only for what was to come.

It was the first chance Tucker had had to look around. His brief impressions when they emerged from under the waterfall were marred by the memory of the massive dark shapes that had spread across the sky.

He saw that the place they had been staying was more a cave than a structure. It was built into the side of a grassy hill. The door was almost completely obscured by bushes, and the smoke from the fire came out through the branches of another bush which diffused it so that it scarcely made any sign in the air above.

When they had walked through the long tunnel he had tried to imagine where they were headed. He had considered that they might simply pass through the mountain and be back in familiar territory. He had also contemplated that they might be going down, landing them in some world underground where magma served to work as the sun. However, as he took in his surroundings he was certain that the place he had arrived was neither one of those options.

On first sight, he had thought the terrain looked like home, coinciding with his initial presumptions, but he now saw that was not the case. The sun burned high above, and there was not a cloud to be seen, but the sky was not blue. It had a purple tinge and for a moment he felt like he had stepped into a little girl's fantasy world. This was enhanced when he realized that the grass was not green, but more on the side of being teal. The bark of the trees was distinctly pink, and the way their branches curved and swirled was unlike anything he had ever seen.

He wanted to stop and take it all in. This world was breathtaking. Ravinna, however, was already making for a faint trail in the trees, every movement indicating the seriousness of their situation. He scurried to catch up with her as she moved behind a line of trees.

"Stand back," she ordered him. There was nothing unfriendly about her tone, but it was clear that it was an order. Up until this point, Tucker had not visualized her as a commander, but in those two words his eyes were opened to her warrior side.

Tucker obeyed with no misgivings, and watched as she opened the bottle Arthyr had placed on her earlier. He had a vague memory of her sprinkling water from the spring on the walls when they had taken the smaller side cave the night before, and it seemed she was doing so again.

"Why are you doing that?" he asked in a husky whisper.

"Covering our tracks. This water will wash away our scent so the dragons are unable to follow us to the hide out. Arthyr regularly purifies the entire area, but I want to be sure that we are not followed in either direction," she explained as she continued to toss droplets on the trail behind them.

"So will you be doing that the entire trip then?" Tucker was trying not to test her patience, but it seemed to him that their progress would be greatly slowed if she had to stop every few feet to sprinkle water on the trail.

"No, just a little longer to create a good amount of separation," she kept at her work, nudging Tucker slowly forward for another twenty or thirty feet. Once satisfied that they were sufficiently far away from the others, she corked the bottle and returned to the lead.

"We will keep to the trees as much as possible. I know this area well, but the dragons have done enough damage to change the landscape in some places, so we will have to keep an eye out. Despite what Arthyr said, there is always the chance that some of them will be hunting here, so keep alert."

Tucker fell into step, observing the scenery while trying to keep up. The height difference proved a problem occasionally, so he had to watch carefully to avoid being hit in the face by low hanging branches. The trail they were following was maintained, but it was frequented by people or animals much smaller than himself.

Ravinna moved with utmost care and almost without a sound. Her muscles were taut, and she responded to the smallest sounds in the forest around them immediately. Every bird call was evaluated, every snapping twig noted.

They traveled stealthily for about an hour before she paused and indicated that Tucker should sit on a small stone bench. "We can rest here," she murmured, her voice soft and enticing. Tucker relaxed immediately as he sank down beside her.

"I must apologize," she said. Tucker was more aware of the way the dappled light fell through the leaves of the trees and cast sparkling lights through her dark hair than he was cognizant of what her words meant.

"Apologize?" he asked, trying not to let her know he had been staring at her hair. "For what?"

"I have neglected translating," she sighed. "I have been so busy trying to pay attention to everything around that I just let you be."

Tucker was at a loss. "What has there been to translate?"

"Why, the birds of course," she was clearly surprised that he had to ask. "They have been most helpful, but I figured you would be confused by their directions and coordinates, so I kept it to myself. Birds have a frightfully large knowledge of mapping. They can pinpoint places precisely," she shook her head in awe. "But it can get complicated if you do not have a head for maps. They were reporting to me the exact location of all the dragons within a hundred mile radius. And some of the other animals were rather," she paused. "Rude. I thought I would spare you their sentiments, but perhaps we should work on your technique."

"Technique?" he felt like one of those kids who takes every statement and repeats it back in the form of a question.

Ravinna hid behind her hair sheepishly. "They think you might be less, clunky?" Her voice rose at the end making it both a question and request.

"Clunky," Tucker stated.

"Yes," her voice was barely a peep. "They are very sensitive to vibrations, and they are not accustomed to someone as large as you passing through. And I am afraid you have incensed a few spiders as well. They are always careful to build high enough that we can pass under them without causing a disturbance, but you are, well, slightly taller than most."

"Let me get this straight," said Tucker. "Are you telling me you can understand what all the animals are saying? That's incredible."

"So you are not angry?" she asked.

154

"Angry? Why would I be...? Oh you mean the bit about me being too big and 'clunky'? No. Embarrassed maybe, but not angry. I don't really know what I can do about my head getting in the way, or the size of my feet. If I tried to crawl on my hands and knees behind you I'm afraid we wouldn't get anywhere very fast. I'm just surprised that you can understand, like, everything."

Her cheeks tinged sweetly pink. Gone was the commander from her facade. "It is not as hard as you might think. The animals who want to be understood are quite insistent. If more people would listen, I imagine they could learn. But most are far too busy."

"So when you were over in my world, could you understand all of our animals, too?"

"No, unfortunately most of them were too concerned with their own interests to pay attention to anyone or anything else. I suppose it shouldn't come as a complete surprise, given the way things exist there in general, but I must admit I was disappointed. Even here there are some who have no interest in sharing their thoughts. Certain domesticated animals are less communicative. Cows, sheep, pigs, these mostly live centralized on their own kind and do not care to be a part of anything larger than their own needs."

Tucker wanted to ask her more, but as in every instance, there was not time.

"We will not rest here for long. There was dragon activity not far ahead, and I thought it best to pause to give them time to move on."

Tucker's face expressed his concern, so when Ravinna looked at him she burst out laughing. The sound reminded him of all things sweet and good that he had ever known. It was enough to even make him forget that she was laughing at him, rather than with him. "No worries," she placed a hand lightly on his arm. "These are not hunting. We would have heard the sounds if something dark was afoot. We are near the first great lake and there are several bathing there. We are quite safe, but I thought it best to leave them plenty of space."

The idea of dragons bathing was absurd to Tucker. He let out a laugh of us own. Whether Ravinna guessed why he was laughing or not, the tension was broken and they lost themselves in mirth. Tucker laughed until his sides ached. He was certain he would be reprimanded by all the mice and deer from here to the great lake for the raucous noise he was raising, but that was of no concern to him.

The sound of Ravinna's giggling mixing with his own, brought feelings of more than just humor at the thought of big fire breathing human hunting dragons sudsing up in a lake. He felt a deep sense of joy at the sound. The feeling was so overpowering that he almost reached out for her, but in that instant a bird flew close overhead and Ravinna froze, completely silent.

"What is it?" she asked in a sing song language Tucker was able to understand.

"Approximately nine miles to the north the dragons are on the move," a high musical voice replied as the bird fluttered back and forth. "By my estimation, they will be passing to the south east of this point in the next 3.5 minutes."

The bird continued, explaining technical information about wind speed and giving a list of coordinates that meant nothing to Tucker even in English. When Ravinna had thanked the bird and sent him on his way, Tucker chuckled quietly. "Well, I can see why you didn't share all that with me before. But it was nice to catch at least a little of it this time. So, should we move out, or wait longer."

"Another couple minutes and the way will be clear. I will go back on silent once we begin to move, but I thought you should have a chance to hear what you have been missing."

Tucker took a look around him and shook his head. "It appears I've been missing an awful lot. Pink trees, bird speech, and dragons. Who knew?"

"Well, I learned things in your world as well. What was that magnificent food you gave me in your truck. I have never tasted anything like it."

Tucker remembered her devouring the granola bar and struggled not to relapse into laughter. "Well, my dad would have called it bird food," he grinned. "Just an average snack food by our standards though. Guess it's good to know there are a few things you don't know everything about."

Ravinna ignored his last comment. She was already pulling her pack on. "It's time," she said, switching back into command mode. "We need to keep moving now that the way is clear. And maybe you could try to duck."

Tucker considered saluting her, but thought better of it. Instead, he fell in line behind her and they continued quickly through the forest.

Chapter 11

Flint knew the road well. When he used to drive log trucks early in his career he had often passed through the canyon. It was one of the most beautiful places he had ever seen in real life. It was hard for him to imagine that anything sinister could take place in the midst of such incredible scenery.

When he came around the corner, he saw Tucker's truck and the sparkle of the lake amongst the trees simultaneously. It felt like being punched in the stomach. The air went out of him and he had to use every ounce of concentration he could muster to keep the bike on the road.

He cruised down to the truck, not noticing the police cars until he was about to stop. He pulled up right where the shoulder began to widen, and left his motorcycle there, far enough back that it would be out of the way of their search.

An officer with a red goatee and dark aviator glasses made a bee line for him the instant he stopped the engine. Flint disliked the man immediately as a matter of principle. As soon as he opened his mouth, he disliked him even more.

"Sir, I'm afraid I'm going to have to ask you to move along. We're conducting an investigation here." His voice was clipped and too high. Flint imagined the jokes his classmates must have made about a voice like that. He also had a strong feeling that those insults were what had driven the man to become a cop, and that if he found any excuse to pull aforementioned classmates over, he no doubt made the most of his authority.

Fighting the temptation to say, "It's a free country," Flint walked determinedly toward the truck, a perfect picture of composure.

"Sir," the officer's voice went higher, and Flint bit his lip to keep from laughing. "I really am afraid you need to be moving along." His hand shifted nervously down to his hip where his weapon was holstered.

Flint put up his hands in a demonstration of his lack of weapon. "Not here to cause any trouble, Officer," he said succinctly, his words as near to polite as he could manage. "This here truck belongs to a friend of mine, and I'm here on behalf of his mother to look into things."

At mention of Tucker's mother, the officer puffed out his cheeks and Flint was sure that if the sunglasses were removed his eyes would have been bulging. "His mother," he said through gritted teeth, "has done quite enough already. We are handling this."

"Aw Terry, quit being such a stickler," a second man in uniform called from over near the cab of the truck. "Don't let Terry scare you off. Bark's worse than his bite."

There was a chuckle somewhere, and Flint proceeded with confidence. "My name is Terrance," the young man's face turned red to match his goatee. "And I am not a terrier."

Flint ignored the muttering, and hurried over to the second officer. "Have you found anything?" he asked, trying to seem nonchalant.

"Afraid not," the second man shook his head in frustration. "Name's Garrison," he put out his hand and met Flint's firm grip with self assurance. "This here's Hobbes, and you've already met Terry."

There was another flurry of indignant protests from Terrance, but no one paid him any mind. "It's a real puzzler we got here," Garrison indicated the truck. "Truth is, we got nothing. Everything's totally clean. Not like someone wiped it down, but just clean exactly the way it should be if the guy got out to take a leak.

"It does look like he mighta picked up a passenger at some point. There's dirt on the floor of the passenger side, but nothing to indicate any struggle. Besides, it's impossible to tell how long the other person was there. Chances are the guy was alone when he pulled over. Plain weird if you ask me." Garrison scratched his head verifying his puzzlement.

"Still think we should bring in dogs," this came from Hobbes who was seated up inside the cab. "Only way to tell where he mighta gone." He spat a stream of tobacco on the ground at Flint's feet. "Course," he continued, "If you ask Terry over there, he'll say dogs gonna be no use. They don't catch the trail of a space craft after all."

Garrison joined in the laughter, and Flint had to bite his lip even harder to keep from letting loose. Much as he had already grown to despise "Terry," he was afraid to alienate any of them if he was going to get results.

"That's not what I said," Terrance pushed his way into the circle. "When will the two of you grow up? The term 'abducted' doesn't relate solely to extra terrestrials. Although, if you ask me, your mamma certainly couldn't have been from around here." He took a good step back when he said those words, just barely quick enough to avoid the angry stream of tobacco Hobbes aimed at his head.

"What's that you said about my ma?" Hobbes demanded. "Do you want me to come down there and...?"

Garrison cut them off. "Not now guys. We got company, remember? Not to mention a job to do. Listen, what did you say your name was again?"

"Didn't say," Flint replied. "Name's Flint."

"Well, Flint," Garrison started again, "what do you think about bringing in dogs?"

Flint's lower lip jutted out as he pondered and he stroked the dark scruff on his chin. "I'd say that might not be a half bad idea. It's not like Tucker to disappear like this. He's a good guy. Dad died quite a while back and he's been taking care of his mom ever since. She's all he's got, and I need to be able to tell her something."

"You can tell her to take her medication," Terrance muttered.

"Terry," Garrison gave him a sharp look. "Sorry about that," he turned back to Tucker. "Terry was the one who had to try to calm her down when she started calling in. Let's just say that woman has some lungs and she wasn't about to let us do anything by halves."

"Terry wanted to put a restraining order on her," Hobbes chortled.

Terrance rolled his eyes and stomped around to the other side of the truck. "Let me just put in the call," Garrison gave Hobbes a look and then walked over to his squad car.

Hobbes jumped out of the cab and came to stand beside Flint. He was a big guy with an obvious gut, but Flint was pretty sure it would be best not to brawl with him. They both looked each other over warily now that they were on even footing. "So what are you really here for?" Hobbes asked.

"Tucker's my friend," Flint stood solidly, feet planted shoulder width apart, arms hanging lightly at his sides. "I'm here on behalf of his mother and myself to find out where he is."

For such a big guy, Hobbes had unusually small eyes. He squinted them, looking decidedly like a hog. "You sure that's all?" he demanded. "Sure you're not here to cover your tracks? Where were you yesterday afternoon?"

Flint could hardly believe where this was going.
"Larry, would you knock it off," Garrison walked back
over to them. "You're almost as bad as Terry some days.
The man's here to help, so let's let him help. You really
gotta excuse these two," Garrison apologized. "Not
fully housebroken."

As if to prove his point another stream of
tobacco jetted out of Hobbes mouth. He snorted and
slammed the door of the truck. "Nothing in there."

"The dogs should be here in twenty minutes.
Until then, let's try to make nice, okay?" he looked at
Hobbes who gave a short nod. "Okay?" Garrison called
over to where Terrance was pouting out of sight.

"Whatever," came the reply.

Garrison kicked at some rocks. He seemed
nervous to Flint and it put him on edge. He wondered if
there was something they were holding back, but he
wanted to keep things pleasant.

He chose his words tentatively. "So, is there
anything you can tell me at all so far? I mean, Nance,
Tucker's mom, she's gonna be asking me all kinds of
questions."

Garrison studied the rocks under his feet more
closely, ignoring Flint's question. He reached down and
picked up a small black stone. It was smooth, almost
shiny. He turned it over in his fingers, testing the way it
felt, estimating the weight. "When I said we had
nothing, I meant it," he said, still not looking at Flint.

Flint had spent plenty of time in small towns.
He had met plenty of small town cops. These were the
type he had been afraid he would find. They were

territorial and cliquish. If Terence had been less of a stickler, he might have been able to make some headway, get some extra information. Hobbes had made it plain that Flint was less than welcome, and despite the show Garrison was putting on, Flint was pretty sure he would happily send him on a wild goose chase to keep him off whatever trail they might find.

They were baffled by the case. Perhaps they had hoped it would be a chance to get fame for their force, but the lack of evidence was too boring. At best, they were hoping to throw him onto some alien pathway, possibly garnering a little tourism out of the deal.

"Mind if I look around?" Flint asked. "Just want to get some perspective on things."

"Be my guest," Garrison put his meet the public face back on. "The guy's boss came and emptied out his load, so there's really not much to see in the truck. Like we said, only prints we found were the vic's, uh, I mean, Tucker's. Then, like we said, it looks like he had a passenger for a while, but far as we can tell, those prints are pretty tiny. It was likely a woman. They're pretty petite, doesn't look like someone capable of hurting a big guy, less maybe she had a weapon..." his voice trailed off and Flint saw the wishful thinking look cross the officer's face.

Hobbes hit Garrison hard in the shoulder. "Stop making this something it isn't," he spat. "You're getting to be as bad as Terry. You really think some little lady offed this guy?"

Garrison laughed drily. "Nah, probably not. But don't you think it's a better theory than that he was heisted by aliens?"

The two men chuckled, and Flint excused himself and went to make a loop around the truck. Everything about the place felt wrong. He knew Tucker picked up hikers from time to time, it was a common practice among truckers, and generally fairly safe. But if it had been a woman, and a small one at that, he had trouble thinking of a reason she would have brought him out here and hi-jacked him. Tom had said the load was all accounted for, and there was nothing else of value to take. Tucker was the kind of guy who would have offered her whatever money he had in his wallet just to help her out in the first place.

As he puzzled over these things, he found Terence sulking by the guardrail. "Sorry if we got off on the wrong foot," Flint extended his hand. "Don't want to mess with police business. Just want to help out a friend."

Terence stared at his hand as though it were a foreign object he had never seen before. "There is such a thing as protocol," he said at length. "Some people have no regard for the way things are to be done." With that he turned back toward the view of the lake and stared off into space.

Flint wondered if maybe this guy had been abducted by aliens himself. There was clearly something lacking in his social skill set if nothing else. He let it be and continued his perusal of the area.

There was a steep drop off all around the parking area. About twenty feet down the trees grew thickly, almost to the point of obstructing the view of the forest floor completely. He knelt next to the railing, thinking how this view would look to Tucker with his fear of heights. He checked the rock formations, searching for any path that might have enticed his friend to go for a refresher hike in the woods.

He stood, walked ten feet back toward his bike, then squatted again to check the view. There was nothing that looked Tucker friendly about this piece of landscape.

Back and forth he walked for a good ten minutes, pausing every few feet to see if there was any easier pathway to the trees. "Any big predators around these parts?" he asked, eyeing a patch of ground that might have been disturbed recently.

Garrison and Hobbes stopped their conversation and looked at him for a minute as though puzzled by his question. "We do occasionally have a bear around," Garrison answered. "But nothing likely to come after a guy. Besides, there would be some sign of a struggle if a bear came at him."

"Been a few big cats sighted as well," Hobbes nodded. "They might like to hunt a man sitting down on the job, but they like to take their time, really figure out their prey. Not too likely they'd swipe a guy taking a stretch by the side of the road. Leastwise I've never heard of 'em doing such a thing."

"All right," Flint was mostly satisfied with their response. "Just thought I'd check. Looks like something might have gone over here, but in an easy sort of way. Thought if he did go this way, the only reason he didn't come back would be if something was after him." Flint cringed inwardly at his own words, but he kept things casual on the surface.

Garrison and Hobbes headed over to check on what Flint had seen, and even Terence cast them a sidelong glance. Flint pointed down to where a faint trail could be traced. It was impossible to tell what had made it. It could have been deer, but it was the closest thing they had found to evidence that anyone might have left the truck.

"Dogs'll be here any minute now," Garrison drummed his long fingers on the guardrail. Flint figured he was irritated that he had not spotted the trail. "We'll be able to get a better idea then."

His words were as good as a prophecy. Not thirty seconds later, an old station wagon pulled up. A tall gangly man with a gap toothed grin and a thatch of sandy colored hair got out and waved a hand at the others. "Skip and Deet are pleased as punch to have a job, boys," he called. There was a distinct southern accent in his drawl but it was obvious that he had been in the area for quite a long time considering the way the officers opened up to him.

"Thanks for getting here so quick, Lenny," Garrison grinned back at him. "Bring 'em on out." He turned to Flint, "Not to worry you now or anything, but these dogs aren't too partial to strangers."

Flint kept his cool. He had never been a dog lover, but he knew better than to show any fear as

Lenny went to open the back of his station wagon and release whatever beasts he had inside. There was a flurry of whuffling and snuffling sounds, then Lenny was followed out by two slobbering long eared basset hounds.

Garrison threw his head back and laughed, pounding Flint in the arm. "Really had you going there, didn't I," he chortled. "Slobber you to death, likely as not."

"All right, what you boys got for us?" Lenny was as eager as his dogs.

"Well," Garrison explained, "Seems we've got a trucker who up and vanished. Thought maybe the dogs could get a scent and help us see where he wandered off to."

"Piece a cake," Lenny leaned down and affectionately scratched the ear of the larger dog. "All right, Skippy ol' boy, let's show these fellows what you can do."

Skip nodded in solemn agreement as though he understood every word. Both dogs followed their master obediently to the truck. "Do you have anything specific for them to smell?" he asked. It works best if there's a personal item, like clothing or such."

"'Fraid all we've got is the truck itself. But from all we can tell his scent should be fairly thick there. Hopefully it'll be enough for them to go on."

"It rained yesterday," the memory came to Flint out of the blue. "What use are the dogs going to be in the face of that?"

Everyone stopped what they were doing and looked at him. The realization struck them hard. "Why didn't I think of that?" Garrison muttered, confirming to Flint that the man was irritated that he kept coming up with the best information.

Lenny scratched his head. "You got a good point there...?"

"Flint," he supplied his name to the question.

"Flint. Yeah, there's a point in that," Lenny went on. "But my boys, they're pretty good at what they do." He eyed the bare patch of pavement and the rocky cliff on the other side. "It's likely the scent will be washed away right around here, but if we can find a place he might have entered the forest there's a chance we can pick up the trail. If it didn't rain too hard, there's likely to be some remnants under the trees."

It was a thin hope at best, but they agreed it was their only option. Garrison held the door of the truck open as Lenny lifted first Skip and then Deet into the cab. The dogs understood what they had to do. Their noses went to the seat, the steering wheel, the clutch, every place Tucker was likely to touch in the process of a normal day. Flint noticed how Lenny's nostrils flared in anticipation, as though he was helping them with his own olfactory senses.

Skip let out a short bark, and Deet howled in agreement letting the men know they had all the information they needed. Flint was fascinated by the process. He might not be the biggest dog fan, but he was impressed all the same.

Gently, like lifting a baby, Lenny brought his dogs back to earth, giving each a good scratching once safely on the ground. "All right boys, now's your time to shine."

Noses to the ground, the dogs searched for any sign of Tucker. It was quickly obvious that Flint's fears had been valid. They meandered back and forth across the pavement around the truck, but gave no sign of recognition.

"Guess we'll have to check that trail Blade spotted," Terence muttered with a sigh.

"It's Flint," Garrison corrected him, working on his public image again. "And it would appear that is our best chance."

"You have a trail?" Lenny looked shocked, maybe even hurt. "Well why didn't you tell us that in the first place? No point in scratching up their noses on this nasty pavement if we have a place to start."

Garrison, mildly abashed, led Lenny to the guard rail and pointed out what Flint had spotted. Without another word to the men, Lenny leaned down and whispered in Skip's ear. He lifted a long leg over the guardrail, then a second, showing the dogs where they had to go.

Deet whined, uncomfortable with the separation and nervous about the prospect of going over the edge. He walked back and forth whimpering softly. Skip sniffed at the railing, then tentatively raised his stubby legs to rest on the top. Lenny scratched his ears to encourage him, then helped him over onto the rocky ledge. It took more effort to convince Deet to come, but eventually both dogs were on the other side.

Flint watched the transaction with amazement. When they began their ascent along the trail, he made to join them but Garrison held him back. "No reason for all of us to go just yet," he cautioned. "Give them space to work. If they pick up the trail we'll know. Then we can go."

Flint was having a hard time figuring Garrison out, but he knew better than to push the issue. He rested his hands on top of the guardrail and watched impatiently as Lenny and the dogs made their way to the tree line. He imagined Tucker making the same trek, and felt another wave of doubt that his friend would have done such a thing. It was so unlike him to go traipsing about the countryside; especially in the middle of a job. And it was even stranger to picture him climbing down this cliff unless there was a very compelling reason.

The passenger made him curious. Tucker had so much compassion. Flint knew he would help anyone who came across his path. If there had been a girl who needed help, he was sure Tucker would have done so. All the same, what reason would there be out here in the middle of nowhere for someone to need his help?

In the midst of his mind muddling contemplations, he heard a sound that brought his attention back to the present. A long low howl came from down the bank. The dogs had caught the scent.

"That's my little Deeter," Lenny hooted with satisfaction. "Come on down boys, we're on to something."

Without hesitation, Flint was over the railing, making his way to where Lenny sat congratulating his dogs.

"You sure about that?" Garrison called. "Sure he didn't just catch the scent of some animal."

Lenny let out an exasperated sigh, but he was too pleased with his dogs to let Garrison's doubt get him down. "Keep in mind, y'all called me down here because you knew what these boys can do. When they're on a scent they don't just go off and give a holler for every squirrel or coon they get a whiff of. Whatever happened here, your missing person definitely came this way."

Garrison looked doubtfully down the ledge, but Terence climbed over, grabbing the chance to take the lead. That was all the incentive the other two needed. Flint and Lenny watched them fumble their way down to join them.

Skip and Deet were both snorting the ground with great interest. The crew assembled at the tree line and Lenny, proud as if his children had just brought home a straight A report card, gave his dogs the signal to follow the scent. "It's hard to tell how well they'll be able to track through here," he cautioned, but there's enough cover from the trees that even with the rain that passed through the scent is still here. We'll just give 'em a little leeway, and they'll take us as far as they can."

Flint was pleased with the dogs progress. He figured the police crew were less than eager to find Tucker, but at least something was happening. Besides, Lenny was the kind of guy Flint could respect. He might not have the rank of the others, but he was a man who knew his business, and trusted what he knew.

They followed the dogs deeper into the forest, and Flint was amazed by how dark it was. It had been a relatively sunny day when they entered, but the trees grew so thickly together that very little sunlight reached the forest floor. He hoped that was a good omen for the dogs ability to follow the trail. The farther they went, the more baffled Flint felt. He could think of no reason why Tucker would have come there.

After an hour of hiking, Garrison stopped them. He was winded. "I think we should take a moment to consider things," he leaned up against a tree, his wavy dark hair sticking to the sweat running down his brow. "Let's look at the facts. One: we haven't found any evidence of a fight or coercion. Two: there is no evidence that Tucker was injured."

"What exactly are you getting at?" Flint asked warily.

"What he's trying to say is, it looks like your friend up and walked off," Hobbes spit punctuating his point. "You ever thought of the possibility that maybe he looked at his life, saw he was nothing but a trucker, and decided to run away?"

"Seriously?" Flint was flabbergasted. "You really think a guy would do that? You think he would just leave his livelihood, his family, and walk off into the forest without a word or a note or anything."

"It's not the first time it's happened," Hobbes snorted. "Grown man sometimes takes stock of things and realizes he's at a dead end. Gotta make the cut at some point."

Flint ignored the obvious slights toward his profession, and glared at Garrison and Hobbes. "Are you suggesting that we give up because he's apparently run away into the woods for the thrill of it?"

"Well, we weren't the ones who said it," Garrison acted innocently. "It's just that we're on a wild goose chase here. We took this case because the mother was bent on making a scene. Now we can assure her he decided he needed some space and has gone on an adventure hike in the middle of a dark, creepy forest. No harm, no foul, and if she wants to hire someone to keep up the search, that's her choice."

"Now wait a minute," Terence broke in, causing him to rise in Flint's estimation. "We have an obligation to look into this. Don't you think it's odd that he traipsed all the way out here in the middle of his work day. He might at least have waited to get paid. Seems to me, we've come this far we might as well figure out where the guy ended up."

"Maybe you have nothing better to do with your time, Terry, but there is still police business to do around these parts," Garrison patted him on the shoulder. "We're short staffed as it is. Can't have our whole force up in the mountains for no reason."

Flint had never been good at keeping his temper, and he could feel a flare up building. He knew that time was of the essence if they were to have any hope of finding Tucker. If they left now, the trail was likely to grow cold before he could get anyone else to come up here with him.

"Look, gentlemen," he forced politeness through his teeth. "I could stand here all day and try to convince you that I know Tucker would never do what you're insinuating, but the truth is, we don't have the time. If you aren't interested in helping me, that's fine, but I'm going to keep looking until I find out what happened to my friend."

Garrison sensed the tension and decided it was time to avert a fight. "Truth is, Mr. Flint, pardon, just Flint, we have no proof of a crime. I'm sure his mother'll want more answers, and she is free to fill out a missing persons report and go through the proper channels, but as I said before, we have no reason to assume this is anything but a guy deciding to take a break. If you would like to hire Mr. Patterson here on your own dime, that's between the two of you, but we have to go."

As much as Flint thought the situation stunk, he saw an element of truth in Garrison's words. For them, Tucker was another random guy who got sick of life and his nagging mother and decided to make a break for it. He nodded solemnly and turned to Lenny. "Well?" he asked hesitantly. "Are you willing to work for me?"

"Got the dogs all the way out here and worked up on the scent. I hate to disappoint my boys when they're on a trail," Lenny grinned.

"It's settled then," Garrison was pleased with the state of affairs. "You coming with us, Terry?"

"Good luck," Terence went so far as to pound Flint on the back in a sign of solidarity, then the officers turned and walked away.

"Guess it's just the four of us then," said Flint. "You want to talk about payment before we continue?"

"No worries," Lenny was all smiles. "Never cared much for that crew anyway. Who knows, maybe you'll be able to give my boys some good publicity. I'm happy to help you out, free of charge, friend. They might have cut me off their dime for the rest of the day, but I can still claim enough hours to pay for the dogs time so it's all to the good."

"You're one of the good ones, Lenny. And I will find some way to repay you for this kindness."

"Just finding your friend would be good payment at this point," Lenny gave a signal to the dogs to continue. "Garrison was right when he called this place creepy. I wouldn't want any friend of mine wandering out here alone all night. Something's not right about all of this."

Flint agreed. The forest was too dark, the air too thick, for his liking. He knew they were hiking through a national forest, but thought a little thinning might be in order, even if just to prevent the risk of a harmful forest fire.

The dogs galumphed ahead of them happily, pleased to be useful in the case. The trail took a steep turn and Flint threw his energy into the hike.

Chapter 12

"It is time to stop for a while," Ravinna's voice broke him from his thoughts. They had fallen into a quick pace, and Tucker found the easiest way to keep up with her was to think about other things.

"Why?" he asked, instantly wary remembering the last time they had stopped.

"No dragons this time," the sound of her voice washed his worry away. "I am hungry."

Her second sentence opened up a new realm of feeling inside his body. His stomach screamed at him angrily. He had no idea how long it had been since they left Arthyr, but according to the loud gurgling coming from his belly, it had been quite a while.

Ravinna slid down to the mossy forest floor. The peculiar teal and orange colors of the moss registered in the back of Tucker's mind as he settled onto the spongy flora. She pulled a round loaf of bread from her pack and broke it in two. The crust was hard and difficult to chew, but the inside had a lovely fluffy texture that melted in Tucker's mouth as he took a large bite.

Ravinna rustled around in her pack, pulling out dried meat for extra energy. "Sorry I have none of those amazing bars you shared with me earlier," she said as she handed him the jerky.

"At this point, it all tastes like manna from Heaven," Tucker chewed with relish. Ravinna set two wooden mugs on the ground and poured a little water into each.

"I am afraid we have to be sparing with our liquid. There are a few streams in the area, but the water is not the best for drinking. I would have gone by the lake to stock up, but with the dragons there so recently it did not seem like the best idea."

"I'm just glad it's only water," Tucker grinned, sipping slowly. They finished their meal in silence. Tucker savored the last bite of bread, counting slowly as he chewed. Ravinna got up and walked over to a nearby tree. She had a knife in her hand and he watched in confusion as she scraped some bark off the tree.

"For dessert," she smiled as she walked back and handed him a small handful of pink shavings.

"I guess if I'm going to trust you with my life, I should trust you in this, right?" he eyed the pink stuff.

"It really is good, try it," she encouraged.

Tucker tasted it tentatively, not certain if he should chew it or swallow it whole. Much to his pleasure it was sweet and slightly chewy. "Not bad," he grinned. "Not exactly maple syrup, but it's good." He finished his serving, then stretched lazily. "Probably not nap time, is it?" he asked hopefully.

"I am afraid not," Ravinna held out her hand to help him up. Tucker accepted her assistance and tried not to blush as the feeling of her hand in his sent warmth through him.

"Thanks," he brushed himself off and put his pack on. "Well, it seems things haven't been too bad so far. Any word from your little friends that we should be concerned about?"

"It appears to be fine, but I will admit that has me worried. According to Arthyr, the dragons have been making regular sweeps of this area every few hours to manage traffic. Their goal seems to be to keep us contained. I believe they're working closely with Karush. He tries to make the people believe he has things under control, that the dragons are our friends again, but I know it is only his way of maintaining power. Anyone who steps out of line is likely to meet a less than friendly winged visitor."

"But we should have some warning before they arrive, right?" Tucker shuddered at the thought of a black shadow approaching unannounced.

"I know they will do their best, but even with a warning, there are few places to hide if they pass above us. Dragons have keen eyesight. It is better not to think about it. Let's get moving. Perhaps we will be pleasantly surprised."

They had not taken more than a few steps when a loud cawing met their ears. "They come! They come!" it squawked frantically as it came closer.

"So much for pleasant," Tucker said as Ravinna took hold of his hand and pulled him through the trees. Her feet blurred as she picked up speed and Tucker stumbled behind her feeling oafish.

There were other birds, other messages, but Ravinna was too focused to translate. All Tucker knew was that the situation was not good and that he would be better off if he had started training for a marathon before this began.

"Here," Ravinna's voice was breathless as she pulled Tucker to the ground behind her. He felt his knee hit something hard, but there was no time to whine.

Ravinna pushed the base of a tree and much to his surprise, it opened up revealing a hollow inside. Ravinna chittered through her teeth, and was greeted by a matching sound from within. It was a tight squeeze, but she pulled Tucker in behind her and the tree swallowed them in its fragrant pink flesh.

It was not as dark inside the tree as Tucker had expected. "We are very lucky," Ravinna breathed in his ear reminding him of the dragon's lair. "We should be safe here. If we are cautious, we can move toward the branches and we might catch a glimpse of the dragons as they pass."

Tucker was uncertain why they would want to see the dragons, but he had decided to trust her and there was no going back on that. He remembered the noise he had heard the night before, and wondered how they could cover their ears in the tight space.

As though reading his thoughts, Ravinna said, "they come silently this time. Their goal is to catch people unaware. They will only make a sound if they find someone, and even then, it is usually at the last moment when there is no hope for the poor soul."

Tucker nodded slightly, just enough for her to know he understood. "Come," she whispered. Her body pressed against him and turned so that she was facing the inside of the tree. He could feel her reaching for the tree and finding some sort of foothold. With great care she climbed the inside of the tree. "Think of it as a ladder. It will squeeze us as we go up, so it is best if we climb together."

Tucker awkwardly shifted closer behind her. She had risen to the point where her head was even with his. With much longer arms, he reached above her and put his fingers tentatively to the tree. It was spongy, and his fingers sunk in at first, but when he curved them, as though holding the rungs of a ladder, the wood solidified.

"This is so weird," he whispered and he felt more than heard Ravinna's giggle.

In the same way, his feet sunk into the tree cautiously finding a foothold. It molded into whatever he needed in the moment. When he was firmly settled on the ladder Ravinna whispered, "Up," her face brushing against his, and together they ascended the inside of the tree.

As she had warned, the space tightened, but he was amazed by how far they managed to climb. When she gave the command to stop they had reached a decent height, and the light was brighter. Tucker was fully aware of how their bodies pressed together within the tree's soft and oddly inviting expansiveness, which enveloped them in a squishy grandmotherly hug.

Ravinna no longer had to hold on to the walls to keep herself in place. She leaned firmly against Tucker to improve her position, and used her hands to push away a hidden window flap. They were bathed in soft light, only slightly diminished by a thin film that remained over the opening she had created.

"They shouldn't be able to see inside," her breathy words tickled his ears. "We can watch safely."

There was little space to move, and Tucker was unable to relax. He could feel the blood pulsing from his heart to every extremity of his body. In the closed in space he was amazed by how each piece of himself came into focus. As much as he disliked heights, he had never been claustrophobic. He had been particularly thankful for that when they passed through the crushing walls of the cave. What he felt now was very different. He was not afraid, but he felt out of control due to the confinement, and it made him nervous.

Several minutes passed noiselessly. When they entered the tree Tucker had taken the silence as a part of their location. It was only natural that the tree offered a barrier of noise protection. However, the longer they waited, breathing as quietly as possible, the more he realized that it was deeper than that. It was as though every creature in the forest was waiting with bated breath.

At first it was hard to distinguish things clearly through the semi-opaque filament that covered the tree's opening, but as time went on, he realized that one of the reasons everything seemed a hazy sort of purple color was because they had risen over the height of most of the trees. He let out a tiny gasp to which Ravinna responded with a nervous pressure on his wrist, warning him to keep quiet.

Even as she did so, he noticed a dark shape was approaching from their left. It gravitated toward them with no visible effort, like a light sucking bubble floating through the sky. Then he noticed another on its right and a third following behind. As they drew nearer he observed an occasional flap of leathery wings, but they were coasting through the sky in no hurry.

The closer they came, the more details he witnessed. The beasts were bigger than he had realized, roughly triple the size of an elephant. Their bodies were anything but aerodynamic, large and round and blacker than black. He now understood what Arthyr meant when he had tried to describe the way they swallowed light. These fellows had clearly been responsible for heinous crimes.

The faces were long with snout like noses, and curved teeth hung down around their lower lips. Their eyes were wide and alert and a furious red. Ravinna's body shook beside him. Whether inspired by fear or rage, he had no way of knowing, but her reaction was strong and he wished he could protect her from the horror.

A memory of the truck turned to dragon lingered in the back of his mind. As horrible as it had seemed, it was nothing in the face of reality. Sharp claws curled from their hands and feet, and long spikes rose out of

185

their tails. Every part of their bodies were built for offense, and as far as he could tell, they had skin so thick it would provide plenty of defense if anyone attempted an attack.

When they were directly in front of the tree, the world went dark, not unlike the moment in the cave when his relatives had played their cruel joke. Every bit of light was eliminated and Tucker had the feeling they were hovering over the tree, perhaps contemplating settling there.

Then the dragons moved on. The dark night was replaced with brightest day. For an hour they stayed, unmoving, marking time by the movement of the sun. The tiny chittering sound came again, and Tucker felt Ravinna's body go soft within the circle of his arms.

"He says they are gone. This was their third pass today. Night will fall shortly. We need to move." Her voice remained low, but the music was back.

Tucker pushed his weight slightly back against the tree and together they moved back down to the bottom. When they reached the ground, Tucker saw the source of the other voice. A large black squirrel with pointed ears was perched on a shelf cut into the side of the tree above his head.

Ravinna looked up at the creature. "Thank you," she said, her voice higher and faster than normal.

"Anything for you, my Lady," the squirrel replied. "Have you something to eat as you go along your way. You will need strength and a place to curl up when it is time to sleep."

"I believe we have everything we need. We would not deprive you of your supplies. These times are hard for all."

"True, true," was the answer. "But if we do not all take care of your safety, there may be no future for any who live in Aristonia."

Ravinna turned sorrowful blue eyes on him. "I have heard they have been burning," she murmured.

Tucker had never imagined the expressions an animal was capable of making. He had noticed that dogs sometimes had a sad look on their faces, and his grandmother's cat was excellent at showing contempt, but the look on the face of the squirrel was deeper than that.

"They do it only for sport," the squirrel mourned. "They can destroy more of the forest in one night than what can grow in a thousand years. Many have been lost for nothing."

The luminous eyes of the squirrel looked as though tears might soon begin to fall. "They do not normally burn so close to home. We have remained safe, but those who have escaped have told such tales that we can only weep with them, and hope our good fortune continues."

"We will do our best to change the future for everyone," Ravinna reached up to grasp his furry paw. "We have a plan. Do not lose hope."

The squirrel nodded glumly. "My home is always open to you," he indicated the tree. "The homes of my family likewise."

There was a scurry of feet, and the door of the tree opened. Tucker nearly fell on top of the hundreds of small creatures that stood alertly on the other side.

"He's so big," he heard one whisper.

"No wonder he makes such a racket," grumped another.

"Surely he can help," chirped a third.

A mixture of squirrels, rabbits, mice, raccoons, and other animals he was unable to categorize moved back to give them room. They were similar to the animals he was used to, and yet more animated. He wondered if they were really different, or if it was because Ravinna's presence had given them voices.

"Greetings, my small friends," Ravinna spoke to them, and he felt an echo in her voice that reached out and greeted each one in the language of its heart. "We thank you greatly for your services. We are forever in your debt, and would be most grateful if you would continue your vigilance as we continue our journey."

There was a chorus of yeses in different shades of voice. "We promise," one spoke above the rest, and again the others hummed their agreements.

Had there been time, Ravinna would no doubt have spoken to each of them, but the sense of urgency had increased with their witness of the evil lurking in the skies. The sun was moving rapidly, and they still had a lot of land to cover. "Good bye, dear friends," she waved.

Tucker wished he could say something, but had no idea what, especially knowing they would not understand him. He shrugged, hoping it would come out as an apology for his size and inability to speak, as well as a demonstration of his thanks. "They understand," Ravinna called, reading his mind as had become eerily common.

With a slight wave of his hand, he turned to follow her. It was getting darker, and he wondered how they would follow the trail. The trees were not as thick here as they had been on the other side of the cave, but he had no idea what the moon or stars might appear like here. The idea of knowing so little bothered him. It started out as a small irritation, but as he continued to hurry behind Ravinna, aggravation blossomed inside him. Sure, she had told him about her own past, and Arthyr had given him a brief history of Aristonia, but there was so much that made no sense, and he doubted whether anyone would have a chance to fill him in on how it all worked. It no longer seemed good enough to accept that there were things he would never know. If he was going to die in this place, he wanted answers.

The darkness grew thicker, and with it his doubts. There was a curious stench in the air that covered over the rich earthy scent that emanated from Ravinna. He dwelt on what he had learned. They had told him compelling stories, but how could he know they were the truth. Perhaps the prophecy had called for a sacrifice. Maybe they knew he was going to die, and that was why he had been chosen. Forget "Tucker the Trucker," he realized he was "Tucker the Sucker." He had fallen for some beautifully crafted story in which he would be allowed to play hero. It was the sort of thing that was too perfect, and conversely too

189

horrifying, to be true. Clearly, the lithe beauty in front of him had no interest in him beyond being a hand to hold a spear. After all, what else could a girl like her see in a guy like him? The cold hard facts stated that she was the daughter of an emperor and he was a lowly truck driver.

He was struck hard by the pure truth of this thought. So hard, in fact, that he stopped moving all together. They had entered a meadow with a small stream which trickled nervously out of the ground and shivered into the trees. Tucker was so tired and thirsty that he no longer cared about Ravinna's warnings.

Night had fallen, and although he could see there was a moon doing a decent job of lighting the way for them, having one question answered was not enough. The stars above were not the stars he used to look at through a telescope with his father. This was not a place where he belonged.

Slowly, deliberately, he stepped away from the trail and toward the water. Ravinna continued ahead, not noticing that he was walking in the wrong direction. He told himself that if she cared, she would have been listening for him, she would have been paying better attention so he would be safe.

He took another step toward the stream, then a third. A twig snapped under his foot, but even that did not stop Ravinna's progress. That settled things in his mind, and he headed quickly toward the sound that would quench his thirst.

Like lightening, the owl struck, flying at his face with an angry hoot. Tucker fought back a high pitched scream, and raised his arms defensively. The bird swooped a second time, forcing him to step backwards.

"Tucker?" the fear and concern in Ravinna's voice were as powerful as if she had knocked him upside the head. She did care.

"Tucker!" she ran and was at his side before the owl could swoop a third time.

It hooted fiercely, only this time, Tucker understood. "Fool!" it rasped. "Very nearly stepped into the water that snaps."

"Forgive him," Ravinna cooed. "He was confused. I am the one at fault. I noticed the smell, but was too intent on the trail to consider the negative effects it might have."

"Water that snaps?" Tucker felt more confused than ever. He realized his mind had been playing tricks on him, but was at a loss for a reason beyond being bone tired and ridiculously hungry.

"Again," Ravinna spoke directly to Tucker now, "I have been remiss in filling you in on all the details. It is easy for me to forget that while you appear natural here to me, things are not natural for you.

"Dark dragons are not the only dangers in Aristonia. You seem so strong that I forget you are as susceptible to temptation as any other man. The grasses that grow here," she indicated the tall grass that had a golden sheen as it swayed in the moonlight, "release a toxin into the air that plays tricks on the mind. They close off joy, allowing the person who smells them to think only the worst. It is a clever trap. Desperation grips the victims, and brings about an abnormal focus on bodily discomfort. The water becomes a compelling force.

"Thankfully, we have friends looking out for our well being," she smiled up at the owl who cooed softly. "Had he not stopped you, it is likely I would have been too caught up in my own head to notice. I have developed a tolerance for the smell, having grown up with it, but it serves to concentrate my focus. I was thinking only of what might lie ahead, neglecting my other senses.

"The water that snaps, as he so aptly called it, was the next step you would have taken. The water appears innocuous, but were you to drink it, you would be slowly paralyzed. The effects are temporary, but if you were to fall forward, rather than back, you would be consumed by Zambuzzi. They are similar to your alligators which I have read about, but they live like fish and only stalk their prey inside the water. Their thoughts are only darkness, and I cannot discern them, but I can tell you without a doubt that they were willing you in their direction."

The more she talked, the more sense it made. The doubts were pushed back, but he detected a whiff of the stench, and was positive that if Ravinna walked away from him again, he would be lost.

"Is there any way to block it out?" he asked.

"Well, you can always try holding your breath," said Ravinna as she maneuvered him back to the trail. "Or, here, I have a better idea," she reached into her pack and rustled things around, then pulled out a small handkerchief. "If we tie this around your face it will diminish the effects. We will be passing through this region along the stream for a while longer, and it would be difficult for you to hold your breath that entire time."

Tucker gratefully tied the fabric around his face. He could still breathe well enough, but the smell he got was Ravinna's lovely scent, rather than the putrid swamp grass. "Good to go," he said, and they resumed their rapid pace.

Chapter 13

Alone with Lenny and the dogs, Flint was pleased to see how much progress they made. As odd as it appeared, Tucker had clearly been heading deep into the forest. He could not fathom why his friend had gotten out of his truck and gone hiking.

At the base of a steep rocky face, Lenny came to a stop. "Dogs seem to think he headed up this way, but there's no way I can get them to climb it. Any thoughts?"

The light was fading. Flint's stomach sank. He eyed the rock wall warily. "What were you thinking Tucker?" he muttered to himself. "Thing is, he's almost deathly afraid of heights," he told Lenny. "I can't think what would possibly have possessed him to climb this thing."

"Much as I hate to admit it," Lenny shook his head, "The cops might not have been off in their suspicions. Seems mighty queer that a guy would change his ways and climb a mountain, but that's what it looks he did. Know if he had knowledge of this wilderness?"

"None I know," Flint scratched his chin stubble in bewilderment. "That's one of the reasons I can't let go of the idea that he was drawn away by a force we haven't discovered. I'm not talking aliens or anything. I mean there are obviously tracks to follow and, besides, the idea is absurd, but I just can't figure it." He took a step back to get a better view of the rocky cliff.

Skip and Deet snuffled around the rocky base. Flint wondered if they had merely lost the trail, in the open where the rain would likely have washed it away. There was no way to envision anything that could urge Tucker to climb in such a place.

He scrutinized the rocks from the bottom up. "Does that look like..." he broke off mid sentence and Lenny moved to see where Flint was pointing. He rubbed his eyes to help verify what he saw.

"Seems to be a cave opening," his voice was awe laden. "Maybe your friend did have a reason for coming out here."

"But how could he possibly have known...and why?" Flint knew his mouth was hanging open, but he could not be bothered to close it.

"I've heard rumors of old mines in these parts. Maybe he had a tip about gold or something," Lenny's eyes gleamed.

"So what do we do now?" the question hung in the air.

"It's getting late," Lenny kept an eye on the sky. "I didn't come prepared to spend the night. Dogs have worked hard, they're hungry. Much as I'd love to get a peek inside, we don't have the equipment. Not sure how your boy managed, but I wouldn't want to risk a climb like that without gear."

Flint weighed his options. He knew Nance would be desperate with worry, and he felt an undeniable eagerness to see Karla again. He knew Lenny was right about their lack of preparation. He only had the clothes on his back and a cell phone that was useless. He had even left his riding jacket with his bike.

Skip and Deet whined to prove that a meal was in order. "Well," Flint gazed up at what he was now certain was a cave entrance, "I guess now that I know where this place is I could get an earlier start in the morning and head up at first light." He considered the gleam he had seen in Lenny's eyes at the prospect of hidden treasure and took a cautious approach. "You game?" he asked casually. "Maybe leave the dogs at home and we can check it out together."

"Sounds like a plan," Lenny jumped on the idea faster than Flint had expected. "We should get a move on now. I don't have a good feeling about staying in these woods at night, if you know what I mean."

They moved quickly. It took more coaxing for the dogs. They were in the mood to have a bite to eat and curl up after a job well done. "Come on, boys," Lenny urged. "We'll have steak tonight. Nice juicy steak. But you gotta race me to the car to get it."

The whole walk back, Flint thought about what he would tell Nance. He had to work hard not to spend all his time thinking about Karla instead. He had trouble putting his finger on what it was that had him so captivated. There was her voice, of course. That infectious lilting voice that lifted him out of the worries of everyday life. Then there was the smile. His mind wandered far off topic until a branch slapped his face bringing him back to earth. He would have to be careful how he explained things. Nance was delicate. He wanted to give her hope, without adding confusion.

It was dark when they arrived at the bank beside the road. In the low light, it looked nearly as treacherous as the rock face they had just put off climbing.

"Bet those cops looked awfully funny climbing back up here," Lenny chuckled to himself. "They're not so bad, I guess, but that Garrison has a way of getting under my skin like you wouldn't believe. I think it's the way he tries to seem sincere, like he's 'Good Cop' in some movie, but you know he's looking for a way to pull a chair out from under you when your back is turned."

Flint agreed with this assessment. He was certain they should not inform the police of their discovery. "I know what you mean. That's kind of why I was thinking maybe we wouldn't tell them what we found. How much work do you do for them? Think they'll notice you're unavailable?"

Lenny stroked his chin. "You might be right. If I know Garrison, when he thinks there's potential for attention, especially positive press about himself, that'll take priority. Let's call it a plan," he extended his hand to shake.

Flint shook it firmly. He could tell a treasure hunt was the stronger pull for his new comrade, but he liked Lenny all the same. If nothing else, the chance of excitement would serve as payment for the help he had given him.

"Can I help with the dogs somehow?" he eyed the climb warily. "Something tells me their stumpy little legs weren't made for a climb like that."

"Ain't that the truth," Lenny nodded. "Skip's a little heavier than Deet, but he's more mellow." He bent down next to the dogs and whispered encouragement to them, then hefted Skip into his arms. "Let him sniff you first, just to get better acquainted."

Flint held still while the big wet nose explored his hand, then his t-shirt, testing to see if he was safe. Then Lenny handed the dog over. "He's a friendly guy, but overly fond of table scraps as opposed to kibble."

Flint made sure he had a good hold on the dog as Lenny picked up Deet. "You take the lead," said Flint. Lenny cautiously began his ascent, Flint close behind. It was a slow climb, but they made it to the top and set the dogs down with a sigh.

"Tomorrow, then," Flint said as he climbed onto his bike.

"Tomorrow," Lenny waved then opened the back of the station wagon and urged the dogs inside.

With a final look at Tucker's truck, Flint started his motorcycle. It roared to life, obliterating his ability to hear momentarily. He strapped on his helmet and sped away.

The way back to Nance's place went quicker than he had expected. The front light was on in anticipation of his return, and he wondered if Karla had stuck around, or if she had other things to do this evening. He pulled up to the curb and hurried to the door.

Karla answered on the first knock, her eyes bright and hopeful. "Nance and I were just having a cup of tea," she opened the door wider, indicating that he should enter. "Would you like a cup as well?"

"Got anything stronger?" he asked. He had been in such a rush he only noticed how cold he was at that moment.

"Coffee?" she asked with a grin.

"Guess that'll have to do," he ducked his head, irritated by how the shyness of his childhood suddenly reappeared in the presence of this charming woman.

"Why don't you come in and sit down, and I'll go get that for you," she smiled, then turned. "Nance, it's Flint, just like we were hoping."

Nance stood when Flint entered the room. "Where's Tucker?" she demanded. "You were gone so long, I thought, surely..." Her voice broke off into a sigh as she saw that no one else was there.

"We haven't found him yet," Flint admitted. "But we're close. Sit down and drink your tea and I'll tell you all about it."

"I don't want to sit down," she almost shouted. "Why do people keep telling me what to do? I'm a grown woman after all. I'm a grown woman who lost her husband. No, not lost. I'm a grown woman whose husband died. It's my son I've lost. My little Tucker." Whether she meant to sit or not, her legs gave out and she fell back on the couch in a crumpled mess.

Karla entered the room in a flurry. She set Flint's cup on the clean coffee table, and hurried to Nance's side. "Nance. Nance. Would you please listen to me. Flint is trying to help." She took the older woman's hand in her own and stroked it gently. "He was only trying to help you relax so you could listen. No one is here to tell you what to do. We only want to help."

Nance hid her face in her hands and sniffled. Karla slipped a tissue to her, and Nance wiped her nose and eyes, then turned her gaze on Flint, her faded brown eyes pleading. "I'm sorry you had to see that, Flint," she said. "It's been an awful day. The police called and said from all they could tell Tucker left us. Just turned and walked away from everything. He wouldn't do that, would he? He wouldn't just leave."

Inwardly, Flint cursed Garrison. He was certain he was the one who had broken the news. No doubt he had neglected to inform her that they had found evidence that Tucker was alive, and nothing to indicate he had been hurt. The fool had told her that her son, the only thing she had left, had deserted her without cause.

"It's not like that, Nance," he soothed. "We all know Tucker would never do such a thing. These cops, they just want to keep their lives easy. Truth is, we had some real success today. There was this nice man, Lenny, who brought his hunting dogs and we were able to find Tucker's trail. When the police gave up, mostly 'coz they were lazy, Lenny and I kept going."

"So where is he then?" Nance demanded. "If you found his trail, why did you come back without him?"

"I was getting to that," Flint took a swig of the coffee. Karla had definitely managed to make it strong. He spluttered, and noticed her cheeks reddening.

"You said strong," she said sheepishly.

"What?" Nance turned to her.

"Oh, nothing," her blush deepened. "Please, Flint, what more do you have to tell us?" she asked, moving the attention off herself.

He took another tentative sip, then continued. "So this guy, Lenny, he has great dogs. You know there was that big rain last night, but once we got into the forest they were able to pick up Tuck's trail. They led us to a big rock wall. At first, we weren't sure if the trail had just washed away at that point, or if Tucker had climbed up it."

"Impossible," Nance shook her head. "My Tucker, climb a rock wall? I love the boy with all my heart, but it's about all I can do to get him up a step ladder to reach something in the attic."

"That's what I thought, too," Flint nodded. "But we stood there, just looking for a while, and we made a discovery."

"Well, what was it?" Karla was fully ensconced in his story. "What did you see?"

He grinned at her with a little wink, "A cave."

The word hung in the air. They all needed time to process what it might mean.

"No," Nance said after several minutes had passed. "I still can't see it. Why would Tucker, my Tucker, pull over in the middle of work, hike out into the woods, and check out a cave? It doesn't make any sense. It is so not Tucker."

"That's what I thought all along, Nance," Flint agreed. "But there it is. The dogs led us very clearly to this cliff. There's no place else he could have gone. We stood there at least ten minutes, letting the dogs sniff around, and they didn't get any other trail than this one. You see? Tucker must have gone there.

"Now, don't ask me how he found it, or why, but I'm certain that if we can get up in that cave, we can find him."

"Well, what about the passenger?" Nance asked. "That officer said something about there maybe being a woman. Do you think that's possible? Do you think he picked up some woman and ran off with her?"

"What?" Flint was astounded by the idea. "Now don't go getting crazy ideas, Nance. I'm sure whatever happened, there is a perfectly good explanation. Lenny and I are going back tomorrow. We'll get an early start, and he has some climbing gear. We're going to find him, and we're going to bring him home."

"I wish I could be so sure," Nance's face crumpled again. "But it doesn't seem my life works that way anymore. You know when I first met Frank, I thought I'd found happily ever after. He was so strong. So solid," her face had a far away look as she spoke about her late husband. "We were young, maybe too young, but I'm so glad we had those years. And then Tucker came along and made life complete. I lived a dream."

Flint caught her gaze. "We're going to find him," he repeated.

"Will you stay here tonight?" she asked in a small voice. "You can have Tucker's room. It would be so much easier not to be alone. And then I'll know for sure when you go."

Flint gave Karla a look. "Don't you think it's better if Karla stays?" he asked. "It's late, and she shouldn't have to drive home at this time of day."

"Oh, don't worry about me," Karla stood abruptly and started cleaning up their cups. "I can stay or go, it doesn't matter either way. My house isn't far. It's really no problem."

Flint wanted to insist that Karla stay. He felt the need to have her near. He was sure things would be easier it she was around.

Nance looked back and forth between the two of them. Making a decision had become too heavy for her to do on her own.

"We'll both stay," Flint was unusually decisive. "It makes sense. That way you won't have to worry about being alone, and in the morning I can leave knowing you still have company."

Nance looked prepared to argue. Flint remembered that she was unusually opposed to having Karla around. It was beyond him to figure out why she had a problem with the lovely girl who was so adept at putting things in order. Perhaps she felt threatened by her presence, as though her cheery disposition would overshadow her to the point that she disappeared all together.

"Well, I guess Karla can sleep on the couch," she looked down at the faded sofa on which she sat. "It's a pull out."

"I'll take the hide-a-bed," Flint rushed in before Karla could gracefully accept the offer. "I'll be up and around early, and I won't want to wake anyone with the light. Karla can sleep in Tucker's room and everything will be perfect."

Flint's new in charge attitude surprised even him, but the ladies accepted his declarations. It was an unusual situation for him. His experience with women was varied, but of a very different nature.

"I guess it's settled then," Karla wiped off the table with a cloth napkin and carried the cups away.

"I don't have any nice sheets for the hide-a-bed," Nance twisted her hands nervously. "You really should've taken Tucker's room. After all, she's only the cleaning lady."

Flint ignored her tone. "Now, let's not have any of that, Nance. I've slept in my fair share of shoddy hotels, and on the ground under the open sky more times than I care to count. This is going to feel like luxury. Just tell me where the sheets are, and I'll get this taken care of."

"No, Flint, I insist. If that woman is going to stay here, she's going to earn her money by doing some real work. We pay her to keep the house, which is highway robbery if you ask me, so she might as well make a bed."

Flint wanted to be sensitive to the current situation, but the way Nance spoke about Karla was getting on his nerves. He had seen nothing but kindness from the girl, even in the face of obvious disrespect.

He checked over his shoulder, but saw that the kitchen door was closed. "What do you have against Karla, anyway?" he asked. "She seems to be doing a fine job, and she offered to stay with you as much as you need until we find Tucker. Seems to me she's doing you a kind service."

"Ha," Nance scoffed. He had never seen her so overly critical. "You call it a service, but we pay her a pretty penny for that service. That's all she is. A hired hand. You saw the way she snapped at the opportunity to stay over night. Paying her by the hour, can you imagine. So some of her other jobs are out of town and she sucks me dry in my time of need."

"I'm sure it's not like that," Flint was shocked by her harsh attitude. "She really wants to help."

Nance gave him a hard look but kept her mouth shut. Karla returned a moment later, and Flint was thankful the scene had ended.

"Would you like me to run you a bath with some of that lavender sea salt Tucker got for you?" she asked Nance. "I'm sure it would do you good to soak and relax for a while."

Flint was afraid Nance would say something about wanting her out of the way, but thankfully she merely nodded. Karla headed for the bathroom and soon running water could be heard.

"You're a good friend to Tucker," Nance said quietly, barely loud enough to be heard over the water. "I thank you for all you've done for us, Flint. But my mind is made up about that girl. And I'll have you know, it's not just my money I worry about. She's got her eye on Tucker, just you wait and see."

Karla breezed back into the room and Nance clamped her mouth shut. "I've got clean clothes in there for you as well," she smiled sweetly, seemingly oblivious to the tension in the room. "Is there anything else I can do for you?"

"Flint will need his bed made up," she gave him a sideways look, but he made no protest. "You know where the sheets are, right?"

"No problemo," Karla was off again, getting sheets out of the bathroom. "Water's just about ready if you want to head in there. I'll make sure Flint is well taken care of." She helped Nance to her feet and led her into the bathroom.

When she came back into the room, she began fixing the bed as though it were the most natural thing in the world. Flint was heartily amazed. "How can you just take all that?"

"All what?" Karla kept at her work, not looking up.

"All that animosity. She treats you like her servant, like someone not fit for company."

"Oh," said Karla knowingly. "That."

Flint waited for her to go on, but she made the bed in silence. "There," she said when it was finished. She looked at Flint who was openly staring at her. "Your bed is ready, sir."

His jaw dropped and she had to cover her hand to stifle her laughter. "It's really not what you think," she grinned, showing a full mouth of shiny white teeth. "She's just a sad and lonely woman. A bit confused sometimes, it's true, but mostly just sad and lonely. She adores Tucker, but he's a grown man who needs to have his own life. If I resented every person in this world who doesn't treat me like a friend, I would have more worries than joys."

"But you're only here to help, and she acts like you're trying to rob her blind with your very presence. It's downright rude."

"Sometimes," her eyes softened as she spoke, "you have to choose joy. I could let it bother me, but who would that help? Should I fight with her and tell her she's being ridiculous? Where would that get either one of us?"

Flint contemplated this. He had always been a fighter. People might have said rude things about him behind his back, but they never said them more than once to his face without dealing with the consequences of his anger.

"And believe me, I've experienced a whole lot worse," she chuckled over an unspoken memory. "But Tucker's a good guy. We were never close in school, but I respected the way he handled himself. High School can be a brutal place for a girl who isn't built like a beauty queen. But Tucker was never one to bully any of us misfits. I even heard him stick up for me a time or two when some of his buddies were being particularly abusive with their words. I always liked the guy."

Flint remembered Nance's other fear and tensed. Karla noticed and quickly hurried on, "not in the way Nance is worried about. Tuck and I are just friends. I'm not here trying to get into his good graces. Just trying to be a helping hand."

"Well, you're a wonder if you ask me," Flint nodded appreciatively. "I don't think I've ever seen a person who can take that sort of abuse like it's nothing. I don't know what more to say."

"It's nothing, really. Just part of the job. She's wound extra tight right now, for obvious reasons. Most people react negatively when things in their world get messy. Besides, underneath it all she's a total sweetheart. She just doesn't want anyone to know."

It took all Flint's energy not to give her a hug right then and there. "You're amazing," he said. "That's all there is to it."

Karla laughed off his flattery. "If you're not careful you'll give me a big head. That's the last thing I need. I'd better go check on her now. She needs to get to bed so her body can rest. All this stress will make her sick if we're not careful." With those words she was gone, leaving Flint feeling very much alone.

He could hear Karla speaking in a low soothing tone to Nance, but it was impossible to distinguish what she was saying. He sat on the edge of the couch and flipped on the television with the remote on the end table.

He scooted back until he was resting against the pillows Karla had plumped for him. He was planning to watch TV to pass the time until Karla came out so he could talk to her some more, but as soon as his head made contact with the pillow it was all over and he fell into a deep sleep.

Chapter 14

Tucker was unsure how they passed the night. It was merely a darkened blur. Ravinna moved like a machine. She never slowed her pace, leaving Tucker to blunder behind her as quickly as possible or risk being lost.

There were several segments of the trail where she indicated he should cover his nose. She was not about to let the same mistake befall them twice. Tucker, for his part, decided that letting go of his own thoughts, and allowing her to lead completely was the best choice. He was useless in this place without her.

Every now and then he wondered how she knew where to go. The moon was much larger here than any moon he had ever experienced, and the stars, spread out in unfamiliar constellations, were brighter. It was dark, especially in the heavily forested sections, but he could feel the presence of the light. Despite the visibility, they were constantly changing direction, as though traveling through some intricate maze.

He admired her more with each passing moment. Contrary to his thoughts early in the night, he was now able to see how much she had gone through. She might be asking him to do something for her, but in comparison, it seemed small when he saw all she had risked. This was not the first time she had made this journey, and the last time she had been alone.

Tucker detected a change in the light around them. They had been heading primarily southeast, and he saw that the sky ahead was turning pink. Ravinna slowed her pace so he could catch up to her. She took his hand in hers. "They will come out soon, we need to hurry. At this pace it will take us twenty minutes to reach the Eastern outpost, but we need to cut that under ten."

The words were foreign to Tucker's current state of mind. He was already pushing his body beyond its normal bounds. He had a job that called for early mornings, but primarily the only other person in his world was his mother. There was little to look forward to in the evenings, so it was no problem to get to bed at a decent hour and have an honest night's sleep before he had to start the day. He could still feel the effects of sleeping on a bench then running most of the day and all night.

"I'm with you," he said, not really sure he believed it.

"Then it is time to move," he detected a smile on her face as she said it. The feel of her hand in his did stir him up inside. With a burst of adrenaline, and a small amount of shame at the idea of this wisp of a girl making him look like an out of shape loser, Tucker set to running by her side, hands firmly clasped.

The ground disappeared beneath their feet as they sped down the mountainside. Tucker considered closing his eyes. They were descending at such a rapid rate that his stomach had lodged itself firmly in his throat, making it hard to breathe. Ravinna seemed unaffected by either the speed or the treacherous terrain. She was light on her feet, sprinting past bushes and trees as if they scarcely existed. At times she bounded like a deer, and Tucker frantically leapt beside her, willing his feet to find firm ground beneath them when he landed.

There was no trail. They followed the curves of the mountainside, skirting any obstacles as they ran. Tucker imagined the dragons behind him, their hot stinking breath propelling him forward. It was the best kind of motivation, and for a moment he edged ahead of Ravinna. Seeing this added speed, she added a burst of her own, hurtling them ever faster toward the bottom of the hill.

They hit the flat land and she whirled him in a one-eighty so they were facing the hill. At what felt like breakneck speed, she hurled him to the ground. It happened too quickly for Tucker to anticipate the instant bruising that was about to take place. He felt them spin, felt her arm bend slightly and then snap like a whip, forcing him directly into a bush.

There was a slight ripping sound as the brittle branches of the bush tore at his skin. Instead of a crash, however, he skidded into darkness. It was like unexpectedly stepping onto ice. His balance abandoned him and he fought to keep his feet from taking him in two directions at once.

It was only when things finally stopped moving that he realized he was still holding Ravinna's hand. He turned toward her in the darkness, and saw the faint sparkling of her white teeth. Even as his eyes fought to focus, he heard a scuffling sound in front of him, and then a match sprung to life.

Tucker and Ravinna blinked in the sudden glare. When his eyes adjusted, Tucker drew in his breath rapidly, and realized he had pushed Ravinna behind him. His body had sensed the danger at the first sound of the rustling, compelling him to shield her. It seemed like a good sign, even in the midst of uncertainty.

When he could see, he was not inclined to move away. Ten armed warriors stood in a half circle in front of him, teeth bared and weapons drawn. No one spoke.

Behind him, Ravinna pried his fingers off her wrist and put her hand on his shoulder. "It is all right," she assured him. "Let me come forward so they can see me."

Hesitantly, and with a healthy amount of foreboding, Tucker moved aside.

A gasp went round the circle and, as one, they fell to their knees.

"Your Majesty," the one in the middle spoke with a shrill voice. "We did not hear that you had returned. We believed there had been a breach. This is the last stronghold that remains without ties to..."

As though Ravinna knew exactly what name was about to be spoken, she rushed on before having to hear it. "I am sorry I had to come to you in such a way. It has been a long journey, and we beg your permission to rest this half a day before continuing on to my father."

"Everything we have is yours," the shrill voice said. "We offer all we have to give, which is frightfully little."

"Stand, my friends," Ravinna's voice was soft. "There is no need for such behavior. We are one in this battle. Anyone who remains loyal to my father is a friend."

They stood slowly, the tallest among them a good head shorter than Ravinna. In the midst of their flight, Tucker had forgotten what sort of people these were. He relaxed beside Ravinna.

As they took him in, this time as a companion to their beloved princess, their behavior was greatly modified. Their faces turned to awe, rather than menace. Tucker felt shy, and hoped the mess he had made of his face was not as grotesque as it had been before. It no longer pained him, thanks to the balm Arthyr had used on him, so he hoped it looked better.

"And who might this be?" one asked, curiosity written on his petite face.

"I know you all have studied the prophecies of Balthazar," Ravinna spoke the name with reverence. The assembly nodded, their eyes never leaving Tucker.

214

"Then let me present to you, Tucker Kenworthy. He is here to help us slay the dragon."

Tucker had never seen a group so astounded. He imagined how they must feel. A story they had always heard about had appeared before them in the flesh. In their darkest hour, they were presented with the one thing they had not believed possible. The thought horrified him. He was not prepared to carry the weight of their hope.

"May we come closer," asked the smallest man. He was roughly four feet tall, and yet there was a fierceness in his eyes that Tucker had never seen in the largest of men from his own world. There was a challenge in his voice that went beyond mere curiosity.

Ravinna glanced at Tucker, nervous for the first time. She swallowed and regained her composure. "Of course," Tucker could feel her attempting to exude a feeling of calm amongst them.

The diminutive warrior stepped forward, but the others remained in position. They stood taller, however, as this outspoken member approached Tucker. Everyone was alert.

Tucker contemplated the possibility of throwing this challenger up over his shoulder like a child. After all, he was so small he scarcely reached Tucker's waist. Fortunately, the fierceness in the man's eyes warned him that such a lack of decorum might do more harm than good. This was not a question of size.

When he was directly in front of Tucker and about two feet out, he stopped and looked him straight in the eyes. "How can we trust you, who have not been born in our lands? Are we to put our faith in someone we have never seen? What makes you so special, so arrogant, to think you can come here and do what our bravest warriors have not been able to do?"

Tucker was at a loss. He could echo this man's words directly from his own heart. He glanced at Ravinna. She nodded, encouraging him to state his case.

"Well, uh," he stammered.

"They can understand," Ravinna encouraged, indicating that she was working overtime to allow everyone to hear whatever Tucker would say.

"What did you say your name was?" he asked his challenger, scrambling for time.

Apparently, this was the platform the little man wanted. He stretched himself to his full height, eyes never wavering from Tucker's. "My name is Vatslavem, from the family of Shelem in the Eastern Mountains. My kindred have been warriors for centuries, bringing victory over darkness throughout this region and far beyond. I, like those before me, have journeyed between worlds, and conquered dragons on both sides of the Cavern Gate. You do not think the men of your world knew what to do when errant dragons were sent their way? Were it not for myself, and my forefathers, they would have been lost.

"Beyond all this, I have seen the great Svyetlo in the flesh. I have encountered him, and lived to tell of his power and might and the great evil that oozes like stench from his pores. I have seen many a great warrior fall at one stroke of his mighty claws. I have seen the

216

fire from his mouth consume an entire forest in one foul breath. And I have seen him tear another dragon to shreds for daring to stand against him.

"So tell me now, who are you to come with such great claims? Who are you to stand where we have failed, and exert authority over us?"

It took every ounce of strength in Tucker's body to prevent him from taking a step back in the face of this tirade. He knew any show of weakness would be the end of him here. "All right, um, Vats..."

"If even my name is too much for you," he said disdainfully, "you can call me General Shelem."

"Yes, okay, General Shelem," Tucker cleared his throat. "Let me say first, that I am not here out of some misconstrued belief that I am in any way better than you. You are right to bring up these questions. They are the same questions I have asked myself. I have no idea how to fight a dragon. Until yesterday, dragons were something I remember from fairy tales when I was a kid.

"I'm not anything special, and I hope not to present myself as being arrogant. I am only here because Ravin asked me to help her. I did my best to assure her that I am just a simple man, but she believes I can be of service, and I promise I will do my best, whatever that might look like.

"It is obvious that you are more knowledgeable and qualified than I will ever be. I am not here to take something from you, or to try to prove that I am superior to you. I just want to help."

Vatslavem took in these words. He measured each one in his mind to see what value it had. Before he could speak, the man who had first addressed them stepped forward.

"You have spoken well," he said in his shrill voice. "I am General Mykel Slaveem, first son of the great Gabrel Slaveem. Like General Shelem, my family has taken part in all the wars of our history, as well as enjoying the glorious era of peace which lasted for many an age under the wise reign of Yaveen and Emperor Karlov. We do not delight in this war, and long for it to be resolved so peace can return. If you can help us in some way, whether small or great, we will stand with you."

A thick silence fell over the cavelike room. Vatslavem took a slight step forward, and, much to Tucker's surprise extended his hand. Tucker put his out as well, not certain if this was going to be a typical handshake as he was accustomed to, or not. They met in the middle. Vatslavem's entire hand was scarcely the size of Tucker's palm, but when they touched he felt the thick calluses and a raw power stronger than any trucker handshake he had ever experienced.

Vatslavem spread his fingers so they covered Tucker's palm, taking his measure. Then he swung his hand back and slapped Tucker's hand full force.

Pain burned in his palm and vibrated up his arm, but Tucker held still, willing himself not to cry out in shock or pain. A grin spread across the face of the little General in front of him, the man who had already killed his fair share of dragons, and seen the Great Beast and lived.

The smile broke the ice and laughter erupted throughout the room. The men gathered around his legs, patting him on the back as high as they could reach. There were other hand slaps, though none quite as brutal as Vatslavem's, and with each one the room roared with laughter.

He was so caught up in the sudden camaraderie that he almost forgot about Ravinna. When his mind came back, he turned and saw her standing to the side. There was a smile on her face, but he also noticed a tear sparkling on her cheek. He determined to ask her about it later.

The patting and hand slapping went on for nearly twenty minutes. By that point, Tucker's hand was nothing more than a numb thing attached to the end of his arm. The raucous laughter was cut short as Mykel cleared his throat.

"Friends," he said when they had all quieted down. "Our visitors have traveled hard to reach us, and still have many miles to go before they reach their destination. We, too, have had a long night. Let us share our food with them, and send ourselves to bed while there is still daylight to burn."

There was a hum of agreement, and the men scattered around Tucker, heading off for their usual morning tasks. He was relieved when Ravinna returned to his side.

"We can speak freely for a few minutes," she whispered when she was close, "I will not translate for them."

"Well, that was intense, now wasn't it?" he sighed. "I felt like I was in front of the firing squad for a minute. You think next time you might prepare me before you throw me down in front of hostiles?"

"I am sorry," she hung her head. "You are right. I left you on your own. I suppose I was hoping, given the past..."

Her tone was off. "I see there's something you're not telling me," he chided.

"It's about Vatslavem," she said, her words coming out in a rush. "We were very close once. My father had thoughts about a union between the two of us. Maybe he even mentioned it to Vats, but it would never have worked. We are both too strong minded to agree on anything."

Tucker nodded knowingly. "Well, that clears a lot up. For all that time spent with them, you sure don't know much about men, do you?" He patted her on the head.

"What do you mean?" she asked.

"Ah Ravin, the guy obviously cares about you. Did you think you could bring another man into his territory and expect him to play nice? You can't be that naive. Don't they have sayings here about a man and his palace?"

"No," she shook her head. "No, you are wrong. We left with the understanding that friendship was the only possibility. But I really thought he still respected me enough to trust my judgment. You said things to make him think, but there is more to you than you are ready to accept.

"Maybe at first I asked you for help because I was getting desperate and you were the first person I met who exhibited the soul I was looking for. Now, things are different. You are here to do more than stand beside us. You are here to lead us. Tucker, you will slay the dragon." Her voice rose at the end and Tucker was taken aback by the depth of emotion in her statement.

"Don't worry, Ravin," he tried to sound soothing. "I'm not going to turn around and run. I'm here to do whatever I can for you all. I gave my word. I just don't want there to be any sort of false pretenses. I don't know the first thing about killing a dragon. And I haven't been much of a leader since I was on the football field. I'm not saying I won't try, but Little General is right, I'm not a super hero."

"Little General, eh?" Ravinna chuckled. "Good thing I am not translating for you right now. You might have to watch your back as well as your front if he heard that one."

"Sorry," said Tucker. "But you have to admit the guy is uber tiny. I imagine he has a complex. Hard to picture the two of you together."

Ravinna punched him in the arm, a flirtatious action that was different from the way she had behaved toward him in the past. "No more comments about my being a giant," she threatened with a twinkle in her eye.

Tucker put his hands in the air. "Truce," he said. "I promise not to infer that you're a giant ever, ever again."

"All right," she made a show of composing herself, straightening her clothes as if she were wearing a dress.

Their conversation was cut short as a man approached them carrying a tray of food. "My apologies," his voice was low. "We're not much in the way of cooking around here. Missing that feminine touch, no offense, Majesty."

"None taken," Ravinna accepted her tray and Tucker followed suit.

This meal was a far cry from the fare they had eaten the day before. There was crunchy dry bread, and a thin soup that seemed to be stocked with whatever slightly edible thing they could forage from the forest. Tucker recognized mushrooms and nuts floating in the thin broth.

"They are not connected to the royal army any longer," Ravinna explained. "Arthyr can still get decent food to prepare for the men, because he remains, albeit in protest, under my uncle's command. There is a divide among the men loyal to my father. Some chose to remain in their positions, feeling they can be the most use on the inside. My uncle might be an idiot, but he is not without wise advisors. They knew that Arthyr and his men would not sit idly by while an interloper took over the kingdom. So they were sent to the most dangerous region to create the appearance that the country was still being guarded.

"Others, like Vatslavem and Mykel, could not bear the thought of service to such a man. They separated completely, taking the bravest and hardiest men they could gather, and set up in a less obvious location. This is actually my first visit here, and I must say I am impressed by how they have concealed this place.

"Unfortunately, in their attempts to battle the dragons, their numbers have dwindled. Originally, there were dozens of these groups spread about the three kingdoms, but this is the only one that remains.

"It is not an easy life for them. They must be separated from their families in order to protect them. My uncle set out to entrap and destroy them all, aiding the dragons whenever he could. He told their families that to be caught helping them was to invite death into their homes. The kingdom has become divided by fear. They no longer trust my uncle, but they feel helpless to stop him."

"What a mess," said Tucker. He blew on the soup before taking a small sip. It tasted awful, but he was so hungry that he finished three bowls.

They finished their meal in silence, their exhaustion getting the best of them. When they finished Mykel came over with a pile of blankets. "We have little to offer you," he said. "I hope you will accept our humble service, and rest well while you are with us."

They thanked him, and took the blankets. There were not even benches in the barracks. They spread them on the ground and curled up, falling instantly into a heavy sleep.

Chapter 15

Flint woke with a start. There was a crick in his neck, but his headache had not returned. It took a moment for him to register where he was. When the faint scent of the musty couch confirmed his location, he picked up his phone and saw that it was 4:30. He had plenty of time to get a few more z's before going to meet Lenny.

Working long hard hours had made him into an easy sleeper. He was the type who could sit down in a chair, lean his head back, and be asleep. It happened almost every time. When it was time to take a driving break, he would pull into a rest area, use the facilities, and kick back for a snooze. Power naps, heavy sleep, whatever the moment called for his body complied.

This time, things were different. He curled up on his left side, but the crick in his neck got worse. He turned to his right side, but a flashing light on the old VCR shone like a neon sign. He rolled onto his back and tossed his arm over his face to block out the light, but a ticking clock came into focus. Each tick, every tock, drove sleep farther away.

After ten minutes of tossing and turning, Flint gave up. He had slept in his clothes, so he simply rolled out of bed and tried to stretch out his stiffness. He felt a stab of worry that he was getting old and had nothing to show for it but the best decked truck for miles around. It seemed little consolation in the face of stiff aching bones. He massaged his biceps, his elbows, and his forearms to get the blood flowing.

Flint quietly headed into the kitchen where he was amazed by how Karla had anticipated everything he would need. There was a pot of coffee, all set to go. A large blue mug with a picture of a smiling cat painted on it was sitting next to a sugar bowl. She had left a note explaining where the bread and butter or milk and cereal could be found for breakfast. There was also a brown paper bag in the refrigerator with "Lunch" scrawled across it. A fleeting thought of what life with a woman in it might look like crossed his mind. He had been the consummate bachelor for years, and yet for the first time he could see the appeal in having someone to come home to at the end of the day.

He drank a big cup of coffee and indulged in six slices of toast with a thick slathering of butter and honey. He went ahead and had a second cup of coffee, then figured he might as well try the cereal. Clearly, Tucker still had a sweet tooth. He poured something pink and sugary with marshmallows in a big bowl. He added milk, thinking of how he would harass his friend about this later, without letting on that he ate some himself.

The time was creeping toward 5AM when he finished his third cup of coffee. He went to the bathroom and gave himself a look over. His hair could stand cutting, and his eyebrows were definitely unruly. The scruff on his chin was looking shaggy, but at least it was clean.

He decided to take a shower, even though he was without a change of clothes. The hot water was deliciously refreshing. It cleared his mind, and when he examined himself in the steamy mirror he thought he might not look half bad with a hair cut.

At 5:15 he went back to the kitchen for coffee number four. He emptied the pot, thankful it was still warm. He was not expecting company at that hour, and nearly dropped the mug on the floor when Karla cleared her throat.

"I didn't mean to startle you," she smiled. "I see you found the coffee."

Flint was at a loss for words. He nodded, lifting the cup to state the obvious.

"I thought you might sleep later than this," she added. "I'd planned to fix some eggs and bacon, but it looks like you've already eaten."

Flint looked down at the pink milk in the bottom of the bowl and felt a flush color his cheeks. He was suddenly very thankful for the almost beard. "Your note was helpful," he stammered. "Just made myself at home, as you can see."

"Is there anything else I can get for you?" she asked. "You saw the lunch in the fridge?"

"Yes," he said, then realized he should clarify which question he was answering. "I mean, yes, I saw the lunch. You really didn't have to do all this. I could've just grabbed a burger on my way out of town."

"A burger? At this hour in the morning?" her eyes sparkled. Her presence was so compelling that her frizzy morning hair and rumpled purple robe escaped his notice. He knew she was teasing him, and he should somehow react, but despite the three cups of coffee he had consumed in the past hour, his thoughts remained foggy.

"Well, I don't want to get in your way if you're getting ready," Karla hesitated in the doorway. "I'll be in the bedroom if you need anything before you go." This time it was her turn to blush at the unintended insinuation.

"Thanks again," Flint called after her departing figure. He muttered something about his idiocy as he grabbed the lunch bag from the fridge and carried it to the living room. He decided to head out, so he would be sure to arrive before Lenny.

He put on his coat and straightened up the hide-a-bed, then went to say goodbye to Karla. She had pulled the door closed, but he could see that the light was on. He lifted his hand and stood like a fool for a full minute before finally tapping so lightly she might have thought it was nothing but a mouse in the wall. He waited another minute before knocking louder.

"Come in," Karla called, her composure had returned.

It had been a while since Flint had gotten a look in Tucker's room, but he was certain it had never been so clean. Karla sat on the bed, a ball of yarn beside her and a half finished blanket spread across her lap. "I like to keep busy," she said, filling the silence.

"It's really nice," Flint said lamely. He inwardly slugged himself for being such a numb skull. "Anyhow, I'm gonna to head off now. If you could tell Nance I'll be back as soon as possible, I'd greatly appreciate it. It really is great of you to stay here like this. I know Tucker will be so glad to know his mom hasn't been by herself."

"It's nothing, really," Karla assured him. "She slept a lot yesterday. Stress was just too much for her, the poor dear. She's been through a lot." She paused. "I hope you find him soon, Flint. I'm not sure how much more she can take."

"Me too," Flint nodded. "Me too." He tried to think of something more to say, some reason to stay and talk to her longer, but he was running out of excuses. "Thanks again," he finished, feeling like a bigger loser than ever. "Be back soon as I can."

"Be safe," she called after him. "I'll keep some dinner for you."

Those last words stayed with him as he headed out. He wanted to find Tucker more than anything, but the idea that someone was waiting for him to come back, with or without his friend, warmed him all the way through. He hardly even noticed the chill in the air as he hurried out to his motorcycle and brought the engine to life.

Flint made good time. It was still dark when he saw the large white expanse of the trailer on the back of Tucker's truck. He wondered how long they were going to let it sit there. He thought it was wrong to leave it like an abandoned dinosaur to rot in the sun. The police had seemed eager for a glory ride, but were clearly not concerned about what had happened to Tucker, or what was to become of his truck.

A chill ran through him, and he wondered how long it would take for Lenny to arrive. He wished he had asked for his number before they parted ways. He remembered the strange look in Lenny's eyes when the idea of a mine had come up, but doubted the man would have come back in the dark to check on something so unlikely. Besides, it would have been dangerous at night.

To pass the time, he decided to take a look at the lunch Karla had packed for him. A strange feeling in his stomach, quite different than hunger, rumbled around as he pulled the bag from the small pack on the back of his bike. With stiff fingers, he opened it up and looked inside. The sun was beginning to send pink feelers across the eastern skyline, giving Flint barely enough light to see.

He felt like a school boy. There was a thick sandwich with toppings he was unable to identify in the low light, a bag of grapes, a large apple, a small bag of chips, three chocolate covered granola bars, and something else wrapped in a piece of wax paper. He chose to it leave it for a surprise, and carefully put everything back in the bag.

Headlights came around the bend, and a moment later Lenny pulled up in his battered station wagon. "Morning friend!" Lenny called cheerfully as he climbed out of the car. "The boys weren't too happy about being left behind today, but I've got a feeling they'd a been even less pleased having to wait for us at the bottom of that cliff.

"Brought us some climbing gear and a few other things to help out today," Lenny grinned. "Hope you got yourself a good night's sleep, 'cause I've got a feeling we're gonna be needing it."

"I'm ready if you are," Flint nodded. He could see that Lenny had been holding back in the talking department the day before, but was hoping to remedy that today.

Lenny moved behind the station wagon and pulled out a large backpack. "Is that your lunch there?" he asked, indicating the bag with "Lunch" scrawled across the front. Flint felt a reply was not required and Lenny went on. "You can go ahead and toss it in here if you'd like. Still got plenty of room, and I'll put it together with mine so it won't get all squashed. Can't believe we didn't take anything to eat yesterday. I very near liked to have starved. Good thing my little wifey cooks up a mean plate of pork and beans." He patted his stomach at the memory.

"We can take turns with the backpack," Flint suggested. "What with you helping me out, and carrying my lunch, it seems only fair."

231

"Sounds like a plan," the bag was now in place on Lenny's back. "Shall we get a move on, then?"

Flint nodded, and they headed for the railing. He glanced back at the truck, looking tired and forlorn in the peachy glow of the early morning sun. He promised himself he would ask Tom if they could move it the next day if they were still unable to find Tucker. Then he skidded down the side of the hill. The trail head was more obscure without the dogs there to scent it out, and with only the dim light of dawn to show the way, but they found it eventually and headed into the trees.

For all that Lenny could talk a man's ear off, he was a good tracker. Even without the dogs there to guide, he could recall every twist and turn of the trail, regardless if there was a clear marking to follow or not. When he was working, he was silent, his entire being focused on the hunt. Flint was pleased by their steady progress.

It was downright shocking how quickly they made it to the cliff. Flint wondered what had made it take so long the first day. He figured it was partly the dogs, partly the attitude of the officers, and partly their unfamiliarity with the land. This time it all flowed, and after two hours of hard hiking they arrived at the base.

The sun was decently high in the sky, lighting the rock face evenly and revealing the cave more clearly. Flint thought it surprising that there were no marks from climbing gear. He used to enjoy backpacking and rock climbing in his youth. However, it had always seemed, no matter how far out he wandered in the wilderness, someone had been there before, leaving remnants of their attempt and often actual equipment in the wall for whoever came next.

"I wish I could explain to you how afraid of heights Tucker is," Flint said to Lenny as they took in the wall of rock in front of them. "As much as the evidence points to him going up here, I'm having a hard time wrapping my head around the idea. How would he even know about a place like this, let alone come here by himself for a little sport?"

"Only way to know is to check it out for ourselves," Lenny's eyes gleamed.

Lenny took off his pack and pulled out an assortment of equipment. He had spikes to drive into the walls, ropes and carabiners, and other bits and pieces. Flint helped sort through things, remembering as he went along, and soon they we're ready for their ascent.

Flint felt a moment of worry as he approached the rock, but as soon as he began he found that the rock was more accessible than it appeared. In fact, he scarcely needed any of the climbing aids. Slowly, he began to see that Tucker could have free climbed if he had wanted to. It was that wanting to part that escaped him.

In less than fifteen minutes, they neared the lip of the cave. For the first time the situation grew strenuous. "Look here," Flint pointed out a section where the rock was loose and had the appearance of being scraped off. "Maybe this is where Tucker climbed up. See how it's all torn to shreds?"

Lenny leaned his direction and took a good look. "No doubt someone was climbing here," he grunted. "And whoever it was got real stressed around this point."

"Well, I can totally imagine Tucker being stressed about here," Flint cast a glance over his shoulder at the height they had reached. "Definitely not his cup of tea."

He avoided the loose rocks and pulled himself up to the lip of the cave. Lenny was there a second later. He whistled long and low as he looked inside before pulling himself up.

"Well, would you look at this place?" Lenny spoke in a hushed, almost reverent, tone. "I knew it was gonna be a trip, but I had no idea it would be like this."

Flint nodded, awestruck. The cave had barely been evident from the ground below, but now that they stood in its gaping mouth, they were amazed by what they saw.

The late morning light sparkled off crystalized walls, throwing rainbows hither and thither around the room. There was something about standing there, looking deep into the hidden areas of the earth, that moved Flint unexpectedly. His whole vantage point on life shifted. He could no longer remember what the drama he so urgently needed to see Tucker about two days before had been. His life before Tucker went missing disappeared, insignificant in the light of the search.

He stood, gasping at what the earth was revealing to him. Here was a great secret. The earth was not supposed to be so exposed, so vulnerable to the eyes of men. Lenny ran his hands over the cave walls, but Flint felt glued to the ground. He thought of Karla, wondering what she would think of this view. Karla, who had not existed for him before yesterday, lingered around every corner of his mind today.

"Amazing," Lenny kept whispering.

Flint shook his head, trying to clear it so he could deal with what had to be done. "Well, it doesn't look like we found a gold mine," he said, trying to speak lightly to break the spell the cave had cast over them. He was not ready to completely give himself over to sentimentality.

Lenny chuckled, "No, I suppose not. But it's sure worth looking at, isn't it?"

When he pulled back and observed things objectively, Flint figured it probably was similar to most other caves. There were the stalactites and stalagmites, the tiny pools of water, and the constant sound of dripping that were typical of all the caves he had ever seen in books or on television specials. Perhaps it was the fact that it seemed undiscovered that made it special, or the mystery of Tucker's presence in this strange and magical place. He was having trouble placing his finger on exactly why he was so astounded, but he could see it had struck Lenny as well.

Light streamed through the opening, but only extended a short way into the cave. Lenny pulled out a couple flashlights and a headlamp so they could see what lay beyond their natural vision. The floor was damp, but there was not enough dirt to record footprints. The remote location in the middle of a rocky wall made it unlikely for animal use, and it was clear that it was mostly empty.

"Hey, come here a minute," Lenny called from a few feet away. Flint hurried to his side. "What do you make of that?" he pointed to the ground with his light. Flint squinted, uncertain what he was supposedly seeing. "Are you getting what I'm getting?" Lenny asked.

"Well, to be honest," said Flint, "I don't rightly know. What do you see?"

Lenny hunched down and pointed to the ground around the pool of water. "Look here, do you see this black stuff?" Flint nodded. "Looks like ash, if you ask me."

"Ash?"

"Ash. Exactly. As in, I think someone built a fire here."

"A fire? So you think it's possible that he was here?"

"I can't say for sure that it was your friend," Lenny replied, "but someone was here. Let's see if there's any other sign."

The men continued to search the floors and walls for any nook or cranny that might hint at the presence of others before them, but the ash residue was all they could ascertain with any certainty in the main room at the cave's opening. Flint swung his flashlight back and forth at the rear of the cave, searching for a way to continue deeper into the earth. At first it appeared as though they were going to be left with nothing more than this trace evidence, but then his light gave him a flicker of an idea.

He moved toward the back of the cave, and observed one of the large rocks more closely. In this area, it looked like the opening to a mine shaft. He could imagine that this front area was cleared long ago, perhaps some ancient inhabitants valued the shiny stones, but then they came to something sturdier, and their path was thwarted.

"What'd ya find?" Lenny called.

"I'm not sure," Flint moved around the rocks. "But this might not be the end."

Lenny hurried to his side, lights at the ready. "Look," his excitement could not be contained. "You're right. It curves behind this rock."

Flint shifted back to Lenny's line of sight and, sure enough, there was an opening between the rocks. "You up for taking this farther?" he asked.

"I thought you'd never ask," Lenny's grin was huge, revealing a gap near the front between large yellowed teeth. "Let's do this," he rubbed his hands together gleefully. "I'll get my pack. We'll want everything along, just in case. Used to go spelunking with my old man, and you never know what you'll find. This old earth is full of secrets."

Lenny returned in a flash, and Flint had already shifted the stone to make it easier for them to fit through. He entered cautiously, with Lenny right on his heels. It was a tight fit. The rocks crowded him on both sides and he fought claustrophobia. However, after about twenty feet it broadened and they found themselves in a tunnel.

Lenny shone his light around the walls. Flint wondered if he was searching for gold veins, but figured there was no harm in it. They walked quietly, listening to the water dripping, as it had been doing for millennia, and the soft echoing of their breath.

Their surroundings changed imperceptibly as they walked. Flint thought his mind was playing tricks on him when he perceived the walls moving gradually inward. The stalactites and stalagmites had thinned at the entrance to the tunnel, but the farther they went the spikes returned, growing from all directions. The height and width of the tunnel was clearly shrinking, and as it came closer together the rocks appeared razor sharp, reminding Flint of a shark's mouth.

"Unless your friend was some sort of straw man," Lenny commented from behind, "I'm not thinking he could have gotten much farther than this."

The cave narrowed visibly ahead of them. They would have to give up the search soon. "Where are you Tucker?" Flint muttered into the darkness.

Tentatively, he stretched out a hand to test how sharp the spikes growing from the walls were. His hand flew back and into his mouth as blood flowed freely.

"I've got some bandages," Lenny said, quickly taking his pack from his back and rummaging around.

Blood poured from the wound, filling Flint's mouth with the strange flavor of salt and iron and something sickly warm and headily sweet that always reminded him of losing teeth as a child. Lenny had a bandage out and beckoned for Flint to extend his finger. Flint looked away as Lenny worked. The cut was deep and clean. Within seconds of securing the bandage it soaked through. It took several tries to get it thick and tight enough to staunch the flow.

"Well," Flint hated the breathlessness of his voice,"I guess we know we won't be getting very far that way."

Lenny's headlamp dizzily followed the motion of his head, casting eerie shadows on the walls. "Nope, that's for sure. I don't know what could have happened to your friend if he was here, but I can't see any way he could have gone farther than this."

Frustration pulsed through Flint's veins. He could feel anger bubbling inside. They had come so far, and all for nothing. He took the flashlight in his hand and beat it against the wall. He knew it was a stupid thing to do. He was trying to protect his hand from another nasty cut, but letting go of his temper always led to trouble. The bulb in the flashlight shattered on impact, and the tinkling of glass was followed by an ominous boom.

"Sorry," he muttered, looking at his feet to avoid eye contact with Lenny and an accidental glimpse of his bloodied finger.

"What. Was. That?" Flint looked up and saw Lenny's eyes widen and his mouth gape as he squinted into the pitch black hole.

"Just lost my temper's all. I'll buy you a new flashlight. Have a bit of an anger problem sometimes."

Lenny swatted his hand in the air as if to silence Flint's apologies. "No," he hissed, "That loud sound?"

His question was followed by a second boom that sent a chill through both men. In their curiosity they had hardly noticed how cold the cave was in contrast to the warm fall day outside, but the icy wind that flowed toward them from the narrow space between the walls caught their attention, and brought a foul sulfurous odor with it.

Flint wondered what he would tell Nance. He was already imagining her tear streaked face as he came back alone. He could picture Karla comforting her, telling her there was still hope, and actually managing to make it feel like the truth. He even imagined a group hug, but the image fractured before he felt the firmness of Karla's body in the crook of his arm.

"We gotta go," Lenny whispered franticly. "I think this place is gonna cave in."

Flint looked at him through hazy eyes. All the fight had gone out of him. He had the sense that he would have made a good family man. He really could have cleaned himself up, changed his ways, and settled in a home.

"Flint? Flint! Flint, come on. Listen to me." Lenny danced around in front of him, arms flailing wildly as a crunching sound filled the air, the sound of stone, grinding on stone. "If he came down here, he's gone now, okay? If you don't come with me now I can't promise to stick around and see what happens to you either."

Flint wanted to answer Lenny, he really did. He wanted to tell him that things were going to work out, but he was pretty certain that was a lie. They were too deep. All those spiky rocks were going to start falling from the sky soon. They were going to be buried alive, and no one would be any the wiser. They would disappear as mysteriously as Tucker had.

Lenny was pulling on his arm now, trying to get him to budge. Flint could never quite say what it was that convinced his body to start moving again. All he knew was that instead of cold air flowing up the tunnel, he noticed that it was hot. So hot, in fact, that it revitalized an old fear he had suffered from in childhood. A house on their street had burned down with the whole family inside. For years he had recurring nightmares of how they must have felt. Even after his father had explained that they would have been unconscious from smoke inhalation long before the flames reached their bodies, he was unable to shake the fear of burning alive. He started to run.

In the rush of adrenaline that propelled them forward, caution was forgotten. Lenny tripped. His flashlight flew from his hand and hit the floor with a crunch and a spray of glass shards. He picked himself up and kept running, the light from his headlamp their only consolation.

The cave narrowed in front of them again. The burning at their backsides subsided, and Flint could see the first signs of natural light. The large boulders pressed cold and firm against their arms, assuring them that they were heading the right way. Then, suddenly, the way was blocked.

Both men stopped, breathing heavily and listening intently. There was nothing but silence beyond the normal cave sounds they had enjoyed on their earlier walk. The temperature was back to normal cave cold, and the stink had subsided.

"We're trapped," Flint stated the obvious, his voice devoid of emotion.

"I have things," Lenny had a note of panic in his tone, but he was fighting to hold himself together.

"What kind of things?" Flint asked.

"Ex...explosives," Lenny's teeth were chattering. "Wa...wasn't sure what we would find. Wa...wanted to be ready, you know?"

"So you brought explosives?" Flint was baffled. "Did you think we were going on a treasure hunt? Really? Did you even care about finding Tucker?"

"Hey, don't get all high and mighty on me. I don't even know the guy. Sure I hope you find him and all, and I gave you all the help I could, but I've gotta make a living too. I..."

"We shouldn't fight," Flint cut him off before he started sputtering. "I'm sorry. You're right. This is my fault. And there's no reason you should care about Tucker, or me, or really about anyone but yourself. It's not important now. What is important, is that we figure some way out of this mess. But seriously, after I hit the wall with a flashlight and all Hell broke loose, do you really think that setting off dynamite is going to help us? It'll only make things worse, far as I can tell."

Lenny thought about that, the light from his headlamp casting odd shadows across his hollow cheeks. "I've got a spade too, and something we can use like a lever. We just have to figure out where the opening should be and I think we can get ourselves out of this."

"We should eat something first," Flint suggested. "We'll need all our wits about us to figure this next bit out."

"All right," Lenny agreed. He reached into his pack and handed Tucker the paper bag Karla had packed for him. "Maybe take it slow," he cautioned. "Hard to say how long this is gonna take."

"Do you think we should save the battery in your head lamp?" Flint hated having to ask the question. He dreaded being in the pitch black, but figured they were in a relatively safe location.

Lenny's eyes shifted from Flint, to his backpack, to the surrounding rocks. "Guess you're probably right," he agreed at last. When they both had their food securely in their laps he reached up with a shaking hand and flipped the switch.

The darkness was not pure. That was the first thing Flint noticed. He had never been in a cave before, but he had heard that when the lights go out the darkness can be so intense people lose all sense of direction. He held his sandwich in his hand and traced the faint outlines of the rocks with his eyes as they slowly came into focus. He wanted to pinpoint the source of the light. That would be the best place for them to start their escape.

As he had expected, it was up ahead, very faintly edging around several large boulders. It was not going to be easy to get those monsters to budge, but if Lenny was as well supplied as he claimed, they should be able to work their way out.

He took a bite of the sandwich Karla had made. His teeth sank into the thick bread, crunched their way through the lettuce, onions and tomatoes, then continued smoothly through the sliced turkey and cheese. There was a tangy burst of mustard flavor, and the perfect mix of salt, pepper, and oregano. It was just a sandwich, but sitting desolately in a cold dark cave, it was the best tasting sandwich he had ever eaten. He pictured Karla standing in Nance's tiny kitchen while he slept like the dead on the pull out couch. He imagined how she must have debated what ingredients to use. Perhaps she contemplated that, as a trucker, he would have simple tastes, well accustomed to roadside diners and their traditional fare. Yet she opted away from anything heavy like mayo, keeping it light and simple and absolutely fabulous.

He began to wonder if he was going crazy. Clearly, he was already delusional. No doubt she opened the cupboards and the fridge, and slapped together something quick and easy. But his heart rebelled against such a lack of care on her part.

"So what do you think it was?" Lenny broke the silence.

Flint wished he could have stayed in his fantasy, but knew Lenny was going to go a different sort of crazy if he was left alone with his thoughts. He had already pegged him as a talker, and if he knew anything about talkers, they have an insatiable urge to get things out in the open.

"Dunno," Flint said around a large mouthful. "But you know how caves are. They're unstable."

"This is no ordinary cave," Lenny disagreed. "I've been in my fair share of caves, but this is like nothing I've ever seen."

"How so?" Flint was curious.

"Well, there's typically a couple types of caves. The natural type and the manmade type. Simple explanation, because there are plenty of different reasons for the natural ones to exist, but the outer bit of this is clearly natural. You can tell by the way it grows. Manmade caves are scooped out clean. Got lines to show you how they were picked, or evidence of dynamite.

"By my best bet, the first pocket is totally natural, but this part here, where it sneaks behind the rocks and gets wider for a bit, has the look of something on the manmade side of things. Remember how it was all sorta smoothed out?"

Flint nodded, though he doubted Lenny could see anything of him beyond a vague shadow.

"Then we got to that pokey bit, and everything got really strange. I can see why folks mighta gotten curious about those pretty stones in the walls out there. Would've been hard for them to get up here, but once they did they'd have wanted to see more. Only there's the problem with how undisturbed the place seems. If they did have a mining operation here, how did they move their tools in place?"

"Maybe there's another entrance," Flint suggested. The idea excited him. If they could find an alternate entrance, they might be able to get out.

"Maybe," Lenny sounded unconvinced. "But it gets all strange again when we come to that sharp and tiny place. Somehow that part has to be natural again. So did they just get tired of their digging? And I've never seen rocks growing out of the walls like that. It didn't feel natural."

"You're contradicting your own argument. Either it was natural, or it wasn't."

"Okay, all that aside, the sound, or at least the first one, was just plain creepy."

Flint could sense Lenny nervously looking down the tunnel. "Yeah, I'm not going to disagree on the creepy part," Flint acquiesced, allowing himself to be sucked into the conversation. "I guess where I got confused was when it got hot and smelly." He took another large and satisfying bite, internally thanking Karla for the work of art he was consuming.

"Hades?" Lenny suggested.

Flint snorted derisively. "Come on, Lenny. Be serious."

"Okay, that might be a bit far fetched, but I got a good dose of fire and brimstone training in my childhood, and that was the very smell and feel I imagined it to have."

Flint opened the bag of grapes. He had read how, when one sense is put out of commission, the other's step in and develop in superhuman ways. He felt the smooth, firmness of the grape between his fingers, then relished the sweet and sour explosion of cold juice in his mouth as his teeth broke the skin. He thought of the food shows he enjoyed watching, and what it must be like to act as a judge, describing how the food made him feel.

"Well?" Lenny had endured the silence for as long as he could handle it. "Any brilliant thoughts?"

"I used to have nightmares about being burned alive when I was a kid. Started when a house down the street burned," he briefly recounted the story. "One of the kids was my age. We went to the same school, but were in different classes so I didn't know her all that well. Sometimes when I had that dream I could feel her holding my hand..."

"Do you really think this is the time for ghost stories?" Flint heard Lenny's fear.

"Sorry," he felt like he was constantly apologizing. "When I was in high school we studied the witch trials, and how they burned them alive, and it brought those dreams back. I never told my dad. It was bad enough that he knew about them the first time. Kind of hard to hide things when you're a kid and you wake up in a cold sweat, screaming.

"Anyhow, when we were standing down there it came back to me. Those darkest memories were on my tail. I keep trying to think if I've ever heard of volcanoes in this area. Those sort of things happen sometimes. Maybe we triggered a magma flow. It's the best I've got."

"You sure got to volcanoes from a strange angle," Lenny mused. "Would've been better if you just told me you saw a documentary about volcanoes once and thought maybe that's what we stumbled on."

"Yeah," Flint popped another grape into his mouth. He was eating them slowly, to try and savor the sensation they gave him each time they burst inside his mouth. "I guess you're right. But what's life without a good scare every now and then?"

"All right," Lenny sighed. "I guess just let me know when you're done and we can start trying to muddle our way out of this one."

Silence descended. Flint wondered if he had offended Lenny. He knew they were in this together, that he would be lost without the man sitting next to him in the darkness. The last thing he wanted to do was to alienate him.

"Sorry," Flint said for about the millionth time. "I'm still trying to figure out how we got ourselves into this mess in the first place. I know I can be inappropriate sometimes. Hazard of the trade, you might say."

"It's all right," Lenny sounded almost cheerful again. "We're both on edge. Down where I come from we're all pretty superstitious. Guess I'm more sensitive than usual."

"Well, I'll save what I have left. Might come in handy if the job takes a while."

"Agreed," Lenny switched the light back on and they blinked in the glare.

"I saw some light up this way," Flint led the way.

Chapter 16

Tucker had another dream. His mother was there. She was wearing the dress she used to put on the third Sunday of every month when he was a kid. It was a pale yellow, with bunches of small blue flowers scattered about, and a lacy trim around the hem, the cuffs and the neckline. It had three quarter length sleeves and the skirt hung below her knees, all loose and flowing, giving her body a sense of movement even when she was standing still.

She wore the dress when she made pot roast with potatoes and carrots and onions cooked in the broth. Sometimes she wore a string of pearls that used to belong to her mother, and sometimes she wore the cameo that Frank had given her for their tenth anniversary.

In his dream, she was standing in a field under a leafless oak tree, wearing the dress. Her hair was pulled back in a loose ponytail, and she looked younger than

Tucker could ever remember seeing her. There was a baby on a blue and white striped blanket at her feet.

His mother was watching the baby and laughing. She had a big hearty back slapping kind of laugh. He felt like he was spying, and he wondered who the baby was. She said something low and so soft that it faded completely before it reached his ears. He was watching her from a hill top through a telescope a great distance away.

He decided to go to her, but when he moved he realized someone was holding his hand. He turned and saw Ravinna. She was so beautiful that he stopped breathing. Gone were the basic clothes she wore for travel, the ones that hid her shape and gave her a childish appearance. Now she wore a gown fit for a woman. It hugged her figure alluringly. It was pale yellow with small bunches of blue flowers.

There was a scream. Ravinna's face paled and she stretched out her arm, pointing back to the field where he had been watching his mother. He put his eye back to the telescope and saw the panic on her face as she wrapped the baby in the blanket and lifted him in her arms. She started to run.

It was only when he stepped back from the telescope that he saw the dragon. It moved slowly, but with obvious intent. He could tell it was toying with her. It opened its mouth lazily, and blew an arching stream of fire that devoured the grass in the field, but left the tree in tact.

He wanted to run to his mother, but Ravinna stood in front of him, blocking his way. When he

251

looked at her, he felt his legs give way. She smiled patiently and shook her head.

His eyes flew open and he was certain his heart was pounding so loudly that anyone in the room was bound to hear it.

"Tucker?" Ravinna's voice was heavy with sleep. He tried to banish from his mind how attractive she was when she appeared so vulnerable.

"I, I had a dream," he whispered, not wanting to disturb anyone else.

Worry creased her face. She rubbed her eyes to clear away the sleep. "What kind of dream?"

Tucker felt a rush of embarrassment. He wondered how best to edit the feelings he had experienced when looking at her. After all, she was a princess, and he was a stranger in her world. "It was about my mother," he said finally. "I wish there was some way to get her a message that I'm okay. See, my dad died when I was younger, and I'm all she has. I think she's worried about me."

Ravinna nodded, with understanding. She did not ask for details. "I am sorry there was no time for you to tell people you were leaving," she sighed. "I feel responsible for so many things, and incapable of fixing them."

"What do you mean?" he asked.

"Well, I feel like I need to protect all the people here. When I first went to find you, though it pains me to admit it, I did not think of you as a person. I know that sounds horrible, but my goal was to find the one who could help us; who could set everything right. No

252

one believed I would be able to do it, but I refused to listen to reason and left against my father's better judgment. He and Adym had a different plan..." her voice trailed off and she lost herself in thought.

"So I went and I searched for so long that I was sure I would be too late," she continued. "When I found you I was desperate. You saw my situation. I was about to return a failure, but then you found me, and I knew you were the one for whom I had been searching."

Tucker was mesmerized by the lilt in her voice. It might have been the sound of her guilt, but her vulnerability helped him see her in a way she had never appeared before. It was a struggle to focus on the content, and not just the tingling feeling he experienced with each word she spoke.

"I must confess," she dropped her eyes and concentrated on her fingers which were laced tightly together on the blanket in front of her, "I never gave a thought to the people you were leaving behind. You could have taken the time to call them, but I could see in your eyes that you were confused, and I, I took advantage of that confusion. I pushed you forward so that you had no time to think. If you had, I was afraid you would think me crazy and refuse to come." She looked up and gave him the full power of her gaze. Her eyes were sorrowful looking sapphires in the soft light that filtered in from outdoors. "I am sorry, Tucker. Do you think you can forgive me?"

Tucker fought the urge to stroke the soft skin of her face. "Of course, Ravin. I know you were only trying to do what was best. I'm glad you did it. I'm glad you pulled me away from my world of conformity and made me take real life into consideration. I know there are good people who are taking care of my mother, but her state is so fragile sometimes." He sighed.

"She would be proud of you," the words surprised him.

"What do you mean?" he asked.

"When you were talking about her, I could see that you feel guilty. Not just for disappearing without a word, but for the life you have been living. It appears you think you have disappointed her with your choices. I just thought you should know that she would be proud of what you are doing here. If she sees any of the things in you that I have seen, she knows that you were meant for more than sitting inside a big metal cage every day."

Tucker pondered her words. He imagined that, coming from a place like this, his truck would look like a prison. He had never thought about it that way, but it reflected the feelings he had experienced when he heard the horrible nickname in his childhood.

There was a loud cough from the other side of the room. Tucker and Ravinna jumped and looked in the direction from whence it came. Vatslavem was standing by the wall. He did not appear to be watching them, but Tucker had the feeling the cough had been intentional. Ravinna stood, rolled her blankets up and pushed them against the wall.

Tucker followed suit. He figured it was time to get ready. Unfortunately, he rose too quickly and hit his head on the ceiling. Not surprisingly, the place had not been designed for people of his stature. Vatslavem did little to hide his derisive snort.

"Are you all right?" Ravinna spun around as he rubbed his head gingerly.

"Seems I grew in the night," Tucker made light of the situation but could feel a bump forming under his fingers.

The room stirred with life as the others seemed to wake as one. Tucker was unsure whether to be thankful for this, or to feel guilty for making too much noise. Either way, he was glad he would not have to face direct conversation with Vatslavem.

"Dusk approaches," Vatslavem commented to the room at large. "We must make ready."

The men stood with a quick easy motion. Tucker was fascinated by the way they did everything gracefully. He wondered if it looked so unusually perfect because they were so small. They were the size of children, but without any of the awkwardness.

Within minutes the room was cleared of all traces of sleep, and the men were fully armed. Some of them bristled with weapons. These were the archers, whose quivers were full of cruel looking arrows, and whose bows were nearly as tall as they were.

"Good Morrow's Eve," Mykel said with a chuckle. "We have had a slight shift in vocabulary in recent days. It makes more sense. How did you sleep?"

"Very well," Ravinna answered for them, much to Tucker's relief. "We thank you for your immense hospitality. Your kindness and brave efforts will not be forgotten."

Something clanged loudly and Tucker looked over to see Vatslavem fishing a metal dipper out of a pot. "I am afraid we cannot risk a fire at this time of day, so the soup will be cold. Not very fine fare to serve to such special guests."

"Really," Ravinna put a hand on his arm. "We ask for no special treatment. We are all family here, all fighting for the same things."

Tucker wondered if he would ever cease to be amazed by this woman. He felt like a bulky awkward mute beside her, but the only one who noticed him was Vatslavem, who eyed him doubtfully.

Mykel ushered them forward to where a short round man had taken Vatslavem's place beside the soup pot. He bent low as Ravinna came closer, and made sure to fish out as many large pieces as he could find for her bowl. Likewise, he filled Tucker's bowl to the very brim.

The slop tasted even worse cold, but they both offered up grateful thanks and ate every bite, sopping what was left up with the stale bits of bread they were offered. The room was filled with the sound of spoons scraping the bottom of bowls, followed by slurping as each man sought to get every last morsel of sustenance before the night watch began.

The instant his bowl was empty, Ravinna put her hand on his arm. "Are you ready?" she asked. "The sooner we are on our way, the better."

Tucker nodded and they gathered their things. Before they could head for the door, however, Vatslavem was beside them. "It is not fully dark," he protested. "We cannot allow you to go out. The dragons like to circle this area before they head back in. They know we are here, but have yet to find our hiding place, so they lurk in these areas in hopes of catching us unaware."

Around the room the others nodded in support of his claim. "Indeed," Mykel chimed in. "It is very dangerous to leave before darkness has completely fallen. We cannot stop you from going," he gave Vatslavem a serious look, "but we would be remiss if we did not advise against it."

"I know you mean well," Ravinna used her authoritative voice, "But we have a long way to go, and we must reach my father by morning. We have wasted too much time already. I had planned to leave by mid-afternoon, but I suppose our bodies knew how much rest we needed. We are fresh now. It is time for us to go."

There was a general rumbling amongst the warriors. Ravinna secured her bag tightly and indicated that Tucker should follow her. "We thank you again for everything, but we must be on our way."

They looked at her warily. Tucker sensed their fear and concern and he wished Ravinna would take their caution more seriously. It seemed that a few minutes more would not put them too far behind, and would provide them with the ability to move more quickly and with less caution.

Ravinna's mind was made up, however, and he was not going to make any stand against her in the present company. Despite the fact that it took every ounce of his strength not to tremble, he followed her to the opening. He saw her hesitate at the entrance, but it was hard to tell if she was questioning her decision or merely uncertain where the exit was. The entire wall was opaque and grassy looking, making it hard to find the place they had tumbled through before the sun rose.

Without realizing they were passing through, Tucker and Ravinna found themselves standing at the foot of the mountain. The sky was a dusty rose, the fading light casting a faint glow over the teal grasses that grew in the field stretching before them. The sun was nearing the horizon, but they had an hour or two of semi-light before night would fall completely.

Ravinna took Tucker's hand tightly in hers, and practically drug him into the trees on the outskirts of the meadow. She was more tense than when the dragons had flown over them the day before.

"I know this looks foolish," she said so softly that he had to bend down nearer to her face. "But I had to show them strength. Once I made my declaration, I could not back down. It is the only thing they respect, even though they sounded against it."

"I think they really were against it, Ravin," Tucker kept his voice as low as hers. "From the sounds of it, I'd say they were partly trying to protect their own hides. They're afraid that if we're spotted out here the dragons will be able to locate them."

She looked quickly up at him. "Do you think that is true? I would not do anything to unnecessarily endanger them."

"I know that," said Tucker gently. "I'm just trying to see it from their view. It's clear that they want to protect you. They're aware of the risks involved in what we're attempting. And at the same time, it's obvious that they want to stay alive. I half expected Little General to follow us out the door."

A sound something like a snort reached their ears. It came from above them. Tucker hunched protectively over Ravinna, thinking perhaps even their softest whispers had brought a dragon on their heads. Ravinna rolled her eyes and indicated that he should look up.

A mere five feet above them, settled easily in the branches of a tree, was Vatslavem. Having been discovered, he swung down and joined them in a single silent move. He landed lightly on his feet, and Tucker felt renewed awe at how fluidly the Aristonians moved.

"You did not really think," he spoke directly to Ravinna, "that I would let you do this alone, did you?"

She ducked her head and would not meet either of their eyes. "Why do you think I never told you I was going to find Tucker in the beginning?"

"I know you think you can do everything on your own," Vatslavem looked about to put his hand on her shoulder, then thought better of it. "But we need each other. We are already so divided. It does no good for anyone. Besides all of that, you are not even armed. What would befall you if you were attacked by dragons?"

Tucker knew it was petty of him, but he wished Ravinna would stop translating. The words were too

259

personal for him to hear. She had already told him enough about their relationship, and now he felt in the way. He could see clearly now that he had no right to her. This was where she belonged, and he was the one who was out of place. Since there was no way to help hearing, he decided to tell himself that Little General was talking in general terms. "We" could be seen to represent their entire people, not just the two of them. He knew he was grasping at straws, but it was all he had.

"There is no time for this," Ravinna looked up. "I know we have a responsibility to our people. That is why I am doing all of this. Having you here only complicates things unnecessarily. I have been through the very heart of Yaveen's Keep which is now the dragon's lair, and passed unscathed without the use of any weaponry. It only loads us down and makes us move more slowly."

Vatslavem bristled at her words. "Well, that's some pretty thanks I get for coming to help you. Vinnichka, please drop this self sufficient act." His voice had risen and Tucker was tempted to shush him. "When has it ever been better to have fewer warriors on a mission?"

Ravinna glared at him. "When it is necessary to do things quietly," she hissed. "We are in a hurry, and you are impeding our progress. We must get to my father as soon as possible. You know what is at stake."

"Then let's go," Vatslavem held out his hand palm up, indicating that she should lead the way. She looked about to argue further, but seeing that it was useless, she turned from both men and started forward.

Tucker ended up in the middle, feeling like he was stuck in a lover's quarrel. He told himself it was better this way, and his spirits sunk lower with the realization.

They stayed beneath the shelter of the trees, avoiding various trails. Ravinna appeared to have the entire map of Aristonia emblazoned in her mind. They progressed smoothly, and the way she was practically skipping down the trail made Tucker wonder if she was gloating.

Then it happened. It was so sudden that there was no time for any of them to think. One moment, they were moving steadily on their way with no worries in sight. Ravinna had been getting the usual communication from the birds and animals of the area, and it looked like they would reach nightfall without incident. Tucker knew he was traveling with the country's best. Ravinna had handled herself on many dangerous missions in the past, and from the speech Vatslavem had given him, he was certain Little General was vastly experienced in all the ways of dragonhood. Nevertheless, the trees in front of them vanished in a roar of flames.

"Get back!" Ravinna screamed as Tucker continued in a straight line, despite the vicious fire.

It made no difference. With a wild screech a new fire engulfed the trees on their right, and before they had time to register the hopelessness of this situation, the trees on their left were ablaze. Ravinna and Vatslavem fell into defensive positions. Much to Tucker's surprise, however, rather than keeping their backs to the unscathed trees, they moved their little half circle so that their backs were being blasted with heat. They had not yet seen the beast.

"He is alone, at least for now," Vatslavem assured them. "We must do our best to keep it that way. If he is joined by others, we will be hard pressed to defend ourselves at this angle."

It was unimportant which of them saw the dragon first. All that mattered was that he was located. In that moment, Tucker understood why their backs were to the flames. The dragon had carefully hemmed them in on all sides, and had they tried to creep back into the forest he would have been there to dispatch of them at his leisure. They watched as he slithered toward them, fire raging closer from behind and on either side.

Sweat trickled down Tucker's face. The heat was oppressive. His body was tense. He had no idea how to fight a dragon, but he was about to get first hand experience, or die without a clue. If that were the case, there would be no one left to tell his mother whether he fought bravely or otherwise. There would be no peace for her, and his last clear memory would be an image of her running and screaming, clutching a baby to her chest.

At first sight of the beast, even as Tucker froze in his dream world of thought, Vatslavem and Ravinna took action. Little General had come well prepared with a hefty arsenal of large weapons. Tucker had been so distracted by the conversation that he had not noticed them earlier. The bow and arrows were quickly passed to Ravinna, and Tucker felt a sword being pressed into his hand.

He had a fleeting thought of his hunting rifle, resting securely in his lock box back at home. It had been a gift from his father, shortly before he died, and he had never used it. Every now and then he took it out, oiled it, and checked that everything was in working order, but he had had no use for it in his life. He would have loved the chance to use it now, but, instead, had to figure out how to hold this strange new weapon.

The hilt was substantially smaller than his hand required for comfort. Fortunately, it was of a fairly basic construction, with no ornamentation like the swords he had seen in history books and fairy tales. The hilt was roughly two and a half inches long with a large ball on the end. He had to hold the pommel in his palm and wrap his thumb and two fingers around the grip.

It all happened so quickly that individual moments scarcely registered. The red eyes of the dragon glittered as it crept toward its victims. There was no sound, save for the crackling of the fire as it rapidly consumed the trees. Tucker noted that Vatslavem had a spear with an angry looking circle of sharp points on the end.

Seeing that they were not caught unaware any longer, clearly not complete novices, the dragon rose from its crawl and towered over the surrounding trees. "Now!" shouted Vatslavem. "It will call."

As the beast lifted its nose skyward, Ravinna let an arrow fly. Tucker watched as the flaps of skin around the dragons neck grew taught, revealing its weakness. The arrow flew straight and true, penetrating the area where throat flowed into chin. What would likely have been a loud howl to alert friends turned, instead, into an angry gurgle. The dragon flailed its head wildly.

Though the bow looked large in Ravinna's grip, and the arrow had seemed long when she let it loose, Tucker figured that the dragon's head must be at least three times the size of the arrow. It had pierced the tough hide, but it had not done deadly damage.

There was a snort of rage and a puff of thick black smoke billowed from the dragon's nostrils, but there were no flames. "You always were the best shot," Vatslavem hooted, clearly enjoying this. Ravinna said nothing, but Tucker shot her a glance and saw that her eyes were surprisingly sparkling with glee.

The dragon fixed them with a glare. It brushed at the arrow with indignation, snapping it in two, but the point remained firmly embedded beneath the scales. It tried again to make its blood curdling howl for assistance, but there was nothing but a hiss and steam.

Vatslavem and Ravinna spread out, edging closer to the flames, but also forward toward the angry dragon. Tucker was paralyzed with doubt. He had no idea what he should do, so he stood, frozen, watching his impending doom approach. His partners could not have asked for a better decoy.

The dragon swung its mighty head back and forth, eyes rolling constantly in a vain attempt to keep all three of them in view. Tucker clenched his sword, wondering what part of the dragon's body might have the appropriate level of weakness. He glanced down at the sword, doubtful whether it would have any effect on the massive creature. It was only two feet long, and while he was sure it was razor sharp, he felt certain it would scarcely get around the scales and through the leathery skin of the beast who eyed him like a tasty niblet.

The dragon flicked his tail with a mighty whoosh, and toppled several trees. One of them nearly fell on Vatslavem. He escaped being crushed, but his view was momentarily blocked. The tail wagged back the other way, and Ravinna dodged forward to avoid being likewise obstructed.

There was a loud snap and crackle. Branches, leaves, and a serious amount of dirt flew through the air. Tucker put an arm up to protect his eyes, and as he did so the dragon lunged forward, claws grasping for his body. At the same time, Ravinna let loose another arrow, knocking out the dragon's left eye.

He lost interest in Tucker, and turned toward Ravinna, searching blindly for the nuisance that had twice foiled his plans. This distraction gave Vatslavem an opening to rush from the boughs of the fallen trees. With the strange spear in his hand, he came up beneath the belly of the dragon and thrust it under the dragon's left arm. There was a squelching sound and an odd tinkling as the scales shattered with the force of the blow. The dragon reared, but the small man held on tightly to the wooden shaft. With no foothold, he was left clinging desperately to the spear with little hope of doing more.

The dragon was in pain, but equally filled with rage. It gurgled angrily, spitting sparks through the smoke. "Tucker, quickly!" Ravinna shouted.

In a daze, Tucker had no idea what she wanted him to do, but he realized that if the dragon managed to lift himself into the air Vatslavem would be done for, and more dragons would likely come to join the fight. Flames were hot on his heels as he ran blindly into the action.

Ravinna was quickly racing in a half circle to get around to the dragon's good eye. "When I shoot him, he will drop closer, and you must reach up and grab the spear. Twist it hard and pull out the heart."

Her words swirled nonsensically around inside his head. Smoke fumes were making everything fuzzy. She could not possibly think he was going to be able to pull out the dragon's heart. He looked up and saw Little General throwing his weight to and fro in an attempt to make the vicious spear twist inside the beast's body. This was made more difficult by the fact that the dragon continued to grasp at him with his claws.

Even as Tucker shuddered, he caught a motion from the corner of his eye as Ravinna shot a third arrow at the dragon. He was blind now, and, as she had predicted, he lunged forward, much lower to the ground. There was no time to contemplate. Tucker watched as Vatslavem's body flailed toward the forest floor. As soon as he was within reach, Tucker jumped up and grabbed the spear. He used the force of his leap to spin the two of them in a one-eighty, and as they swung around he heard a slippery sound, followed by a noise like pulling fruit off the vine.

Everything happened in an instant. The spear ripped the heart free from the dragon's body in a massive gush of black blood. However, the dragon was falling toward the ground so quickly, that the spear plunged back into the cavity, heart and all, and jammed through its body as it crashed heavily on top of Tucker and Vatslavem.

Tucker had a vague memory of being at the bottom of a doggy pile in football practice. The boys would scream as they leapt onto the top, forcing him lower into the grass and the dirt. There was so much heat at the bottom of the pile, and the weight of those wiggling grunting bodies, and the smell of sweat and dirt and stinky socks. He remembered telling himself over and over, as he slowly suffocated, that this was fun.

Being crushed under the body of a dead dragon was anything but fun. There was a sulfurous smell, mixed with something both metallic and acidic that would have choked him if only he could breathe. Unlike the warm bodies of his teammates, the body of the dragon was hard and cold, each scale like a razor sharp fingernail digging into his back. He tried to move, but his body did not respond to the warning voice that his brain tried to send through every synapse.

A faint groan sounded near his ear. He could not turn his head, but he managed to open his eyes enough to see that he was not alone. A small body was curled up next to him, only partially crushed under the dragon's weight because Tucker's body was so much bigger that it created space for the tiny man.

"Tucker?" a breath of fresh air spoke peace into his brain. He might die, but it would be a beautiful death as long as the voice was there. "Tucker, if you can hear me, try to move your hand so I can see where you are. I am going to try to lever this beast off of you, but I will have only enough strength to hold it briefly, and want to make sure I lift in the right place."

The voice was muffled, but he understood the words. He willed his arm to move. Apparently he had thrown one arm over his head in the course of the fall. He figured that one must be closest to freedom since some light filtered through from that direction.

The scales cut into his arm as he shifted it slowly. His hand felt like it was on fire where it had gripped the spear but he refused to concentrate on the pain. He needed to breathe, and getting his arm out was the first step toward drawing a full breath.

"Very good," Ravinna cooed. "You will have to move quickly when you have space. I know it will be difficult, but you must do as I say."

Tucker liked hearing the power in her voice. He could accept and follow her directions. It was easier not having to think. The weight would lift and he would move.

The body beside him groaned. He realized he was going to have to pull Vatslavem out as well. The light dimmed as Ravinna jammed the branch into the small space next to Tucker's fingers. He heard a grinding sound as she pushed a stone into place under her lever.

Slowly, the light expanded, and the weight lifted from his arm. He pulled it back and wrapped it around the broken general. Ravinna's breathing was strained as she pulled on her lever. Hot smokey air rushed into Tucker's lungs. He choked and moved simultaneously. The dead weight lifted, and a surge of adrenaline, like the last gasp of a drowning swimmer, propelled him to action. He pulled Vatslavem with one arm, and pushed himself forward with the help of his legs. They emerged into the middle of an inferno.

Ravinna's hair flew wildly in the wind of the fire, and she glowed amongst the blaze. They did not take time for a joyful reunion. The flames had reached the head of the beast, and they could hear its skin bubbling.

"If the flames reach the throat before we are away, we are done for," she yelled. "There will be an explosion. Quickly, after me."

Tucker scooped up the limp body of the bloodied warrior and followed her at a desperate run. He could not allow himself to think of anything. He focused on the sound of his feet thudding heavily into ground.

They ran hard, and then the ground rocked as the promised explosion tore through the air. Tucker fought to maintain his balance. If he fell he would crush the broken body cradled in his arms. Bits of tree debris sprinkled around them, but they had gotten far enough to avoid further injury.

Smoke seared Tucker's lungs. His mind wandered, searching for happy memories to block out the present. Trees flashed by on every side, their shadows flickering from the distant inferno. Slowly the light dimmed and the air grew fresher.

"We can stop now," Ravinna's hand on his arm coupled with the sound of her voice, halted him. They were back where they started, like a tribute to Vatslavem's warning.

Ravinna led the way into the room. There was no fire to warm the place, only a few candles. "Hello?" she called tentatively to the empty space. There was no movement. "Hello?" she called anxiously again.

"Sorry, sorry," rasped a voice from the corner. "Just wanted to make sure you were safe before answering. They have been known to send beautiful young ladies into the hideouts of men to tempt them, before entering with swords."

There was a scuffling sound, and the owner of the voice appeared. He was about medium height for their kind, but surprisingly round considering the food they had been eating. He walked with a limp, which helped to explain why he was the one left on guard duty.

"So because there is the possibility of danger, you hide?" Tucker was surprised by the anger in Ravinna's words.

"You do not understand," he held his palms upward. "The idea is to make them believe they have found an abandoned hole. Were they to stay, I have ways of escaping to warn the others so they would

270

never return. Or if they do, it would be well prepared to do battle. There is a tunnel," he indicated the area he had just vacated.

"I apologize," it was Ravinna's turn to look humble. "I was not trying to attack your honor. I am only concerned for our friend."

Tucker had almost forgotten the small burden he carried. Vatslavem was completely still in his arms and weighed little more than a large house cat.

The man, who had been bowing low whilst talking to them, looked up to see of whom they spoke. When his eyes recognized the body of Vatslavem, torn by the dragon's claws and crushed from the fall and the weight of the dragon that Tucker had not been able to protect him fully from, his face disintegrated in horror.

"Quickly," he gasped, "bring him nearer the candles."

Tucker went as fast as he could, setting the body gently on the blanket the man spread quickly on the ground beside the flickering light. The guard set to work immediately, removing the torn and bloodied clothing.

"Light a small fire," he directed Ravinna. "We will need to boil water to clean the wounds."

She gratefully took action. There were already the makings of a small fire in a pit by the wall. Tucker wondered if they had a similar method of distributing the smoke as he had seen at the last outpost.

"They leave me here for two reasons," the man explained to Tucker as he began to gather things from around the room. "I was injured early on in the fight against the dragons. I used to be a warrior with the best of them," his eyes misted as he said this. "But after my injuries made me unstable in battle, I trained as a medic. I am too slow to dodge dragons on the field anymore, but I'm quick with a needle and thread."

It took an interminable amount of time for the water to boil, but the man never stayed still. He carefully removed fragments of cloth from the cuts on Vatslavem's body with a tweezer-like instrument. Ravinna carried the pot to them the instant it boiled. She kept herself busy by dousing the flames and wandering about the room carefully avoiding what was going on in the corner.

"Name's Stow, by the way," the round medic informed them. He was more than content to work and speak at the same time. "He's lost quite a lot of blood, but he's a strong one." The more he worked the more confident he became. "Hand me that cloth again," he instructed Tucker.

"So, will he live?" Ravinna spoke tremulously from the far wall.

Stow grew quiet, but he nodded. Tucker saw he was holding back, but Ravinna seemed contented enough. She came a few paces closer, and rested her hand on Tucker's shoulder.

"He is in good hands," she whispered. "We have done all we can. We should go."

"What?" Tucker spun to face her, confused. "We're just going to leave before he wakes up? I'm sure we can do more to help."

"The best thing we can do is to get to my father before things get any further out of hand," her voice had an icy edge to it.

"It is best if you go," Stow confirmed her words. "I thank you for your help, but she is right. You can do nothing more here. I know what I am doing."

Tucker oscillated between the two of them helplessly. It was useless to imagine himself a great warrior when no one listened to what he had to say. He tried not to respond out of hurt feelings, but it was hard to take orders right and left without any good reason.

"Please," Ravinna's voice was her own again. "They were right, we should have waited. I can admit that I was wrong. And it has been a heavy price to pay," she glanced down at the battered body of Vatslavem. "But this only shows how important it is that we reach my father and Adym quickly."

Tucker wanted to leave a parting message for Vatslavem, but had no idea what to say. He looked at Stow with pleading eyes. "I will explain it all to him," Stow nodded. "He will understand that you had to go."

"Thank you," said Tucker, standing up to join Ravinna. "Do you think we should bring weapons with us now?" he asked. "Just to be on the safe side?"

"They will only slow us down," she shook her head. "Besides, we will be traveling in the dark. It will not matter so much. It is speed that matters now." She passed into the fresh air without another word.

Tucker waved to Stow, hoping the gesture would convey the respect he felt, rather than his confusion. Then he quickly followed Ravinna outside, not wanting to be left behind.

They stood at the base of the mountain, peering into the forest. A bright glow from the fire still raged on the horizon. "Do you think other dragons will come to check it out?" he asked.

"It is not likely. If there had been a fight to join, they would have been there, but they care little for one that is already lost. The explosion consumed the body, so there would be nothing for them to eat either. Perhaps in the morning they will come to inspect the damage, but that is all." Her voice was flat.

His mind burned with an insatiable need for answers. How would they put out the fire? Where were the rest of the men? Were they safe out there in the night? They continued to stand unmoving, so he decided to try one of them. "So what caused the explosion?" he asked.

Ravinna turned to look at him as though surprised to find him beside her. "Explosion?" she asked, confused. Then the light dawned. "Oh, yes, that. Well, you know that dragons breathe fire, right? In order to do this, they have in their long necks a sack filled with highly flammable liquid. When they are alive they control how much of this liquid escapes, which explains why their heads do not explode every time they spit flames. When I shot him through the neck, I punctured this sack, along with his windpipe, making it impossible for him to call for help, as well as limiting his ability to burn us alive. However, when the flames reached that part of his body they ignited all the liquid at once, causing his body to explode."

Before Tucker could respond to her clinical description of their experience, she had walked away. "We will have to alter our route to avoid the fire," she explained. Having never even seen a map of Aristonia, this information was useless to Tucker, but he was glad she was confiding in him. "We will also have to move much faster."

Tucker had never been much of a runner. He was fine for a sporting event like football or basketball or even soccer, but track had never been appealing to him, and cross country had sounded like a sick joke. He remembered hearing that a couple of his old high school friends had decided to run a marathon. They had made some wagers and decided that one of them would train for six months, gradually increasing the miles he ran every day, while the other one would train for only two weeks and they would see which one did better. Oddly enough, to his memory it was the one who had only trained for two weeks that came out ahead. It had never made sense to him, but he suddenly found himself in a similar position, albeit with even less training and more desperation than a bet for motivation.

Ravinna bounded ahead, lithe and graceful, with moonlight glinting off her hair as she raced through the night. Tucker was sure every animal in the forest was cringing at the sound of his feet tromping heavily behind her. He sent out thought apologies every time he saw some shape fleeing from their path into the deeper darkness.

They soon left the glow of the fire behind. Tucker let go of all sense of direction, trusting completely in the apparition who led him with such focus and drive. His whole body went numb, and he stopped thinking entirely. Keeping up was the only thought allowed. If he slowed down at all he would stop, and if he stopped, he would never start moving again. So he ran, knowing that his life truly did depend on it.

Chapter 17

Flint hated to admit it, even to himself, but his arms were aching. It was impossible to tell how much time had passed. Even looking at his watch, he was no longer certain if it meant AM or PM. His life was focused on shifting dirt and rock one way, and then another in a desperate attempt to find a way out of the cave before it became their grave. His knife was now dull and would be useless for anything other than dirt scraping in the future.

Lenny groaned. "Poor Skippy and Deeter. I hate to leave them alone this long. They're likely to be digging holes again. I gave 'em a good breakfast 'fore I left, but this is ridiculous."

Lenny leaned against the wall of the cave, taking the light with him. Flint sighed. "We're not doing your old dogs any good if we give up now and stop working," he waffled between sounding gruff and desperate. "Now, I need that light if I'm going to keep moving things around over here."

"I say we call it break time," Lenny put his head on his knees, obscuring the light. "If we don't get some sleep we're not going to be able to keep this up."

Flint searched his brain for something motivational to say. The truth was, he had sunk so low over the past few hours that he was empty. With the exception of Nance, who he knew was going crazy while she waited for word of her son, there was no one out there expecting him. At least Lenny had his dogs. He thought he remembered him making a reference to a wife as well.

At the thought of a woman, he came up with an idea for how to drum up inspiration in his exhausted companion. Flint knew if Karla was waiting for him on the other side it would keep him going. "I thought you said you had a wife," Flint nudged Lenny with his shoe. "What about her? Don't you want to get back to her? And, come to think of it, can't she feed the dogs?"

"The boys never took too well to Annie May," Lenny sounded sorrowful, his voice muffled by his knees. "She won't go near 'em when I'm not around. Afraid they'll bite, even though I've tried to assure her they're just big pushovers."

Flint had trouble imagining the floppy eared hounds intimidating anyone.

"Trouble is," Lenny went on, "She won't give 'em table scraps. Don't know how many times I've told her just to let 'em lick her plate and they'd be friends for life, but she's afraid they'll ruin her plates, and very near runs past the boys to get those blasted dishes in the wash."

"See," Flint tried to sound bright. "You've got all sorts of reasons to get yourself out of this mess, Lenny. A wife that loves you, two devoted dogs...what more could a man want?"

"Worst bit is," Lenny went on as though Flint had not spoken, "My Annie May's due any day now. I told her this would be a quick job and I'd be back by dark. Left her all alone with no car and a baby about to arrive."

Flint heard tears trying to weasel their way into Lenny's voice. The more the man talked, the more ridiculous their situation appeared. They had to get out. As much as it would pain him to tell Nance they had not found Tucker, he would get through that. When things were taken care of to the best of his abilities, he determined he would ask Karla on a date. Not just some night out at a bar, but a real date with flowers, and dinner in a nice restaurant, and maybe a movie or something cultural.

"Snap out of it, Leonard," Flint pulled out his big man on the truck voice. "We've gotta get you home so you can help your wife have that baby."

Lenny's head jerked up as if Flint had slapped him. "My momma only called me Leonard when she was real angry," he regarded Flint cautiously.

"Come on, Lenny," Flint urged more gently. "Work with me here, buddy."

Lenny shifted around so his headlamp illuminated the area they had been working on.

Progress had, indeed, been made. With the light in place, Flint gripped his faithful blade in his raw, blistered hands, and began to scrape dirt from between the rocks.

Not only did Lenny stop complaining, he stopped speaking all together. He worked beside Flint, scooping dirt away and looking for anything that might present itself as an opening out of their predicament.

Flint dared not even to sigh, for fear that Lenny would snap in some new way. Their only hope was to keep diligently at their task. The only people with any idea where to find them were the police they had dealt with the day before, and he knew it was unlikely they would be heading out to help any time soon. If they were going to get out of this alive, they were going to have to do it themselves.

He had a memory of Karla promising to keep dinner warm. He wondered if she had meant it, or was saying it to be polite. It was long past dinner time, and his stomach growled loudly driving the point home. Flint contemplated taking a snack break, but after the effort it took to get Lenny working he decided not to risk it. If they kept at this it was only a matter of time until they would break through.

Chapter 18

When they first heard the dreaded screeching, Tucker thought he had fallen asleep and it was his alarm. Then he realized he was still running. He was so deeply zoned out that he was aware of nothing.

There was another great squawk, this one deeper, and he looked up, noticing that the sky was a warm pink, splashed here and there with puffs of orange clouds. He pulled his head down and searched for Ravinna. She had increased her speed to a blinding rate.

Tucker thought it unlikely that he could make his body move faster than the breakneck pace he had been miraculously keeping up all night. Then two calls came at the same time but from different directions and the reality of what he was hearing sunk in. The dragons were coming, and they were making no secret of it. This was not good news.

He spun his head around wildly, but could see no sign of them. That was his only happy thought. He spotted Ravinna as she was about to disappear into a massive garden of dusty red rocks. Amazingly, his feet picked up speed and he hurtled himself, like a mad man careening toward certain death, after her.

He tried not to identify how many dragons were following them. He even attempted to delude himself into thinking they might not be after them at all, but instead were merely out for their morning flight, sharing the latest dragon gossip. He cringed imagining they might be speaking of their fallen comrade, the dragon he had had a small part in destroying. He was not ready to call himself a dragon slayer, but no matter how he looked at it, his hand had helped to twist the weapon that pulled out the dragon's heart.

All he could see were the tips of Ravinna's dreads as she whipped around one of the mammoth rocks. Tucker raced after her then lurched to a standstill. They were on the edge of a precipice, overlooking what was either a huge lake or a sea. The drop off from the cliff was staggeringly high.

Tucker's breath caught. They were trapped and dragons were coming. He gladly accepted Ravinna's hand as she slipped it into his. The things he had wanted to tell her would go unspoken.

Then they were falling. At least, Tucker was falling. In that fleeting moment, as the ground ceased to exist in front of him, he had the horrifying realization that Ravinna had purposely jumped. There was no sense in flailing, but Tucker's legs seemed destined to hit the water running after a night of mindless movement. Ravinna, on the other hand, was straight as an arrow, toes pointing downward as if in a ballet pose.

At the last moment, Tucker plugged his nose. He was certain it was pointless, but it was the only thing, in the midst of the madness, that made sense. His feet tore at the water a fraction of a second before Ravinna slipped down next to him. Despite his thrashing, she did not release her grip.

The water was surprisingly warm and wrapped smoothly around them as they cut through the surface. The searing pain followed by a quick death, which Tucker had anticipated, did not come. They bobbed to the surface. Ravinna's face remained serene as Tucker gasped greedily for oxygen.

"We are almost there," her voice slipped through his trauma and drew him back to the present. "Can you swim?"

Had he not been fighting to keep his sanity, Tucker would have laughed long and hard about that question. It seemed the sort of thing she should have asked before they jumped. Given the circumstances they had been through over the past couple of days, however, it struck him as par for the course. He limited his response to a drippy nod.

That was all the encouragement Ravinna needed. She squeezed his hand briefly, then pulled him under the water as the screeching resumed in earnest.

Tucker had mostly been telling the truth about swimming. He could swim, but that was different from being a swimmer. It was just like how he could run without being a runner. His experience in the water was primarily the result of hotel swimming pools on family vacations and icy cold swimming holes in the river. It quickly became evident that what Ravinna was asking him to do was another marathon, this time underwater.

They moved deeper beneath the surface of the sea. Everything blurred. Ravinna kicked firmly with nice even strokes. Tucker did his best to mimic her movements. He had a thought of what the other truckers he knew would think of him in this situation. This was a Tucker no one had imagined possible for many years.

He felt invigorated as they plunged amidst the flowing arms of watery plants, and the myriads of fish that flitted away at their approach. It grew darker, and panic struck like a steel wall. He needed to breathe. He needed oxygen in a tangible way. He writhed away, fighting to return to the surface. Ravinna, for all her ability to compel him, was no match for his strength.

Rationality left his mind as the need for air drove out every other thought. Ravinna was like a dead weight as she clutched his hand and fought to bring him deeper. He was not able to process the idea that she might be trying to drag him to his death. It was irrelevant. All he knew was that he must breathe.

The water grew lighter, less opaque. He could see the air. It was there, just above him. Then his mind registered something else. The air, or more precisely the sky, was not clear and empty. Rather than being inviting, it was full of dragons, their distorted cries bouncing off the surface of the water and reaching him from every angle.

His body and mind were split. His lungs begged for relief, his mind pleaded that he stay hidden and safe. There was nothing to be done but surface, by this point. With one frantic kick he surged up, Ravinna still tugging at his hand. Just as his mouth was about to open, there was a new pressure on his body. Something had wrapped itself firmly around his left ankle. It exerted such extreme downward force that he was certain his lungs would burst.

Down, down, down they went. Darkness closed in and all the fight left Tucker's body. He was beyond exhausted. He was tired of fighting, and of failing and of feeling useless. He let go and pulled in a deep breathe.

His eyes flew open. His head was above the surface of water so black he could not see his body where it floated beneath it. Ravinna's face glowed pale, but happy, beside him. Before he could think his way out of it he kissed her. She did not back away, but met his caress softly, thoughtfully.

Then reason returned and he pulled back. "I'm sorry," he muttered. "I just...what happened?"

Ravinna acted as if nothing out of the ordinary had taken place. "You panicked. It is not surprising given the circumstances. Thankfully, we are no longer alone."

His eyes flew to hers then scanned the darkness. Ravinna giggled and a spout of light erupted in front of them. Unlike the angry orange flames that had destroyed the forest, this fire danced around them like fireworks. It fell in cool white sparks that hissed softly as they landed on the water.

Ravinna let go of his hand and floated on her back away from him, gracefully propelling herself toward the source of the light. Tucker treaded water, watching in wonder as she drifted beneath the starlike sparks that shimmered on and above the water. Then she was on her feet, emerging from the darkness into another shower of sparks. He saw her take something in her hand, then realized it was a burning torch, illuminating a large dark shape.

"Tucker Kenworthy, please allow me to introduce you to Adym," her voice was musical with delight and he could not help but be swept up in her euphoria. He paddled toward her, and she reached out her hand to pull him from the water. Slowly, as though not wanting to frighten him, the great dragon, the only son of King Yaveen, lowered his head closer to the light so Tucker could get a better look.

The face was both similar and completely unlike the dragons he had witnessed. He could sense immense power but also the utmost gentleness in the gaze of the huge green eyes. Sharp teeth curved around the edges of Adym's mouth, but rather than appearing sinister, it looked more like a grin.

"It is a privilege to meet you," the dragon spoke with a deep earthy voice. It reminded Tucker of the way Ravinna smelled. It was so natural and fresh and honest in its smoothness. "We have been eagerly awaiting your arrival."

"The honor is mine," said Tucker, hoping his voice would not betray his trembling.

Ravinna, who was still holding his hand, squeezed it in encouragement. "Come, we must go to my father. He, too, is eager to meet you."

"I'm such a mess," Tucker was painfully aware of how bedraggled he was. Ravinna looked at home, as if undisturbed by the night of fighting, running, then swimming until he almost forced them to drown. He had no idea how she did it. And there was more. He had felt inadequate since his arrival in Aristonia, but now he also felt unworthy. Ravinna had been leading him to safety, and he had been so full of doubt that he had risked their lives. If the Emperor had any idea, Tucker was sure he would be furious.

"No worries," Adym's voice warmed him. It was different than the way Ravinna effected him, and more powerful. All his insecurities were laid bare, and yet forgiven without exception. "Karlov can wait. Rest and be refreshed, then, when you are ready we will meet you in a more respectable way."

Understanding dawned on Tucker. It had been Adym who had pulled him here. The great dragon had seen his weakness and rescued him. He felt even more ashamed, yet there was no judgement in the soft, low voice.

"Ravinna, his room has been made ready. I have other things to attend to now, but if you would be so kind as to take him there, I would greatly appreciate it."

"Of course," her voice carried a respect that was new to Tucker. For the first time, she was neither in control nor defiant. "Let's get you cleaned up," she snuck a glance at Adym. "And I guess you should rest before you meet Father. I am sorry I rushed you. I am so eager for you to meet him, especially after what we have been through these last few days."

Adym gave her an affectionate nudge with his long snout. "See you soon, Princess," he said, then turned and disappeared into the water.

Tucker was surprised to see a pink tinge coloring Ravinna's cheeks. "It's amazing, isn't it?" her voice full of wonder. "Somehow, he always knows exactly what to say."

"So you like being called 'Princess,' do you?" Tucker asked. She made no verbal response, but continued to avoid his gaze.

She lead him quickly down the passageway. Tucker respected her silence. He was again amazed by how undisturbed she appeared after all that had transpired. While he felt like his body was about to fall to pieces, she walked smooth and steady as though it was a normal day. The only evidence of their rigorous journey could be seen in the way her clothes hung loosely around her small body, weighted down by water, and the way the loose strands of her hair curled.

Tucker made note of the passage they were walking along. The walls were clearly manmade. They were decorated in intricate carvings that breathed history. If he had not been utterly exhausted he would have wanted to study the stories on the walls. They reminded him of the ones he had seen near Yaveen's Keep, but these were more intricate.

"Here is your room," Ravinna held a door open which Tucker had not noticed. "Please, forgive me, for rushing you so much. What Adym said was right. You should rest. Everything you need is here. Take all the time you need, and when you are ready pull this cord and I will come."

There was a rope hanging down the wall just inside the door, and she pressed it into his hand to make sure Tucker would not forget where to find it. She could see that he was nearly delirious with his need to rest, but before she left she rose on her tiptoes, pulled his head down and kissed him on the cheek. Then she was gone.

The world spun around him, and Tucker's legs felt like jelly. All the exhaustion he had been resisting washed over him as he stumbled through the door and grasped the back of a chair. The door closed quietly of its own accord, and Tucker breathed in deeply as he sought balance.

The skin of his cheek tingled where Ravinna had kissed him, and he allowed his thoughts to return to the moment when they emerged from the water. He imagined the feelings he had experienced there were similar to how being born felt. There was the rush of life giving air that filled his lungs, the realization that he was not dead, and then the beautiful warm pressure of soft lips willingly against his.

Tucker forced his thoughts back to the present. He knew he had to meet her father soon, and the thought made him excessively nervous. He wanted to be at his best for such a monumental occasion. He looked quickly around the room and noticed a bed that looked soft and inviting, a small table laden with fresh fruits, breads and cheeses, and a tub with steam rising around the edges. Beside the tub, there was a large fluffy towel and what he assumed to be a fresh change of clothes. He wondered vaguely if they would fit him, but decided he would deal with that issue when the time came. He decided to clean himself up while the water was warm.

He half dragged himself across the room on rubbery legs, and eased himself blissfully into the hot water. It was a shock when he felt the water bite into the lacerations on his back and arms. The night had been so intense that he had forgotten the injuries he suffered in the battle with the dragon. In his mind, his part had been relatively small, but the injuries it had cost him were significant. He slid further under the water, disregarding the burn, and longing to have it all wash away.

It was tempting to fall asleep in the comforting embrace of the water, but Tucker knew that would be foolish. He had nearly drowned once in the day, and was not ready to face such a pathetic end. He pulled himself out and wrapped up in the towel, then sank blissfully onto the bed. He was asleep the moment his head hit the pillow.

Chapter 19

"I think I see more light," said Flint, scrambling to get a better angle. "Look, look!"

Lenny, whose head had sunk lower in the last few minutes, perked up at these words. "Where?" he asked eagerly. "Do you really think so?" He scooted closer, frantically pushing dirt back.

"Turn off your lamp," Flint directed.

Lenny complied and things got a lot darker, but it was quickly obvious that what Flint had said was correct. They had managed to get through the excess rubble and were finally scraping at the rocks directly blocking them inside the cave.

With renewed energy, they worked at the larger rocks. "Too bad we can't use the dynamite," Lenny said wistfully.

Flint paused. "I was wondering about that," he looked over at Lenny in the dark. "Why did you bring dynamite along? What were you expecting to find?"

Lenny was quiet, his hands still in front of him.

"Well?" Flint asked again.

"Okay, to be totally honest," Lenny sighed. "I really do wish we'd found your friend, but it was the cave that called to me. I love my dogs, and I adore my Annie May, but we're having a wee bit of trouble making ends meet these days. The boys at the station toss me a job every now and again, but it's not often they need a tracker. We've sniffed about a thing or two for them, but the checks only cover food costs.

"When I saw this here cave, I'll confess I thought we might finally have hit the jackpot. Annie May's been looking for work, but jobs are hard to come by, 'specially when you're pregnant. So, yeah, I was hoping we might find gold in these hills."

"But, seriously," Flint put a hand on the other man's shoulder. "Dynamite? Even if we did find gold, that probably isn't the best way to go about getting at it."

"I s'pose you're right," Lenny agreed.

"Well, we might not have found gold, but I think our luck is about to change," Flint turned back to the rocks. "I think we're about to find our way out of this mess."

As if to prove his words were true, Flint put all his weight against one of the rocks and gave a big push. Much to the joy of both men, the rock shifted. It was only a small movement, but it was enough to propel them into a fresh frenzy of action. They forgot the risk of anything falling down on top of them, and put all their force into pushing the huge stone.

The rock groaned as it inched forward. Lenny counted, "One...two...three..." and on each "three" they threw themselves against the rock. Dirt and gravel fell in their hair and scratched their faces, but they were oblivious to it and kept pushing. The progress was slow, but it continued to scrape forward with each lunge.

"One...two...three!" Lenny shouted. With one last colossal shove, they slammed against the rock and it hurtled free. However, even as it moved everything began to shake. Frantically, Flint pushed himself out of the hole pulling Lenny behind him.

With a sickening crash, the rocks tumbled back over the opening. Lenny howled as his foot was crushed, but Flint kept pulling him, afraid that he would be sucked in and smashed completely otherwise. With a fierce tug, he freed the man, and drug him across the floor of the cave. Once they were clear of the danger zone, he collapsed, panting with relief.

Lenny groaned and sat up, gingerly testing the damage done to his foot. "Sun's come up," Flint huffed. He looked at his watch. "Past noon I guess."

"Annie May's gonna kill me," Lenny moaned.

"Annie May's gonna kiss you for a week," Flint corrected him. "You think you'll be able to walk?"

"Won't really know till I try," said Lenny.

Flint forced himself to his feet then reached his hand down to pull Lenny up. The tall thin man stood uneasily, tentatively testing his injured foot. "More worried about the climb down this hill than anything," he admitted, taking a limping step. "Once we're down I

293

can rig up a walking stick or a crutch if need be, but I'm afraid there's no way I can climb."

Flint hit his forehead with his palm. "I'm such an idiot."

"What?" Lenny's concern was obvious.

"We've got a whole pack of climbing gear, but it's still in the hole. No way we're gonna clear that out again to get it."

Lenny lost his balance and teetered against Flint. "Feel like I'm out of the frying pan and into the fire," his voice shook as unsteadily as his body.

Flint helped the injured man sit on the ground, then paced the cave trying to figure out the best plan of action. He hated the thought of leaving Lenny alone, but without the aid of ropes it would be next to impossible to get him down the cliff. They had eaten most of the food they had along during their small breaks, but he knew it would be bad to leave Lenny with no supplies.

Flint wandered to the edge of the cave and looked down. He shook his head. The drop was too far for Lenny to go over the edge. He would likely break both his legs in the process and be in worse shape, immobile and easy access for wildlife.

"You'll have to leave me here and go for help," Lenny said weakly. "It's the only way. I'll be all right. Won't take you long. And if you're worried about finding the way back, use the dogs. They'll be more than happy to help if you explain it to them."

Flint wondered if Lenny was delirious, but when he turned back to him his eyes looked clear. "Go," he

294

said, his voice stronger. "The sooner you go, the sooner you can get me out of here."

Flint chuckled at that. "If you're sure," he said.

"I'm sure," said Lenny. "Get out of here before I roll myself off that cliff and make you carry me home."

"I'll be back as soon as possible," Flint assured him.

"Make sure you are," Lenny forced a smile.

Flint fished around in his pocket, remembering he had shoved one of the granola bars there. He handed it to Lenny. "It's not much, but hopefully it'll be enough 'til you can have more of your sweet Annie May's pork and beans."

Lenny accepted it gratefully, and Flint made his way back to the edge of the cave. He lowered himself carefully, then waved to Lenny as he disappeared down the side of the mountain. Again, he was impressed by how easy the wall was to scale. If Lenny had not been injured, they would have been half way to the road.

"On my way," Flint called the instant his feet hit the ground.

"Be safe," Lenny hollered back. "I'm not going anywhere."

Flint barely heard those last words because he was already running. He had been awake for well over twenty-four hours, but he knew he could not slow down. He had to get back for help quickly. Even as he ran he went over his best options. He had no idea how to find Lenny's wife. He would rather contact her than go to the police station. In the end, however, it seemed his best bet was to go with the men who could easily get the equipment they would need to move the injured man from the cave. Much as he hated to admit it, he was hoping he would find Terence rather than Garrison. At least Terence would take the situation seriously.

His breath came out in quick, burning bursts. He muttered to himself about getting too old for such business. In general, he would rather lift weights in the gym than go for a run. He started to worry that he might not get back to the road before he collapsed. The prospect of collapsing out in the dark woods was inconceivable. He berated himself for every mistake he had made over the past couple days. Things could have been done better, smarter. He was under qualified for what he was doing. He ran and ran and with each footfall became more certain that he had made a wrong turn and was going to get lost.

Then, as if out of nowhere, the roadside hill was ahead of him. Adrenaline surged and he pushed himself to keep running right up the side. With aching fingers he grasped the guardrail and pulled himself over, then tumbled to the ground, his body shaking violently.

He laid there while several minutes passed. The shadow of Tucker's truck grew and slowly covered him. Flint had to get moving. Lenny was counting on him. Nance was no doubt beside herself with worry. Karla... he had no words to describe what Karla might be thinking. He only hoped that, when he saw her again, he would be able to articulate the ideas in his head and not freak her out.

A car drove by, tires squealing around the corner. Flint took it as a sign. With shaking hands he used the guardrail for support. He was weak, but there was no time to waste. He stumbled drunkenly to his motorcycle. He was relieved to find the key was still in his pocket. He let the engine roar briefly, before swinging onto the road and heading back to the nearest town.

Chapter 20

Tucker did not dream. He did not move. He slept hard and awoke with a start. He had no idea how long he had been sleeping, or where he was. Everything ached, yet the bed he was in was more comfortable than any place he had slept in his life. He was afraid to move; afraid that if he did the sweet softness of the spell would disappear.

He breathed in deeply. Everything smelled fresh, a mixture of citrus and floral. Then he caught a whiff of something else. It had been a long time since he had eaten a real meal, and he felt a jolt as his stomach rumbled loudly at the scent of food.

At long last he allowed his eyes to open. He looked around the room, and saw the table covered with fruit and bread and cheese. With a groan he sat up, and pushed himself off the bed. His legs were wobbly, but he made it to the chair beside the food.

He picked up a slice of bread, lifted it to his mouth and took a bite. It was firm, hearty bread with a nutty flavor. He chewed slowly, feeling the need for composure. Then, realizing there was no one to see what he did, his animal hunger took over. He went into a feeding frenzy, devouring the food with pleasure. It was simple fare, but Tucker had never eaten anything so delicious and filling.

He had been satisfied with most of the food he had eaten since his arrival, but the drinks he had been served had left much to be desired. He was overwhelmed by a great thirst, but when he sniffed the liquid in the glass he worried the fabulous breakfast he had consumed might come back up. He set it down as far away as possible, but changed his mind. Holding his nose as he used to do when served powdered milk as a child, he tossed the stuff straight back.

Much to his surprise, the liquid cooled the aching in his throat immediately. He released his nose and experienced a sweet and minty flavor. It was not what he had expected, but it was not bad either. It left his mouth tasting fresh and clean, as though he had drunk children's mouthwash.

When everything was gone, Tucker allowed himself to think. He tried to piece together the events that had brought him to this cozy and magnificent place. Images of flames and water, trees flying past in the darkness, giant beasts both evil and good, and then the memory of the sweetest kiss, flashed through his mind.

"The Emperor," he said to himself. "I've made him wait." He looked around frantically in search of the clothes he had noticed the night before. He saw them on the floor by the tub, and hurried to see if they would fit.

On a whim, he tested the temperature of the water. It was not icy cold, but only slightly above room temperature; a sign that he had slept for quite a while, but not unreasonably long.

Tucker picked up the clothes nervously. They were similar to what Arthyr and his men had worn. Simple, but clean and neat. The shirt looked a decent size, but he cringed at the thought of it coming down only to his belly button. He pulled it on over his head, and, much to his surprise, it fit perfectly. It was designed to drape loosely over his body, allowing for easy movement, and it did exactly that, hanging down well below his waist. To his great delight the trousers were a perfect fit as well.

He looked with despair at his ruined work boots. They were so soaked that he knew it would be useless to wear them. His dirty socks were still sticking up out of the tops of them, having basically glued themselves to the inside of the shoes. As fabulously as the clothes fit, it seemed impossible that the delicate looking boots he saw leaning against the wall would cover his feet. It was one thing to add extra fabric to a pattern and slap clothes together, but something else all together to make a pair of boots to fit a person the size of which has never been seen.

The boots felt good in his hands when he picked them up. They were sturdier than they looked, yet lightweight. He imagined they would be useful when trying to maneuver quickly away from a dragon. He pulled on the long socks before slipping his right foot into the proper boot. The fit was so exact that it was as though they had been made uniquely around the shape of his foot.

Now that he was fully dressed, Tucker noticed there was a mirror on the wall near the bathtub. He stood up and examined himself in the glass surface. A scruffy beard was forming after so many days without a shave. It had mostly obliterated the remaining bruises from his fall. Lying in bed with wet hair had made his slightly wavy light brown hair a mess, but after wetting his hands and running them through it he decided he looked decent. The clothes suited him so well that he thought it might be time to change his wardrobe. He had never worried about fashion, but as he looked at himself in this setting it fit who he was becoming.

He sighed. "Are you ready to meet an emperor?" he asked his reflection. "Are you worthy of such an experience, Tucker Kenworthy? And what would this man say if he knew you," he pointed to himself, "had kissed his daughter?"

He ran his hands through his hair again. "It's time," he said, then turned and walked to the cord by the door.

It was obvious that Ravinna had been waiting for him. She was at his door before the sound of the bell had come to an end. She knocked gently, an action which clearly took effort. Tucker opened the door and they both froze, taking in the image of the other.

Ravinna was a reinvented woman. It looked as though someone had taken the wild waif Tucker found by the side of the road, and given her a Hollywood makeover. Her long dark hair had been intricately braided and twisted in coils around her head. There were no longer any signs of dreadlocks. Her traveling clothes had been replaced with a long burgundy colored dress of soft material that smoothed out the thin lines of her body and gave her a luxurious appeal that was hard for him to resist. The only part of her that remained unchanged were her eyes. They were the same vibrant blue he remembered, mysterious, and liquid, and ever so inviting.

"Are you ready?" she tilted her head slightly to the left as she looked up to meet the steady gaze of his brown eyes.

"Ready as I'm gonna be," Tucker shrugged. "Would you say your father is a violent man?" the shaking of his voice betrayed his worry.

"Violent? Daddy?" her laughter shimmered in the air making Tucker feel light headed. "Do not worry, Tucker. This is not a test. Everyone is eager to meet you."

"Everyone?" he gulped. He had a horrifying vision of being presented to the king and his court of well dressed courtiers. "I'm not going to be expected to give a speech or anything, am I?"

"Oh, come on, Tucker. You will be brilliant, I promise," the look in her eyes and the sweetness of her voice helped to even out his wildly beating heart. As long as she stood beside him, he was sure he could

302

handle anything. After all, together they had killed a dragon, what could be so bad about meeting her family.

"All right, let's go," he agreed.

Ravinna took him by the arm, and while he was concerned that might be overdoing it, he was thankful for her presence. The passageway seemed interminably long, and far too short at the same time. He wanted to get it over with, but when they reached the large wooden doors at the end of the hallway he wished Ravinna was tall enough for him to hide behind. He knew he was being stupid, these were his friends, not enemies, but his pulse rate was back on the rise.

Despite the great height of the doors, the main handle was almost too low for Tucker to reach it comfortably. Ravinna reached out her hand and pushed it down, then pulled the door open. It drifted smoothly open, and the room stretched out before them.

Tucker had an aunt who liked to travel. She had spent time in Europe, and brought him back a large picture book. There was information about history, wildlife, culture, and architecture mixed in amongst the photos. He had spent countless hours imagining what it must have been like to live in those ancient days. He used to look at the pictures and dream of standing inside the grand palaces and beneath the vaulted ceilings of the cathedrals in those distant lands. The sight that met his eyes made him feel as though he had stepped back in time and right inside one of those pictures.

The room was vast, hewn from stone in the heart of the mountain. What might have once been stalactites and stalagmites in a natural cave were shaped into intricately carved columns. At the end of the room was a raised section upon which the

Emperor and his Empress sat on large wooden thrones. Two young women sat in smaller chairs alongside them. Even from a great distance, Tucker could see that they were the most beautiful women he had ever seen, in person or otherwise. They were clearly Ravinna's golden sisters, but they were as unlike her as night was from day. While Ravinna had a beauty that was as natural as breathing, these two were like shining stars of utter perfection. He could imagine a man becoming lost and never reviving his senses if he looked at them for too long.

He tore his eyes away and noticed the long green tail for the first time. It wrapped around the pillars and slowly widened into a sleek reptilian body. The neck curved around the last column and he saw the face of Adym smiling down at him from near the ceiling.

The only thing missing from the room to make it look like those European throne rooms of old, were the stained glass windows. The only light in the room came from the massive chandeliers that hung from the ceiling every ten feet.

They stepped through the doors onto a thick velvety rug that spread from the doors all the way to the dais where the thrones were set. Ravinna gripped his arm tightly, and he let her lead him. The room that looked so huge upon first entry, was only about fifty feet long but the ceiling was as high as the room was long which added to the grandeur. Tucker hoped Ravinna could not feel him shaking.

They arrived at the base of the stairs. The hidden Emperor Karlov rose from his throne. He was tall in comparison to the other men of Aristonia, but without the help of the dais Tucker would have towered over him. The man appeared younger than Tucker had expected, but when he looked into his shining blue eyes he saw ages within them that he could not begin to fathom. He was overwhelmed by their depth, and felt compelled to bow.

"No need for such formalities," the Emperor's voice was deep and melodic. He felt emboldened by the words, and rose again to his full height, seeking confirmation in the kind and timeless gaze. "You are our guest and our friend. Welcome." He threw his hand back as if encompassing the entire party in the words of his welcome. "I am Emperor Karlov. This is my wife Celestina, and these are our other daughters: Sirena and Tanzia."

"Pleased to meet you," said Tucker, willing his voice to stay steady. "Your daughter has said much about you."

The Emperor roared with laughter. "I hope you did not believe half of it. Always been a lovely story teller," he looked at Ravinna with infinite love.

"Were I to speak of you for an age," Ravinna smiled, "I would not begin to tell him half of all you have done."

"And yet here we are, hidden underground. A small remnant of all that once was great about this land," Karlov hung his head. "I am afraid, you come to us at a sorrowful time in our history."

"Now Karlov," it was Adym who spoke. "Do not allow yourself to wallow. We are not so desperate as that. Time must play out as it has always been planned. We would all wish to forgo pain and tragedy, but then we would not appreciate the beauty of new beginnings nearly so much."

"You are true, dear Friend," Karlov nodded. "Forgive my momentary lapse into self pity." He winked at Tucker as though it were some big joke, but Tucker saw a flash of deep sorrow behind the frivolity and wondered what more there was to the story that he was yet to hear. "Please, come and join us," the Emperor motioned toward two chairs that Tucker had not noticed. They were on the dais, but were turned to face the other four. "Ravinna has told me what she has put you through to make it this far, so please take a seat."

Tucker and Ravinna climbed the stairs and took their places. Even though everyone was looking at him, he was surprised that he was calmer than when they entered. He was thankful there was little left of the bruises on his face to betray his clumsiness, and the wounds from the dragon fight were concealed by his clothes.

"We must make our move soon," Ravinna said once they were seated. "It is time to take action. The dragons are beyond reasoning with. The few who remain honest and loyal have gone deep underground, just as we have. We have to stand up and fight."

Tucker noticed that Ravinna's sisters turned pale in the midst of her speech. They clearly did not understand their tall dark sister. He had to smile at the irony. Here were these exquisitely beautiful creatures, living deep beneath the world they once ruled, yet they were still more comfortable sitting back and letting life drift by than taking a stand if it would cause them to look less feminine. It only made him love Ravinna, with all her spirit and vitality, a hundred times more.

"We are all aware of your sentiments, my dear," Karlov spoke slowly. "And we are grateful that you have managed to find and bring Tucker here, though you went explicitly against orders not to do so."

Ravinna tapped her foot impatiently. It looked to Tucker as though she was going to leap back out of the chair at any minute. "They are not just sentiments!" she protested. "Have you seen what is going on out there? The forests are being laid to waste. Villages scarcely exist anymore. The seas have been ravaged beyond recognition. Svyetlo is determined to destroy everything, and here we are, sitting under ground, discussing how this can be overturned peacefully. It. Is. Not. Possible." She stomped her foot making her point reverberate around the room.

"Lower your voice, child," her mother spoke for the first time, her tone shrill. "This is no way for a lady to behave!"

Ravinna rolled her eyes and threw her hands in the air. "Would you rather I sit placidly in beautiful clothes and let the world fall down around our heads?" she demanded. "We have tried standing peacefully against them, we have tried reasoning with them, we have even tried burying our head in the sand and pretending that life is still bright and beautiful when lived out under ground, but all the while Aristonia is dying."

Tucker tried to look at everyone at once. He wanted to see the effect her words were having on them. In all their conversations, she had never told him she was a renegade in her own family. Her mother and sisters were repulsed by her actions and defiance. Her father listened, but his expression remained cautious. The most interesting reaction came from the dragon who seemed both curious and excited by everything Ravinna did. Tucker wished Adym would speak up.

"And what do you think, Tucker?" Adym asked as if sensing his thoughts.

The question took him by surprise. The air seemed to leave the room as he struggled to find his voice. "Well," he began hesitantly. "I'm not from around here, obviously, so I don't really know how your world looked before. It's clear that things are a mess up there, but I'm the last one to ask how to fix anything. I have, however, come to trust Ravinna. She loves Aristonia, and cares deeply about what is happening."

Adym nodded his heavy head throughout the speech, considering every word Tucker spoke. "And do you, yourself, feel ready to kill a dragon?"

Having these words spoken to him by a dragon was more than Tucker had ever expected. He was impressed not only by the size of the creature, but by the immense capacity for emotion that he saw in

Adym's monstrously large eyes. The abrasions on his body, caused by his last tussle with a dragon, burned under the intensity of Adym's gaze.

"Honestly, sir," Tucker cleared his throat. "I feel very inadequate."

Ravinna cast him an angry glare. "He was very brave in his first dragon attack," Ravinna spoke as if wishing to correct some error. "Yes, he will need some training, but he has the size and the strength and the courage to do what needs to be done. "

"I know, you think we have acted foolishly," the depth of Karlov's voice had a magnetic effect. They all leaned closer, waiting to hear whatever new idea he would reveal. It was a trait Tucker knew any politician would kill to have. "You would have resisted Karush to the death, and would not have been wrong to do so. You would have sent our warriors out to do battle immediately, and would likely have saved some lives even as others would have been lost. No one doubts your heart, your intentions, or your bravery, Ravinna. However, you are wrong in believing we are hiding and waiting for the bad things to disappear."

Tucker felt Ravinna holding back. He thought she was going to have another angry outburst, but when he turned to her, he saw something different on her face. Tears were welling up in her glorious blue eyes in response to her father's words.

"We know our plan is distasteful to you," Adym spoke. "You would have us push forward in a display of power and force them into submission. But that is not the way to create change. As much as we plead, as

309

much as we push, as much as we reason, the dragons have chosen Svyetlo, and the people have accepted Karush."

The room was silent. Adym's words carried a gravity that brought them all near the point of tears. Tucker was confused by the meaning of the sorrowful undercurrent that he was unable to discern.

Adym turned to him now. "You are wise to be hesitant, but I trust Ravinna's observations. You are very nearly ready, and when the time comes you will kill the dragon as you were always intended to do. Unfortunately, this task will be different than what you may have been led to believe."

"No!" Ravinna howled. "Can you not see that this is unnecessary? He is here. There is more than one way to read the prophecy. There is more than one way to right the wrongs and bring the world into harmony." Tears poured down her face and her full lips trembled.

Karlov rose from his chair and walked to his daughter's side, taking her hand in his. "However you choose to read the prophecy, there is only one way to destroy the beast. He must be beaten at his own game and be shown for what he is in the eyes of all. If you like, you may go with your mother and sisters and leave us to explain."

Tucker waited for her to put up a fight, but she did not. Her head hung low, and she sat completely broken. Karlov kissed her forehead, then beckoned for his wife and daughters to join him.

There was something different on the faces of the ethereal beauties now. They were torn in their expressions between compassion and pride. Karlov passed Ravinna's hand to the Empress Celestina and she gently pulled her daughter to her feet. Ravinna succumbed, allowing Sirena and Tanzia to stand on either side of her, arms linked with hers, as they followed their mother from the room. Tucker stared vacantly after them.

Karlov sighed wearily and sunk back into his chair. His timeless face appeared more lined than it had before. He and Adym exchanged knowing looks, leaving Tucker feeling excluded.

"May I ask what this is all about?" asked Tucker. He felt small with Ravinna out of the room. He was a stranger in this land, and despite being in hiding, he was in the presence of two of the most powerful inhabitants of Aristonia.

"I am sure you have been told some of the history," Karlov began. "Ravinna informed us that Arthyr spoke with you, and that she filled you in on other aspects of the current situation. However, both of them, as well as the group of warriors you met most recently, wish to see things differently than they really are.

"It would be wonderful if you had come to us during a time of peace, so you could understand how it began. Indeed, in my own fallibility, there were times when I was swept up in the peace that reigned for so long, and doubted the possibility of such extreme evil. I wanted to believe that if we kept our minds and hearts open to truth, if we continued to be kind, gentle, and reasonable, things would not reach the proportions

Balthazar foresaw. Alas, despite all I had witnessed of the hearts of man and beast, I was mislead into believing that, given the ideal circumstances, they would chose the best options for their lives."

"I see you think we are speaking in riddles," Adym lowered his head to look deeply into Tucker's eyes. "So let me paint this as plainly as possible. After many years of living in peace and harmony, everyone grew complaisant. They all knew that they were blessed, but began to see their blessings as their own doing, rather than as the benefits of living in harmonious community with those around them. When they began to trust in their own wisdom as the key to success, they lost their concern for others."

"When the dragons began to fall under the velvety tongue of Svyetlo's deceit," Karlov took up the story again, "we humans were slow to react. At first, it seemed a distant threat, like a single gray cloud in an otherwise clear blue sky. We knew the great power and wisdom of Yaveen, and expected the dragons would return to reason. Their ways might change, as society is in the habit of progressing, but we saw no great risk in the decision of a small minority opting to break with tradition."

"For our part," Adym flowed back into control so easily that Tucker scarcely noticed that the speakers had changed. "We knew the risk was too great to send the dissenters to your world as had happened in the past. Early on, Yaveen had sealed the cave almost completely, in order to prevent the likelihood of escape. While the weapons in your world would no doubt destroy a dragon quickly, it would cause too much speculation. The last thing we needed was a war amongst worlds. Our kind has fallen into the land of superstition and it is better to keep it that way, at present.

"We, too, wished to solve things by appealing to reason, but those who had tasted the power offered by Svyetlo were no longer interested in lives of peace, but only in increased wealth and power. They made a compact with Karlov's brother, Karush. While we had seen the risk of such a thing happening, we had not foreseen the extent to which the two would ally themselves."

"Karush had long been a question of concern," Karlov agreed, "But in the days shortly before he made the pact we had been speaking a good deal more than usual. I love my brother, and know he is capable of great good. I would do anything to see his heart change back to what it was in our youth. Unfortunately, I did not realize the depth of his envy until he asked for the hand of my daughter, Sirena, and I denied him. I know I made the right decision, but he saw this as a slight on my part. He went behind my back and told Sirena that I had given him permission to take her. He spoke to her vanity, and she accepted his offer.

"He persuaded her that they would have the grandest wedding Aristonia had ever seen, and that their union would be the key to holding everything together. However, he convinced her that it must remain a secret from everyone until he could prepare things. He was convinced that, with her by his side, he would be able to gather the approval of the people.

"Once her promise was secured, he went to Svyetlo and made his dark deal. Again, there would be a pact between man and dragon, only this one would be at great cost to any who disagreed with the terms. Karush waited until he knew Ravinna was away, then promised one of the cooks a place of honor if he would slip sleeping powder into my drink the next evening. I fell into a deep tortured sleep, and my dear Celestina stayed by my side, bidding Karush to speak to the people, and inform them that I would be well soon.

"Karush took this as his moment, and, instead, informed the crowds that I was on my death bed and had given him Sirena as a sign that he would be the one to lead the people to victory from the heart of darkness. He told them that he had spoken with Svyetlo and an agreement had been reached. If they would provide the dragons with fresh meat, and inform them of any green dragons hiding in their midst, they would be left in peace.

"The people cheered on every count, and considered themselves blessed. While some mourned my health, most believed that it could not have come at a better time. They were ready to fight or flee, and they saw Karush's offer of a safer life as the best possibility."

"But what happened when you woke up?" Tucker asked eagerly. "And why didn't Sirena point out that his words were wrong?"

Karlov looked heavily at Tucker. It was not easy for him to relate the darkest hours in the history of his

314

world, and the treachery that had been committed within his own home. He looked to Adym, silently asking him to continue the tale.

With an understanding nod, Adym obliged. "Sirena had also been deceived. Karush did intend to marry her, but he forbade her returning to her family. He lied and told her that her mother and sister had also taken ill, and that his concern for her safety prevented him from allowing her to visit them. She begged him to contact Ravinna, but he fabricated stories about her demise. Knowing that her sister could be foolhardy, she believed them, and wept in her room while Karush had her family put in chains and removed to the dungeons.

"To most on the surface, everything appeared to be improving. Their problems with the dragons disappeared over night. However, as news spread to the outposts, the men sensed there was something wrong. When they questioned Karush's new guard they were given no answers. Many of them were called back on false pretenses and met their ends before they arrived home. Karush declared that they had broken the treaty with the dragons, and made it clear that disobeying any of his new proclamations would result in similar fates.

"Like sheep, the people flocked to his promises, and did his bidding willingly. Anyone speaking against the new orders was reported. They were determined not to be seen as dissenters.

"When Yaveen saw what had taken place amongst the men, he and I discussed our options. We knew that forcing people or dragons to see our logic, would make us no better than Karush and Svyetlo. If

315

they wanted to choose this life of sorrow, as much as it pained us, we would not deny them their rights. It was decided that Yaveen would retreat to the deepest part of the Keep and remain there to insure that the gateway was not broken. The other remaining portals had long since fallen from use, and were forgotten so there was little need to deal with them. I left him then, to see if I could discover what had happened to Karlov.

"Ravinna and I arrived at the same time. She was oblivious to what had been happening, having been out inspecting the far boundaries of Aristonia, and seeking to reinforce good relations with the other kingdoms. At that point, the dragons were hunting primarily in the night, so I was able to fly by day, and therefore found her shortly before she arrived home. I told her what I knew, and together we discovered the whereabouts of her family.

"She was able to get to Sirena, and slowly pieced together what Karush was up to, without seeing him. It was difficult for her to persuade Sirena that she had been deceived, but she eventually convinced her to invite Karush to her chambers to sing for him without informing him of Ravinna's presence.

"Karush, naturally, came to see Sirena in the evening, and when she sang he went into a trance. While under her spell, Ravinna came out and questioned him. She learned the entirety of his plot, and exactly where to find the rest of her family. Sirena was horrified to learn how cruelly she had been deceived. She agreed to go with Ravinna to rescue their family. Perhaps, one day, Ravinna will share this story with you herself. She is an excellent teller of tales when she has a mind to do so," Adym grinned as he spoke of Ravinna and Tucker felt more at ease than he had since her departure.

"Adym was kind enough to bring us here," Karlov explained. "It was a long forgotten palace, covered by time, with the secret entrance through which you came. We relocated, and cautiously informed people we knew we could trust. Karush had a hard time explaining the disappearance of Sirena, and eventually told the people that she was spending the time before their marriage in confinement so she could make herself as perfect as possible for the grand event. In this way, he hoped to prevent questions until he could locate her.

"You have met two of the few groups who know we are here. For their own safety, they do not know the location of our hideaway, but we keep in contact through connections within the animal kingdom."

This final comment reminded Tucker of the unusual language issue he had faced since his arrival. "So why is it that I can understand you both without Ravinna being here?" he asked.

"Ravinna is not alone in her gift," Adym smiled gently as only an enormous dragon can do. "I, too can speak the language of all men and animals. Even those who do not intend to reveal their opinions are open books to me. Ravinna has come across some minds locked to her sensitivity, but I do not have this problem."

Tucker was baffled by the thought. "It seems I still have much to learn," he said in awe. "But if that is the case, why did you wait so long to react. Why didn't you take action sooner and prevent all the bad things from happening. You have made it clear that you and your father are more than strong enough to enforce your rules. I can see why Ravinna's frustrated that you let it get to this point."

Adym looked so intently into Tucker's eyes that he thought for sure he could hear more than just the words he spoke, but could actually read every thought inside his head. "There are times when no amount of either strength or reason are enough," he said. "There are times when everyone must deal with the consequences of their choices. I do not delight in the suffering I see around me. In truth, like Ravinna, I weep. But there is a time coming when everything can be made right. A scar will remain, but hope will return."

A shiver ran down Tucker's spine and the hair on his arms stood on end. The words sounded innocuous, but he could tell something sinister was about to come. "So what, exactly, is the purpose of me being here?" he asked. "You've given me a lot of information, some rather different than what I've heard from others, and I need to know what you expect from me."

"I am sure you have heard something of the prophecy," Karlov stroked his beard thoughtfully, "but it is no doubt that you heard it only in part. It is so easy for ideas to become distorted by time and interpretation.

"Adym and I were present when Balthazar spoke. We not only heard the words that were written, but were able to read the lines in between as well. It is true that the division between visions and reality is sketchy at best. He was able to give us no direct timeline, but as things took place, it was not hard to see that what he had predicted had, indeed, come to pass."

"The place where things get tricky," Adym took up the story, "is when he spoke of how things would end. Given what Ravinna has told us, and what we have seen ourselves, we trust that you are the one he spoke of who would come to our aid and would help us kill a dragon. The issue lies in which dragon you are here to kill."

Tucker's mind flashed back to the fight the evening before. When he thought about it, he realized he had already helped to kill a dragon. Was it possible that this was all that would be required of him? He had come, made an appearance, helped to kill one nasty bugger, and now he could go home. It sounded like a nice, neat little story. He could be happy with that, although he had a secret hope that he might still manage to get the girl. His daydream was short lived.

"In his prophecy, Balthazar was very clear on this point," said Karlov. "A man would come to our aid, and would kill a dragon. The loss of this dragon would come at great cost. Where he was unclear was exactly which dragon this would be, and to whom the cost would be great."

"Wait a minute," Tucker put his hands up in the air in protest, sensing that things were about to go in an objectionable direction. "I'm not here to call myself a hero, but something in what you're saying doesn't sound right. Did this Balthazar character say there would be a happy ending if I managed to do my job?"

"There is much in the world that seems beyond our control," Adym circled the question. "We cannot force others to agree with our opinions, no matter what we do. We can only give them the option to believe. This is one of the deepest mysteries in life, and the one most often incorrectly manipulated."

"Okay, I get the fact that us going out and forcing people to see that Karlov is alive, and explaining to them that they've been a bunch of idiots and gotten themselves into an awful mess won't work, but what are we supposed to do?" Tucker demanded. The more insecure he felt in his purpose, the stronger he stated his concerns.

"Ravinna would have us ride out in a blaze of glory," Karlov spoke of his daughter fondly. "She went to find you with little more than a spirit of good intentions. She is so pure of heart and mind, that she would do anything in her power to stop the darkness that has fallen over our land and our people.

"While the idea even frightens her, she would suit you up in full armor and have you face Svyetlo boldly. It is clear that she cares for you, and worries for your safety, but she holds such faith in the prophecy that she believes you would be able to commit this great act, and come out unscathed. With their vile leader dead, she hopes the power he held over the others would loosen, and they would listen to reason. I have no doubt she has a similar plan in place for Karush, although his part in this is dealt with minimally in the prophecy."

"But we have seen, all too well, that hearts, once hardened, do not melt easily. If Svyetlo is toppled, another will rise in his place. He has an abundance of minions with hearts as cruelly deformed as his own," Adym's head sunk as he spoke these tragic words, and Tucker leaned forward to hear him better. Then the great head lifted and the deep green eyes engulfed him. "There is no grace without sacrifice," he said solemnly.

Tucker had been struggling not to catch the drift of where they were going. He could see from the beginning, even in the slump of Ravinna's shoulders when she left the room, that it was a place he did not want to go. He shook his head, denying them the opportunity to speak the horror he saw coming.

"Until they know we will stop at nothing to make things right, they will not hear what we have to say," Adym continued. "Even then, there will be those who refuse to listen. When I traveled to your world in search of open hearts, I was poorly received. The dragons refused to see any purpose beyond their own. They felt no reason to concern themselves in the affairs of others.

"It pained me so deeply to witness how far their pride had taken them. They cared only for life as far as it brought them gain."

"Wait a minute," Tucker broke in. "Who is to say that they will listen even if we do go through with this crazy plan of yours?"

"There is no one to say they will listen," Karlov agreed. "But it is only in this way that we can reveal the better option. A life given has far greater power than a life taken."

Tucker wanted to put his hands over his ears and to start humming. He wanted to drive out the terrible images that flooded his mind. He might be nothing to them but a simple truck driver, but he would rather die in an insane attempt to make things right, than to become a puppet executioner.

"I give myself because I love them," Adym's eyes drilled into Tucker's until he thought he would scream. There was such innocence, such love, in the look that it was like a slap in the face when connected with the words.

"You cannot," he sucked air through his teeth trying to calm himself so he could get out what he needed to say. "You cannot expect me to kill you..." his voice faded into the dark corners of the room.

Chapter 21

It took Flint less time than he expected to reach the Cow Creek Police Station. Garrison sat behind a desk, flipping idly through a stack of papers. It was as small time an operation as Flint had expected.

Garrison scarcely took the time to glance at Flint. He wrote something at the bottom of one page, then slipped the papers inside a file and reached for another.

Flint cleared his throat. He fought the urge to pound his fist on the table to demand attention.

"Any luck finding your friend?" Garrison asked, still not looking up.

"No," Flint replied, "but we have other problems now."

"We?" Garrison asked quietly. "Not sure what problems you're mixed up in, but I'm pretty certain they don't involve me. Cow Creek's a quiet town. Don't need anyone coming here causing problems."

Flint gritted his teeth. "I'm not trying to start any problems," he said evenly. "I'm saying there is a problem. Lenny's been hurt, and I need some help going back to get him. It'd be good if you'd let his wife know, too."

Garrison rolled his eyes. "Oh, that Annie May's had Terry tied up all day. Hobbes suggested she just collar him like one of the dogs and lead him on that wild goose chase," he laughed. "Far as we can tell, he up and left her. Bit surprised he didn't take his beloved hounds, but he's not the first man to run away in the middle of the night, and if you ever heard a woman go on about everything and nothing to the point you'd like to shoot yourself in the head just to make the voices stop, then you have a small idea of what that woman is like. Dogs were his only solace, but she's so scared of them it seems likely he thought he'd leave her with them just to get the best on her in the end."

"Look," Flint let his hands smack flat on the table. "I'm not gonna spend all night persuading you to help me. If you're going to keep being a pumped up idiot, fine. I just need to find Lenny's wife and see if there's a medic in town to help me get him home."

"Calm down," Garrison stood reluctantly. "Don't go and get your panties in a twist. I'm an officer of the law, you know. It's my duty to check up on a man that's been hurt. I just don't want to see police time being wasted again. We spent a whole day looking for that guy and ended up with a whole lot of nothing for our time."

"Well, you won't end up with nothing this time," said Flint, playing it as calmly as he could. "You'll end up with a man in need of hospital attention. Now, can we please get going?"

Garrison slipped on his jacket casually and signaled that Flint should walk out the door first. "And what about Annie May?" Flint wanted to know.

Garrison rolled his eyes, but did unfasten his radio from his belt. "Terry? You out there?"

"Affirmative," Terence barked.

"You still with Scary, I mean, Annie May?" he chuckled when he let up the talk button.

"Correct," came the reply.

"Well, it seems there might be something to her story after all. Got that trucker here, says Lenny's been hurt. Don't have any other information, but it might be enough to get you a little extra leash so you can get back here and help us."

"I heard that, Officer Garrison, and don't you think for one minute that I'm gonna let you just bully us around like we're hicks from the sticks." There was no doubt that she had more to say, but Terence retrieved the radio.

"Be right over," he snapped, and the radio went silent.

"Oughtta be here in about five," Garrison said lazily. "So, why don't you tell me what you and Lenny're mixed up in."

Flint's patience had worn thin hours ago, and Garrison was the kind of guy who pushed his buttons. He wanted to stay calm, wanted to keep his fists in their places, but he was itching to throw a punch at the pompous grinning face to the point that he had to take several steps away to regain control.

"Well," Flint put on his best patronizing voice. "After you boys skipped out on us and gave up on Tucker, Lenny and I were able to follow his trail all the way to a cave up in the side of the mountain. We didn't have the right equipment, and the dogs needed attention, so we decided to come back the next morning and check things out. We're pretty certain he did end up in the cave, but still weren't able to find him. The cave was extensive, but in the end it got too small for us to continue. On our way out, there was a cave in. We spent the night trying to dig our way out. We were able to make it eventually, but as I was pulling Lenny out there was another minor cave in, and his leg was crushed, so he couldn't climb down. That's the whole story."

"Hmm," was all Garrison replied. He was running out of excuses to use against Flint. He kicked in the dirt and tapped his radio nervously. Flint knew being a trucker made him look like a lower class citizen to the man in front of him, but a report of police negligence in the case, would not reflect well on Garrison, and they both knew it.

They were spared a long drawn out silence by the arrival of Terence and Annie May. From his time spent with Lenny, Flint had developed several ideas of how his Annie May might look. He realized, after how far off his image of Karla had been from reality, that this was not the best plan, but in the case of Annie May he was dead on. She was a petite creature, whose pregnant stomach suck straight out like a basketball under her shirt, with curly fly away red hair, and large startling blue eyes. Her small round face was heavily freckled, and her clothes had an overly worn second hand look. She was a fiery imp, even if her wardrobe was on the shabby side.

"You," she fired at Flint. "You're the one who dragged my Baby off and never brought him back. Where is he?" She held on to the "is", her voice hissing shrilly.

Flint had not expected this sort of attack, and was taken aback by her fury. He had definitely been right about the fiery part. "Listen, ma'am," he held his hands open before his chest. "I'm not sure what Lenny might have told you, but we were just out looking to find a friend of mine. Unfortunately, things went wrong. Lenny's fine, just hurt his foot is all. I can take everyone right back there, no problem, and you'll see that he's just fine."

She ground her teeth together and her eyes continued to flash, but her posture relaxed slightly. "Well, you better," she humphed. "Left me out in this hole all by myself with those crazy mutts of his."

"So where do we go?" Terence was happy to have Annie May focused on someone else.

"Right back where you were with us the other day. If we go quickly, we should be able to get there by night fall, but I suggest we take a medic along. His leg is hurt pretty bad."

"He better be all right when we get there," Annie May had trouble holding her tongue for more than a minute. It was no wonder Lenny talked nonstop when given the chance.

Garrison was already making the call to get a medic along for the trip and he sent Terence in to get some gear from inside the office. "He'll be just fine, Miss Annie," he soothed once things were in motion.

"Oh, it's Miss 'Annie' now, is it? What happened to 'Scary?'" she sneered. "Don't take me for some country fool. It won't bode well if you do."

Flint might have felt sorry for Garrison if his feelings had not been perfectly in tune with Annie May's. He scratched his ear nervously, ready to be doing something, besides standing around waiting. He considered calling to check on Nance, but thought better of it. He doubted hearing he had survived a mine cave in would bring her much relief since he had no news of Tucker. He longed to hear Karla's cheery voice on the end of the line, but was sure she would likewise be disappointed. It would be better to discuss things in person.

Finally, the medic arrived, a burly guy that Garrison introduced as Mike. Flint was no longer concerned with details. He felt a responsibility to help Lenny out of the mess he had gotten him into, and then he was going to have to deal with the ever expanding mess his life had become.

"Well, let's get this show on the road then," Annie May tapped her foot anxiously, her stretched out belly bouncing with the rhythm.

"Now, you don't really think you're coming along, do you?" Garrison's eyes widened. "You're nine months pregnant, woman. Stay home and keep an eye on all those mongrels, and we'll get the little mister back to you safe and sound."

"I am going with you," she said in no uncertain terms.

"I've got some tape in my bag," Mike muttered low enough that only Flint could hear him. Flint refused to be amused.

"There's no room in the van," Garrison did not relish the idea of having Annie May there to give her two cents the entire time.

Flint was uncertain exactly where Lenny would hang his hat on the issue, but decided the best way for everyone to get some peace was if he offered Annie May a spot on his bike. He expected her to refuse, but it would show her that he was not the bad guy. "I've got an extra helmet," he ventured, speaking softer than usual due to his hope that she would ignore the offer.

"Well, hand it over, and let's get a move on," she held her hand out, and Flint reluctantly walked to the motorcycle and pulled the extra helmet from the pouch under the seat. He gave it to Annie May, who had followed him.

"We'll lead the way," he shrugged and the others climbed into the emergency van with Mike at the wheel. Flint slung his leg over the seat and noticed the first hesitance on Annie May's face. In that moment, he realized that she was just a woman, worried about the fate of her husband. Lenny had probably told her he would be home in time for dinner, and she had worried herself sick all night. Any woman would have been frantic in such a situation. She had his respect.

"Go ahead and put your arms around my waist," he hoped his voice was soothing. "The easiest way to feel balanced is if you turn your head in the direction of each corner. That way you know what to expect when your body leans."

She nodded shortly and climbed on behind him with determination. Her short arms had to stretch to make room for her belly, and they gripped around his middle tightly, making it hard to breathe. Flint was thankful the ride would not be long.

Things went smoothly, and soon they were gathered beside Tucker's truck. "I think he should be able to walk with crutches once we get him out of the cave," Flint explained. "But getting him down is gonna be a trick."

"Don't worry," said Mike. "Got it covered. Just focus on getting us there."

Flint nodded. He chose not to be annoyed, and went with the flow. He wondered if patience would ever get easier. Appreciating being patronized was not natural for him.

He checked to make sure Annie May had her balance back. She had been trembling by the time he stopped, and he expected she was relieved knowing she could drive her own car on the way back. "Alrighty then," Flint rubbed his hands together, feeling chilled in the late afternoon light. "Here we go."

The strenuous hike was a blessing. He kept the pace brisk for Lenny' sake, preventing conversation. A serious gnawing rumbled in his stomach, but he ignored it as best he could. He had a fleeting thought of the dinner Karla had prepared the night before. He hoped she would come up with something left over for him when he arrived, even though he knew he would bring disappointing news.

The sun was sinking fast, and it was as dark as midnight inside the thick forest. Flint worried that he might not remember the trail as he should. There were so many little splinters along the way. It was nothing but an assortment of animal tracks, making it difficult in the dark to be certain of landmarks.

Flint had been so focused on making sure they rescued Lenny, that he had almost forgotten about Tucker. As the temperature dropped, he thought of his missing friend and wondered for the thousandth time what could have caused him to disappear. He had a sinking feeling that he had passed the same rock twice, and despair set in. If he was thinking rationally, he knew that none of this was his fault, but as he led the group deeper into uncertainty, it was hard to remain rational.

"You're sure you know the right way?" Annie May had been silent since stepping off the bike, but despite the effort it took to keep her pregnant body in line with the rapid pace, her worry was getting the best of her.

"We should be there soon," said Flint gruffly. If they lost their confidence in him, he would have no hope of finding the way and they would have to go back empty handed and return in the morning with the dogs. They were counting on him. Lenny was counting on him. And Tucker? He could only hope for the best where his friend was concerned. It was out of his hands.

He heard Garrison muttering to Mike, and figured he had slowed down too much. He picked up his speed, hoping they would reach the cave before the sun went down completely. As much confidence as Mike had in himself, Flint knew it was going to be a challenge to get Lenny down. While it was relatively easy to climb up the side of the cliff, it was still treacherous, and it was going to be even harder carrying someone.

His spirits were at an all time low, when the rock wall loomed before them out of nowhere. "Lenny, we're here," he called out into the near darkness.

"Flint? Is that you," the voice was weak but cheerful.

"Lenny?" Annie May half wailed. "Lenny?" she was sobbing now. Her tough exterior broke in the face of relief.

"Annie, Darlin'? What on earth are you doing out here?" there was shock and joy mixed into Lenny's voice. "Flint, I thought you was gonna bring help."

That was enough to bring Annie May out of her tears. "You think I couldn't come right up there and pull you down all by myself?" she demanded the dark hole above their heads. "I'm the best help he brought, even with this big ol' belly in the way. These jokers aren't worth a quarter of their pay checks."

Lenny chuckled, "That's my girl."

"Okay, enough chit chat," Garrison took control. "Terry, set up the lights. Mike, let's see what you've got."

Mike was lower on swagger, having carried all the equipment by himself throughout the hike. He took long, slow breaths, trying to obscure how winded he was. He pulled his equipment out and carefully arranged things on the ground.

"How you holding up, Lenny?" Flint called. "This could take a while."

"Been worse," Lenny had regained the good humor that had been dampened while they were stuck behind the wall of dirt and stones. Flint imagined he had slept over the past few hours. The dizzying effects of his own exhaustion washed over him. His presence was superfluous in this phase of the rescue, and he decided it might not be a bad idea to sit down and grab a nap.

Annie May and Lenny chatted back and forth, as Flint eased himself to the ground, resting his back against the rocky wall of the cliff. The instant his eye lids fell he was asleep.

Chapter 22

Tucker felt as though all the air had been sucked from his body. He had risen to his feet unconsciously, and stood looking from Karlov to Adym in abject horror. "I have to agree with Ravinna," he said once he could breath. "This is madness. It makes no sense. What can possibly be gained by killing you?" His voice broke as he looked into the gentle eyes of the magnificent dragon. "They will think we've stooped to their level, and that they've won."

Adym nodded, "we did not expect you to think as we do. Your heart is good, Tucker. You want to make things right without hurting anyone. We tried this as well, but it has become evident that they are past listening. They must see."

"Could you tell me again what you think they will see? As far as I can tell, they'll see you die. They'll be overjoyed. They'll continue on their evil killing rampage. There'll be no one left to help the innocent. The end."

"You see it this way," Karlov spoke gently, as if trying to explain a difficult concept to a young child, "because you focus on the surface. You have observed bits and pieces, but as a stranger to our land, it is no surprise that there are things here that baffle you. And you are not alone in this misconception. Ravinna, and the warriors you have met, carry the same doubts. They believe that the power of their own hands can exterminate evil. Sadly, fight as they may, evil can only be overcome by good."

Tucker covered his eyes with his hands, trying to blot out everything. Nothing made sense anymore. He wished Ravinna was beside him. The power of peace and reason had vanished from the room. He needed her sweet voice to calm him, her earthy scent to soothe his frayed nerves.

"I need time to think," he clenched his teeth. "Just tell me, when were you planning to carry this crazy plan out?"

"Karush has been searching desperately for Sirena," said Karlov. "He planned to marry her tomorrow, and has prepared a party of grand scale to celebrate the occasion. His allies, both dragon and human, are all expected to attend. From our sources, we gather that he intends to clothe his 'bride' fully, so those in attendance are unable to realize that it is not Sirena. After all, this alliance is part of what endeared him to the common people when he took power, and he fears that if he fails on this point they will see it as a weakness."

"So are you trying to tell me that you want this to happen tomorrow, when everyone is gathered?" Tucker's voice wavered.

"Yes," Adym replied solemnly.

"Tomorrow," Tucker muttered. "Not asking much, are you? I guess I realize why it was so important for Ravinna to get me here quickly. Would have been nice if she had mentioned the timeline so I could have been prepared." He sighed. "I guess I don't have many options though, do I?" he asked no one in particular. "Would it be okay if I think things through before we go further?"

"Certainly," Karlov nodded beneficently. "Time is of the essence, naturally, but we want you to feel comfortable with the situation before we rush you into it. Take a few hours to rest and refresh yourself. When you are ready, we are at your beck and call to discuss what needs to be done."

Tucker nodded his thanks, then walked away without making eye contact. He was afraid he would see disappointment in their eyes, and was not ready to deal with that sentiment. The walk down the carpet to the main doors felt much longer this time, and he could not breathe normally until he was on the other side.

The door closed behind him with a boom, and he struggled not to sink to the ground then and there, fully overcome by despair. He had no idea how he had believed it might be possible for him to kill the mighty dragon, Svyetlo. It looked ridiculous even with months to train. However, he was certain he could never be prepared to take the life of anyone as good and true as Adym, regardless of the reason.

On shaky legs, he arrived at the door of the room which had been prepared for him. Ravinna was inside, pacing nervously. When he opened the door she flew to him, her face a mask of fear and dread.

"You know, then?" he asked, his head hanging low. "You know what they want me to do?"

Ravinna took him by the hand and led him to the bed without a word. She pulled him down to sit beside her and took his head into her delicate hands, pressing her forehead against his. "Yes," she whispered, the sweet smell of her breath intoxicating him, wiping away some of the doubt, "I know. But there is still time to make things right. I have a plan."

Tucker had no desire to hear more plans. All he wanted was to pull her into his arms and feel her lips yielding under his. He wanted to pretend they had met under different circumstances. His hand rose, unbidden, and stroked the soft skin of her cheek.

"Ravinna," he said her whole name for the first time, but she put her finger to his lips, silencing him. His hand fell uselessly by his side. She conceded halfway, pulling his head down and kissing him on the forehead before leaning back so she could look him in the eyes.

"Please, Tucker, let me tell you my plan."

He felt the blood moving properly through his veins again, and allowed himself to be drawn in by her pleading blue eyes. "Okay," he sighed, "Let's hear it."

Ravinna smiled with relief. "So, they have not convinced you completely? That is good. I do not know how much they told you, but I can guess most of it. Have they revealed how they want it to take place?"

"They let me come back to think," Tucker admitted. "When I realized what it was they were proposing, I needed some air. All I know is that it must happen tomorrow, to coincide with the wedding celebration."

"And that is exactly where we are going to change things," despite the desperateness of the situation, Ravinna's eyes sparkled. Tucker could see how much the thrill invigorated her. "At present, it is my uncle's plan to make the crowd believe some other girl is my sister. I am sure that even in the short period of time you were in her presence, you could see that such a ruse would never work. But he is foolish, and believes that if a woman is fully covered then any woman will do.

"I might not get along perfectly with my sisters, but they all adore Adym, and believe this plan is a mistake. Sirena has agreed to take part in our attempt. Just as I have special skills, like the ability to translate, my sisters are likewise gifted. When Sirena sings, she has great power. Not only is her voice the most beautiful sound any ear has ever heard, it also can put those who hear it into a trance. My plan is to have her present as herself. If Karush is dense enough to believe the people would not recognize the poor bumbling girl wrapped up in gauze is an imposter, then perhaps he will not realize the real thing when he sees it.

338

"When the time comes for her to speak her vows, she will sing instead, and her voice will lull them into a trance, giving you the opportunity to sneak in unnoticed and kill Svyetlo. By the time the trance wears off, we will all be present and will stand behind my father and Adym in a show of power. With one leader slain, and the other leader shown for the liar he is, they will be forced to turn from their foolishness. Arthyr and his band have been making their way here behind us, and I believe Mykel will bring the others, though I am afraid Vatslavem will, be unable to join them. The greatest warriors will be present to stand against evil, and the darkness will fall. It must."

Her eyes burned with the passion of her plan, and Tucker felt lighter at the thoughts she had birthed in his mind. He remembered how easily the heart of the last dragon had succumbed to the vicious spear when he had thrusted it deep into its chest and turned it violently. He imagined that, under the spell of Sirena's voice, the great Svyetlo would stand helpless before him.

"Your plan sounds perfect," he agreed. "Why don't the Emperor and Adym agree? I'm sure, if you explained it to them they would see this is a better option. We would be able to get the attention of everyone with as little bloodshed as possible. And it wouldn't be a matter of force, which they seem to be repelled by. It would be a show of strength that reveals how they've been heading the wrong direction. You're brilliant."

"Unfortunately, they see things differently. Their minds are made up," she twisted a lock of hair that had come loose from the intricate braiding. "I would honor them in any way I could, to my very death," her eyes penetrated through any defenses he might still have believed himself to possess. "But if there is a way to prevent what they suggest, I will not cease to try."

"I just have one last question," Tucker felt unreasonably nervous. "If they were against your search to find me, and yet truly believe in this prophecy, how did they intend to go about it? I mean, did they think I would stumble upon this place on the right day and everything would work out?"

Ravinna's laughter bubbled freely, filling the air infectiously. Tucker found himself laughing without having the slightest idea why. When she finally paused for breath, he drew her attention back to his question. "Well?" he asked.

"I am sorry to laugh at you," Ravinna was still struggling to catch her breath. "I know you were not trying to make a joke, but the idea of you accidentally finding us of your own accord was laughable. You must see that.

"No, their idea was less subtle than that. Adym intended to go himself. He has visited your world many times, and is surprisingly good at traveling inconspicuously. I am sure that is hard for you to imagine, but he has his ways. I do not know exactly how he would have approached you, but he would have been very convincing, don't you agree?"

Tucker shuddered at the thought. Having met him as he did, he was fond of Adym from the beginning, but he could only imagine what his response would have been had the massive dragon appeared magically in front of him in the context of his daily life. He laughed again, and Ravinna joined in. It felt good to let loose and see the world in a freer light. Her plan sounded excellent, and Tucker harbored the hope that they would be able to achieve success without any harm coming to Adym.

"So have you tried to tell them your plan?" he asked. "I still think that if they were behind this idea it would solve the whole thing."

"It is like I said before. They are not willing to listen, because they believe themselves to be right in what they are doing," she twisted the hair around her finger absentmindedly. "And I must tell you that I do not doubt them. I am sure they know what they are saying, but I am too selfish to accept it. I do not want to face the loss it would bring us if I can find an alternative on my own. You see, that is the real reason I went to find you. I knew that if I were the one to bring you here, if I introduced you to this place, and to the people here, you would trust me and see the reason in my words. I respect my father and Adym above all others, but the truth is, I want them to be wrong in this."

Tucker thought about what she had said. He could see that, even in the face of the brilliant plan she had formulated, she had doubts. "I will speak to them again, alone," he told her. "I think it is best if you keep your distance at present. Go over the plans. Make sure Sirena is comfortable with everything you are asking of her. I will learn more of what they want, so we can be prepared whatever the outcome. You might see yourself as selfish," he lifted her chin so she would meet his eyes again, "But I know your heart is good and true. We will work together for the best."

"Go then," she nodded. "I will meet with you after dinner to discuss our final plans. I only ask that you keep what we have discussed to yourself. If they discover that we are still planning to try something they will stop us before we can begin."

"Of course," Tucker agreed. He knew it was a risky move, but he found the attraction too strong for him to stand. Besides, given the circumstances, a hug of solidarity seemed appropriate, or so he told himself. He drew her quickly to himself and held her briefly, letting her feel the strength in his arms and the steadiness of his heart. Then he pulled back without another word, and left to speak with Karlov and Adym.

He passed quickly through the long corridor, pausing in front of the massive doors. He had no way of knowing if they were still waiting for him, or had gone away. If the latter was the case, he would have to figure out how to summon them. He tapped lightly on the door, surprised by the anxiety he was experiencing.

There was no response, so he pushed the handle and carefully opened the door. The room was empty and he felt at a loss. He wandered amongst the columns, studying the intricate designs carved into them. Unlike the mural like carvings in the hallway, these seemed strictly ornamental. He could see no rhyme or reason, but was in awe of their delicacy. His fingers traced the looping shapes and the crisscrossing spirals and lines.

"It is a dying art," the deep voice caught him off guard. He had heard no one enter, and yet Adym's head was hovering just above his. The dragon's eyes were thoughtful as he considered the columns.

"I guess people are too busy for things like this, these days," Tucker said, wishing he had a more clever response.

Adym chuckled softly. The sound reverberated gently off the walls and warmed the room. "Ah, my new Friend, you have much to learn. Of course, I cannot blame you for your ignorance. This is not the work of any man. This is the script of the dragons."

"You mean, this says something?" Tucker was dumbfounded.

"Indeed," Adym sighed. "I know you have been told that things were not always as they are now, but you cannot really understand it. The dragons were once beautiful elegant creatures. They delighted in all forms of life, and they captured their lives and stories in these intricate patterns you see as nothing but design. I so wish you could have seen this world when it was young and they were all pleased to live in praise." Adym sighed, and a sweet smelling smoke wafted from his nostrils. It reminded Tucker of the time he visited a monastery on a school trip. It had a heady smell that carried his thoughts far away, and he had to work to pull himself back.

"But," Adym continued, "if everything goes according to plan, there is hope that the old ways can be restored. There will be peace and harmony and laughter. I often wonder if they miss laughter," he spoke more to himself than to Tucker. "There was a time when flying through the skies on a sunny day was a symbol of jubilation. We would laugh and weave through the clouds with transparent joy. Now they content themselves with the sound of screaming on every side." He lapsed into silence, and Tucker avoided his pain filled eyes.

"Are we ready?" Karlov entered the room as quietly as Adym had come. Tucker wished he was less jumpy. He followed Adym back to the dais and this time took the seat next to Karlov when it was offered.

"So?" Karlov questioned. "Are you ready to hear our plan?"

Tucker nodded. He was afraid to speak. If he opened his mouth he worried he would betray the alternative Ravinna had shared with him, and he was desperate to see to it that her's was the plan that succeeded.

"All right, then," said Karlov. "The festivities will begin early in the morning. Already the guests are arriving. By morning, Avilista, the capital city of Aristonia, will be packed. The ceremony is meant to take place in the amphitheater outside the city walls. It is in a large open field, the only location where men and dragons can gather easily. It will be a nervous peace, but the pact between Karush and Svyetlo is strong, so there will not likely be any carnage during the day, although the possibility of a public feeding of the dragons would not be a surprising show of strength at some point."

Tucker cringed. He envisioned tiny men being dressed like miniature gladiators, then tossed into the clamping jaws of vicious dragons. It was not a sight he wished to behold.

"The main event will begin mid-afternoon," Adym took up the thread of the plan. "By then, everyone will be in attendance. They have no reason to fear an attack, but it is likely they will have warriors in place around the arena, and possibly a few dragons flying circuits to keep up appearances. One of the ways Karush has brought people to his side, is by convincing them that he is the one who stands between them and death at the claws of the dragons. "

"Our plan," said Karlov, "is to wait until everyone is gathered and the ceremony is underway. It is the event of the century, or so it has been proclaimed, and none will want to miss it. Your size would make you too obvious, so you must not enter the arena until the moment is right. Ravinna, however, will already be inside. She will disguise herself and enter early to be part of the crowd. She will give us the signal and then we must move quickly."

"We believe Svyetlo will be given the place of greatest honor, and will be on the dais alongside Karush and his shrouded 'bride.' I will carry you and Karlov to the center of the arena."

Immediately, Tucker saw that this plan would make it impossible for him to carry out what he had discussed with Ravinna. If he flew in on Adym, he would have no time to attack Svyetlo first. And if

Sirena was able to put everyone into a trance, they would enter to find the crowd senseless.

"May I interrupt?" Tucker asked nervously. The other two nodded agreeably and he continued. "I'm wary about the idea of flying in like this. Not that I don't trust you to carry me, but I worry that everyone will be confused if I come in then turn around and...and..." there was no way he could bring himself to finish the sentence.

"What would you suggest?" Karlov asked. "You are so much taller than everyone else, that if anyone saw you in advance they would be alerted to our coming and we would be walking into a prepared battle. Our goal is to prevent bloodshed as much as possible."

"I understand that," Tucker nodded, "but you have already said Ravinna will be there, and she, too, is taller than most. "I think the best idea is for me to go in tonight." He was creating his own plan now, and wished he had discussed this possibility with Ravinna. "If I am already in place, waiting hidden for the right time, there will be no confusion, and no chance of being seen."

Karlov and Adym considered his idea, while Tucker held his breath.

"Your idea has promise," Karlov stroked his beard thoughtfully. "This would give us the opportunity to address the assembly before you act. We will have the element of surprise on all counts."

"So you will watch and wait," Adym agreed. "We will enter the arena and allow everyone time to accept what their eyes are seeing. I will address

Svyetlo, and when the time comes I will signal you to come forward..."

"Let's just leave it at that," Tucker spoke quickly. "There must be some proverb about not planning things out too much or they will all come to ruin, right? And if not, there should be."

Karlov could not resist a grin at Tucker's nervous speech. "Okay, we can see your point. The only thing left is to be assured that you know how to kill a dragon. It is not the easiest thing to accomplish, even when the dragon goes willingly."

Tucker had been hoping to avoid this part of the discussion, and yet he knew it would be useful when he carried out Ravinna's plan and killed Svyetlo. While he would not be a willing victim, he would be paralyzed which should be similar.

Karlov rose and walked behind his throne. Tucker followed unwillingly, growing more nervous with every step. There was a large wooden box, the length of the four thrones together, and carved similarly to the columns.

"What does it say?" Tucker asked Adym, hoping to buy more time.

There was a curious sound in the back of Adym's throat. Again, the sparkling spray of lights filled the air, and as they circled their heads a sound more beautiful than any Tucker had ever heard emerged from the dragon's mouth. There was a melody and harmony dancing amidst the lights, that slowly swooped from a joyous proclamation into a melancholy minor chord as the lights slowly died. Tucker noticed the trademark dragon grin on Adym's face, and realized he had heard his true voice for the first time.

"And the interpretation?" he asked.

"Here lies the weapon that was formed by Balthazar," Karlov said, lifting the heavy lid from the box. "When tomorrow is complete, you will know the meaning of Adym's song."

Tucker was disappointed, but there was no time to dwell on it. Karlov lifted two mighty weapons from the box. Unlike the tiny sword and the strange spear Vatslavem had used, these weapons were clearly built for a man of Tucker's size. He realized with awe that it was more than that. They were built exactly for him.

His hand fit perfectly around the shaft of the spear, as though the slight groves had been worn in the wood by his own hands. There would be no slipping and splintering this time. He studied the fearsome claw at the tip, and wished he were ignorant of the purpose of this cruel instrument. There was a sword as well. This too, seemed to have been created to fit him perfectly. The metal was light but the blade was excessively sharp.

"You must take the spear and plunge it here," Adym indicated an area of his chest where Tucker assumed his huge heart must be beating peacefully. "The skin is thick, and protected by scales, so as you thrust you must also twist the spear. The blades will scrape away the scales, then slide easily into the flesh. Continue to twist until you get to the heart. Then you must use all your strength to sever the heart from the veins and pull it quickly from the body. If these steps are not conducted completely, it is likely the dragon will not die. The heart is very large and can continue to sustain the body as it regrows, so you must be thorough and pull it all the way out."

It amazed Tucker how clinically he spoke of his own demise. It seemed impossible that this dear dragon could really ask him to do something so brutal, so irrevocable. His mind flew back to the dragon he had helped kill with Ravinna and Vatslavem in the forest. He had known nothing of the art, and wondered if the dragon had died from his actions, or from the explosion. Every thought that came to his mind was ghastly, and he wished the instructions were finished. Then he remembered there was also a sword in his hand.

"So why do I have the sword?" he asked. "Did Balthazar mention that as well?"

"By the time he had fashioned the weapons in accordance with his visions, he had grown weak," Karlov explained. "His whole life had become obsessed with the preparations, and he had forgotten the details of the vision itself. We begged him to reveal more, but he told us that when the time came, the man who carried the sword would know what he had to do."

"Hmmm," Tucker muttered. "Not the most useful information he could have passed along, since this is the first time I've ever held a sword that wasn't the size of a child's toy, but I guess we'll have to wait and see, like with everything else."

"You should rest," Adym said with concern. "The amphitheater is not far away, but if you wish to

349

conceal yourself there before morning there are not many hours left. If you wish, dinner can be delivered to your room so you can have some time to yourself."

Tucker was relieved by this suggestion. He had the feeling that eating in the presence of Ravinna's mother and sisters would not be relaxing. He was a trucker, after all, not a well educated courtier with knowledge of proper etiquette. "Sounds perfect," he agreed. "And will I see you again?" he asked Adym. "I mean before..."

"I will carry you to the amphitheater," Adym assured him. "Do not weep for me, my small Friend. I know what I am doing, and I am not afraid. Trust me when I say it will be for the best. When it is completed you will understand."

Tucker had not realized that tears had come to his eyes. He dashed them away irritated by his weakness. He knew there was another plan. It would turn out right in the end, because it would go according to Ravinna's instructions.

He left the room, and hurried back to where Ravinna awaited him. She saw that the meeting had been difficult. "It was awful," he choked on his words. "They spoke like it was the most natural thing in the world. And the weapons...and when Adym spoke, I mean really spoke..."

At the mention of Adym's true voice Ravinna wept with him. "But we must not despair," she gripped Tucker's hand firmly. "While you were away I spoke again to Sirena. Everything is prepared. It will work, Tucker."

"Oh," he said, pulling himself together, "They said they would send my food here. I'm sure I would make a mess of myself if I had to eat in front of those ladies. We decided I will leave in the middle of the night. They had planned that I would fly with your father, but I changed their minds. This way I can be there in advance, and you can let me know when to act. Then, when Svyetlo is in hand, you can signal them."

"You see," Ravinna forced a smile. "It is possible. I will leave you to eat and rest, and will spend the time with my family as is expected, but I will return before you leave." She squeezed his hand to reassure them both that everything was falling into place exactly the way they wanted it to.

Tucker sighed as she walked out the door. Exhaustion swept over him like a tidal wave. He moved to the bed and decided the best thing would be to get a little sleep before dinner. He was going to need all his strength to pull off the events to come.

Chapter 23

Flint only meant to close his eyes for a minute or two. It had been more than a long day. It had been a list of long days full of disappointment. As far as he could tell, only an instant passed before Annie May was shaking him awake.

"Flint?" she said cautiously, her voice far lower than usual. "They got him out. He's going to be okay. Sorry I was so angry with you earlier. Really, I shoulda been thanking you for helping me find him."

Flint rubbed the sleep from his eyes. He knew he should respond, but his mouth was not ready to form words. Everything felt heavy, including the darkness surrounding them.

"Hey, Flint," through his blurry eyes he saw Lenny giving him a thumbs up. His leg was wrapped and splinted and he was leaning on a crutch.

Flint stumbled to his feet and felt the blood rush to his head. He steadied himself against the rocks, then moved toward Lenny. "You all right," his voice slurred.

"Been better, but at least I'm out, and had me another granola bar, so I'll live long enough to eat some a Annie May's magic beans," he gave his wife a wink and she blushed in a way that made her look pretty.

"Looks like it's time to run along," Mike said, putting a hand on Lenny's shoulder to check that he was steady.

Garrison was standing looking thoughtfully up at the cave. Darkness had fallen heavily, but the moon lit the side of the mountain making the black hole appear even more sinister and mysterious.

"What do you boys suppose caused that cave in?" he asked.

"It was mighty strange," Lenny admitted. "It goes quite a ways back, but then it got too narrow for us to keep moving and we had to turn around. Just before we left there was this booming sound and an awful smell. We started moving pretty quick as this heat rushed around us, but when we got to the opening it was all sealed up."

"I've never heard of any volcanic activity in these parts," Terence mused.

"Good thing we brought you along then, Terry," Garrison jibed. "It's always useful to have someone who knows everything around."

Terence ignored him. "I was only thinking that if there is something strange going on down there, it might be smart to look into it. Could be there was a sink hole that your friend found and got sucked down. If there's a volcano, or even hot springs, they can sneak up on a man, and he's done for before he knows what hit him. This place isn't normally frequented by hikers, but it'd be best to block that cave off if there's a risk."

Garrison rolled his eyes. "If you want to come all the way back out here on your day off, go for it. We'll even let you bring some warning tape to mark it off if you think it's so dangerous, but we've spent too much time on this. Lenny looks good to go, so let's head back."

Annie May stuck close to Lenny's side as they progressed down the mountain. Garrison had taken the lead, and Flint was happy to let him. He had had more than his share of being the center of attention. He hung back outside the light of the lamps so he could think by himself.

The hard part was going to be breaking the news to Nance. There was no way to make things easier for her. He had no concrete information about Tucker, and his own disappearance was another embarrassment added to her worries. The confidence he had built up while he was digging to save his life had ebbed into exhaustion and disappointment.

Something bothered him about the cave scenario. What Terence said might be right, but there should have been more sign of Tucker in that cave if he had been trapped there. As they drew closer to the road he made up his mind to go back to the cave one last time. He would get a hotel room closer to town and call back to let Nance know he was all right but still searching. Just maybe, if he could come up with something more concrete than a hole in the ground that was impossible to pass through, he could return in less disgrace and make a better impression on Karla.

He found breathing easier once his mind was made up. He was even able to rally himself enough to join the men in helping Lenny up to the cars. When they got safely to the top, Mike checked Lenny over inside the emergency van, and Flint stood with the others waiting for the word that all was well.

"Lenny and I would love to have you over for dinner," Annie May had become a different person. She smiled earnestly, her blue eyes entreating him to accept.

"That's sweet of you, Annie May," said Flint, "but I think I'm gonna get a room, order room service and crash."

Annie May nodded. "Just know the offer's there. Any time you're in the area."

"Thanks," he muttered.

"Everything looks good," Mike reported to Lenny loud enough that everyone could hear. "You should come into the clinic tomorrow for a better cast, but what you've got should hold for the time being."

"Looks like we've got things wrapped up," Garrison was back to business. "I'm sure Annie May will take good care of you, Lenny. Flint, thanks for your help in tying this up. Y'all go home and get some rest and try not to get into any more trouble."

Flint could tell Garrison just wanted everyone to disappear so he could go back to his quiet state of affairs. The case had become an annoyance since there was no chance for personal recognition. "Nice knowing you then," he said sarcastically. He headed to his bike and was gone before anyone could respond.

There was one small dodgy hotel in Cow Creek. The lights on the vacancy sign were burned out, but he had a feeling they would have rooms available. Their idea of room service was pizza delivery, which suited him just fine. He took the battered room key and hurried to the room. He stared at the phone for a while, then decided to order the pizza first. He ordered an all meats pizza, knowing his body was famished even though he had gone past the point of hunger hours ago.

He sat on the bed. Except the short nap in the middle of Lenny's rescue, he had not slept in almost two days. The digital clock informed him that it was nearly eleven. He had ordered his pizza just in time.

The phone sat there, waiting patiently for the call he was dreading to make. His head was so fuzzy, and sleep so tempting, but he knew he had to do it. Besides, it would be at least half an hour before his pizza would arrive. He considered writing what he was going to say, but knew that would make it sound robotic.

"Just get it over with, Flint," he told himself angrily, gripping the receiver in his hand. He dialed the number from memory, thankful that he had known Tucker before the era of cell phones. His battery had long since died, and all those neat lists of numbers were out of reach.

It took an age for the line to connect. The phone rang. It rang a second time and Flint could hear his heart pounding in his ears, too loud and fast to mean anything good.

"Hello?" Karla's voice was tired and apprehensive. It might have been the connection, but Flint felt an insane hope that she might have been thinking about him, worried that he had been gone two days without word.

"Karla," his voice came out an unrecognizable croak. He berated himself and carried on before she got confused by the strange voice recognizing her in another woman's home. "It's Flint."

"Oh, Flint," there was a flood of relief in her voice that warmed his heart more than he thought imaginable. "What happened? Are you okay? Did you find Tucker?"

The questions flowed so quickly that he had trouble getting a handle on what she was saying. When she stopped to catch her breath Flint stuck to the basics. "Sorry I wasn't able to call before. Me and this other guy got stuck in the cave. We're okay, but we didn't find Tucker. I'm going back again tomorrow, just to make sure."

"Are you sure that's wise?" Karla asked. "If there was a cave in, it's probably not a safe place, especially if you're going alone."

"It's for the best," Flint said with as much strength as he could muster. "Look, Karla, I'd be really thankful if you could tell Nance that I haven't forgotten my promises to her. I'm still looking for Tucker, and I'm hoping to have better news soon."

Karla was quiet on the other end of the line and Flint worried that he might have been too stern with her. After all, the woman was only trying to be thoughtful. "All right," she said eventually. "But I'm worried about you, Flint. Do you think I would be any help to you at all? Nance was able to remember the number of her sister, so she's not alone. I've been staying around, because thankfully she's finally realized I'm here to help and not to steal the money she doesn't have. But if I could help you somehow..." her voice broke off and she waited for Flint's reaction.

The idea stunned him. He had to wrap his head around the thought that Karla was eager to help him. At the same time, he wondered if having her there would be more a hindrance than a help. As much as he longed to spend time with her, he knew that what he was going to do was dangerous and he had no desire to put her at risk. On the other hand, he wanted to keep her interested and was worried that if he denied her this opportunity she might change her mind about her potential feelings for him.

It was too much on so little sleep. "It's very sweet of you, Karla," he said honestly, "But I think I need to do this alone. There is some danger, and I would never be able to live with myself if you were hurt because of me. The best thing is for you to keep helping Nance, and I will do my best to be back soon. I seem to recall you promising to have dinner waiting for me, and I would be much obliged to you if that offer was still standing when I come back."

"All right," Karla agreed. "If that's what you think's best. But be careful, Flint. And when you do get back, I'll have the best meal you can imagine waiting for you. Any requests?"

"Surprise me," Flint grinned as the sparkle came back into Karla's voice. The only way he could describe his feelings to himself was that hope was blossoming up inside his chest. He remembered the phrase from an English class in high school, and only now was he able to understand what it meant.

"Can't wait," said Karla. "See you soon."

"Yeah, soon." Flint hung up before his mouth got him into trouble. At the same time, there was a knock on the door. The pizza had arrived. He paid the delivery boy and brought it to the small night table. With unimaginable glee, he opened the box and revealed the pooling grease that was a thing of beauty after all he had been through. The dingy hotel room was no palace, and the pizza was certainly not any original Italian masterpiece, but with the hope of food and rest and the warmth of new love springing in his heart, Flint was certain no moment in his life had ever been sweeter.

Chapter 24

There was no way to mark the passage of time. Sleep was only an estimate. Even the temperature of the food could not do the trick. It had not been there when he went to sleep. It might have come immediately thereafter, or much later. Either way, it was warm when Tucker awoke.

When he thought of the awful soup that the warriors with Mykel and Vatslavem had to eat, he felt guilty at the beauty of this fare. He had to wonder how they acquired good food in hiding, but his stomach growled so loudly that he figured it was better not to worry, and just enjoy, because he had no idea when this opportunity would arise next.

He made short work of the pile before him. There was pasta with a rich red sauce that reminded him of tomatoes, but not exactly. There were herby bread rolls and thin sliced meat and cheese. There was a salad with leafy greens and bits of vegetables he did not recognize. Then there was dessert, a pile of light sugary cakes that dissolved into happiness inside his mouth.

The offering of food had just been consumed when a gentle tapping sounded at the door. Ravinna pushed it open without waiting for an answer. She was dressed more simply than the night before, but her clothes were suited for a common person to wear to a wedding.

"Are you ready?" she asked in place of a greeting.

Tucker looked at the empty table then back up to her. "Ready as I'm gonna be, I'd say." He walked to her, feeling gratefully refreshed. "You look amazing."

"I only hope it will be passable," she indicated the soft blue fabric she was swathed in. "It is quite old. I used to wear it often when I was out in the woods and my mother refused to let me wear trousers."

Tucker tried to imagine her scurrying through the woods in anything so elegant. It was hard to keep a straight face when blessed with such an absurd image. "I'm sure it'll do just fine," he assured her. "Before we go, I wondered if it might be possible for me to write a message for my mom. You know, just in case things don't go perfectly for me..."

"Of course," Ravinna agreed. She went over to a stand beside the bed and opened a drawer that contained pen and paper. "We can leave your message here with a note for my mother to have it delivered if we do not return."

Tucker sensed she was trying to placate him, but her motives were unimportant. He thought for a moment, rubbing the feathery end of the quill pen against his chin, then focused on writing. It was a short note, a few words of love and vague explanation, but he felt immensely better to know she would not be left to wonder. "So is everything ready?" he asked when his task was complete.

"Yes," she lowered her voice. "Adym will take you and I there now. I told him it would be easier for me to conceal myself as well, and then mingle with the crowd as they arrive. This will give us time to come up with our signal. Are you ready for this, Tucker? I mean, really ready? I know we have discussed it, and I know there is no reason to suspect it will go differently than we have planned, but do you feel ready? Even under the spell of Sirena's voice, Svyetlo will not be an easy dragon to kill."

"Let me worry about that," he took her hands in his, hoping she would not think him too forward. "I am well rested, even better fed, and as ready as I can ever be in the face of something completely foreign to me. We just have to leave it at that and hope for the best."

"Okay," she sighed, pulling only one of her hands away, and turning him toward the door.

Together, they left the room without looking back, and made their way to the watery entrance where they had first arrived. Adym was there waiting. He was not bothered by the sight of them holding hands, yet Tucker was thankful Karlov and the rest of the family were not present to witness their familiarity.

"Hopefully this will be less traumatic than the last time I helped you through the water," Adym grinned toothily at Tucker. "Ravinna will help you into position when you are both ready."

Ravinna moved over and took hold of a thin rope that hung down the dragon's side. Even with Adym lying on the ground his back rose over Tucker's head. Using the thick scales as footholds, Ravinna climbed to where a harness system was fastened between the leathery wings. Tucker hesitated briefly, trying not to imagine how the world would look from the back of a dragon, and even less how it would appear once they were airborne. He was thankful it would be dark outside.

He grabbed the rope in both hands, closed his eyes, and climbed carefully. Had Ravinna not been settled comfortably above him, he knew he could not have forced himself to make the climb. She greeted him warmly on his arrival, and showed him how to slip his feet into the harness, instructing him to hold on to her waist as she would be holding the front straps.

"We do not control Adym," she informed him, "but without hand holds, it can be slippery, and the last thing we need is for one of us to go falling to our deaths before we arrive."

It was the worst thing she could have told him, but Tucker willed himself not to show his squeamishness. He focused on the gift of being able to wrap his arms around her as they flew, letting the smell of her hair put him into a rapturous trance.

"It will only be wet briefly," Adym assured them. He descended into the water before Tucker could consider anything more. He held his breath for dear life as they plunged beneath the black waves. Adym, however, had spoken the truth. Unlike their previous journey, they passed from the water in one powerful surge. Tucker had a fleeting memory of a documentary he once saw about deep sea diving. He knew that if the divers surfaced too quickly they ran the risk of their lungs bursting. Adym had no regard for research. He moved with such speed and grace that there was not even a chance for the pressure to build up before they were bursting through the surface of the bay.

All Tucker's hopes for the darkness of night were banished by the startling brightness of the moon. As fast as they had traveled through the water, their ascent into the sky was even more rapid. He barely had time to recognize the heights of the cliff that he and Ravinna had leapt from, before they were spread out like a topographical map beneath him. It reminded him of an edible map of the Mediterranean region he had made for a geography class. It helped to imagine the mountains below as the frosted ice cream cones and muffin tops from that long ago project.

The wind blew wildly and, although Ravinna was likely screaming the words, he could scarcely hear her as she explained to him that they had to go extra high to be above potential dragon guards. She likewise informed him that Adym was the fastest and most capable flyer that ever sailed through the skies. He wished he could appreciate these facts, but instead concentrated on the way her body felt, pressed closely to his. If he ducked his head closer, the loose strands of her hair blotted out the land that zipped past beneath them.

Then, as quickly as it had begun, Adym was bringing them back to the ground. "We are here," Ravinna said cheerfully, patting Adym's neck in thanks. "So you do not cut yourself sliding down, use this to sit on." She handed him a small piece of cloth made of sturdy material that reminded him of a wet suit. It was only then that he realized a similar piece of material had been situated under the harness that held them in place so they were not injured during the ride.

He closed his eyes tightly and slid without thought to the grass below. Ravinna was quick to follow. She patted his back lightly, a sign that it was time to open his eyes. He was thankful she had not said anything aloud.

Adym curved his long neck around to face them. There was a gravity in his look that Tucker had not seen before, even when discussing the details of how he should be killed. "I am afraid I must say goodbye to you now," he looked at each of them fondly. "This day is likely to try us all beyond the point we believe we can stand, but do not lose heart, my small Friends. This is goodbye only, not the end." Then, with a swooshing sound he was gone before they could reply.

Tucker noticed Ravinna wiping her eyes, but pretended not to see, just as she had not mentioned his fear of heights. "We must move quickly," she said stiffly.

"If you are already here, how will Sirena be moved into position?" he asked, realizing a potential hole in their plan.

"She is here already," Ravinna moved toward the walls of the great amphitheater.

Given different circumstances, Tucker would have stared in awe at the massive walls of the structure they were approaching. There was so much that he wanted to discover and explore, but it seemed his time here would be short and brutal. He moved quickly to keep up with his guide. As they got closer he noticed a group of figures gathered near the entrance gates.

The figures took clearer shape, and he realized they were guards. Anxiety washed over him and he reached out to stop Ravinna. "It's the guard," he whispered brusquely.

"I know exactly who it is," there was humor in her voice that made Tucker wonder if maybe the last laugh was on him.

"Who goes there?" a voice called out. Tucker wanted to grab Ravinna's arm and force her to run back toward the shelter of the trees.

Ravinna, however, was running down the hill at great speed, as though prepared to attack. Tucker could only follow, not wanting to be the one responsible for letting her rush to her death alone. His mind churned, trying to identify the familiar sound of the voice. They sped down the hill and were soon standing before Arthyr and Mykel with their men, minus Vatslavem and Stow. There was also a ghostly looking figure wrapped in layers of creamy colored satin and lace.

"How?" he found himself a man of few words.

"You did not think we could do this alone," Ravinna smiled demurely. "I knew you would not be ready to piece everything together from the beginning, but my stops had a specific design. I was not simply resting, I was gathering reinforcements." She turned to Arthyr. "Were you able to acquire what we discussed?"

"It was a challenge without you there to translate," he said good-naturedly. "But Tucker made a good impression on your woodland friends. They have generously supplied enough fluff to stuff the ears of half the audience if necessary." He lifted a bag from the ground which was filled to bursting with downy fur.

"We must move quickly," Ravinna took the bag from him then turned to Mykel expectantly.

The general signaled two of his warriors to come forward with heavy earthen jars containing a foul smelling muddy substance. Ravinna smiled brightly and took a pinch of the fur, rolled it between her fingers, then dipped it into the mud. "You must all take enough to fill your ears completely. The mud will harden quickly in your hands, so form them quickly. Immediately before Sirena begins her song, put it into your ears. The surface will soften and the fur expand to dilute the power of her song."

Obediently, the warriors stepped forward and began to make their own ear plugs. "You will need them as well," Ravinna directed Tucker. "The last thing we need is to have our dragon slayer fall under my sister's spell." He felt some underlying fear in her words, and wished there was a way he could let her know that he was not about to fall for either one of her sisters, regardless of their skills and beauty.

"The sun will rise soon," Ravinna reminded them. "Were you able to secure the entire guard?"

"Not a problem," Arthyr grinned. "They were plenty surprised to see us, mind you, but they are well subdued now."

It was enough for Ravinna. "Good. And we have those prepared to replace the bridal guard as well?" Two men stepped forward in the special uniform of the royal guard. Ravinna nodded, pleased. "And you, Sirena? Are you prepared for what you must do?"

The shrouded figure responded with a voice that could have won over the heart of the hardest man, crystal clear and melodic, "I am ready." Those three words were enough to make Tucker aware that Ravinna had not been telling tall tales when she spoke of her sister's power. She took his hand possessively, as though aware of the strange sensation the voice sent through his veins.

"I will put Tucker in place, then we must assume our positions and wait," she looked around the group assembled. There were those who had questioned her authority, those who had thought a woman incapable of leading them anywhere but to the table, but they stood beside her now, and she was visibly moved. "I thank you all for being here. This plan will work if we stick to it exactly."

A rumble of agreement ran through the ranks of men. Only Tucker noticed the tremble in her voice when she spoke the words she had repeated so many times, as though in an attempt to assure herself that what they were doing was possible. As they moved away from the group, he squeezed her hand to affirm that he, too, was with her one hundred percent.

A small entrance around the wall from the main gate was guarded by two men. "You may return to the others," Ravinna instructed them. "You must have protection for your ears as well." They accepted her order and left immediately.

Ravinna pushed open the door. She had to duck, and Tucker bent nearly double to enter. The passage inside was not any higher, and it was almost pitch black. Tucker recalled their walk through the cave and reminded himself that he was not claustrophobic. Light filtered in steadily, and he saw Ravinna straighten up. Soon, he was likewise standing. The passage turned and they entered a small chamber.

"This area was designed for the guard to keep an eye on things during competitions. Since the changes in the dragons, we have not held the games, so they have not been used in years and are rather musty, I am afraid." Tucker was tempted to laugh as she apologized for the thick air and moldy smell that lingered in the room. "However, as far as my uncle knows, the whole place is well guarded. And he is correct, except you are the guard, and not his precious pets." She laughed mirthlessly. Tucker hoped it was a sound he would not have to hear again. He preferred her joy to be real. "I will be there," she pointed to a tower on their right. "The moment Sirena steps forward and begins to sing, I will raise my right hand to signal you. You must seal your ears immediately, then wait to the count of one hundred. By that time, you should see the effects on the crowd. Svyetlo will be on your left, when you come out of the door at the bottom of the stairs," she indicated a doorway he had not noticed before. "You must move quickly, and as you do, I will signal Adym and my father to approach. Svyetlo must be dead before they arrive, so they do not carry through with their plan. Do you understand? This point is absolutely imperative."

"I understand," he answered, not wanting to sound patronized by the question. "I have the weapons ready, and will move as fast as I can. How long will Sirena be able to keep everyone under?"

"For a week, if need be. She has powerful lungs. But it should not take that long," she smiled, relaxing somewhat. "I should leave you now. They will begin arriving soon. I can already see the sky changing. I must hide so I can enter with the crowds and be less conspicuous. I also need to help Sirena. She is very sensitive, and I want her to feel as comfortable as possible."

Tucker could see worries crowding in on her again. "Go, and try to rest easy. Like you've been telling us, the plan is good. It's going to work Ravin. When this is done, you'll see."

She started to speak, but before she could, he pulled her to himself and silenced her fears with a kiss. He could see how easy it would be to get used to having her with him. She was stiff at first, her mind still working out her fears, but as he ran his fingers over her hair, she relaxed and responded to the sweetness of his caress.

When he let her go, whatever words she had been planning to say had escaped her. "Good luck," she said rather lamely.

"See you soon," Tucker waved easily, and let her leave without further interruption.

He watched her cross the field, and admired the way she observed every angle as she moved. A vision of his mother passed through his mind, and he wondered what she would think of the amazing woman who had found him. He hoped they would have a chance to meet. They were from such different worlds, but in the few short days they had been together he had discovered how much bigger life could be, and how empty it would be without her in it.

He wondered, fleetingly, how his mother was doing. He was certain his disappearance had come as a shock. At the same time, he believed that when she knew what he had been through she would understand how it had been for the best. His mind and heart were so full that the time passed quickly. The sky became a veritable rainbow of colors. He heard the calls of welcome the birds sang to the coming day and wondered how Ravinna would translate their heart song to him.

He watched as the crowd arrived. First trickles of people filled the arena floor, then dark shapes filled the sky as the dragons joined the assembly. He had not seen Ravinna return, and wondered how Sirena was

feeling as she prepared for her role in the day's drama.
It would clearly be a very long day.

Chapter 25

Flint woke when the first rays of sunlight found their way through the blinds of his hotel room. The plain white walls were a lonely sight. The single painting of a cottage in the mountains reinforced his emptiness.

He got up quickly, and took a fast hot shower. He had been so tired the night before that he had not even bothered to rinse off the grunge that covered his body from his night spent in the cave. When he checked out a few minutes later, he added an extra tip, suggesting they might want to buy new sheets. The receptionist grimaced, making him want to leave faster.

There was a tiny drive through coffee shop on the edge of town. He had noticed it when he first came to the police station. He made that his breakfast stop, then drove into the hills with a resigned focus. It seemed unlikely that he would find Tucker. His friend was gone, but he was going to do his best to make absolutely certain.

The sun shone brightly as he drove, denying the dark feelings that filled his heart. Though it would have made it more miserable, he had hoped for rain. He pulled over beside Tucker's truck and gave the side of it a good smack as if in some superstitious ritual to bring luck on his mission. Then he hurried down over the edge and onto the now familiar trail.

Chapter 26

Tucker had to admit that the spectacle before him was incredible. The people were dressed exquisitely. Their clothing had a richness to it unlike anything he had ever seen. It represented more then just another era in time. He had never paid attention to fashion, but there was an element of depth and delicacy in the design that was unrepresented in his world. The vivacious colors and joy filled faces made it hard to imagine that these party goers were under the spell of Karush and his wicked schemes. He hoped there was room for repentance in their hearts.

Beyond the human entourage, he was captivated by the dragons. There was no denying their beauty. Their sparkling scales reflected the morning sun in shades ranging from a vibrant scarlet to a burgundy so deep it was almost black. As long as he ignored the vicious gleam in their eyes, he could believe they, too, might be won back to the side of purity and goodness.

His eyes scanned the crowds, searching for Ravinna. She had been wise to choose a place in the tower to observe the festivities. Had she stayed in the crowd, she would have towered over the revelers. Instead, he found her seated in a corner of the tower box, scanning the crowd. He wondered if she could sense him watching her, but knew the distance, and the design of his hiding place made it impossible for her to see him. Even so, he noticed her glancing frequently in his direction in the midst of her scrutiny.

The festivities began with a blast of music distinctively foreign to his own time and place. He listened with delight to the ancient tones filling the amphitheater with trills of joy and laughter. Had he not known the horror hidden behind the celebratory spirit of the event, he would have been taken in entirely, but he knew he must stay attentive to more than the events the crowd was following.

The entire assembly began to dance. Dragons spread their wings and wheeled through the sky in a brilliant display. Flowers rained from above and Ravinna was obscured from his vision amidst the fluttering rainbow of petals. If he had not been paying close attention, he would have missed the slight movement of her hand. He only barely got the small balls of fluff stuffed inside his ears when the first notes of Sirena's song filled the amphitheater.

Everything had been designed for a perfect acoustic performance, and her lilting voice powerfully struck the ears of all who were not protected. The effects were immediate. As Tucker began his slow

376

count he watched the eyes of the crowd turn glassy. The dragons floated to earth. Both man and beast swayed in unison to the enrapturing voice he could only faintly hear.

Warriors drifted amongst the dazed crowd as his count reached one hundred. Tucker's heart thudded in his ears as he checked the position of the sword in its sheath, and lifted the vicious spear in his hand. His time had come.

The door opened easily. He took the stairs three at a time. Bright sunlight blinded him when he threw open the tower door. Ravinna had told him where Svyetlo would be, so he spun in that direction without waiting for his vision to clear. He knew the time would be short between the song's beginning and Ravinna's signal to Adym and Karlov.

He moved too quickly to realize something was wrong, even as his sight returned. There was room for nothing but focus. Ravinna's screams and the warriors' shouts fell on deaf ears as Tucker rushed unwittingly toward the very alert dragon. Gripping the spear firmly, Tucker lifted his head and was nearly struck down by what his eyes beheld. He may have been able to see past the foul characters the other dragons had disguised in their cartwheeling party antics, but there was no masking the pure evil that Svyetlo embodied.

This dragon bore no resemblance to Adym. His head was three times larger, the teeth curved in a ghastly grimace that was a mockery of Adym's teasing grin. The dark eyes were black holes surrounded by a blazing red fire. Tucker had no time to grasp the

377

immense size of the beast. He was frozen, transfixed by the mocking glare.

The screeching voice scratched away the protection inside Tucker's ears, grating directly on his nerves. He tried to remember the bliss of Adym's true voice and the warmth it brought, but it was hard to concentrate on anything in the face of the beast. The dragon was making a speech, but with Ravinna so far away, there was no one to translate the mocking words.

As if to prove his point, the dragon rose to his full height, casting a dark shadow over the crowd. Tucker watched the shrouded form of Sirena quiver, but she bravely continued singing, keeping the crowd under her spell. Even the warriors cringed at the sight of the massive dragon. Svyetlo croaked another sinister comment, and with one claw he impaled the witless Karush and flung his helpless body across the stage. The great beast glared down at the crumpled form and croaked in a more human tongue Tucker surprisingly understood, "Nice doing business with you, but it was not enough."

Quicker than a striking snake, his head spun and leveled with Tucker's face. Razor sharp fangs dripped venom, and a sulfurous stench accosted his nostrils. "And so, my little Foe, what did you think would happen? Did you think you would come here and spoil my fun? Killing them now would be no sport at all. Perhaps I should eat your little singer here? But I have a feeling there is more at hand. Come out, come out wherever you are, Adym. Or are you so afraid of me that you leave this ankle biter to do your duty?"

Svyetlo raised his mighty head and sprayed a terrible flame into the sky, so bright that it rivaled the rays of the sun which stood directly above them. It was too much for Sirena. Her voice faltered into a scream and she ran for one of the escape doors on the dais. With a lurch the crowd came awake, stunned and baffled by what they saw.

Seeing the earplugs were pointless, Tucker pulled them out and was accosted by the shrieks of the crowd. The dragons were equally anxious, spouting flames in their nervousness as their wild eyes sought the meaning of the confusion that circled around them.

Before Tucker could register everything that was happening, Svyetlo was in his face again. "Well now, isn't this fascinating?" he screeched as though they were having a confidential conversation. "It seems you have been abandoned. It looked a clever plan, didn't it? Woo us to sleep, then come and kill me like a drugged animal." He lifted his head and chortled, sending angry red sparks heavenward. "I am disappointed in Adym, though. He should have known he could not win this battle."

As he said these words, a rushing of wind arose, and Adym swooped over the edge of the amphitheater in a wave of cool, soothing green. Karlov glided off his back to settle gently on the dais between the two great beasts. Seeing how much smaller Adym was compared to the monstrous Svyetlo, Tucker's heart sank. His eyes scoured the crowd until they found Ravinna. She had been halfway to him when Sirena stopped singing, and now the crowd was slowing her progress immensely.

He wished that yelling and telling her to stay back would do some good, but knew it was useless.

"And so here we meet," Adym's voice calmed the crowd and they froze again. Even Ravinna stopped. "It was not quite the way I had planned, but few things in life ever are." Adym glanced sadly at Tucker. The mercy and love displayed in the deep green eyes was enough to break his heart. Despite his betrayal of the trust Karlov and Adym had put in him, he felt no condemnation.

"Sorry to disappoint," Svyetlo cackled, "You weren't really so foolish to think I would die so easily."

The world had been rushing past Tucker from the moment Ravinna first told him her plan by the side of the road. He had been on a wild roller coaster ride, traveling at breakneck speed through a story that did not seem to be his own. Now, everything switched into slow motion. He saw Svyetlo's tail swing in a gentle arc. The metallic spikes on the end caught the rays of the sun sending rainbows across the sky. He detected a movement of Adym's head, an angle that set his features askew with pain. Then he shifted outside his body as the tail struck him hard and sent him flying into the air. He was not able to discern the pain of his deceit from the pain that threatened to tear him in two. He was aware of only one thing: he had failed on all accounts.

When his body hit the ground, he realized things were still happening around him. Svyetlo's laughter sent a wave of flames across the sky, and the dark dragons joined him. Tucker was sure they would start the entire forest on fire without a second thought. At any moment, they would begin a feeding frenzy and end everything.

"Tucker!" Ravinna was at his side, her hands cool on his skin. He looked into her eyes, wondering what she would say. However, there was no chance for her to speak because Svyetlo was crowing his victory to the crowd.

"You see," he grew in the face of Adym's pain. "You see!" his shrill voice clawed higher. "You cannot stop it. Your only hope is to join me. Look at this place. Okay, so the people are a little disappointing, but this can all be ours. Yaveen is gone. You no longer have to pretend to go along with his old fashioned ways. Join me and enjoy life for a change."

"There is no joy in your choice, Svyetlo," Adym's voice was firm. "There is no hope, no love, and, in the end, no choice."

"And where was the choice in the old ways?" Svyetlo demanded. "There were only rules: the way of your father, or nothing. I have offered them a life where they can be the kings of their own destinies. There is nothing that can stop us here, and when we are done with Aristonia, it will be easy to move and take the next world. They put too much trust in their weapons, their science, their truth. Look at this one. He is so small and pathetic, yet even he came to trust his own strength." In one fluid movement his claw swept down and he lifted Tucker's broken body from the ground.

The world spun, literally and internally, as he hurtled skyward. Ravinna's scream came from such a great distance that he wondered if she was there at all.

In a flash, all he knew was the heat of Svyetlo's breath and the cruelty of his glare.

"There is no return from this decision," Adym spoke grimly. "There is only pain."

"Pain!" Svyetlo mocked. "Perhaps for you, but he looks like a delicacy to me. Almost a full mouthful." Tucker fought down nausea in the face of Svyetlo's acrid breath and tried to look anywhere but at the vicious teeth. Unfortunately, the distance from his current position and the ground was far from encouraging.

"Perhaps I can offer you something more appealing," Adym stared unflinchingly into the greedy black eyes.

Svyetlo cocked his head. "And what, pray tell, might that be?" he asked. "Everything is mine. At one command, this place will be cleared of any life I choose to end. What could you possibly offer me?"

A new panic surged into Tucker's brain. This, then, was the moment he had been dreading since he first realized Adym and Karlov's plan. He struggled against the deadly grip that held him, fighting through the pain. He wondered why Ravinna did not have her bow in hand to strike out the eyes of this beast, or why the warriors, recently so brave, stood motionless in the face of the atrocity about to take place.

"You will need both your hands," Adym spoke softly. "You must release Tucker."

Svyetlo snorted. He sensed a trick. "What, exactly, are you proposing?"

"It is simply, really," Adym smiled and Tucker wondered if anything had ever been as sad and beautiful as the face of this loving dragon. "Put him down, and I shall give you what you have always wanted most. The choice is yours. If you kill him, there will be no more choices, but if you let him live, I will give myself over to you to do with as you will."

A howl went up from the gathered dragons. They could taste their greatest victory. "Where is the catch?" Svyetlo eyed Adym closely. "Once you are dead, I can kill them as easily as while you are alive. You've had stupid ideas in the past. I had to laugh when you thought you could convince the outsiders to return. Such foolishness. But this? This is the greatest idiocy I have ever heard. It's too easy."

Adym's gaze did not waver. The grip around Tucker's body loosened. He wondered where Karlov was. He could not see him between the dragons, and worried that he, too, had abandoned his dearest friend in the end. Helplessly, he felt himself being lowered to the ground.

Svyetlo dropped Tucker in an unceremonious heap, a worthless offering in the face of Adym's proposal. The ground beneath him trembled as Svyetlo advanced on his willing prey. Tucker was surprised by a feeling of calm. He became more aware of Adym's strength than he had been before, and had the shocking realization that if Adym chose, he could destroy Svyetlo. It was as clear to him as anything had ever been, and he knew that Adym was equally aware of the power he held, but he did not use it.

Instead, as the darkness swept closer, his eyes scanned the crowd with a look of utmost love and understanding. "The choice is yours," he said. The words echoed around the perfectly formed amphitheater, filling the ears of every creature present. There was no obstruction that could stand against his message of hope, even as Svyetlo leapt, with a fierce snarl and slashing claws.

Tucker was sure he screamed. His throat was an open sore of agony as the unthinkable played out before him. He longed to block out everything, but his eyes were locked on Adym's, and he could do nothing but stare as Svyetlo attacked. The green dragon's gaze was asking him for more, but he could not grasp what. The air was rent by the screaming of the crowd. Tucker fought to breathe as he watched the light flicker out in Adym's eyes. Svyetlo crowed as his nemesis went limp and sank to the ground in a pile of scales. A movement on the left drew Tucker's attention away from the brutal scene. Karlov stood gravely, tears streaming down his face, Tucker's spear in his hand.

Despite the pain, Tucker knew what he must do. The spear was already in the air, and he caught it in a desperate grip. The dragons howled with hideous glee, chanting in a fearsome language Tucker could no longer understand. He knew in that moment, without even seeing the rush of blood, that Adym was dead. Ravinna was frozen in horror, and he realized that she had not been able to translate for him from such a great distance.

Eyes glazed with hatred and power, Svyetlo lifted his head in a wild bellow that rocked the sky. His cruel white fangs dripped blood. Tucker's body protested, but the adrenaline pumped through his veins as he ran toward the crazed dragon. Fire rained on the stage around him, but he pressed forward, gaining speed.

Svyetlo bent low, checking to make certain his prey was dead. Tucker saw a clear, reachable target. With every remaining ounce of strength, he thrust the spear into the depth of the darkness, twisting it sharply and ignoring the pandemonium that was breaking out around him. The giant head lunged in shock and a different howl blazed from the mouth of the dragon. Flames encompassed the limp body of Adym, and lit the floor of the dais on fire.

Svyetlo reared in rage and Tucker was lifted from the ground. He had a fleeting thought of Vatslavem's body twisting back and forth, and knew he must get his feet on something solid to complete his task. Svyetlo's claws scrambled toward the irritation on his chest. The battle was nearly over, and Tucker could taste defeat, but he threw himself into a spin and the blades did what they were forged to do. The great arteries gave way in a mighty surge and the heart was severed. As Balthazar had spoken, when the time came he knew what to do with the sword. He pulled it from its sheath and thrust it through the dragons fully exposed neck, piercing the fuel sack.

As the spear came loose from the dragons chest, Tucker fell. His natural instinct was to let go of the

385

spear to try to soften his landing, but in the back of his mind he fought to remember all he had been taught about killing dragons. He knew that if the removal of the heart was not complete he would have accomplished nothing, and Adym's death would have been in vain. So he clung to the spear with what little strength he had left and plummeted to the ground.

Chapter 27

Flint had no idea what he hoped to find. The entrance to the cave had become so familiar. He touched the walls. He searched the floor with his flashlight. He examined the remains of what might have been a fire and contemplated banging his head against the walls. It looked like a lost cause.

The second cave in had not been as serious as the first. He could see, from this vantage point, that it would not be difficult to move the dirt and stone and enough to enter the passageway. The memory of that sharp and narrow entrance irritated him. Then he remembered the dynamite. Lenny's bag was still down there. If he could get through, he might be able to blast the hole open. It was risky, but he wanted to feel like he had tried everything before he gave up completely. He owed that much to Tucker and Nance.

He missed having Lenny around to fill the air with something besides his frustrated thoughts. He threw himself into the work, hoping that being occupied would keep him motivated.

The rocks did, indeed, move more quickly than before, and there was soon a stable enough hole that he could enter. He found the bag, and slung it onto his back. The flashlight showed him that the rest of the tunnel appeared stable, so he eagerly proceeded. The walls narrowed around him, and soon Flint found himself face to face with the razor sharp rocks that had ended his previous exploration.

He took the dynamite from the bag, studying the hole. He had limited experience with dynamite, but he hoped he would be able to move far enough away to avoid being stuck in another cave in if his plan went wrong.

The beam of his flashlight revealed layer after layer of sharp rocks. "Well, let's see if this works," he said to no one in particular as he tossed the dynamite as far into the opening as he could. It struck the ground with a dull, echoing thud.

Flint rolled out the fuse. He heard an eerie sound emerging from the hole. The hairs on his arms stood straight on end. His fight or flight instinct told him to run, but he felt compelled to move closer in spite of it. The noise grew, and the air was rent by an angry wordless scream. It echoed around the tight walls of the cave. Flint dropped the flashlight to cover his ears.

Everything went black, but the scream continued to reverberate around the cave and through his body.

It died slowly, and as soon as he could uncover his ears, he fumbled through the dark in search of the flashlight, hoping that it had not broken. His hands had just clasped the cool metal cylinder when a blinding light replaced the darkness, throwing Flint to the ground.

Chapter 28

Tucker had watched the running of the bulls in Spain on television once. He had hated every moment of the cruel sport, but had been unable to tear his eyes away from the graphic scene. The frightened bulls had looked so sad and desperate as they raced in search of escape. Anyone who got in their way was trampled or gored and tossed back into the crowds that lined the streets. Then the poor exhausted bulls were thrown into an arena where they were taunted and tortured until they died in the midst of applause.

There was no applause now, only the frenzied flapping of wings and the panicked gasping of the crowd. His body had bounced when he hit the ground, rescuing him from the crushing weight of the defeated dragon. Tucker mused that both sides had some of the idea right. Perhaps if they had stuck to Adym and Karlov's plan things would have turned out differently, but deep inside he knew they had seen it coming. As carefully as Ravinna had planned, he realized they had been aware of her thoughts. His betrayal had not been a surprise, but even so, he had been forgiven for his treachery, and had been given the chance to make things right.

He felt intense heat and saw flames simultaneously. A sense of knowing filled him. He had been wrong on many occasions recently, but he felt certain that death was near. Svyetlo's dying breath had lit the stage and Adym's broken body on fire. By piercing the fuel pouch he had slowed the speed of acceleration, but it was only a matter of time before the explosions began, obliterating anything in their path. He realized, sadly, that there was no hope of introducing Ravinna to his mother.

"Tucker!" His mind was conjuring her voice. There was desperation in it, yet he felt at peace.

"Quickly, someone help me pull him away." Rough hands gripped his arms and legs, sending needles of pain through his body. "And someone take that awful spear out of his hands. The beast is dead, we have no need of it."

Tucker registered that his body was moving, but he was incapable of accepting what was happening. He gripped the spear tightly, remembering that the heart must be completely removed from the body if the death were to be final.

"It is okay, my Son," Karlov's rich voice was close to his ear. "You can let go now. Mykel, take the spear so that we can show him he has done his job well."

The spear was gently pried from his fingers and he felt himself being settled onto a stretcher. "Faster," Ravinna sounded frenzied. "The explosion is coming. We must be far away before that happens."

Tucker could not tell if his eyes were open or closed. Everything was so dark, but every now and then he caught fractions of faces covered in dirt and soaked in sweat. They moved faster, and his body undulated painfully with each pounding step. Then they were running while fire rained around them.

The explosion was two fold. The first threw them to the ground, and Tucker realized his eyes were open. The sky turned red, and the great heat seemed to light the clouds on fire. The second came quickly thereafter. It rose into the sky like the grand finale of a fireworks festival. The lights shot out, cool and white, and spiraled across the sky in a brilliant display. Little jewels of light spun on the wind, glistening rapturously. Tucker realized, without shame, that he was weeping. Tears soaked his dirty face, mingling with sweat and blood.

All around him, people and dragons froze to watch the awe inspiring spectacle. The sparks did not fade, but grew brighter as they swept the angry red from the sky and consumed the dark clouds. The sun shone again, but was no match for the twinkling stars that drifted through the sky.

Then the air filled with song. Ravinna lifted her hand to hold Tucker's and pointed with the others at something rising over the horizon. There was a whisper on the wind as the song continued to swell.

"Yaveen."

The great silver dragon swooped over the trees, his mouth open wide. The song poured from him, and as he passed over the amphitheater everything was washed clean. The fire was gone, and the walls gleamed fresh and pure.

Tucker felt the cool breath touch his skin. A peculiar feeling moved through his body. The broken bones grew solid, the rips in his flesh smoothed out, and pain was replaced by a freshness he had never experienced.

"Yaveen," the name drifted from his lips.

When he reached the far side of the valley, the great Yaveen turned and swept over once more. This time he perched on the edge of the amphitheater, looking down at the remnants of the nightmare that had unfolded. Tucker realized then that, while everything else was clean, the carcasses of the two mutilated dragons remained.

Yaveen looked up, and his gaze took in every creature present. "The choice has always been yours," a ripple of understanding washed through Tucker. He was not alone in the feeling. Yaveen opened his mouth and a white flame exploded over the corpses of Adym and Svyetlo.

Tucker threw his arm over his face, but Karlov removed it. "This will be worth watching," he said. "It is nearly finished."

When the glow from the flames subsided the scene had changed. Svyetlo and all his fierce beauty had been reduced to a hideous shrunken lizard. In the next moment he turned to ash and blew away. Adym, on the other hand, had grown more lovely than ever. His shiny green scales had turned to gold, and shone brilliantly beneath the sun. The scars remained, but his face was so serene that he appeared to be only sleeping.

"Well done," Yaveen whispered, and Adym's eyes opened. The scattered audience gasped in awe as father and son rose as one into the sky.

Karlov let out a long soft sigh and patted Tucker's arm. "Now," he said, "it is finished. I told you it would be worth seeing." The old smile lit his face.

"You knew all along, didn't you?" Tucker asked when he found his voice.

"Some things are worth knowing," Karlov said softly, "even when they bring pain along the way."

All around people and dragons were shaking their heads as if awakening from a dream. A change had passed over them. Tucker looked around in wonder. The dragons were more varied in color. What had once been a sea of darkness was now a mixture of yellows, greens and blues, with only a few dark streaks in between. The change in the people was not as obvious, but there was a lightness in the mood that had not been there before.

"Every choice we make leaves a scar," Karlov answered Tucker's question without him having to ask. "But wounds can heal."

"So what now?" he asked.

"Now, you must return whence you came. You have done your job well, but there are those who need you on the other side."

Tucker wondered if his heart could take much more in one day. He looked over to Ravinna, and knew everything he felt was written on his face.

"I belong here," she said softly, lifting one hand to touch his face. "There is much to be done in the wake of what has taken place today. There is much to rebuild."

Tucker's head turned between Karlov and Ravinna, as he wracked his brain for some way to make things work out differently. "Can I at least come back and visit?" he begged desperately.

"When the time is right," Karlov smiled, "You will always be welcome here. You have done us a service that none other could do."

"And is Adym really okay?" he could see his list of unanswered questions stretching on into infinity with no chance of relief. The great field was clearing already. There was little left to indicate the things that had taken place. He wondered where Sirena was, and if the things his eyes had seen were true.

"I am more than all right," Adym was suddenly in front of them, appearing from nowhere. "You have done better than you ever could know, Tucker. We are deeply grateful to you, but Karlov and Ravinna are right. There are people searching for you, who need to know you are all right. You will return one day, but there are things you need to do there first. It is time for me to take you for one more ride." His eyes sparkled with such joy, that all Tucker's worries washed away.

"Ravinna?" he asked as he stood and stretched his hand out to her.

"I am sure you do not need my help to be brave enough to fly this time," Ravinna smiled coyly. "You have slain the vilest dragon that ever lived, and no one who does that can worry about something as simple as flying."

"Please?" he asked. "If only to say goodbye."

"You still do not see," she sighed. "This is not goodbye, Tucker. And in case you are afraid you will forget that this is not the end, let me leave you with this." She pulled his face to hers and kissed him so sweetly that his legs gave way beneath him, and she had to support his weight. With a delighted laugh she pushed him away and he fell against Adym's side. "See you soon," she smiled, stepping back and accepting her father's arm.

Tucker accepted that arguing was pointless, so he took the rope in his hands and climbed Adym's back. It seemed higher than before, but he felt no fear.

"'Til we meet again?" he said uncertainly, from his perch on the golden dragon.

Karlov and Ravinna nodded and waved, but they were already shrinking before his eyes as Adym lifted skyward. This time, Tucker took in the landscape beneath them with interest. He saw the paths he and

Ravinna had traveled, and remembered how much each step along the journey had cost.

They arrived at the waterfall too quickly. Tucker remembered his first entrance into Aristonia, and the horrors of Yaveen's Keep when he had passed through it. Adym slowed, and a gaping hole opened before them. Instead of piles of gold and broken bodies, however, he saw that everything was clean and gleaming freshly like Adym's body. They cruised through the passageway and when they reached the place the glowing pool had been, they stopped.

"Yaveen," the name escaped Tucker's lips like a prayer as he slid down Adym's side and stood face to face with the ancient silver dragon.

There was something of Adym's smile in the face of Yaveen, and something he could not place, but that he knew he would always remember. "Thank you for all you have done, Tucker. Your faith and bravery will not be forgotten. Do not worry about the things you leave behind. They will be as you remember when you return. You have many questions, but now is not the time. There is someone looking for you on the other side. Go, and carry what you have learned with you."

Tucker nodded. Words were useless. He was certain Yaveen knew everything in his mind.

"Here is something to light your way home, and to bring you back when the time is right," Adym spoke a blessing in the dragon language, then his laughter sent sparks into the air revealing the opening to the passage Tucker had to traverse. There was no time to delay. He looked into their eyes, one set sparkling and green, the

other deep shades of grey, then turned and followed the
sparks.

With each step he took, the walls spread out
before him, and as he passed through they closed
behind him. He grew cold as he walked away, but the
return path was sealed, allowing no turning back. He
did not check to see what lay behind, but moved
steadily onward until he reached the point where the
walls grew smooth.

He stopped, and looked curiously down at a
body lying on the ground. The last sparkling light
circled over the flashlight next to the body, and Tucker
picked it up and turned on the switch as the spark went
out. A small green stone fell neatly into his pocket.

"Flint?" he said uneasily, shaking his friend's
arm. "Flint, are you okay?"

Flint squinted into the light of the flashlight.
"Tucker!" his face radiated pure joy. "Tucker! Is it
really you? Where...? How...?"

"Never mind all that," said Tucker soothingly.
His voice had acquired a new quality through his
experiences, and he noticed that Flint relaxed visibly at
the sound of it. "Are you alright? Can you walk?"

"I think so," Flint rubbed his head with his hand.
"I was looking for you and then there was this scream,
and this crazy light, and..." the words tumbled from
him.

"You must have hit your head," said Tucker.
"Don't worry, we'll get out of here and everything will
be okay." He wondered what in the world he was going

to tell everyone, but knew there was no use worrying about it. When the time came, he would know.

Flint had lost his voice. There was no explanation that could answer the questions in his mind, so he accepted that he would have to satisfy himself with having Tucker back.

They walked in silence to the edge of the cave. Flint paused, curious to see what Tucker would do, but his friend continued over the side as though climbing down cliffs came naturally to him. This change in behavior added to his bafflement. "Will you tell me some day?" he asked when they reached the base of the rock wall.

Tucker looked deeply into his eyes and smiled. It was fresh and real for him, but he knew the others would find his experience foreign and unbelievable. He saw acceptance in Flint's face, and knew that was the best he could hope for. "When the time is right," Tucker said.

Flint let it go. They walked in companionable silence through the dark woods. When they reached the road it was Tucker's turn to pause. "My truck..." he said, his mouth gaping. "How long have I been gone?"

Flint sighed, puzzling it through in his head. "Three maybe four days," he said at last, somewhat uncertain.

"And no one moved my truck? Has Tom been here," he was amazed as the details of normal life rushed back with mundane clarity.

"Oh, don't worry about that one," Flint snorted. "Man's like a vulture. He came right quick and cleaned everything out. Then there were some lousy cops that couldn't take the time to get all the way out to find you. Truth is, I think Tom was hoping you'd magically appear, which is sort of what you did by the way, or be declared missing so he might buy the truck cheap off your mom. Either way, he wasn't gonna spring to have someone come get your truck until he was certain he could gain something out of it."

"Figures," Tucker shook his head. "But no matter. Where you headed?"

"Back to your place I guess. Your mom's been worried something awful about you, and I promised Karla I'd come back by," he mumbled the last part.

Tucker jumped on it right away, noticing the tinge in Flint's cheeks. "Karla?" he shouted in glee. "Oh, Flint! That's perfect. You have no idea. Just perfect. Well come on then, let's get going."

It was only then that Tucker realized he was back in his old clothes, the keys to the truck still in his pocket. He reached in and pulled them out, and as he did he felt the stone. He held it between his fingers and a warm glow passed through his body.

"See you at home then," he called over his shoulder to Flint.

"Yup," Flint replied, and his motorcycle roared to life.

Tucker climbed into his truck trying to look natural. He felt suddenly like everything in this part of his life was fake, but he would have to go on pretending for the time being. He opened the door and caught the scent of Ravinna in the air. His heart longed for Aristonia.

The drive home seemed unbearably long. He kept telling himself this was where he belonged. Everyone had said so, after all, but it felt wrong. This life felt empty. He was Tucker the Trucker again. The old moniker nagged him.

Lights were on in all the windows, and he noticed his aunt's car parked next to Karla's. He pulled his truck off to the side of the road. He wished Tom had hauled off the trailer, but he had to settle with having the whole thing parked in the street for the night.

Flint pulled up and Tucker waited for him. He noticed Flint blushing. "She's a great girl," Tucker grinned, slapping him on the back. "I'm telling you, I couldn't be happier."

"Do you really think she might be able to fancy me?" Flint felt like the words were wrong, but he wanted to sound more dignified than his typical trucker self. He felt Karla deserved more.

Tucker's smile widened. "If the smell I can detect coming from that window is any indication, I'm certain of it." Tucker led the way to the door and threw it open with a surge of joy. "Mom?" he called out. "I'm home."

Acknowledgments

This book has been a long time in coming, and would not exist today were it not for the encouragement and assistance of many people. Through the help of family and friends, and countless hours editing, revising and, enlisting the help of anyone who had the time to share their advice, I am so excited to see this story continue on its journey.

I particularly want to thank Angela Nord, Amy Chang Sarchet-Waller, Janet West, and Diane Everest for their valuable editorial comments and reviews.

A huge thank you to Jennifer Cazey Daniels of Happy Little Book Nook Publishing for her interest, excitement, and willingness to enter into this publishing venture with me.

Also a special thanks to Jen Edwards @dustanddots for providing the land of Aristonia with a fabulous map.

About The Author

Sarah has been writing stories for as long as she has been able to form letters with a pencil. She has traveled the world, taking photos, gathering ideas and experiencing places and cultures that help to shape her creativity and landscapes. She currently lives in Oregon with her husband, and their dog. She is also the author of One Week in November.

For more information about Sarah, you can connect with her through her Instagram account: @transientdrifter

51428246R00252

Made in the USA
San Bernardino, CA
23 July 2017